F
3 C
P

6

6

# EVIE'S ALLIES

After having her heart broken not once but twice, Evie Yeo has sworn off men and is focusing on her job teaching at the village school. Her class is much bigger now that evacuees have come to Lymbridge and if she thought her previous boss – the mother of her scoundrel of an ex-fiancé – was bad, she's in for a tough term as new headmaster, Mr Bassett, is already proving to be more difficult. Wartime is a time to come together, but when a familiar face returns, Evie might find that her broken heart isn't as easy to forget as she'd hoped...

# EVIE'S ALLIES

# EVIE'S ALLIES

*by*

Kitty Danton

**Magna Large Print Books**
Long Preston, North Yorkshire,
BD23 4ND, England.

British Library Cataloguing in Publication Data.

A catalogue record of this book is
available from the British Library

ISBN   978-0-7505-4389-7


First published in Great Britain in 2016 by Orion Books
an imprint of The Orion Publishing Group Ltd.

Copyright © Kitty Danton 2016

Cover illustration © Richard Jenkins

The moral right of Kitty Danton to be identified as the author of this
work has been asserted in accordance with the Copyright, Designs
and Patents Act, 1988

Published in Large Print 2017 by arrangement with
The Orion Publishing Group Ltd.

Magna Large Print is an imprint of Library Magna Books Ltd.

Printed and bound in Great Britain by
T.J. (International) Ltd., Cornwall, PL28 8RW

For my husband, Mark,
a man of many outstanding talents

## Chapter One

The smell of the verdant gorse and heather on the Dartmoor hills, crags and gullies that Evie loved so much, currently cloaking them in breathtaking shades of gold and purple, wafted through the open bedroom window. It was a scent that revelled in a West Country summer but that also gave a reminder that the harsh weather of a moorland winter was only a few scant months away.

Evie breathed in deeply. She was getting ready for the first day of the autumn term at Lymbridge Primary School.

It was early still, very early, but Evie had barely slept.

As she fumbled for the skirt and cotton blouse she had laid out the night before, while doing her utmost not to wake her slumbering sister Julia who didn't have to get up for another fifteen minutes or so, Evie remembered the start of the summer term, her very first day as an infant teacher.

Although it was barely five months ago, it felt as if a lifetime had passed since that day. Now, if she cared to think about it, her old self seemed shockingly naive and childish, a completely different Evie.

But, like today, back on that spring morning Evie had been suffering from a broken heart and a disrupted night's sleep.

Or, she thought ruefully, what I considered a

broken heart might feel like, the silly and babyish chump that I was. How innocent, and how foolish.

Evie knew differently now.

Her hasty engagement to Timmy Bowes, and the painful discovery that as Timmy left to fight for king and country he'd been nursing an agonising secret in the shape of Tricia Dolby and the unborn baby he'd fathered, had felt dreadful at the time.

Faint rays of September sunlight dappled Evie's bed through the window high up in the eaves as she tried to pull her pin-curled hair into some sort of order, Julia having insisted the previous evening there should be at least one day this coming autumn term that Evie stood in front of her class of five- and six-year-olds with properly styled hair.

Evie avoided her reflection in the wood-framed mirror. She knew there were shadows under her eyes and her eyelids looked puffy. She had lost weight and, Evie fancied, her face looked as if the bones underneath were just a bit too close to the smooth surface of her skin.

Timmy wasn't to blame for this, she knew.

It was her own fault.

No, it wasn't, Evie immediately chided herself, with a shake of her head that sent the bouncy curls dancing into disorder. It was Peter's fault!

Peter and his inconstant heart.

*Her* fault had been to fall for Peter.

Was no man she cared for able to hold himself back where other women were concerned? Or was it Evie that was the problem? Perhaps she made other women seem more attractive by comparison.

At these grim thoughts Evie felt defeated. As she stared down at her unstockinged feet, she fancied they looked sad too.

Evie sighed and dropped her head further as she leant her weight on to her hands, holding the edge of her and Julia's dressing table. A lone tear fell, its edges breaking into a minute splash as it struck the wood. Suddenly weary almost beyond measure, Evie felt her shoulders quiver as she allowed herself the luxury of giving in to her silent desolation.

Twenty minutes later Evie was at the breakfast table at Pemberley, the guest house where she lodged as a PG, or – more properly – a paying guest, staring at the mark her deep red lipstick had left on the rim of her tea cup. Normally she wouldn't wear make-up to school, but today called for special measures to bolster her spirits, she had decided, as she felt so low. The lipstick, a present to Evie from Timmy's mother to say thank you for Evie's gracious behaviour when she had stepped aside in the summer holidays and Timmy had finally made a honest woman of Tricia Dolby, was the best booster to Evie's frazzled spirits that she had been able to think of.

As she heard the first sounds of her fellow guests beginning to stir upstairs, Evie took her tea cup and saucer through to the kitchen, and after rubbing the lipstick mark off with her finger, quickly rinsed and placed the crockery on the tiered draining rack. She picked up her newly knitted cardigan and her handbag, and then the sandwich wrapped in paper she had made while she was waiting for the kettle to boil for her morn-

13

ing tea, and finally she grasped a large jug with just a little milk in it (she'd chosen the large jug to avoid any danger of splashing her clean clothes).

She hurried out of the door, hardly pausing to notice the splendid morning that promised a wonderful Indian summer over the next month or two.

Evie wanted to delay having to face anybody for as long as she could.

It was a short walk to the school, down Pemberley's graceful arc of a sun-bleached gravel drive and then in at the school gate, a mere stone's throw away along the single lane that wended through the village.

Evie went to find the key to the school block in its accustomed hidey-hole in the wall, but no matter how she felt and fumbled around, and then peered with crooked brows into the dim recess, the key was resolutely not there.

'Miss Yeo. Young lady, as you might be able to surmise if you stopped day-dreaming and bothered to think about it, the classrooms are unlocked already.' The arrogantly high-handed male voice sounded as if its owner had called to her from within the vestibule outside the classrooms. Evie couldn't help but note that the owner of the voice couldn't be bothered to put his head out of the door to speak to her directly.

Evie pursed her lips and blinked as she let out a slow breath. This was, she knew, the unwelcome sound of Mr Leonard Bassett, the new temporary headmaster at Lymbridge Primary School.

And, unfortunately, also one of the recently

14

arrived paying guests at Pemberley. This was following the vacating of two spacious bedrooms now that Peter was working in London and kindly Mr Smith had moved out to go to Berkshire to be with his bride. And his new wife was Mrs Bowes, who was Timmy's mother – or more precisely, Mrs Smith, as she now was. Evie would have to get used to calling her former headmistress Mrs Smith, she knew, but it felt very odd still to think of her as anything other than Mrs Bowes.

For the time being, Mr and Mrs Smith were renting a small house close to Stoke Mandeville Hospital, until Timmy would be well enough, following his searing back and head injuries of several months earlier, to be sent to the new recuperation hospital that was being shoe-horned into a once-grand house called The Grange that was reasonably close to Lymbridge. It would soon begin to take its first patients.

There was a Mrs Bowes still – but this was Tricia Dolby, of course. Although heavily pregnant, Tricia had returned to her job at the dairy parlour after the wedding, hoping to get in another month or six weeks of work before Timmy's baby arrived. Evie believed the plan was that once Timmy was installed at the recuperation hospital and Mr and Mrs Smith had taken up residence in Mrs Smith's pretty cottage, then Tricia would move in with them.

Evie didn't mind at all having a new superior she must report to at Lymbridge Primary School. It hadn't always been easy working for Mrs Bowes (actually that was quite an understatement). And at least now Evie was no longer Timmy's fiancée

15

and so she wouldn't have to begin the new term while keeping up the same ridiculous charade she had had to maintain the previous term – for reasons too dreary to dwell on – of trying to keep secret the philandering behaviour of her head-mistress's beloved son.

Evie was all too aware she still had an awful lot to learn before she could claim to be anything approaching a fully rounded infant teacher, as so far she'd only had the one term of teaching experi-ence. In fact she was very relieved to have been offered the autumn term teaching after that, as money had become tight for her over the summer. This was because the previous term had been a temporary posting. And so too was this autumn term, as it had been made clear to her by new headmaster, Mr Bassett, who obviously thought of Evie as merely a make-do-for-now answer to the problem of appointing an infant teacher.

Presumably at some point during the autumn term the Board of Education would 'take a view', as by then Mrs Smith would be clearer as to her own plans and would know whether her sabbatical needed to be extended or not. It was still unusual for a woman teacher to be newly married, Evie knew, but Mrs Smith had to be close to fifty and so she wasn't a typical newly-wed. And if she wanted to teach, Evie felt, then the feisty head-mistress would make sure that was exactly what would happen.

Evie knew there had been a bit of a set-to with the education authority many years earlier when Mr Bowes had walked out of the family home unexpectedly following an unfortunate liaison with a young lady, and Mrs Bowes, as of course she was then, had demanded her old job back at the local primary school even though Timmy was only a small boy. It hadn't taken long apparently for the local authorities to see the error of their ways and to buckle to Mrs Bowes's will.

But if Mrs Smith were to make her leave of absence permanent, then Evie assumed that the new headmistress or headmaster would want to appoint their own infants' teacher, and it was by no means certain that either Mr Bassett or Evie would keep their posts under a new regime. So Evie had told herself firmly that the best thing to do in the meantime would be to throw herself into this autumn term of work and learn as much as she possibly could, but not to assume in any way that she was close to being made a permanent member of staff. All experience was valuable, and it might be that afterwards she could get a job at one of the other local schools if she had a good autumn term teaching at the primary school she herself had attended as a child.

All of this was fair enough. However, Evie did very much mind having to report to Mr Bassett for the few months until Christmas.

Hard to age but very probably not yet thirty, as far as Evie was concerned Mr Bassett's crime was that he treated her as if he were a grand old man and she a mere flippertygibbert. He was bumptious and conceited, and he never appeared to be the slightest bit interested in anything she had to say. And those were his better points, Evie felt.

Her best friend, Sukie, had tried to point out to Evie the fact that Mr Bassett seemed suave, and he certainly was good-looking, but to no avail.

Evie acknowledged that it wasn't Mr Bassett's fault that an eye problem had meant he was unable to join up – within minutes of their first conversation Sukie had got out of him that he couldn't see with the lower part of his vision, and that doctors were divided as to whether this was an optical or a neurological issue. Still, Evie felt, he was a man inordinately fond of his own extremely dull opinions, and as far as she could see he didn't really have anything much to talk about other than cricket.

She had taken a firm dislike to him on sight, definitely aided by the fact that the day he'd moved into Pemberley – at the same time as a young journalist called Paul Rogers (who had rarely been at the guest house since) – was one of the unhappiest of Evie's short life.

And nothing Leonard Bassett had said or done in the ten days or so since arriving in Lymbridge had persuaded Evie that it would be pleasurable for either of them to work together. It was irritating that Mr Worth, who ran Pemberley as a guesthouse with his wife (well, it was Mrs Worth who did most of the running, although Mr Worth tended to overlook this), and Evie's fellow PG Mr Wallace, both appeared to think Mr Bassett a fine fellow.

Today, the fact Mr Bassett had just proved himself to be an earlier bird than Evie in the morning was nothing short of plain irksome, as she prided herself on being up with the lark nearly every day.

'Good morning, Mr Bassett,' Evie said primly as she marched up the three stone steps and con-

18

tinued straight past him in the small entrance hall and on into her infants classroom, making sure she avoided directly looking at him. And how frustrating it was that the corner of her eye revealed that he'd already lost interest in her, and instead he now appeared to be deep in concentration as he gazed at something written on an officious-looking clipboard, replying to her good morning with something sounding suspiciously like a mixture of a sigh and grunt.

Evie swept into the infants classroom, and then realised that in her grand entrance she'd forgotten to put her sandwich and jug of milk for their tea into the old-fashioned cool-box in the poky staff kitchenette. Drat. She went back into the entry vestibule, and was relieved to note that Mr Bassett was now in his own classroom, meaning she didn't have to talk to him just at the moment and she could stow away what she was carrying in peace.

Evie's classroom was spick and span and ready for the new term. She and the school caretaker, Mr Cawes, had spent a good hour the day before arranging the tiny wooden desks and chairs in various new configurations, Evie ignoring his increasingly testy exclamations of 'new-fangled nonsense', 'I'll be damned' (alternating with 'I'll be jiggered'), 'whatever next', 'the maid's done it now' (this escalated to 'the maid's done *it* now'), all of which Mr Cawes muttered only half to himself in his broad Devonian accent as they pulled the desks and chairs this way and that.

It was a daring new arrangement she'd decided on eventually, and Mrs Smith would have been quite shocked if she could see the new placement of furniture, Evie conceded to herself. Mr Cawes apparently thought likewise; he had peered around after Evie had declared their arranging over in obvious disapproval with many a dubious shake of his whiskery head. And after she had insisted on her way and returned to Pemberley, she thought suddenly that Mr Bassett might not approve either, although he hadn't commented one way or another to her after he'd been to check the school the previous evening.

What had provoked this upheaval in the infants classroom was that towards the end of the previous summer term Evie had found herself wondering if desks in a line were really helping her pupils, many of whom were still only five years of age. While she could see such a way of seating could be a better arrangement for the junior pupils, who were seven years and upwards, as sitting in a more regimented manner might quell a little distracting chatter, it seemed to be asking a lot of her small pupils when they couldn't see each other's faces. And so Evie had broken up the rigid rows of desks into what she hoped would be less intimidating clusters so that four children could sit facing each other, with the desks in four little groups in a semi-circle around her teacher's desk.

Also new to Evie's classroom was a big chart on a large piece of hardboard Mr Cawes had found for her and painted white. The two young WRVS (Women's Royal Voluntary Service) PGs at Pemberley, Tina and Sarah, had been instrumental the previous week in carefully transposing Evie's unruly pencil sketch of what she wanted into a simple but nonetheless professional-looking grid, along with the various names of the pupils and categories of lessons. Tina and Sarah had made such a wonderful scoreboard to lodge the competition scores at the village's Revels that Evie had organised in high summer, that she had co-opted them in this latest endeavour.

Once she had their agreement as to the grid-making, Evie had persuaded her younger brother James to cart the board from the school to Pemberley for Tina and Sarah to work on, and then lug it back to the school a few days later. Evie was rather proud that she'd not had to bribe James to help her, but she thought he probably hoped he might run into her glamorous best pal Sukie.

Down the side of the board in alphabetical order were the Christian names of each of Evie's sixteen pupils for this coming term. Five of her previous class had moved up to the juniors now they'd been in the infants class for two years, but another nine children from the village of Lymbridge or the surrounding farms were now old enough to join the school.

Along the top of the grid were the categories, such as handwriting, spelling, sums, gym, history, geography, science, painting and nature. Evie had begged Mr Smith to see if he could wrangle her some card in a range of colours and some blunt scissors from an art supplies shop when he was next reporting to the Board of Trade in London, and she'd been delighted the previous week when he'd sent a package down for her, especially as it contained twenty such pairs of kiddies' scissors and, thrillingly, quite an array of thicknesses of card in a rainbow assortment of colours. Goodness knows where he had managed to find such a treasure trove in these times of scrimping and saving. As Evie had thought before, it was very handy having a friend in a high place.

A day or two earlier, Evie had made a template in a star shape and cut out some samples, sticking a single star of a different colour at the top of each column, making sure the green star was above the title nature, on the basis that lots of leaves and grasses were green. As nearly all of her children wouldn't be reading big words yet she had also hunted around in some old picture books she and her siblings had enjoyed as children and had cannabalised a few suitable illustrations to go underneath the headings. She had also got Tina and Sarah to put in '1 + 1 = ?', 'My name is ?', 'C.A.T. spells?', 'Today the weather is...?' etcetera in the boxes immediately underneath the headings. If that didn't make it clear what each column referred to, then Evie wasn't sure what would.

The plan was that stars would be earned by the pupils for good behaviour or excellent work, with the aim that everyone should get at least one star per subject over the term. At the end of the term Evie would award a prize to whoever managed to get the most stars. The stars would be stuck up on to the scoreboard with a little flour and water paste, already prepared in a washed-out glass jam jar with the metal lid firmly screwed on. Evie was hoping such a mild glue would make the stars easy to remove at the end of term, meaning that the board could be re-used for the spring term. This theory was yet to be tested, however.

Evie had divided the remaining coloured card into smallish sections, and on it she had outlined in pencil smaller stars from her template. It would be chaos, she knew, but she thought the children would enjoy cutting out the stars with the small round-tipped scissors as a way of easing them into the new school year, after which she would award everyone a star for their morning's work, and then put the rest of the homemade stars into another jar, a large one this time, so they were ready to be stuck to the grid as harder-earned rewards over the coming weeks.

Evie had asked Mr Bassett the previous Friday if he played the piano, and he'd had to admit it was something he couldn't do. Evie wasn't very good – and certainly nowhere near the dab hand as a pianist that Peter had been, or even able to match Mrs Smith's rather heavy-handed skill in this respect – but over the summer she had been practising hard on the piano at Pemberley under the tutelage of ancient church organist Mr Finn, and Evie's reward had been that she made vast improvements to her still slim repertoire. While she practised and her fingers fumbled around on the black and ivory keys, Evie had had to force herself not to remember the happy times when Peter had played Pemberley's piano. This was a plan that mostly hadn't gone too well.

Anyway, the day before, she and Mr Cawes, with rather too much huffing and puffing and the pre-requisite muffled swearword or two, had also manhandled the ungainly school piano from the juniors classroom into the infants classroom. 'Well, I'm blowed, Evie. Mrs Bowes was an 'ard

23

taskmaster, but she's a little 'un compared to yer. Me knees and me back are rightly sore,' Mr Cawes said pointedly while ostentatiously rubbing his lumbar region, and then Evie had had to promise she would stand him a stout the next time she ran into him in The Haywain, at which he looked somewhat mollified.

Mr Cawes had attached hooks for string on the back of the hardboard grid and hung it on the wall. Evie hadn't had the heart to point out that he'd nailed in the hook on which the grid hung so high up that every time she wanted to reward one of the pupils named towards the top of the grid, she would have to stand on a chair to do so. However, she decided not to suggest that he lower the hook as she'd found herself having to discourage further conversation with the elderly caretaker with his nosey questioning comments about her and Timmy, and 'that daft Dolby maid, mad's a brush an' wi' a belly t' size o' Christmus'. Evie realised it may have been rash of her to mention the stout if this was the result. A bit of a stretch to stick a star on the grid was a much more welcome outcome than having to fuel the old man's demand for scurrilous gossip that he'd likely be sharing down at the village pub before the day was out.

Alone this early morning in the quiet time before the new term got under way, Evie tried to compose herself as she took the seat at her teacher's desk, and then neatly wrote the name of each of her pupils in alphabetical order down the side of the first page of the register for the forthcoming school year.

The church clock struck eight and Evie realised she had nothing else she needed to do before the first pupils arrived, which wouldn't happen for at least another twenty minutes or so. She sighed and tried to sit in quiet contemplation – she had read an article in a magazine recently extolling the value of 'quiet contemplation'. It can't have been more than thirty seconds before she sprang to her feet and headed briskly to the classroom next door.

'Mr Bassett, I'm shipshape and ready for my pupils now, and I have some spare time. Is there anything you'd like me to do?' she said.

Her temporary headmaster was standing with his back to her as he stared morosely out of the window in the direction of the moorland tors. There was a silence.

Still waiting for a reply, Evie crept forward. Mr Bassett looked wrapped in the deepest of thoughts and Evie felt she'd never seen anyone look so far away. She didn't think he had heard her. Then she was taken aback and slightly shaken to see what looked to be a tear glistening on his cheek. Horrified, Evie halted abruptly, and then tried to back soundlessly out of the room, unfortunately bumping into a desk that was slightly out of alignment.

Mr Bassett jumped at the unexpected sound of the desk's legs scraping on the parquet floor. He turned quickly to look at Evie, who said hastily, 'I do apologise for barging in, Mr Bassett, but I have a spare few minutes and so I was wondering if you would like a cup of tea?'

'No, Miss Yeo, I don't think I do, thank you,' he said flatly. And without ado, Mr Bassett turned once more to gaze on the majestic view of the moors, his back square-on to Evie.

It was impossible not to take this a some sort of rebuke, and Evie returned to her classroom feeling distinctly unsettled. It wasn't so much that anything particularly threatening had happened, but more that she sensed that whatever was affecting Mr Bassett was so very much outside Evie's experience that she didn't know what she should do. Whatever the matter was, though, it was deeply troubling to Mr Bassett.

Still, Evie didn't have the inclination to brood for long on her headmaster. Mr Bassett might not be looking forward to the day ahead, but the parlous state of her own see-sawing emotions felt too all-consuming for Evie. And with that, she allowed herself the luxury of dwelling on the happier times of preparing for the village Revels, and as she turned to gaze out of her own classroom window she caught her breath and her heart bumped uncomfortably against her ribs at the sight of the Nissen hut at the bottom of the school field.

For there, hidden from prying eyes, was where she had stolen two thrilling kisses with Peter while the Lymbridge villagers enjoyed themselves at the Revels just a matter of yards away.

Only lasting a matter of seconds, nevertheless those secret moments were the high point of Evie's life. To think about them sent a giddy whirl of emotions and sensations racing throughout her mind and body.

It wasn't long before the children started to arrive, full of energy and chatter. Evie realised she was very pleased to greet her pupils from the previous year.

Even though really it was only a matter of weeks since she had last seen them all together, it was noticeable how much some of them had grown. Almost everybody looked suntanned and healthy. It was obvious that lots of time had been spent running around outdoors during the summer holidays. Evie could remember that back when she was a child during the warm weather, she and her sisters and brother had only come inside to eat or to sleep. Evie saw that there also appeared to have been a mass loss of milk teeth amongst her pupils, as nearly everyone seemed to be sporting gappy smiles.

As had happened last term, it looked like little Bobby Ayres was set to be the imp of the class. He arrived gingerly carrying a small cardboard box. He opened it carefully to show Evie a dormouse he'd found the previous day. Evie thought it very lucky that the poor dormouse had survived so long (it actually looked surprisingly content, curled up and dozing on an old flannel), but she didn't want to tempt fate. She promised Bobby that the minute everyone had arrived and she had got everyone seated and taken the register she would show them all the dormouse, after which Mr Cawes could release it behind the Nissen hut as it was 'much kinder to let wild animals live outside'.

Bobby's face clouded for an instant and then threatened to crumple, but he cheered up when Evie promised that as a special treat he could go with Mr Cawes to set the small rodent free. And with that Evie put the box on the rather high window ledge as she thought the dormouse might appreciate a little privacy to do whatever dormice do when unexpectedly plucked from their habitat.

Evie said to her infants from the previous term that they could play for five minutes at the far end of the playground and that Mr Cawes would be with them to keep an eye on things. Marie and Catherine, two evacuees from Plymouth who now lived with Evie's parents, were the first to scamper to the side of the playground. As the other infants began to follow, Evie told them she would be calling them all in soon but first she wanted to show the new pupils their classroom and where they could get a drink of water from and find the lavatories and so on. It was probably a good idea, Evie decided, if she made all the newcomers use the diminutive porcelain toilets and then wash their hands. She knew that some of them would be feeling frightened, and too scared to ask to go if they needed.

As she led her little troupe of new arrivals into the schoolhouse, Evie noticed that Mr Bassett had cheered up remarkably from earlier. He seemed to have a nice way with the children, and was promising the juniors a cricket innings later in the morning. Evie also noted that nearly all the girls looked less than enthusiastic at the prospect, although it was hard to tell if this was because they'd been told they had to play, like it or not, or because Mr Bassett had said the girls could field while the boys bowled and batted.

It took Evie what felt like a surprisingly long time to get her new pupils settled. After everyone had used the toilets, she put two of her new children at each of the groups of desks, and one at the final group. And then she called in her older pupils and allocated them seats, attempting to make sure that in each set of four she had a mix of the shy and the forward youngsters, and the new and the old, in the hope that each set of four would balance out and that no one group would seem too raucous or withdrawn.

Holding the open box steady, Evie then went to each group to allow them a peek at the dormouse, putting a finger to her lips as she did so to encourage the children to be quiet. After she had drawn attention to his little pink paws and his tail curling across his tummy right up to his nose, his paper-thin ears and his curly whiskers, she asked them to take a good look as they were each going to try to draw the dormouse later in the morning. Fortunately Evie had an illustrated book on wildlife on the bookshelf behind her desk that would help out too in this respect as it would remind the little ones what they had seen, and with a bit of luck it would detail habitat and food, and so she could turn a chance event into a combined nature and painting lesson.

She then handed the box over to Mr Cawes, who'd been hovering just inside the classroom door, and he and Bobby Ayres set off towards the playing field with their tiny quarry.

Evie was just about to shut the classroom door behind them and start explaining to the rest of the class exactly how they would go about the cutting out of the card stars, which would then be collected to be used as rewards, when a lithe furry body squeezed through the closing gap between the door and jamb.

It was Keith, the school cat.

Evie laughed out loud, and so did the pupils who already knew the puss.

Keith had spent the summer living over at Blue-bells, Evie's parents' house at the far end of the village. She – and it was a she, and not a he, despite her boyish name – had clearly been spoilt and had had a good summer, as Evie could see in her sleek coat and filled-out body as she cavorted by. How had Keith been able to sense it was time to return to school? Evie had planned to collect her at lunchtime, if she could persuade Mr Bassett to watch her pupils as they ate their packed lunches. But now Keith had obliged by saving Evie a job. Perhaps cats really did have something of the 'other world' about them, as some of the elderly folklore-loving village women had tried to persuade Evie when she herself had been young.

The infants were delighted to see Keith too, and it wasn't long before the tabby and white cat was introducing herself to the new pupils.

As Keith's famously booming purr rang out, Evie thought that the school term had got off to a reasonable start that morning, all things considered. But it probably was a good thing the dormouse had made such an early exit. Keith was a dear, but cats were cats, and an already captive dormouse would have been nothing short of a delicious temptation.

## Chapter Two

At the end of the school day, Evie made sure to walk home to Pemberley at an opportune moment while Mr Bassett was talking to a parent and was thus distracted. She didn't want to have to start waiting for him, or he her, as they went to and fro between their home and the school, and so it was best that any sort of routine was never started.

Back at Pemberley, Evie expected to see her sister Julia as she normally finished a little before Evie. But although Julia's battered bone-shaker of a bicycle was propped up near the back door, with her seen-better-days canvas Post Office delivery bag dangling over the handlebars, there was no sign of her sister anywhere. Mrs Worth, Evie's landlady, said Julia had been in and out, and that although she had changed, she hadn't wanted any tea and nor had she said what time she would be home.

Evie went to their room; as she'd slept so little and been up so early she thought maybe she would have a nap, but even though she lay on her bed for ten minutes, she just didn't feel sleepy.

She sprang up and decided to head for Blue-bells, the Yeo family home, as she didn't really want to risk lolling about in the sitting room and having to talk to Mr Bassett, even though he didn't seem to be anywhere around either.

As she turned out of Pemberley's drive, as luck

would have it, Evie's other sister, Pattie, was walking past on her way back to Bluebells.

Not quite a Land Girl as such, Pattie was working on various farms, concentrating at the moment on helping with coppicing and dry-stone walling. Although some farmers felt it was too early in the year still, work was just starting on the coppicing on the top of some of the ancient earth-covered barriers marking the edge of fields, which meant trimming whole trees, or otherwise selected branches, right back so the young shoots that would spring forward as the weather warmed after the cold of winter could then be woven into wattle fencing. Although it could be a bit of a wrestle when it came to the weaving part of the process, if done properly it was an effective and a very robust, long-lasting way of keeping livestock where they should be.

Pattie, who wasn't yet nineteen, had previously been a part-time barmaid at one or other of the local public houses. As Pattie had seemed to be drifting rather, Evie had been very worried that the government would send her to work in a munitions factory in a more industrial part of the country, but now that Pattie was employed on the land that danger had almost definitely been averted.

And her sister looked to be thriving, Evie couldn't help but notice with the minutest twinge of jealousy. In contrast to Evie's current wan complexion, Pattie appeared strong and brown-skinned, with winsome little freckles speckling her nose for the first time, and the strenuous work had slimmed and toned her, while her hair had appealing shades of light and dark from having been in the sun so much.

'You're looking very bonny, I must say,' Evie said.

Hearing a slightly off note in her sister's voice, Pattie glanced at Evie, and realised that Evie was still a long way from the perennially cheerful older sister she had been until earlier in the year. Pattie was unaware that Evie had had her heart recently broken by Peter – only Evie's best friend, Sukie, was in the know as to *that* – and so Pattie assumed it was because it was still only a matter of weeks since Timmy had married Tricia that made Evie sound so uncharacteristically out of sorts.

Pattie placed a comforting arm around her sister's shoulders, while waving her two bruised, blistered and scabby hands in front of Evie's face. 'Yes, beautiful all over. Obviously. I know Linda swears by udder cream for hands, but I think even the best and most udderiest of udder creams would have a challenge in sorting these flippers out.'

Planning on making a playful comment about their friend Linda, who was a farrier, and her staunch belief in the efficacious powers of the udder cream that was ordinarily used on cows to keep their teats healthy for milking, Evie was taken aback when she looked properly at Pattie's hands. She gasped when she realised what a dreadful state her poor sister's mitts were in, with barely a patch of skin that appeared to be unscathed, and with what looked like every nail broken and un-even. 'Poor you, lovey. They look as if you've really

33

been in the wars, so very painful and unpleasant,' commiserated Evie.

'Oh, they'll be fine. At any rate, I'm told that once I get used to the hefting of the tools, I'll get calluses to replace the blisters and cuts. The Land Girls tell me that then the main problem is in putting on stockings, as they catch and snag all too easily on the raggedy hard skin.'

For a moment Evie wondered if her sister was joking, but to judge by Pattie's earnest expression this wasn't the case. Pattie was one of those people who tended to put up with things and get on with life while ignoring minor inconveniences. So, thinking that she must, all the same, ask Linda for some of the udder cream for Pattie to use just in case it was as magical as her friend promised, Evie decided that sympathy was the most appropriate response. And maybe a little gentle joshing. 'Well, to judge by what was in the shops in Plymouth last week, which was practically nothing, none of us will be wearing stockings anytime soon. And meanwhile, fortunately, I hear your photographic modelling session for the *a la mode* manicure advertisement has been put back a week, although the rumour from the dinner queue is that there is a chance you might be asked to fill in if they need photographs of a farmer's scaly paws...'

'You daft old maid, you!' responded Pattie, with a friendly nudge of her shoulder against her sister's.

They chatted for a little about the coppicing and dry-stone walling, with Pattie explaining that before this, she'd had no idea that something they all saw everyday in and around the village and local farms was actually very skilled. For years, they'd derided Timmy's best friend Dave Symons, who was a professional dry-stonewaller, for being dim and boring.

'Well, he came to teach us how to do it, and the truth of it is that he can wall at a cracking pace and he has a knack for seeing which stones will fit with which, and so I'd be thinking he makes a pretty good living as he must be in great demand from the farms round here. And I couldn't believe his coppicing. Actually I was seeing him in such a different light, and he was so impressive, that I nearly had to tell him that he was an absolute master of his craft. Fortunately, I then remembered that if you give him an inch he tries to take a mile. And that he's an ugly old trout,' said Pattie with an enviably demur expression, 'and so I kept my trap shut as otherwise he'd probably ask me for a drink. And that way would lie madness.'

Evie laughed as she could only too well remember Dave Symons's octupine arms when in a moment of weakness she had agreed to meet him at Easter, just after Timmy had left to fight, and how her sisters had squirmed when she'd described those minutes squeezed with him into a nook in the snug of The Haywain and the evasive action she'd needed to take. And to compound the indignity, he'd also broken the news that evening in a tipsy slur that Timmy had been most assuredly very free with his favours as far as the Devon lasses were concerned, and not at all faithful to Evie.

It wasn't a pleasant memory in any respect, and so Evie now turned the conversation to their middle sister, Julia. 'There's something up, I'm sure of it. She's usually so talkative and reliable, but these last few days, I don't know. I hardly see her, even though we are sharing a bedroom, and she's evasive when I do. I'm trying a new approach, which is not really talking to her about anything specific, in the hope that she'll say something off her own bat... But the silence is deafening so far. And in fact, if I look at her while she's sleeping, I fancy she even looks then as if she's dreaming about being up to no good.'

Pattie agreed this was a peculiar state of affairs, although to be honest she herself hadn't noticed anything particularly different about Julia. 'But I know Mother always calls her the dark horse of the three of us, and that she's the most determined of all when she's really set her mind on something. She so sensible, though, that I'm sure it's nothing untoward.'

Pattie's words were so reassuring and eminently sensible that Evie immediately felt as if she had been reading too much into nothing.

While Evie was the oldest and the most forthright sister, and Pattie was the youngest and flirtiest, it was a Yeo family tradition that Julia was the reliable and always-stable sister, prone neither to swings of mood or excitability. Those were the traits of the other two sisters, and Julia was one of those kind and caring people who made everyone around them feel as if the dark days of the war were perhaps indelibly fused with the glimmer of the light of humanity. It would be horribly unsettling to everybody, Evie was sure, if Julia was doing anything that would upset this comforting balance.

But before Evie and Pattie could speculate further, their mother, Susan, hailed them as they were passing the village shop where she worked. She had some logs that a farmer had given her in return for a little book-keeping Susan had carried out for him, and so she wanted a hand hauling them back to Bluebells.

As Pattie asked her mother what dimness had made the farmer drop the logs off at the shop rather than at the family home (Susan saying she couldn't begin to guess), Evie ran to get her father, Robert, brother James, and the Yeos' evacuee boys, Frank and Joseph, who were several years older than their evacuee girls.

And with one burlap sack apiece to lug the logs down the lane to Bluebells, soon the fire wood was being piled up not so tidily in the large front porch out of the way of any forthcoming wet weather. Shady, the Yeos' family dog, got under everybody's feet, and then with calls of 'don't you dare, Shady!' the family left him happily sniffing around the logs while clearly pondering whether he would get away with cocking a hind leg against them.

As she walked towards the kitchen Evie thought to herself that when she got her mother alone she might ask whether she'd noticed any change in Julia. Evie wasn't being nosey, more a concerned older sister, she tried to convince herself.

But then she acknowledged, before Susan could do this for her as Evie knew would most certainly be the case, that really she was nosey first and a concerned older sister second.

It was a good-natured, slightly raucous teatime at Bluebells, even though the food was rather dull, being homemade bread with a scraping of butter and two boiled eggs apiece from the hens that the Yeos were keeping on the fenced-off village green, the green having long been given over to food production for the whole village. Some people had built sties for a pig or two, and there was quite a variety of outbuildings for poultry and several goats. The goats had proved to be masters of escape, and very greedy, and so although at first some people had tried to cultivate vegetables alongside the various runs for the animals and poultry, the general consensus now was that it was only livestock on the green, with vegetable production being much more likely to give a good rate of return for the effort expended on it if it were instead in people's gardens, hopefully well out of the way of the mischievous goats.

Earlier in the week Susan had attempted to make some hawthorn syrup for the four evacuees, although using the word syrup would be perhaps to oversell the eventual concoction, owing to the meagre amount of sugar that she had been able to add. To judge by the faces of the evacuees and the crescendo of their moans as they were each made to force down a spoonful after their tea, the syrup tasted as foul as it looked. But grimace all they could, Susan insisted come what may that each evacuee swallow it down without more of a fuss as 'it'll do you good', adding that the government were keen on children having a whole range of extra nutrients and vitamins, and the Yeos were lucky enough to live close to where there was a plentiful array of hawthorn bushes around. To judge by the horrified expression on all four of the evacuees' faces, Susan's enthusiasm wasn't convincing anyone.

Evie smiled – she could well remember when Susan had been equally firm with her ten or so years earlier, a confrontation that would usually end with an 'Evie, if you don't stop making a fuss, you'll be doing the washing up for the family for a whole week. On your own.' Quite determined as a child, Evie had made the decision to put Susan's threat to the test. Just the once, mind.

At teatime, Robert, along with Evie's fifteen-year-old brother, James, sat at the end of the table, their heads close together as they looked at the newspaper. Evie saw for the first time how much James was coming to resemble the older man; there was no doubt they were father and son, as they were now disconcertingly alike in both looks and demeanour. Evie knew she herself favoured Susan, as she and her mother shared the same brunette hair and slender frame. Julia had Robert's squarish, strong build, whereas Pattie didn't look much like either of her two parents as she was fair and on the short side.

What was exciting Robert and James so was that there was a story in the *Western Morning News* that the following week horse racing and also boxing matches would be officially allowed to start once more. Most sporting events had been curtailed after war had been declared in 1939, but now, two years into the war, the government were keen to keep morale as high as possible, with the result that many public events were being encouraged to resume. Keeping morale high also extended to women encouraging each other to look as good as they could at all times – Hitler might be a heinous man, but he wasn't going to stop lipstick-wearing, for those lucky enough still to have lipstick, or the nightly pin-curling.

Robert announced that he wanted to take the whole family to the races. While it looked like Newton Abbot racecourse, which was the closest proper racecourse to Lymbridge, would remain closed, Robert had heard there were plans afoot for a local steeplechase in a month or two, provided somewhere suitable could be found on private land, which would give time for anyone with suitable horses to fitten them up a little, although the shortage of time for the fittening and the availability of quality mounts would mean that the race-course would be shorter than usual and the obstacles the horses would jump over less challenging.

Everybody at Bluebells that afternoon thought a trip out to the races – or race, most probably, as the entrants would have to be local as there would be no spare petrol to transport horses by lorry or trailer, which would mean there would be a natural cap on numbers – would be fun, and a good opportunity to catch up with acquaintances who might not often have need to visit Lymbridge. There was even a rumour that as it was an exceptional year, women jockeys might be allowed to race against the male riders!

James was very interested as to the precise ins and outs of how betting worked, and the manner in which odds were arrived at. Evie could see that he wanted to know more than Robert really was certain about, but that Robert was quite keen to seem as if he knew all there was to know about horse racing and the Tote. Susan also thought similarly to Evie to judge by the conspiratorial look her mother was darting her way, with a smiling shake of her head when Robert tried to sound very authoritative, and her pointed, 'Yes, that's all very well, James. But you have to have some money to place a bet in the first place,' to which James grabbed a potato from Susan's basket on the floor near him and waved it around to puzzled looks from the rest of his family.

Evie thought she'd have a word with Linda, as being a farrier she'd know the state and whereabouts of the local horses. Evie had ridden a lot in the past, as she had been small as a teenager and quite a skilled equestrian, and so had earned pocket money from riding people's difficult ponies thanks to her knack of calming them down and getting them going well. And she missed horse riding, which had for a long while just seemed too frivolous an activity to do.

Evie knew she wouldn't want to take part herself in a real race as she wasn't brave enough to attempt fixed fences while galloping pell-mell with other horses and riders around her, but she wondered if somebody might want a hand in bringing on the horses that would be raced, trotting them up and down the hills to build muscle now that fox hunting has also had to make way for the war effort. Evie thought that if Sukie could find a ride actually to race, then she'd probably leap at the chance, as she was pretty fearless in the

41

saddle, and if it meant she could race on equal terms with the men then she'd almost certainly be keen to have a bash. There was definitely something of the daredevil about Sukie and she would enjoy pitting herself against the local lads.

And then the potato-waving started to make sense when, just at the moment that Julia bustled in, James announced to the family that he'd got himself, and Frank and Joseph too, a day or two's work sorting potatoes at a local farm. The potato sorting was clearly news to Frank and Joseph, who immediately became ridiculously over-excited at the thought of earning a little pocket money of their very own as they'd never really had any before. Frank was now old enough to go to secondary school in Oldwell Abbott, where James was a pupil, and Evie was pleased to see Joseph's happy face – he had been a bit down in the dumps since his brother left Lymbridge Primary School. In fact Joseph had been so morose that for the past few days Evie had made an effort to keep reminding him it wouldn't be too long before he'd be at the 'big school' too.

Then Evie caught herself and Pattie both scrutinising their sister. But aside from slightly bright eyes and pinkish cheeks, she looked every inch the Julia they knew and loved. With her habitual warm smile she greeted the family, and then she knelt down and listened carefully to Marie and Catherine as they showed Julia how very much their reading was coming on.

It was only later that Evie wondered if her sister hadn't perhaps made a strategic move by surrounding herself with the two small girls, thus

42

neatly avoiding the possibility of any gentle interrogation.

When had she herself become so suspicious of how other people behaved? Evie berated herself. Was this the legacy she was to be left with following her experiences with Timmy and Peter? Dear Julia had never done anything to warrant such outright misgiving, she told herself.

About seven o'clock Evie got up to go, Julia indicating that she would stay a little longer. Evie's early start was now making her feel quite sleepy, and she was looking forward to an early night.

It was not to be.

Back at Pemberley, the sitting room was abuzz with news as everyone sat around with cups of tea. Fellow PGs Mr and Mrs Wallace had realised they were missing their old home and their friends in Canterbury too much, and so they had decided that they were going to return there. This was even though Canterbury's location, relatively close to the White Cliffs of Dover, meant that often the German planes flew overheard and there was still a high chance of bombs dropping, although – thank goodness, as the painful cost had been desperately high earlier in the year – Plymouth, not many miles from Lymbridge, had been mercifully quiet on the bombing front for several months.

As Evie thought over this announcement from the Wallaces she realised she would miss Mrs Wallace, who had been enviably fashionable and also most supportive of Evie's Make Do and Mend sessions with the local sewing circle she'd organised at the massive dining-room table at Pemberley. Mrs Wallace had even paid Evie to do some mending for her and to make the odd commission or two.

But these thoughts as to the Wallaces were pushed to the side abruptly when Sukie and Linda arrived unexpectedly, Sukie perching precariously on the handlebars of Linda's bicycle, and the pair of them roaring with laughter as they made such a tremendous racket scooting up the drive that Evie rushed to the front door to see what the fuss was about.

'What on earth's going on?' Evie asked in a concerned voice. 'It's gone eight o'clock, and although I don't want to sound prim, it's late for you to visit for a Monday night.'

Linda was flushed and breathless from having peddled herself and Sukie to Pemberley, but after saying that her own bike had had a puncture and they'd been too excited to fix it before seeking Evie out, Sukie indicated to Evie that it was Linda who had the news and so Evie knew she would have to wait until their friend had managed to compose herself. Sukie had smiled conspiratorially at Evie, and at this Evie relaxed. Whatever it was that Linda wanted to say, it didn't look like it was going be bad news.

It turned out to be extremely good news.

'Evie, my sweet. You'll never guess,' squeaked Linda, gasping for breath still, and unattractively red of face. She seemed unable to go on.

Evie ran to the kitchen for a glass of cold water.

'Sam's popped the question,' Linda wheezed, once she'd gulped down the cool drink while standing on the drive still, with her bicycle propped against her and not having bothered to change out of her work britches and sturdy boots.

Evie flung her arms around Linda, as she cried, 'Congratulations.' She knew that this was what Linda wanted most in the world.

Mrs Worth and Mrs Wallace, and Tina and Sarah, were grouped at the doorstep, keen to see what all the noise was about.

Evie turned and told them, 'Linda's going to be married!'

And with that Linda and Sukie were bustled into the kitchen so that everybody could hear all about it. Mrs Worth put the kettle on, and Julia arrived back home to find a kitchen unusually full of chatter and laughter, and with everybody only thinking about Linda.

Sam Torrence, a young farmer who was painfully shy, and Linda had fallen for each other over the early summer when she had visited his farm to attend to the hooves and legs of his workhorses, used for ploughing and cart-pulling. At first, although Sam was obviously keen, Linda had had to work hard at making it very clear to Sam that if he were interested in thinking of her in a romantic light, then she could be persuaded to think likewise of him. And although initially Sam had seemed dense (actually incredibly dense, in Evie's opinion) as to what Linda was driving at, eventually the penny had dropped in Sam's honest but slow-witted brain, with the result that they had been walking out together for the past couple of months.

'I saw Sam earlier,' Linda explained. 'I was working at the Millets' farm just over from his as

45

I was giving their cows a trim and once-over, and so when I finished I popped across to see Sam while he was ploughing in his east field. And he just asked me out of the blue if we should make it official! After I'd made sure he'd not had a bump on the head, or been at a pint or two of Knock 'em Dead – as I've never known him to be decisive about anything before, or have much of an opinion one way or another – I said yes, and when should we be thinking regarding the official bit? And he said what about before Christmas; his mother had been married in the autumn and she and his father had been very happily wed,' gushed Linda in a much more rapid voice than her friends were used to, to general smiles from all who were in the kitchen. 'And I said yes, let's get married before the snow comes! And then he kissed me, even though he was still holding the horses at harness in the plough. I could hardly believe my ears! It was a wonderful kiss too.'

Evie thought it all whistlestop quick. Sam and Linda had been going steady for barely a couple of months, but Evie also felt they were perfectly suited to each other and so there probably wasn't much point in a long engagement. And in these times of war, when some people were quite often meeting, marrying and conceiving a baby in only a matter of days, this relationship looked positively long in the tooth, Evie supposed. With a bit of luck Sam hadn't been at the notorious Knock 'em Dead scrumpy made by The Haywain as, if he had, he'd never remember what he'd said to Linda. Sam wasn't the brightest – privately Evie thought him verging on the boring – but he was incredibly kind and honest, and blessed with a strong and fit body made muscular from all the work he did on his farm. It was obvious to anyone who saw them together that he absolutely adored Linda, and she him. And if Linda thought Sam was good enough to marry, then Evie did too, she decided.

Mr Worth had brewed some elderflower champagne earlier in the summer from the pretty trees that dotted the once-imposing gardens at Pemberley. Mrs Worth had pointed out that really it was 'elderflower sparkle' at best, as only wine made in Champagne in France could be called champagne, to which in quiet rebellion Mr Worth had written 'Elderflower CHAMPAGNE' in large letters on ready-glued labels he'd then quickly moistened and slapped on each bottle. And so, after a hurried scurry about to find suitable glasses, there was something special to drink to toast Linda and Sam's happiness.

After a quick confab, Evie, Sukie, Pattie and Julia promised their friend that their wedding present to her would be to provide a wedding outfit for the Big Day, at which point Linda choked on the bubbles going up her nose from the champagne and promptly burst into tears.

While Julia foraged for a clean hanky for Linda, and Pattie stroked Linda's arm while smiling broadly, Mrs Wallace drew Evie aside and said in a low voice, 'Come to my room when Linda has gone – I've a satin housecoat I hardly wear that you might be able to do something with.'

No sooner had Sukie and Linda been waved off than Mrs Worth said she had a further announce-

47

ment, which was that there was to be a new lady PG, a Mrs Sutcliffe, who would be moving to Pemberley the next week.

'Goodness me,' said Evie as she and Julia undressed later in their garret room, 'what a lot of change. I'll rather miss Mr and Mrs Wallace when they go, but I wonder what the new PG will be like.'

Julia added that Tina and Sarah had whispered on the Q.T. to her just as the fuss about Linda's news died down that they were thinking of leaving the West Country also, and heading for London. There was such a shortage of clothing and bedding for people in the capital who had lost their homes, with a mammoth operation underway to source and supply replacement items. And so although Plymouth had also been badly bombed and Tina and Sarah had been involved in doing similar work locally, the two WRVS girls felt that perhaps they could do good for more people if they were to relocate to London.

'Mrs Worth will have a conniption when they tell her as she's desperate to keep all her rooms filled to avoid any chance of Pemberley being requisitioned,' said Evie, and Julia nodded in agreement. 'It's this war. You just get to know someone, and realise you like them, and you feel almost as if you are all close allies banded together against the biggest possible threat we can ever face, and then off they go to somewhere else and you never know if you'll see them again.'

Evie wasn't quite clear in her mind whether she was talking about the Wallaces and the WRVS girls, or Peter.

And then, before Julia got too sleepy – she cycled for miles delivering post each day to outlying moorland farms and remote cottages and she tended to drift off almost immediately after her head touched the pillow – Evie added that the satin housecoat belonging to Mrs Wallace had proved to have distinct possibilities. She thought that it could either make the skirt part of Linda's wedding dress, as the dressing gown's own skirt section was cut to be quite full (clearly it had been produced before the war, as now it was all utility clothing with no wasted material), or else it could do for the bodice, leaving material over that could be used for something else. Evie would decide which option would be best when she'd managed to scavenge some material that would work for the corresponding other part of the dress.

A low snore from Julia's direction told Evie she'd not been quick or interesting enough in describing the options the housecoat offered.

Evie wriggled further under her own eiderdown, and she fell asleep just as she remembered she had failed either to pin-curl her hair, or to put her sleeping scarf on.

But what was more odd about this was that while Evie could be erratic in bothering (or not) with her hair before bed, Julia, who for months had been religious in her nightly ritual of pin-curling, had this evening also neglected to follow her normal routine, with the result that in the soft moonlight from the night sky Evie could see Julia's tresses lying wantonly across her pillow. It was the only time Evie could remember such a thing happening.

## Chapter Three

A week or so later, Evie was sitting at Pemberley's kitchen table after supper to pen some letters. She decided to write to Timmy first.

Although it had been horrible when she had found out about his infidelity when they were engaged earlier in the year, and it had hurt Evie dreadfully at the time, they had become much closer since they were no longer engaged to one another.

This was an irony that wasn't lost on Evie, especially as in fact she had then been instrumental in ensuring that Timmy and Tricia, who was carrying his baby (a baby, Evie felt she'd never forget, who'd been conceived during Timmy and Evie's engagement), had ended up together. Indeed the parents-to-be had married while Timmy was lying in a hospital bed at Stoke Mandeville in Buckinghamshire, with Evie and Sukie as witnesses. Timmy and Tricia weren't quite love's young dream, but Evie hoped sincerely that they would find a way to be happy together.

Life was very strange sometimes, Evie mused as she looked at her sheet of Basildon Bond paper before she leant forward to begin writing. The way things worked themselves out seemed to happen regardless, despite whatever one might do to influence events one way or another.

*Dearest Timmy*

*Your mother's last letter to me said you are continuing to improve, with less severe headaches and some quite good and painless movement in your arms, and that it might not be too long before you can join Tricia and the rest of us back in Lymbridge. The recuperation hospital is near enough that we will all be able to visit you, and quite often too. I think your improving health is absolutely wonderful news, and I am so very, very pleased for both you and Tricia, and the coming baby too, of course.*

*I thought you might like to know that Linda is now engaged to Sam Torrence, who has a farm about three miles away, and they will wed well before Christmas (Linda being very keen they tie the knot before the harsh weather comes, as you know how miserable a moorland in winter can be). Linda will be moving in with Sam and his mother. Apparently Sam's mother is very pleasant, although Linda thinks she might have something of a battle on her hands because his mother serves very large portions of food (one of the ad-vantages of living on a farm, in my view; I am always hungry these days!), as of course Sam works very long hours and is always carrying heavy things about. And so Linda is worried that too many home-cooked meals of those dimensions might mean she won't be able to fit into her work breeches. But I suppose this might not matter for too long as although Sam is happy for Linda to keep working as a farrier, which she is really pleased about, she says that if she falls pregnant she probably will have to stop, as then – very sensibly, I think – she'd be terrified of being kicked in the stomach by a horse when she is shoeing it.*

*Knowing that you've been no stranger to the bookies in the past(!), I thought you'd like to know that there's going to be a small point-to-point (or what will pass for one at least) now that the racing ban has been lifted at last. It's going to be on a portion of what will be the airfield; it's being cleared as I write, and will be positioned close to the recuperation hospital end of the airstrip. Apparently the land has been worked over and levelled, ready if they need it for either a hangar or for soldiers to be billeted there, but this further development is unlikely to happen until the New Year, and so with the land not doing anything much it's said to be the ideal place for the race.*

*(Incidentally, we're all somewhat agog at the moment as there are rumours milling about every evening in The Haywain, which Mr Cawes is very happy to fill me in on, that we might end up with rather a lot of recruits being billeted around here, for various sorts of training as we're so close to the sea. And, as you know of course, the moors offer all sorts of rugged terrain too. No one's quite sure what it all means, but there's definitely been a more frequent number of important-looking chaps walking around with scrambled egg on their caps than we're used to. There's also a rumour that the Polish airmen that will fight on our side could be stationed here – Pattie and most of the young ladies around her are very excited at the thought of this, needless to say!)*

*Anyway my father and James, and our two boy evacuees, have volunteered to build the obstacles for the point-to-point. Father told me that James drove a hard bargain over what his payment should be for the work. And I think James has been coaching Frank and Joseph in this respect too as I hear they weren't back-*

52

ward in coming forward either to talk about their payment. I think when you come home you'll notice how much James has grown up – he is practically a man now, and I'm sure that in time you'll find him a pleasant chap with whom you'll be able to go and have a pint.

You would laugh though. Linda put Sukie and me in touch with that farmer Bill Tucker, who you'll remember used to have that stable of hunters. He's had a couple of goodish horses turned away for the past year at least, but he's allowed us to bring in two to fitten them up – they've not been ridden for almost two years and aren't at all sure they want to be ridden by us just now. Mine especially... Anyway, Sukie is going to ride hers in the race – it's a daft old mare, but she likes it and it's very fast and seems to be clean as a jumper, although to be honest we've only had it over a few tiddly fences so far and it doesn't seem to like ditches much, although that just seems to spur Sukie on that bit more.

Mine is – wait for it! – going to be ridden by Dave Symons in the race. Yes: Dave Symons! And I say good luck to him as it's got a screw loose and it's had me off twice already, and from what I can see, based on my one time of watching him ride it out, he's not that good in the saddle.

So, if you're still a betting man (and I'd be guessing you are) I'd advise putting your money on Sukie, rather than Dave Symons, even though I know he's your best pal.

Warm regards to you and Tricia – I saw her the other Saturday afternoon when we were both on the bus to Plymouth, and she seemed well.

My best wishes, Evie

53

She was still alone in the kitchen and so Evie thought that while she was about it and had her writing paper to hand, she'd write quickly to Mrs Smith, to let her know how things were progressing at school.

*Dear Mrs Smith (how odd it seems to be calling you that – I think there's a little bit of me that will always think of you as Mrs Bowes!),*

*I've just written to Timmy to say that I saw Tricia on the bus to Plymouth the other day, and she seemed well, although I did notice that she's quite large now. Anyway, she asked if I'd heard from you. And I think she's looking forward to having the baby now, as she explained she's getting very tired and her ankles are painfully swollen.*

*In my letter to Timmy I mentioned also that there's going to be a point-to-point race in early November and Timmy's erstwhile partner in crime Dave Symons is going to ride in it. Having seen Dave ride out the other day, I think it may prove fortuitous that the race is going to take place right next door to the new recuperation hospital, as the medical skills of the doctors might very well be required.*

*I also thought you'd like to hear a little about the school. It's all proceeding reasonably smoothly, although having Mr Bassett in the room next door is most definitely not the same as having you writing on the blackboard in the juniors classroom or invigilating a spelling test or playing the piano.*

*I have very much enjoyed teaching this past week or two – it seems easier this term than last for some* reason, but I think that's more down to the fact that the pupils I have at the moment are all sweet children who really want to learn, rather than because I have developed any new skills as a teacher, much as I would like to believe otherwise.

The juniors like Mr Bassett well enough, I suppose, and he seems an able teacher. That's not to say that they don't miss you very much too, of course, and I am sure that they all hope that you will soon be back at the helm of Lymbridge Primary School, giving them what-for when they don't know their eleven times table off pat.

Still, I'd be fibbing if I didn't confess that I have found Mr Bassett somewhat dicey to get on with – he barely says a word to me, either at school or when our paths cross at Pemberley (which happens surprisingly infrequently). And sometimes when I am talking to him, he seems only to be staring out of the window, and is not at all aware of what I'm saying. I don't know whether he is like that in the classroom with his pupils. Joseph is in his class, as you know, and although I've given Joe plenty of chances to say if there seems anything odd about their new teacher, so far all he can think to say is that he and the rest of them feel it is wonderful that Mr Bassett likes cricket so much as he organises lots of bat-and-ball sessions, and even nets practice on a Saturday morning in nets he's put up on a bit of unused parking space at Pemberley behind the rhododendrons. Goodness knows what Mr and Mrs Worth think about all and sundry turning up at every weekend for a spot of bowling!

I had a postcard from Timmy a couple of days ago. His writing isn't what it once was, but it's certainly such an improvement on what he could manage just *this summer, and it cheered me no end to know that he has made such great strides. I am sure you and dear Mr Smith, and the doctors (and Timmy too, of course) are delighted with his progress.*

*I must go now or otherwise I will be late for bed. But I am very much looking forward to the day when you and Mr Smith, and Timmy too of course, return to Lymbridge – I do hope this will be soon.*

*Most affectionately yours*

*Evie Yeo*

Evie had two stamps in her purse, and she quickly addressed envelopes for both letters and stamped them, and left them on the hall table. With a bit of luck whoever was next going through Lymbridge would see the letters waiting and pop them into the post box outside the village shop for her.

As she walked down the drive the next morning on the way to school, Evie smiled when she thought of Timmy and Tricia, and how Timmy would cope with a wife and a new baby. He and Tricia barely knew each other – once, in an awkward conversation, Tricia had described to an incredibly curious Evie the conception of the baby as merely a quick fumble as they stood against the wall behind the church hall. And everybody acknowledged privately, although thankfully not vocally, that Tricia's humble upbringing and her job as a maid in a dairy parlour were a far shot from Mrs Smith's previously much snootier middle-class aspirations for the type of person her son's wife should be – after all, there had been a time when Mrs Smith had felt very short-changed at the prospect of Evie, who had gone to teacher training college, as her future daughter-in-law.

Timmy had confided to Evie though, after he'd released her from their engagement, that he'd felt he had to do the right thing by Tricia – and Evie felt Timmy was honest and rather brave to acknowledge this so openly to her – in large part because his injuries meant he might never be able to father another child. This hard-to-accept fact made the coming baby very precious indeed to Timmy and his mother, even if the forthcoming arrival of he or she had at first seemed a very unwelcome surprise.

Timmy had been candid when he'd added that he and Tricia weren't in love with each other, but Timmy had assured Evie that they were committed to being the best parents they could be to their baby, and so Evie was never to think that the ending of her and Timmy's engagement had been in vain or was in any way trivial. He promised Evie with all his heart that he would try to make a good life for his new family from now on, and not waste time with recriminations or unhappiness for the course his life had taken.

When Evie heard Timmy's comments, she was relieved. For now, although it hadn't seemed so in the spring, she knew that she had never really been properly in love with Timmy, or he with her. Their engagement had followed what had felt at the time like an exciting whirlwind romance. They had been caught up just as much in the public sense of excitement caused by other people getting engaged when their loved ones were about to leave to fight, as Evie and Timmy had been in each other.

Certainly they had found each other fun and they liked each other well enough to think that in time they could be a good match for each other. But there had been an element of pragmatism in the proposed union. Evie was well educated and nicely presented, even though her family were in more reduced circumstances than they had been when she was a youngster, the years of the depression having taken their toll on many West Country businessmen such as Robert, whose village garage had failed in the 1930s. As far as Timmy was concerned, Evie had a lot more going for her than most of the single girls in Lymbridge, and Timmy had felt that Evie would in time be accepted by his fearsome mother. Meanwhile, Timmy and his mother had a good position in Lymbridge society, but Timmy's relationship with Evie was brought into balance by Timmy being less clever than Evie (a fact he would readily own up to), although one of Timmy's better points was that he was always immensely charming, and so Evie, with her brains and good looks, lent Timmy a certain cachet that he openly admitted to all and sundry he didn't have on his own. In short, there was something about Evie that Timmy felt lent him an aura of class.

What had shocked Evie when she thought about it later in the summer was that the reasonably chaste kisses she and Timmy had shared, although pleasant enough, had in no way ignited the throb of passion that swept across her when Peter had taken her by surprise with his sudden kiss – now *that* had been a revelation, as a flustered Evie had never previously dreamt that such feelings were possible.

Evie drew in her breath as her body responded to the memory with a ferocious intensity.

Unfortunately, this feeling was quickly followed by the horrible and inevitable tummy-sink of knowing Peter could never be hers.

Her expression darkened as she remembered that it had all been disastrous as far as Peter had been concerned. Evie had kept her engagement to Timmy secret from him and he'd been very hurt when, of course, it had all come out. Normally she was a very honest person, but when she met Peter Evie had been embarrassed that she'd committed herself to a callow person like Timmy, who had already made another woman pregnant, and so somehow she never found the words to mention the existence of her fiancé when she and Peter had chatted. And very quickly afterwards, it was too late for Evie to broker that particular conversation. She felt very ashamed of her failure of good sense and in the way she had behaved over the whole affair.

After the welcome end of the engagement with Timmy (Susan having always been suspicious as to the merits of their relationship, as a good mother should sense when a daughter might be getting married for the wrong reasons), Evie had felt herself delighted to acknowledge that she was now an unattached woman who could be a free agent in matters of her heart.

It was with all haste she had raced back to Pemberley from Timmy's bedside at Stoke Mandeville hospital to tell Peter she could now be his, only to find Peter had been suddenly moved elsewhere by whatever department it was he worked for, and that he hadn't left a forwarding address. Even the redoubtable Sukie hadn't been able to think of a way that Evie could get in touch with him. Peter had always kept what he actually did in the war effort closely under wraps with the result that Evie knew woefully little about his life outside what they had shared at Pemberley.

Then a chance meeting between Evie and Peter in London a while later (ironically on the very evening of Timmy's wedding to Tricia) revealed a terrible truth.

For Peter had been so convinced that Evie would marry Timmy, that when he'd unexpectedly run into his childhood sweetheart, Fiona, immediately on his return to London, they had resumed their relationship. Within weeks (and with undue haste in Evie's opinion), everyone assumed Peter and Fiona were set to marry.

Tears threatened as Evie remembered now how she had run from Peter at hearing this devastating news, although not quite before they had kissed passionately in an intimate sitting room late at night at The Ritz on London's Piccadilly.

As she had forced herself to leave his arms, Peter had called to her in an anguished tone, but she hadn't dared to look back at him or to listen to anything else he might have to say.

Since then there had been total silence: no visit, no letter, no telephone call, no nothing.

Evie could only think that it was clear Peter felt that Fiona was the woman for him. And that Evie was to be consigned to nothing more than a blip in his past.

Whatever pain Evie thought she'd felt when Dave Symons told her about Timmy and his philandering was simply nothing compared to how demolished and abjectly depressed Evie had felt since that terrible evening at The Ritz.

She was tortured with despair and jealousy. Ill behaviour on her part had led to the scuppering of a relationship with a man she was sure was perfect for her, and she him. Evie had never met Fiona but she detested even the sound of her name.

And the worst of it was that Evie had to act all the time now as if everything was well in her world, or at the very least as if it would be once the dust had settled after Timmy's marriage. It was imperative that her friends and family never found out about Peter, as of course Evie had allowed him to kiss her when she was, in a technical sense at least, still engaged to another man – scandalous behaviour that wouldn't do at all. It was all so complicated. At the time of the first kiss, her parents and Mrs Smith had been unaware of Timmy's infidelity, and Evie had been living the charade of being a happily engaged fiancée. What a mess it had all been.

Only Sukie had been let in to the secret of Evie's all-consuming feelings for Peter, and Evie knew that Sukie would die rather than say anything that might compromise her best friend. Evie wasn't at all proud of giving in to Peter's kisses, thrilling as they were, and so she had sworn Sukie to secrecy.

It might seem very old fashioned, but in Devon in 1941 Evie knew that, once lost, a young woman's good reputation could never be resurrected. And although Evie felt certain she would never fall in love again or marry now she had carelessly let Peter slip through her fingers, nevertheless she didn't want to become tarnished goods, especially as this might have an unforeseen effect on Julia and Pattie's own marriage prospects. Evie's family would of course want to protect her in any event, but it only took one inopportune word and then the cat would be out of the bag. Evie simply couldn't take this risk.

Oh Peter, what have you and I done? How could we get it so wrong? I think you did want me, and I certainly wanted you. But I should have been honest with you from the moment I first met you about my engagement to Timmy, and the emptiness of that relationship, and then we wouldn't have got in such a tangle, Evie chided herself. I don't know why I wasn't completely straight with you from the very first day, and now I am paying a dreadful price. Although it would have helped, naturally, if you hadn't flung yourself in Fiona's direction with quite such alacrity.

But then Evie realised that if she had been clearer about herself being engaged to Timmy, then Peter would never have dared to kiss her, no matter how much he might have wanted to. He was very polite and proper, and it was impossible to imagine him ever overstepping the invisible boundary set by an engagement ring.

Gloomy as it was, Evie thought, at least she had those exquisite stolen kisses to remember in secret private moments. And no one could take those away from her.

Evie realised with a start she was standing in her classroom. Her thoughts had been so powerful that she could remember virtually nothing of her short journey to school, or even what the weather this September morning had been like. With a sigh she pulled out her chair and sat down. She needed a moment to compose herself before she could risk seeing Mr Bassett.

After a minute or two of staring morosely at her teacher's desk, she pulled from her handbag the notes that she had made the previous evening concerning the annual Goosey Fair in Tavistock, which would be taking place quite soon. She planned, with the parents' permission, to take her class to the fair one evening after school finished, and she thought that they could do some work on it beforehand, starting first thing that morning. Besides being a lot of fun for the children, as there would be colourful sideshows and lots to talk about in the classroom afterwards, it was a good opportunity to bring local history and traditions alive for them, even if it might have to be done in a very simple way in order for her youngest pupils to feel involved.

The annual harvest festival was looming too, and so Evie decided to send each child home with a note to say that she would be preparing a harvest festival table in the classroom, and it would be nice if each child's family could contribute something, even if only something very small. Then, on the Friday afternoon before the church service to celebrate the harvest, she and her class could carry everything from their harvest table to the church and rearrange their display beside the bigger one that the rest of the village would have contributed to.

Both Goosey Fair and the harvest festival would also provide the opportunity for her pupils to do some more painting. Evie decided to see if she could borrow Mr Worth's camera, as it might be nice to take some pictures of the children going about their school day, with a painting lesson probably making for nice photographs.

Feeling soothed at these calming thoughts of lesson plans and suchlike, although she could feel a slight flush on her cheeks still, Evie decided she was now calm enough to be able to say good morning to Mr Bassett.

'Evie? Evie! Come and say hello to Miss Frome,' rang the commanding voice of Mrs Worth as Evie walked through the front door at Pemberley that afternoon after school.

Miss Frome proved to be a demure-looking woman in her mid twenties, although Evie was more than a little surprised at how firm her hand-shake was.

She was the new PG, and Mrs Worth very obviously felt she was a young lady of good character and breeding, to judge by the fuss that was being made of the afternoon tea Mrs Worth was preparing in welcome, with the excited rattle of the second-best tea service and the hot buttered crumpets sending out a delicious aroma.

Evie felt like saying to Miss Frome – there'd been no mention of a Christian name, even though Evie had introduced herself as simply that,

64

and Miss Frome only looked to be a couple of years older – that she shouldn't think for a moment they had afternoon tea like this every day. During the week, Mrs Worth would nudge them towards the third-best crockery, with the second-best being reserved for Sundays, and the very best only for Really Important Visitors. And Evie couldn't remember the last time they had had crumpets, let alone a generous amount of butter to go with them.

'Have you been to Lymbridge before?' Evie asked politely, which gleaned a terse, 'Not really' in response.

Evie tried again, 'Do you come from Devon?' This time the reply was simply, 'No'.

It took the arrival of Julia and her gentle smile and kindly manner before there was any sense of a softening atmosphere. And before long Miss Frome was happily chatting away about being a bespoke dressmaker from Brighton, but that her fiancé had asked her to move to an area that was likely to be safer from German air activity.

Evie wasn't sure that Dartmoor was the ideal choice in this respect, with Plymouth having seen such incredibly heavy bombing earlier in the year – it was a strategic site for merchant shipping as well as a large naval base, and there were also a lot of airfields around too. But, she decided, it was probably kinder to keep quiet about this.

Miss Frome mentioned she had once been on a weekend holiday to Dartmoor when she was a child but that she hadn't been back since and nor did she have any relatives living locally. Evie decided to give the new PG the benefit of the doubt, and so she told herself that to choose somewhere to live on such a slender knowledge was a brave thing to do.

Evie felt for a moment that she didn't have either the inclination or the energy to make much more of an effort with the new PG. Those depressing thoughts of Peter just before school started had cast an unwelcome pall over the rest of her day that she was finding most difficult to shake off. And Evie had had a busy afternoon as the Women's Institute had sent one of their canning machines to Lymbridge (these machines were being loaned around the country to make sure that as much food was preserved for winter use as possible), and so following a hasty lesson just after lunch on the various sorts of food and how they could be preserved by canning, Evie had taken her infants to see the process of canning. She had thought beforehand that they would be interested in the process, but actually they had been rather bored as there wasn't nearly as much to look at as Evie had anticipated. And so the jaunt out of the school gates hadn't turned out to be one of Evie's better ideas.

However, as she sipped her tea Evie noticed that the jacket of Miss Frome's suit was exceptionally well cut, and as she was always keen to improve her own needlework skills it wasn't long before she was complimenting the young woman on her clothes, once Evie had established that Miss Frome had made them herself.

And when Miss Frome added that she had designed her outfit as well as making it up, Evie's ears really pricked up. This was a skill that she

66

would give her eye teeth to perfect.

The teatime ended with Evie believing Miss Frome to be just a little shy and to be suffering a wrench from leaving the area she knew well, rather than merely stand-offish as she'd first seemed.

At supper that evening Paul Rogers ate with them. It was the first time he had done so since moving in. Mr Rogers was a freelance journalist, and he had been doing some evening shifts at the *Western Morning News,* and in addition had been away travelling around West Cornwall on various stories, and even up as far as Bristol on the Somerset border and on into South Wales. As he chattered away about this and that it became clear that he and Mr Bassett turned out not to have been previously friends as Sukie had suggested to Evie might be the case, but that they had simply arrived at Pemberley in the same taxi.

To judge by his expression, Mr Rogers was about as keen on Mr Bassett as Evie was, although he seemed rather taken with Miss Frome. Evie hoped Miss Frome would be more quick on the uptake than she herself had been when she first met Peter, and would slip the word 'fiancé' into the conversation before too long.

Anyway, Mr Rogers proved to be a cheerful chap who was very talkative and who had a real knack of lightening the mood and making every-body feel more cheerful. Evie thought he and her father, Robert, would get on like a house on fire over a pint of scrumpy down at The Haywain.

Mr Bassett remained his usual taciturn self as the meal progressed, looking towards the window and speaking only if spoken to. Evie felt at one point that she should make more of an effort with him, and so she tried to get him to tell Miss Frome and Mr Rogers about the nets for bowling practise and how excited some of the boys were at the school now there was the prospect of a little specialist coaching, even at this unusual time of the cricketing year. But Mr Bassett gave Evie a coolly appraising stare, and was little more than monosyllabic on the subject.

Julia caught Evie's eye and raised her brow, and the sisters shared a look. Julia then tried to bring Mr Bassett into the conversation, her cheeks reddening slightly when she was rebuffed just as firmly.

To fill the slightly awkward pause in the conversation caused by Julia being thwarted, Mr Rogers started talking about a story he was working on at the moment.

The government had announced that a donation of £6,000 could be used to buy a Spitfire for the Air Force, while £20,000 could secure a bomber which the RAF would then use to fight.

'How extraordinary,' said Evie.

And Mrs Worth added that she had never heard the like.

After a quite lively discussion, the consensus around the table was that although £6,000 was a very large amount of money, the war must be costing a fortune as so many planes had or were being lost.

Lying in bed later that evening while Julia slept peaceably, Evie couldn't stop thinking that it was an exciting thought that anybody could buy a

68

Spitfire provided they could raise enough money.

Wouldn't it be wonderful if Lymbridge could do its bit in this respect?

Evie decided to have a word with Mr Rogers. Perhaps together they could come up with ideas on raising money, which he could then publicise. Over the summer she and Peter had joined forces to put on the summer Revels in Lymbridge, which had proved to be a surprisingly effective strategy in Getting Things Done, and so although Evie didn't find Mr Rogers in the least bit attractive in the way that she had been drawn to Peter, she wondered if Mr Rogers and herself might be able to work together just as rewardingly to raise money for a Spitfire.

It was with great frustration that although she tried to time her breakfast the next morning with when she thought Mr Rogers would be having his that Evie discovered that he had been telephoned during the night by his news desk, with the result that at first light he had left Pemberley once again for what looked as if it would be several nights away.

## Chapter Four

The next few days were a general flurry of activity as Evie got the schoolchildren, the juniors as well as the infants, to prepare a harvest table at the school. It was decorated with drawings of local vegetable produce and some rather frightening attempts at corn dollies, as well as various floral decorations gleaned from two nature walks around the village.

Rather to Evie's disbelief on these walks – the teachers having joined forces, walking the thirty-two children in the school in one group – Mr Bassett proved to be rather good with the secateurs and then surprisingly willing to carry the branches he'd cut.

Soon there were some aromatic hawthorn, blackthorn and crab apple branches artfully arranged on the table in the small foyer between the classrooms, around which the children placed the various harvest offerings. After a bit of bribery, Evie having gone off the idea of getting her kiddies to help move and then rearrange the offerings, James had agreed to transport the whole table to the church on Saturday afternoon and set it up just as it was at the school in order that at church the following morning the pupils of Lymbridge Primary school could show their parents all that they had collected.

Evie was rather proud of herself as she taught her infants the Latin names of the branches Mr Bassett had cut and carried back for her. Before long she no sooner had to point to the crab apple just as she'd be getting everyone in at the end of playtime, than her class would yell back (she encouraged them, this one time, to shout out as loud as they could, rather to Keith the cat's surprise the first time it happened) *Malus sylvestris*. Or *Prunus spinosa* when she waved a hand towards the blackthorn, although when she got to the bit about explaining that this particular tree was also known as a sloe, she could see that she was losing the attention of her tots as she was maybe offering them a bit too much information on the subject.

Meanwhile, the recuperation hospital at the Grange had at long last opened its doors to the first patients, and this meant that Sukie was now back working full-time in the administration department following the delay in the hospital's launch that had led to her having to be there part-time over the last month or two.

As Sukie explained when she and Evie were riding out, which they were doing now every tea-time in the crisply shortening evenings, it wasn't a moment too soon.

'Honestly, Evie-Rose, the powers that be had cut my hours so much as there wasn't much on the filing or note-taking side that I could do until we were open for business – and there are only so many bandages and dressings that one can count and record, after all – and I was almost on the point of having to get some bar work to tide me over. I hadn't budgeted for such reduced circumstances, so it's all been very testing. So far there's not too many patients, but they will be coming to us from quite a number of other hospitals, so I hear,' she said. 'Of course I'm keeping an eye out–'

'Naturally!' chipped in Evie, knowing what was coming in the way that old friends always do.

Sukie's withering gaze in her friend's direction turned to amusement when Evie's horse, a rather large grey gelding, took umbrage at being asked to walk through a puddle, his quick swerve causing Evie to lurch precariously in the saddle.

'At least he's on my side! Give him a little tap though with your whip behind your leg as he's just playing up and we can all see that he knows better manners than that and so he's just having you on,' advised Sukie, who was the more experienced rider. 'As I was saying before being so rudely interrupted by both of you, when I *casually* perused the doctors and anaesthetists at a general meeting of all the staff this morning, I confess to being disappointed. Not so much eligible when all is said and done, as negligible so far, I'm sad to report.'

'In that case, I'm pretty sure that there's a wonderfully handsome and incomprehensibly single consultant who's obviously much in need of a glamorous and beautiful belle, and who must right at this moment be packing his bags ready to make his way to the Dartmoor Recuperation Hospital where the woman of his dreams is already ensconced,' Evie said, trying to cheer up her friend.

'Don't I wish it!' said Sukie.

And with that the friends urged their horses into a short, fast canter up a steep bridleway, before turning around to do it again as it was an excellent way of building muscle. They then headed to a moorland spring with a pebbly base and stood their mounts in it for ten minutes as Sukie had been told by one of the nurses who'd previously helped fitten hunters in North Devon for stag hunting on Exmoor that they had tried to take the hunters for a splash about in the sea every day as the cool water was so good for their legs.

Sukie looked at Evie, and then began in a careful tone, 'To judge by your slightly blue look of these current times, I don't suppose yorn Peter has been in touch?' Evie shook her head, causing the headscarf she'd knotted over her curls in order to keep her hair out of the way when she rode to slip backwards slightly. Then Sukie positioned her head in such a manner that Evie was in no doubt her friend was looking directly at her and trying to gauge her expression. 'Evie-Rose, dearest, has enough water passed under the bridge for you to tell me what happened at The Ritz after I'd done the decent thing and made myself scarce, leaving the two of you together?'

There was a silence between them as Evie wondered what to say. Looking down at her horse's dappled neck and his darker gunmetal mane, and below him, the clear moorland water and the brown and grey stones of the bed of the stream, Evie took a moment to fiddle with her mount's mane, and then she sighed.

So far Evie hadn't spoken a word to Sukie about what had occurred between her and Peter, knowing that her tears and silence were more eloquent than anything she could have managed to utter in those first few painful days. Perhaps now was the time to come clean.

'Well, we were both incredibly surprised to see each other, as you can imagine,' explained Evie. 'I told Peter about the ending of my engagement, and that you and I had that very day been to Timmy and Tricia's wedding, and I described to Peter also how after Timmy had released me from our damn fool engagement I had rushed back to Pemberley to tell him that if he were interested in

73

me, I was at long last an unencumbered woman.

'Peter looked horrified at what I said to him. It then turned out that he thought I was all set to marry come what may, and so when he was directed away from Dartmoor for whatever department he works for, it sounds as if he bumped into his former sweetheart, Fiona, pretty much the moment he arrived in London. He told me that she'd jilted him for somebody else but when they met by accident she was now once more on her own. From what I can tell, within days it seems, all was back as it once was between them, with a pressing understanding that this time they'd see it through to the ring, and on smartish to happy families.'

Sukie was unused to the bitter tone in Evie's voice. 'Evie-Rose, no!'

'As it dawned on me what he was saying, I could feel I was going to cry. That was if I didn't pull my hair out in a temper first at the injustice of it all – honestly, I could have screamed in frustration. But I wished Peter well in as cheery a voice as I could, and then I tried to get out of that silly sitting room before howling my eyes out. But he grabbed me and we kissed. For those seconds, I was in pure, total bliss. But then I came to my senses, and I think he did too. And so I pushed him away and ran as fast as I could up to the bedroom that you and I were sharing. Peter called out to me, but I couldn't allow myself to look back. And the rest you know.'

'Peter Pipe, what a stupid, stupid, stupid man,' said Sukie with vigour, as her horse tossed its head up and down as if nodding in agreement. 'If he'd left you a way of getting in touch rather than going off with his tail between his legs, or if he'd put up a bit of a fight for you instead of being so damn properly behaved and stepping meekly aside for the likes of that fool Timmy Bowes, this could all have been averted. As it is, both of you are left in an awful situation, as I can't believe that Fiona is much cop – well, she couldn't be next to you, could she? – and I'm sure that right at this minute both you and he are equally miserable and unhappy. The silly, feeble ... um ... er ... um ... man,' finished Sukie rather lamely.

And then as their horses touched companionable noses together, Sukie passed a clean hankie across to Evie, whose eyes were welling with salty tears.

On the Sunday evening, after evensong, Evie co-opted the help of Pattie and Julia, Linda and Sukie, and PGs Tina and Sarah to help her dole out the offerings from the morning's harvest thanksgiving to the poorest families in the village. Rev. Painter had buttonholed Evie that morning on the church steps, wondering if she would be able to take care of this annual ritual for him, and Evie hadn't been able to think quickly enough of an excuse so that it should be somebody else rather than she who did all the running around and making sure that the food was divvied up and delivered safely to the needy.

It actually turned out to be a much more rewarding hour or so than Evie had expected, and it wasn't long before she felt distinctly churlish for dragging her feet over it earlier.

At one house there was a family who were listening to their battered radiogram when Evie had tapped on the door. Evie's words of explanation were interrupted by the national anthem being played on the live broadcast.

Evie felt unbearably touched when she saw every single member of the family stand up to attention in silent respect as the familiar notes rang out from the tinny-sounding, cloth-covered loudspeaker.

London and the BBC might be many miles away, but the patriotic feelings inspired by the national anthem were celebrated across the land in what seemed like every home, Evie felt, from the most lavish to the incredibly lowly. She knew that at Bluebells, although the whole Yeo family would remain quiet in respect as the anthem played, they wouldn't have stood up. Evie wasn't quite sure why, but she felt both humbled and spiritually enriched as she looked around at the open faces of this poor but proud family who were unafraid to show their simple patriotic devotion.

And for the first time in quite some while, Evie also felt that although she was undeniably very sad at the moment about her failed romance with Peter, there were nevertheless some things that made life worth living. In fact, she was nothing short of privileged to be sharing this moment of what was really some sort of outpouring of faith in a ramshackle and rundown Devon dwelling with such ordinary but clearly good people.

For just a few seconds, a feeling of peace and acceptance washed across Evie.

As she walked home slowly afterwards, Evie realised it was the best she had felt since that evening at The Ritz.

After the festival produce had been safely delivered, the young women all reconvened at
Pemberley. It was time to see how they were
getting on with making a wedding trousseau for
Linda.

Evie had had the foresight to ask Miss Frome if
she would join them. When Evie had made sure
that Miss Frome, who still seemed rather shy, had
been introduced to everyone, at last she admitted
to a first name; it was Annabel, and so Evie quickly
said, 'What a lovely name – it's one of my favourites.' She was rewarded with a tentative smile in
return from the slightly awkward new PG.

The reality was that they hadn't got very far in
helping out as regards to what Linda would be
wearing on her Big Day. There was the satin
housecoat from Mrs Wallace, of course, although
no decision had been made as to how best to uti-
lise it, while Mrs Smith had sent down to Pemberley some brand-new delicately crocheted lace
gloves. And that was it.

Evie suggested that Annabel look over what they
had. It was a very brief look, and then a professionally scrutinising glance was cast in the
direction of Linda's quite substantial frame. In
response Linda stared downwards at her own
body, almost as if seeing it for the very first time.
She twisted around to inspect her rear, and finally
looked at herself from each side in the tall mirror
above a small semi-circular table set against the
wall. It didn't seem that Linda was terribly enamoured by what she saw.

Annabel said, 'This is going to need cleverness and invention,' and with that she examined more carefully the satin housecoat both inside and out, paying special attention to the seamwork, as she held it up to a nearby lamp to inspect closely. Then she looked up and added they would need to obtain some backing material as the housecoat fabric was on the fragile side, and a firmly sewed lining would reduce the danger of the top silken layer splitting when Linda sat down or danced.

Linda looked dejected as she was rather sensitive about the size of her behind, but not quite dejected enough to distract Evie from noticing that Julia seemed to have done what was by now fast becoming one of her trademark disappearing acts.

At first Evie wondered if her sister was in the lavatory but after ten minutes and no reappearance from Julia, Evie became increasingly suspicious, even risking a raised-eyebrow look at Pattie at the same time as she inclined her head very slightly towards the door and then towards Julia's empty seat. Pattie raised her brows and nodded back almost imperceptibly in answer.

It was fortuitous that Mrs Worth bustled into the dining room to see how they were getting along, because when they mentioned the need for lining material she came to the rescue. Unbeknownst to Evie, earlier in the week Mrs Worth had been sorting through the contents of old packing cases in the attic and had come across a battered but much-loved dressing-up box her nieces and nephews had played with more than fifteen years previously, and so Mrs Worth said, 'Evie, why don't you and Pattie pop up to the

78

attic and fetch the dressing-up box down here as there might be something useful there you can purloin and make something of? It will all need a thorough wash of course, but you may be able to find the odd treasure there amongst the jumble.'

Once the box was in the dining room it proved to be a veritable Aladdin's cave. Everything was grubby and quite a lot of it was a bit moth-holey, but there were riches nestling amongst the tangle of clothes and trinkets.

Aside from a sizeable quantity of old costume jewellery that had become enmeshed together, and some dresses that were probably the height of fashion in the early 1920s and a collarless cotton men's shirt or two that had presumably been Mr Worth's, there were several pure silk petticoats and an array of sizeable bloomers that had seen better days (Evie and the others had to make sure they didn't catch each other's eyes as it would have been unforgiveable to snigger when Mrs Worth was being so charitable). There were also some damask off-cuts from what probably had been curtains, and quite a lot of curtain nets. But the real find was a large white fox stole, even though it was distinctly tatty in places and one end seemed to have been rubbed against blue paint while the other sported the hideous dried-out face of the poor white fox, with his accusing red glass eyes staring vindictively out at them.

Everyone watched Annabel as she looked at the haul with narrowed eyes, and carefully inspected this piece of material and then that.

'Linda,' she said eventually, 'I think we are sorted. It all needs new life breathing into it, of course, but we can save the buttons from the underwear and the shirts, and the housecoat is big enough to make your whole wedding dress as long as you don't want too long a skirt, or sleeves. If you are happy with that then we will have enough to make you a panelled bodice, lined with the cotton from the shirts, and I can cover the underwear buttons with scraps of the silk, as I should have enough there too to make you some pure silk underwear which will feel most luxurious. The bodice and hip part of the dress can be made strong enough with a sturdy lining to withstand all manner of cavorting around, and it will look to have an unusual amount of flounce as those curtain nets can be used to make both frothy petticoats and a short veil. You can wear those lovely crochet gloves your friend has sent you, while the fur stole can be cut down to make a shoulder wrap to keep you warm as the church is likely to be draughty so late in the year, and I thought the wrap could be held closed with a feature clasp made of some of the costume jewellery. There's a pretty blue necklace that could be adapted to be of use for this, and so then you'd have your something old and something blue. And a large nip of something mightily alcoholic right before you go into the church should stop you shivering if it's a blowy or chilly day.'

'That lucky brute Sam Torrence won't know what's hit him – and I think you'd better make sure he's sitting down when you take the dress off for your wedding night as I think he'll pass out at the sight of you in silk undies,' laughed Sukie, causing everyone to chuckle along with her.

Linda beamed around. 'How wonderful it all sounds – thank you so much. Goodness knows what I'll do about shoes, but I might put a note on the church noticeboard and ask around at all the farms I go to – you never know, but somebody may have some shoes that will make my clodhoppers look suitably dainty and that will work for my something borrowed.'

Evie said, 'And I have the something new for you, which is a pair of cream stockings – I bought them years ago in the January sales in Spooners, and I've been saving them for whoever was the first of us to marry. James will make the clasp for the wrap, I'm sure, as he's good at that sort of thing, while Julia will of course do your hair and make-up. And if Annabel oversees the rest of us as we set about making up your outfit, I'm damn convinced we can make you look like a princess, or else we'll die in the attempt!'

Julia came into the room bearing a welcome tray of tea just as her name was mentioned, and she looked so casual about it and so much her everyday self that for an instant Evie doubted that she'd been mysteriously absent for what had been really quite a long time.

That week it was also the ancient Michaelmas celebration in Tavistock, the infamous Goosey Fair. Evie had asked Pattie and Julia if they could organise their workday so that they could come along with her and Mr Bassett when they took the children after school to the fair, as she thought it might be wise to have reinforcements to make sure that nobody went missing. Mr Bassett hadn't been

81

going to bring his class, but then he had had a change of heart, which Evie put down to her powers of persuasion. It was nice that the whole school could go on an outing, but it did mean that a few favours had to be called in so that the children would be looked after properly. Anyway, at Evie's request, Julia was her normal obliging self and was quick to agree, and Pattie only took a little cajoling even though she said an evening with over thirty elevens-and-under was absolutely not at the top of her list of the best ways of having fun.

When Susan heard about the outing she said that she and Robert would come too. At this James decided he might miss something if he weren't there, and his parents agreed he could have an afternoon off from his school in Oldwell Abbott, as could Frank, and so for the first time in what felt like ages the whole Yeo clan were doing something together, as the other three Yeo evacuees were pupils at Evie's school and would be going too.

Over tea on the Monday, Robert, who was very good at spinning a yarn, told the four evacuees about Goosey Fair, saying it had been going in one form or another for over 700 years and had been held every October to trade Christmas geese in time for them to be fattened up for the Yule table, and that geese were still bought and sold at the fair. The local hostelries would serve cooked goose, and there'd be fair stalls and sideshows.

The youngsters looked at him agog – it all seemed most exciting, and especially so seeing as it was on a school night; bedtimes during school weeks were rigidly adhered to at Bluebells. And

82

the promise of a hot roast-meat sandwich made it all sound doubly-enticing, even though Evie suspected there would be precious little meat in each sandwich.

Robert's job was checking that local farms were getting the highest yields possible for the war effort, and fortuitously he'd been able to arrange that one of the farmers he visited regularly on his rounds would be able to collect everyone from the primary school at lunchtime. It wasn't going to be a dignified journey to the fair as they would all be squeezed harum-scarum into the back of a flat-bed truck, along with some geese in their cages, but although everyone would be tightly packed together the children would have wooden boxes to sit on there and back, he'd been promised.

The evening before the outing, Evie reminded all the parents collecting their children after school that their offspring must be wrapped up very warm the next day as they would be outside for quite a long time, and the truck might not have a covering on it while, of course, they would be coming home in the dark.

And on the Wednesday morning, she walked her infants over to Switherns farm, which was very close to the school, so that the children could see a goose, and compare it to a duck, a chicken and a turkey, all of which were also on the farm. An unexpected bonus to the farm visit was that there was a brace of pheasants swinging in the doorway of a shed, a male and a female; they had been killed on the moor a couple of weeks earlier by one of the Harris hawks the farmer used for hunting, and were hanging up for their meat to tenderise.

Although the children were obviously fascinated with the idea of a hawk trained to kill (well, they were killers naturally, so perhaps it was more the case that the hawks had been trained to return to their handler, Evie told her pupils), the farmer advised against the group disturbing the hawks perched on their posts in a darkened stable – they might not take kindly to youngsters staring at them, he said.

On the way back to the school, Evie was struck by how calmly the children had looked at the birds, both dead and alive, and talked about them all with no obvious signs of emotion. She thought it was because they were country children who had learnt already that there was little room for sentimentality or squeamishness with regards to livestock and the provision of food. It was amazing how quickly the evacuee children came to feel likewise, Evie noted. Animals could be fluffy and sweet, and poultry noisy and amusing, but the implicit understanding was that if they were earmarked for food, then there was going to be a time when their lives would be cut short so that they could go to the table, and nobody was to make an unnecessary fuss about it.

The mood of wartime Britain was all Dig for Victory – nothing should go to waste if it could be helped. And the children seemed to understand and accept this.

Evie felt she herself had been much less sanguine at their age. As a child she had fallen for a piglet the Yeos had homed in their orchard for fattening. He'd had smooth pink skin and a little ginger topknot sprouting between his ears, and James,

84

little more than a toddler at the time, had named him Bucket. He was full of playfulness, and Evie had taught him to do several tricks and to come to her when she called. Poor Bucket had rooted around in the orchard at Bluebells for nearly a year, becoming big and muscular. And then one day the children had returned from school to find the orchard gate swinging open and no welcome snuffling sounds of the porker exploring amongst the fallen apples. It had been a salutary lesson, and Evie hadn't been able to face either bacon or sausages for quite some time afterwards, and Susan had got quite cross with her when she had refused to eat the roast pork lunch on the following Sunday, despite the tempting smell of the sizzling meat and golden crackling.

None of Evie's pupils seemed put off their own lunches by the visit to Switherns. And after they had finished eating, the thrum of the farm truck's engine as it came down the road and then drew to a halt outside the school gate indicated it was time to go.

It was a very excited bunch of children who were lifted up into the flat-bed rear part of the truck and then squeezed together under Evie's command on to the box seating. Everybody laughed when they noticed the captive geese didn't look thrilled about their new travelling companions.

While Robert, Susan and James set off to cycle over to Tavistock, Evie and her sisters travelled with the children to ensure good behaviour, while Mr Bassett went in the cab alongside the farmer.

Evie hoped the two men were having a pleasant chat. She was increasingly concerned about Mr

85

Bassett. She felt that in the evenings he was prone to seeming a little too happy after his evening constitutional, yet a little too subdued and withdrawn each morning before the pupils arrived at school. There was something morose and fathomless about him that made her worry, as did the way she was never quite sure what sort of mood he would be in. Evie hoped that a break from routine like this outing might cheer him a little, as the day before she had found him crouching in the quiet spot behind the Nissen hut when he should have been watching the children's playtime shenanigans. He'd been looking very isolated and private, with his head heavy in his hands, although he sprang to his feet when he realised Evie had come to find him and he even attempted to smile at her as he hurried past to go and keep an eye on the playing pupils. The fact that he'd tried to smile in her direction, when he was normally so taciturn, was probably the most disconcerting thing about it all, Evie thought to herself.

Tavistock proved to be virtually unrecognisable from the small market town that it ordinarily was. The pavements were busy with people milling about as they looked at the various stalls, and there was quite a hubbub of noise coming from many directions.

The farmer dropped the school party off handily near the public conveniences, where Robert, Susan and James were already waiting for them.

Nearby was a gaily coloured merry-go-round and a hurdy-gurdy, and while Patty and Julia organised everyone into spending a penny, Evie negotiated a cut-price rate for all the children to have a ride on the merry-go-round at the same time (this should only be ridden once the children had all been to the lavatory, she thought; and before she gave them each the toffee apple that Susan was now sorting out. If anyone felt queasy from going round and round at least they won't have eaten anything sweet immediately beforehand, and Evie knew there couldn't be any unfortunate accidents from the excitement of being on the merry-go-round if everyone had just emptied their bladders.)

Just before they had left the school Mr Bassett had told Evie to take a whole £20 from the school's kitty to pay for everything.

Evie had borrowed Mr Worth's camera, and so she grouped everyone together in front of the carousel and took a couple of photographs. And then she took a couple more when the merry-go-round had the whole school on board, with the children happily calling out to each other the names of the horses they were riding. She made a reluctant Mr Bassett climb on to the ride too, and then Robert said if Evie made smart and jumped up too, he would take a photograph of everybody at Lymbridge Primary School to mark the Goosey Fair outing of 1941.

Not long afterwards, autumn dusk fell quickly, bringing with it the faint underlying whiff of wood fires burning, and soon there was a faint hiss in the air as newly lit gas Tilley lamps stuttered and then burned as they swayed gently from the hooks above the heads of the crowd in the chilly air. Evie pointed out to her infants how the shadows thrown by the lamps might change if any gusts of wind caught the lamps and made them move.

She asked the children then what they could smell, and this caused a furious debate. As far as Evie was concerned the air was full of the smell of chestnuts roasting and toffee apples; it was an aroma that danced across the background waft of a country area that always reminded Evie of her childhood and brought the knowledge that it wouldn't be too long until Christmas, with its damp autumn leaves turning into mulch and smoky home fires. But some of the children insisted very loudly that the most pervasive scent was that of goose POO!

As she marshalled all the children together so that they could go and look at the fair's geese, Evie was very glad there were so many grown-ups keeping the children in some sort of gentle order as there were abundant distractions all about them.

It was James who really came into his own, and he proved to be a great boon to the outing as he taught everyone how to play table skittles, guess the weight of a goose (this brought back breath-catching memories for Evie of the cheeky piglet in a similar competition at the summer Revels, the piglet being the unwitting agent of those surprise kisses with Peter), catch a floating duck with a fishing line, ring toss, shove ha'penny and tombola. James made sure to tutor even the littlest children to throw a ring-toss hoop in roughly the right direction. Finally, each child was encouraged to delve into a lucky dip in a tea-chest filled with sawdust. Evie thought that her younger brother, although still only fifteen, had all the makings of being a wonderful husband and father when he was a bit older.

They all stood and watched a group of teenage boys, presumably from a Naval school, dance a hornpipe, Susan making sure that James didn't say anything too saucy that young ears shouldn't hear; clearly he didn't think the dancers looked very manly in their white uniforms piped with navy blue, their short flared trousers, white pumps on their feet and small white hats perched on their heads.

The potentially sticky hornpipe moment segued into another dicey minute or two at the Punch and Judy show as it was altogether a much more risqué prospect than the afternoon show the children had enjoyed at the Revels, with a script riven with adult innuendo, and so a quick-thinking Evie hurriedly rallied the troops by saying by-golly-gosh, she was peckish and was everybody else as hungry as she? Because if they were, then it was time to go and get something to eat. The children decided unanimously that yes, they were all absolutely starving, with their tummies thinking their throats had been cut. Phew, thought Evie, thank goodness for that, as otherwise there could have been some very awkward questions if the children had been allowed to listen to too much of what this Punch and Judy had to say for themselves, and there would have been many parents taking A Dim View.

Robert had organised rounds of sandwiches for everyone at a busy public house, and they ate their food, with the hot meat oozing delicious roasting juices despite the thinness of the slices to eke it out as far as it would go, standing in a small courtyard that was in front of the door to the public house, smelling whiffs of beer and scrumpy and tobacco smoke drifting out from the main bar each time the door was opened.

Pemberley's usually absent PG, Mr Rogers, hoved into view clutching a pencil and reporter's notebook, and he proceeded to flirt shamelessly with Evie, seemingly not to care a jot that her parents and her sisters were standing only feet away. He told Evie that he was writing a 'colour' piece on the ancient fair for one of the national broadsheets. Evie mentioned that she had taken some pictures earlier of the pupils and the merry-go-round, and Mr Rogers said that he would be very interested in seeing the photographs once the film had been developed. If there were any that were in focus and were suitable to accompany his article then Evie would get the going rate and her name would be credited beside the image if she allowed a photograph taken by herself to be used.

Evie said that there were still some pictures left on the film in Mr Worth's camera to be used up, so Mr Rogers posed her under some brightish lights strung high above a stall selling rope halters for horses and cattle, and implements for grooming, and snapped several pictures very quickly.

As Evie made to talk to him about the Spitfire and raising £6,000, he diverted her attention by asking for a bite of her sandwich, insisting she hold it to his mouth as his hands were otherwise occupied with the camera and his notebook. Evie laughed at such a trumped-up reason for making her get close to him, but she found him quite

90

amusing and so was happy to flirt back a little. She wasn't serious about it, but she supposed that she had better start making a little effort where men were concerned, as they couldn't all be such heart-breakers as Timmy and Peter, surely to goodness?

Susan was just starting to direct pointed looks at Evie, bush-telegraphing that she'd gone far enough with Mr Rogers and so that would be enough for now, thanking you muchly, when Mr Bassett, who had been content to bring up the rear of the group and chivvy along any stragglers throughout the visit, said that for their last treat they were going to watch The Great Kludini, an escapologist, at which Mr Rogers turned and gave Susan a cheeky half-bow and drifted off into the crowd, making a funny face at Evie as he did so.

Evie and the children thought the escapologist unintentionally hilarious. He'd asked for a volunteer to tie him up in all manner of ropes, and so a sailor jumped up and in a split-second professionally trussed him with a variety of professional and quickly twisted seamen's knots.

There was a valiant struggle for ten minutes, accompanied by grunts and wheezes, and a lot of energetic wriggling around. And then The Now Not So Great Kludini had to beg the sailor to help him out of his heavy rope bonds to a barrage of cheery catcalls and ribald comments. He had the grace to give the crowd a shame-faced bow of acknowledgement and then raised his clapping hands in the direction of the laughing sailor in an acknowledgment of having been well and truly kippered.

It was getting cold and was time at last to head

91

for home. As Robert and Susan directed the children to the farmer's truck, counting them up on to its flatbed in order to make sure nobody had gone missing and that they all got on board safely, Sukie darted across the road to Evie, grabbing her arm.

Evie jumped as she hadn't expected to see her friend. She thought Sukie had been promised a date that evening with someone who'd drop the soiled hospital bandages and linen off over in Oldwell Abbott for specialist laundering.

'Evie-Rose, sweetie,' Sukie hissed in an excited undertone in Evie's ear, her breath misting in the nippy air, 'you'll never guess who I saw at the hospital today, walking down a corridor as plain as plain could be.' There was a silence as Evie couldn't imagine what, or who, had got Sukie so obviously excited. 'Go on, guess!' urged Sukie more vehemently.

Evie shook her head, her curls burnished by the soft glow of the Tilley lamp she was standing beneath.

'It was Peter!'

Evie stood completely still, and for a moment everything around seemed to be as if underwater, moving slowly and remotely around her, only with the hurdy-gurdy blaring out its mechanical tune uncomfortably loudly.

'Peter?' she whispered in confusion. This made no sense at all.

'The very same. I've no idea what he was doing there and I don't think he saw me, as I was behind him. But once I'd placed my letters in the To Post rack and turned around to speak to him, he'd disappeared, and nobody I asked seemed to know that he'd even been there. All the same, I know I saw him,' Sukie replied in a still excited tone.

The farmer was obviously keen to drive his charges back to Lymbridge, and he was tooting his horn loudly to get Evie's attention. 'Young maid, if you'm not be gettin' up yer rit now, schoolmistress or no, I'm off and you'll be left on yer lonesome, d'you 'ear what I be tellin' yer?' he yelled out of the window, although to Evie's ears it sound as if it were coming from a long way away and very probably from down a deep tunnel.

In a daze Evie nodded farewell to Sukie and then clambered up into the cab to sit alongside Pattie, who was eager to get back to Lymbridge herself as she had a date that night with John, who had extended his summer job into the autumn, helping Barkeep Joss out behind the bar at The Haywain. Pattie had boasted earlier in the week that John was proving to have a very fine touch in the brewing of Knock 'em Dead, apparently. Evie had joked back in that case Barkeep Joss would never allow him to leave Lymbridge, to which Pattie replied, 'Suits me.'

As the farmer revved his engine ostentatiously, more to clear a pathway through the pedestrians milling around in front of the truck than actually to drive forward, Julia and Mr Bassett were already in the back of the truck keeping an eye on the children.

Pattie noticed that her eldest sister looked exceptionally pale, and when she asked Evie if she were feeling all right, her sister said in a distracted voice that she thought she might have eaten something that disagreed with her and that she might try to nap just for a few minutes. She didn't think she was up to talking to anybody just at the moment.

Evie turned her head towards the window as the farmer began to inch his way through the busy throng.

Indeed Evie did feel unwell, as if her tummy was sliding inexorably downward, and she felt uncomfortably hot and discombobulated as she stared unseeing out of the steamy window.

Sukie must be mistaken. Surely?

## Chapter Five

By the next morning Evie, feeling extremely list-less after another troubled night, had convinced herself that Sukie had misinterpreted what she had seen. It must have been merely someone who looked a little *like* Peter.

There was no reason at all for him to be back in the West Country. As he had let slip that disas-trous evening at The Ritz, he had an important job which had meant him being recalled to Lon-don, and to judge by the Savile Row suit he'd been wearing that night, Evie assumed that he must work in some capacity for the War Office and would be based in Whitehall.

However, Evie's petulant mood merged into the background as she discovered that everybody at school the next day was just as out of sorts as she.

By the time all the pupils had been delivered

94

home after Goosey Fair it had been past ten o'clock, which was very, very late for Evie's five- and six-year-olds on a mid-week school night.

And although Goosey Fair had been a lot of fun for the children, it was soon glaringly obvious that they simply hadn't had enough sleep before having to get up for school the following morning, with the result that short-tempers, tantrums and tears were to be the order of the day.

The upshot was that Evie soon had to give up on her proposed lessons on sums and handwriting, instead deciding on a painting session in which the children had to reproduce their favourite thing they'd seen at the fair. Later, she sat them cross-legged on the floor around her and read them a story about animals in the jungle, during which she encouraged them to make the noises of the appropriate beasts. Evie could hear uncontrolled chattering from the adjoining classroom, and evidently the juniors were as tired as the infants and unwilling to work quietly.

Although Mr Bassett and Evie agreed over their lunchtime cup of tea that it was important the children took part in the local traditions, they concurred that the outing had exacted a toll on everybody. They decided that while the children were out in the playground, Mr Cawes could clear the desks and chairs to one side in Evie's classroom so that all the pupils could relax and let off a little steam after lunch with a spot of country dancing. Mr Cawes made dramatic use of frowns and grimaces when Evie explained what had been decided, although she made sure she laid the blame for the extra work the elderly caretaker had to do firmly at Mr Bassett's door.

Evie plonked out some basic traditional tunes but really it was just an excuse to while away an hour or two rather than any serious attempt at polishing the dancing skills of the pupils. Mr Bassett had made himself scarce, which didn't do anything to improve Evie's up-and-down mood as she had to organise the dancing for the whole school and not just her own class, and when some of the older junior boys started to get a bit boisterous, she felt there was a severe danger she would lose control of the lesson.

That evening at Pemberley, the house felt very strange as Mr and Mrs Wallace had moved out earlier in the day. Although neither had been the sort of people anybody would describe as the life and soul of the party, it was the case that one or other of them had nearly always seemed to be around, and now the generous proportions of the once-grand guest house felt eerily empty without them.

Evie felt disconcerted at any rate, although the Worths and the other PGs seemed less so. But as far as Evie was concerned wartime meant more people coming and going than she was used to, and this was a distinctly unsettling experience. People would form what felt like close alliances quickly, but then suddenly they would be broken, with no promises that anybody would ever see each other again.

A spare piece of linen Evie had been hoarding had come in handy though as a goodbye present for the older woman. Evie had embroidered some pretty yellow and purple pansies on it and thus made Mrs Wallace a handkerchief envelope in which she could keep her clean hankies tidy. Earlier that morning when Evie had knocked on the Wallaces' bedroom door to pass her small present over before leaving for school, Mrs Wallace had obviously been very touched by the trouble Evie had gone to on her behalf.

Julia agreed with Evie when she said that Pemberley felt oddly empty with the Wallaces gone.

Still, the Yeo sisters were soon diverted from their reduced numbers at supper as Robert popped over to tell Julia and Evie that he had been sold a pup at the fair with the result that he now felt a right twerp. He had purchased a very smart-looking watch from a market trader, only to find when he got it home that it didn't have any workings inside! He also had an amusing story about something or other that the unit of the local Home Guard, of which he was a staunch founder member, had got up to, and Julia and Mrs Worth laughed along with him.

Evie smiled a trifle half-heartedly at her father's escapades, as by now her mind was continually drifting towards Sukie's hasty whisperings. Luckily Julia was chattering away to Robert, saying that she had really enjoyed the Goosey Fair and actually she thought it the best one she had ever been to, thus unintentionally making sure Robert didn't notice that his eldest daughter was miles away.

Evie was also distracted by what felt like an increasingly pressing problem. For, although the school outing to Goosey Fair had gone well, she had decided to write to Mrs Smith to properly air her concerns about Mr Bassett.

Once Robert had left, Evie realised she was bone-wearingly tired, although Julia seemed to be full of energy and bounce. Evie decided to wait until the next day before actually putting pen to paper as she wanted to compose a careful letter, and she felt she needed an early night before she would be able to do this properly.

The following evening Evie sat down at the kitchen table with a cup of tea before her, as well as her trusty leather-bound writing case with its substantial brass-coloured zip winding around three sides. Evie's expression was brooding and her hands felt unpleasantly clammy with anxiety.

*Dear Mrs Smith*

*I do hope I find you all well, and that it won't be long until you are once again in Lymbridge making sure we are all minding our Ps and Qs.*

*I am very sorry to bother you with what I very much hope is only a small trifle, when I know what a worrying time you have been having with dear Timmy's health. But I feel I must confide in somebody. I really don't know what to do for the best, or quite who I should speak to about it, if not to you.*

*I'll come straight to the point, which is that I am extraordinarily worried about Mr Bassett, and how things are going at the school.*

*I have always found Mr Bassett to be a somewhat strange person with whom to form a professional relationship. I can't quite put my finger on it, but for rather a lot of the time he doesn't seem properly involved with either the school or his pupils.*

98

Sometimes I hear him teaching a very good lesson, and so I know he is a talented and inspirational teacher when he is in the mood. But quite often he isn't, and then he is prone to leave the children to their own devices. I do admit, however, that Joseph likes him, and certainly he's given me no indication at all that there's any sort of problem.

My brother James also thinks Mr Bassett to be a fine fellow, as Mr Bassett asked James to help him construct the cricket nets at Pemberley, and I believe they found plenty of mutual interests to talk about. James would be biased though, as he let slip that Mr Bassett gave him a whole pound note for his help with the nets.

However, one time at the school recently I heard a lot of chattering from the juniors and rather obviously there was no work being done. I poked my nose around their door, only to find they had been left on their own for quite some time. Mr Bassett was nowhere to be seen, with none of his class knowing where he was. I put a senior in charge of my class briefly as I set to look for Mr Bassett, and eventually I found him standing in the cold behind the Nissen hut, chilled to the bone as he hadn't put his jacket on (you know how cruelly the wind can whip around that corner). When I talked to him Mr Bassett looked at me for a minute as if I was a complete stranger and he didn't know where he was, although admittedly he then rallied and went back into his classroom as if he had only been absent for a second or two.

What's even worse is that was the second time I have found Mr Bassett lurking around behind the Nissen but when I expected him to be with the children.

Aside from what the pupils might get up to in his absences (which, if bad behaviour escalated, could

99

lead to a matter of safety and somebody being hurt), I can't help feeling concerned that his class might be slipping behind in the curriculum. Mr Bassett does so many games sessions that although the children are looking fit and healthy, I can't believe they are where they should be in their spelling or their sums.

He's pleasant enough, I suppose, if I ask him a direct question about anything, but he never asks me to do anything or offers any guidance as to how I might improve my own teaching. Generally, I feel that Lymbridge Primary School is increasingly like a rudderless ship, and I'm sure it must be only a matter of time before some of the parents will start grumbling.

Also, from a purely selfish point of view, I am concerned that the blame for this lassitude might be laid at my door in the not too distant future, bearing in mind how new to teaching I am.

As I say, I am so sorry to burden you with this. But you have been the essence of the school for such a long time, and so I believe you are the person who deserves to know what is happening even though you are otherwise engaged at Stoke Mandeville with Timmy.

It's all very sad. Any advice you can give me on how I should proceed would be very much appreciated.

My very best regards to you and Mr Smith, and to dear Timmy too,

Evie Yeo


It wasn't more than a day or two after the letter had gone that Evie was called to the telephone after supper. It was Mrs Smith.

'Evie, hello, and thank you for alerting me to this parlous situation,' the older woman's familiar

100

imperious tones rang out. Evie couldn't help but smile because although Mrs Smith sounded anxious and almost of another era, as far as Evie was concerned she represented sound sense and security. Mrs Smith went on, 'Are you able to talk freely or is Mr Bassett nearby?'

'Mrs Bowes – er, Mrs Smith, I mean of course, how wonderful it is to hear from you, and there is only myself and Mr Worth in the house at the moment as everyone else seems otherwise engaged,' replied Evie. 'I am so sorry to have bothered you, but I think I was tired and fretful, and I felt I had reached a tipping point.'

'Yes, I see,' said Mrs Smith. 'Evie, we'll talk more at the weekend. Timmy is being transferred over to the recuperation hospital within the next day or two, and Mr Smith and myself will be returning home to Lymbridge. Meanwhile I will telephone the Board of Education to discuss the situation. Please don't say anything to Mr Bassett just at the minute, will you? I just wanted to put your mind at rest, my dear, that your concerns have been heard and taken on board.'

They then spent a couple of minutes talking about Timmy and the logistics of moving him from one hospital to another. It seemed as if this might be a more complicated process than anyone had expected.

The conversation finished with Evie promising that she would go to see Tricia the very next evening to break the news about Timmy moving imminently to the recuperation hospital, which was very close to Tricia's parents' farm-worker cottage where Tricia was currently living.

Tricia was unavailable by telephone and Mrs Smith confided to Evie that she felt a little awkward about writing to Tricia while she was lodging there with her parents. Apparently Tricia had let slip to Mrs Smith that even though she and Timmy were now legally man and wife, her parents were most disapproving still about the forthcoming baby being conceived out of wedlock.

Evie could see exactly why everyone was feeling as they did as regards Timmy and Tricia, but she thought too that the Dolbys probably should make an effort to be grateful that the ultimate result of what had happened was that Tricia had ended up making a match for herself that was further up the social scale than the wildest dreams her parents could have had for her. And then Evie chided herself for being uncharitable; Robert and Susan would have had a lot to say on the matter (and for a very long time), she knew, if it had been she who had fallen pregnant with Timmy's baby without a wedding ring on her finger.

As she hung up the telephone receiver after her chat with Mrs Smith, Evie felt soothed and relieved. At least now another adult, rather than she alone, was aware that there might be a problem at Lymbridge Primary School.

The next evening when Sukie and Evie rode out, there wasn't much time for talking as their fittening programme meant they had built up now to four ten-minute canters with only five minutes of walking in between. Evie didn't want to talk much anyway as Sukie made it clear, unfortunately, that there was nothing further to report on the Peter front. There had been no repeat performance of a surprise appearance, and whoever Sukie had seen, he seemed now to have disappeared as if in a puff of smoke.

This training session was without doubt the hardest yet. They cantered their mounts up and down hill (oddly it was proving much more difficult to keep the horses cantering down the hills than when going up them, something that had always puzzled Evie as she would have expected the reverse to be true), with the result that the friends were both perspiring and pink-faced by the end of the final canter. A short rest and then after Sukie checked the timings on her wristwatch it was a sharp gallop, before finishing with taking in four sturdy stone walls as obstacles, Evie making sure to head for the lowest part of each wall as she wasn't a terribly brave jumper, although her horse seemed reasonably trustworthy in this respect.

By the time they had brought the horses back to walk Sukie and Evie were laughing with exhilaration and their horses' necks and chests were damp with exertion, while there was a foamy build up of sweat between their mounts' hind legs. It was the last time the horses would be ridden out at speed before the race on the coming Saturday, although Sukie had promised Dave Symons that she would coach him over a few obstacles the next evening on the grey that Evie was now riding.

To Sukie's mild irritation, as both horses would need washing down and then walking around to dry off which would take her a considerate amount of effort and time, Evie said that she needed to be dropped off at Tricia's home, and so perhaps Sukie could take both the animals back home and put them away, with Sukie leading Evie's with the reins over its head.

'Sorry, Sukes, but I really do need to see Tricia to tell her that Timmy is almost home and that she'll be able to move into the Smiths's cottage very soon, and I can't telephone her as the Dolbys don't have one, and I don't know how long I'm going to need to talk with her. Obviously I asked Mrs Bowes – drat, Mrs *Smith* – to time it for when the horses would be most sweaty, and so that's worked well for me, if not for you. And of course at least you have the luxury of knowing now that I owe you a tremendous favour that you'll be able to ask me at some time in the future. I've no doubt you'll not let me forget it...' Evie was now standing beside the grey and she let the words hang as she ran her stirrups up their leathers so that they wouldn't bang against his flanks as Sukie led him home.

Sukie, who was annoyingly one of those people who still managed to look glamorous with wind-blown hair, a sweat-beaded brow and mud-splattered clothes, leant down and gave Evie's jodphured behind a slightly too sharp tap with her whip, causing Evie to let out a yelp.

'A *very* tremendous favour, don't you dare forget, Miss Yeo!' Sukie reminded her friend as she manoeuvred both horses around in the lane before making them both walk out smartly on a long rein in the direction of home.

Evie smiled at their retreating rears, the grey's tail flicking across his own flanks as well as the rounded quarters of Sukie's mount, and then she went and knocked on the dilapidated porch door to the rundown home where the new Mrs Bowes had grown up. Evie hadn't warned Tricia she was coming, and just at the point when she couldn't hear the retreating hoofbeats on the tarmacked road any longer, Evie realised she should have asked Sukie to hang on for a moment just in case Tricia wasn't there.

But after what seemed like an incredibly long pause, Evie could hear lumpen footsteps slapping down the stone-flagged corridor towards her, and then Tricia was blinking at her around the door.

'Hello, Tricia. Oh, my goodness, I am sorry to disturb you out of the blue like this, Tricia, as you look as if you've been having a nap.' Tricia's hair was all over the place and oddly peaked above one ear, and her face was sleep-crumpled on one side.

She snorted vehemently in agreement at Evie's words, and cast a very suspicious look in Evie's direction, causing Evie almost to forget what she had come to say.

She gathered her thoughts and ploughed on. 'I do hope you are feeling well and not too worn out. I've come to tell you that yesterday I had a conversation on the telephone with Mrs Smith, which was to do with the school actually. And she said Timmy is likely to move down to the recuperation hospital any day now, and that she and Mr Smith will be moving back to their cottage too and so you can move in with them very, very soon.'

'Thank bloomin' 'eck for that. My ma and pa baint lettin' up wi' me for a second, and I need to follow yorn advice and git well away from yere the minute I can, else there might be murder and

105

then Mrs Smith would 'ave a whole lot to say 'bout *that*,' Tricia cut into Evie's words with more than a hint of rancour. 'I does a whole day at the dairy, and then another whole day of cookin' an' cleaning yere rit after, it feels like. It's rightly too much, an' I'm at the end o' me tether. An' I'm so big I'm flummoxing 'bout summat dreadful.'

Tricia had clearly had a difficult time since her marriage, and Evie sympathised privately that nobody would ideally want to start their marriage being heavily pregnant but having still to stay under the same roof as disapproving parents, and with a husband lying paralysed in a hospital a long way away. Evie didn't think that Mrs Smith would necessarily be easy to live with either, but she thought benevolently that Mrs Smith was very kindly beneath her bluff exterior, and it was certain meanwhile that the baby would be spoilt rotten whenever he or she deigned to arrive, and that after the birth Tricia certainly wouldn't be expected to work at the dairy parlour or to take over the heavy housework at her new home. Evie was surprised at how kindly she felt towards Tricia, considering how angry with her she had once been.

'Would it help you if I had a word to see if my father and James could bring your stuff over to Mrs Smith's for you? That would save you a job, and leave you free to concentrate on putting to one side what you'll take, and then unpacking and getting yourself settled in Timmy's room,' said Evie, who was promptly taken aback when Tricia burst into wet and noisy sobs.

'Nobody's nice ter me, other than you, can you

106

believe?' (Regretfully, Evie could believe that was the case, knowing how disapproving a small country community can be.) 'An' I tear-up at t' drop of an 'at,' said Tricia in explanation, wiping her eyes with the front hem of her ratty and misshapen old cardie. 'An' you and me are the last people to be nice t'other one, an' I don' know wot to think. I 'aven't much, mind, and so I'd only need yorn James if you think 'e'll do it, not that I can pay 'im.'

'Don't you worry about that, Tricia – James'll be happy to help for nothing, I'm sure,' Evie said, crossing her fingers behind her back in the hope that James really wouldn't put up a fuss at Evie volunteering his services for free yet again, as normally he was very keen to ensure a good monetary return for any help he gave anyone. Still, Evie supposed, if he baulked at the prospect she could get Sukie to ask him; James would be putty in her hands.

Evie asked Tricia in a bit more detail how she really was, and after a few minutes of chitchat Evie turned away from the porch to go, thinking she must try and help Tricia get some new clothes as she couldn't go around looking like that when she was living at the Smiths's. Tricia would be embarrassed if either Timmy or Mrs Smith said anything to her about her scutty wardrobe, Evie was sure. She thought that Mr Smith might be the one to ask for help in this, and now that Linda's wedding dress was pretty much finished maybe the sewing circle could be persuaded to turn their attention to helping out Tricia. Mr Smith had never yet failed her when she'd asked him for help in the past, and

Evie was sure that he would be keen to smarten Tricia up a bit, even if only to keep Mrs Smith sweet and even-tempered.

'Lawks-a-mussy, I never ev'n ask'd you in! What a rit ol' bugger, although Ma would've 'ad a conniption at t' thought of you'm sittin' on t' best chair. But whatever is Mrs Smith gwain' t' think of me manners?!' wailed Tricia, as Evie headed away from her down the front garden path.

Evie thought that both Mrs Smith and the new Mrs Bowes would each have a bit of negotiating before them as to what they thought of the other's behaviour, but she tried to be positive and generous of spirit as she stopped and turned back to face Tricia again.

'Well, the good thing about you moving into Mrs Smith's house is that I very much think that Mrs Smith will want to answer the front door herself, even if it is to someone calling in to see you. And Timmy is a good-natured chap, I promise you, and so I'm sure he'll help you with what his mother will expect from you otherwise,' said Evie in what she sincerely hoped was her most authoritative and convincing tone. She added as firmly as she could, 'And do remember, Tricia, that you are not beholden to any of the Bowes – they must know that as it turns out they are very lucky that you are pregnant with Timmy's baby. I think you can be certain they will all treat you well, as that's the sort of people they are, in my experience. And it is in everyone's interests that you are happy, remember – you are the mother of Timmy's child, and so you can stand tall and unashamed. I'm sure you will make a wonderful mother. And when push comes to shove, that is what Mrs Smith will learn to love you for.'

Tricia's 'Harrumph!' was cut in half as she withdrew back into the grubbily untidy hallway Evie had glimpsed behind her and brought the outer door to a not particularly gentle close.

Evie realised she had been holding her breath as she turned around to begin the trudge back to Pemberley.

On the Friday right after school Evie popped over to Mrs Smith's cottage to see if she and Mr Smith were back yet. But the cottage looked forlorn and empty, and the garden alarmingly run to riot.

Evie dropped into Mr Cleave's on the way back to Pemberley as he was supposed to be keeping the garden in order. He was having his tea, but when Evie mentioned that Mrs Smith would be back 'any time now', he pushed his plate aside and leapt up with an alacrity that was surprising for a man who boasted of pushing eighty, to pull on his folded-down gumboots, presumably keen to instill a bit of order and put a few plants to bed for the winter in the dying hours of daylight. Mrs Smith would very likely have words to say if the garden wasn't as she'd hoped to find it, and so Evie could quite understand the speed at which Mr Cleave had stood up.

Evie had earmarked the Saturday morning for topping and tailing the work on Linda's wedding ensemble, helped by Julia and Pattie, and under the watchful eye of Annabel.

It turned out though that Sukie had other ideas. She joined Evie for breakfast at Pemberley and suggested that instead maybe Evie wanted to help take the horses for a half hour's gentle hack that morning to relax them before the race in the afternoon, and then help her with the prerequisite leg-trimming, tail-washing and mane plaiting-up, and cleaning the tack.

Evie declined with more than a twinge of regret, saying that even though it was a lovely day and ordinarily she'd love to be helping Sukie, she really needed to concentrate on what needed to be done for Linda's Big Day, especially as there was now a growing problem over Linda's wedding shoes, or to be more precise, the glaring absence of them.

Sukie gave Evie her tried-and-tested imploring look, usually an infallible method of persuasion, especially when accompanied with a heartfelt, pleading 'Evie-Rose! My dearest Evie-Rose!'

Evie looked at her friend with the sternest expression she could manage as she pointed out that Dave Symons could get his own horse ready – and if it were a question of wedding shoes or no wedding shoes, Evie knew where her loyalties lay. Also, Evie added, it wouldn't matter if the horses weren't plaited-up, especially as Sukie wasn't the best with a needle and thread, and mane plaits could be very wiry to sew, even for an experienced groom.

Sukie stuck out her lower lip in a visual protest that would rival the best that Evie's five-year-olds could do. To distract her, Evie asked how Dave Symons' ride over fences had gone. Sukie shook her head with a laugh, and replied that she'd nearly had to get Linda out afterwards with her equine tooth-rasper as he'd got so left behind when jumping that his long-suffering horse's teeth must have been pulled every which way.

'Still, I think that grey does have a sense of humour. He puffs himself out so much when the saddle is girthed, so the daft critter Dave Symons assumed I'd given the girth a second tightening. It was an assumption he won't be making again, as he nearly came to grief before we'd even left the stable yard when the nag side-stepped a puddle and the saddle slipped,' said Sukie, and she couldn't help but smile at the memory.

'Yes, that horse is a cheeky lad, and I've found him surprisingly quick to avoid getting his feet wet in a puddle. Clearly he's not a fan of water. I wonder if Dave Symons knows that Father and James have dug a ditch on the course and I hear they've lined it with a waterproof tarpaulin that they are probably hard at work sloshing water into right at this very minute.'

Evie and Sukie couldn't help but smile at the thought that perhaps this didn't bode too well for Dave Symons and the grey gelding in that afternoon's race.

The morning's sewing went to plan, and although the problem of the wedding shoes remained, Evie decided to try and think of a solution another time.

And so it was with good humour that Evie and all the Yeos except Julia headed off for the airfield just before noon. It was a fair step out to get there, especially as the evacuees weren't yet used to striding out along the country lanes in the ground-covering manner of the locally born children. Julia had told Pattie she had errands to run but would come to the airfield as soon as she could.

It was a fine autumn day, sunny but with a breeze that made the autumnal leaves crackle and dance and sent some of the browner ones drifting downwards when caught in the stronger flurries of wind. It was the very best sort of riding weather, and Evie thought that the lowish sun would highlight prettily the different colours of the horses' coats and the racing silks of the riders.

When they arrived at the makeshift racecourse, the Yeos agreed that there was quite a gathering at the air field, and that several local bookies looked already to be doing good business.

The Haywain had a stall (naturally, as they never missed an opportunity like this), and looked to be doing a roaring trade too. And for the more refined race-goer, if they went inside a small canvas marquee then there was a tea and cake table that had been provided by the Oldwell Abbott branch of the Women's Institute. Susan promised Frank, Joseph, Marie and Catherine each a slice of cake, at which Evie and her mother had to share a smile, as to judge by the children's wide grins, this was a more exciting prospect than watching the horses gallop.

The course, which wasn't roped off, consisted of six fences, including the dreaded ditch filled with water (which had been dug as close to the perimeter of the airfield as possible, presumably so that it wouldn't be a danger to aeroplanes on the airfield if the ground sank after it was filled in). The obstacles had been positioned in a rough circle with big numbers to the side of each fence

112

so that there could be no mistake in the order they should be jumped in. The competitors would go round the course twice.

Evie was surprised to see from a large black-board that there were thirty-six entrants overall, and this meant there were enough runners to make three races.

The races were divided into ponies of less than 14.2 (this race was called the Wellington Flier, and had nine runners), mares (the Spitfire Chase, with fifteen runners) and geldings (the Hawker Handicap, with twelve). There were three tiny silver-plated cups, provided by the Worths, and an engraver on hand who had already placed the name of the race and the date on each cup, and who would hurriedly add the winner's name and horse before the cup would be awarded by the Rev. Painter, who would make the presentations to the winners at the end of the afternoon.

Runners and riders looked to be quite a motley crew, but everybody seemed in a jolly mood, although some of the more nervous riders were sneakily sipping from hip flasks in order to give themselves a little Dutch courage. As always, the adult riders looked more apprehensive than the pony riders. Most of the horses had had blankets over their backs that had been slung behind their saddles as they were being led around, to make sure they didn't catch cold. Many of them were sweating with excitement as they sensed they were in for a gallop, yet although it was sunny it wasn't a warm afternoon.

Robert, a race steward, explained on a battered loud-hailer that it was thirty minutes until the ponies were to be taken to the 'paddock' (a squarish patch between four buckets weighted down with stones that marked each corner) and there, after the runners had been led around for anyone who wanted to bet to have a look, at his whistle the riders would mount and be led around the paddock a couple more times so that all the punters could get a good look up close of the runners under saddle. At a second signal from Robert they could canter to the first fence and show it to their horses before returning to gather behind the starting line, which was a white line painted across the turf made with the Worths's contraption for marking out their grass tennis court. Once the horses and riders were assembled, Rev. Painter would drop a white flag to start them off.

The pony riders didn't seem to be paying Robert much attention, which made Evie and her sisters smile as it was clearly irking their father, provoking him into comical expressions and waving arms, and an increasingly loud voice.

Just then Evie saw Mr and Mrs Smith walking companionably across the field in her direction. She ran to them, really pleased they were now back in the area.

'Hello, hello!' she cried, and hugged each of them. 'Is Timmy back too?'

'Yes, he arrived this morning, and he seems delighted to be here in time to place a bet. We've just been checking that he is getting settled into his new ward,' said Mrs Smith.

Evie laughed, and went to find him in the hospital. She noticed Tricia plodding slowly across the air field in the opposite direction with some of her friends, and so she waved and, once she had Tricia's attention, pointed to where Tricia could locate Mr and Mrs Smith so that they could tell her about Timmy.

Evie found Timmy on the ground floor of the hospital, his bed in a bay window, with rather a lot of injured servicemen sitting in chairs around him in their dressing gowns, with blankets folded over their knees. Evie realised that the course had been laid out in a way that the hospital patients would be able to see clearly all that was going on, if they were near to one of the large and imposing sash windows with their big bays that overlooked the air strip. And although Timmy couldn't have been at the hospital for more than a few hours, he already appeared to be making friends and seemed very much at home.

'Timmy!' Evie called, and as he glanced up and gave a welcoming smile, she was gratified to see that he looked much better than when she had last seen him in August, and that he was once more wearing the stripy pyjamas she had made for him.

When Evie had first heard about his life-threatening head and back injuries, and then when he had been struck down by fever once he had arrived at Stoke Mandeville, she had despaired that he would never again seem like the Timmy who had gone off to fight. What a relief to see him now much more like his old self.

Timmy grinned broadly as he eagerly beckoned Evie toward him, and she leant down and kissed his cheek. His eyes were both equally open now; the last time Evie had seen him he'd been unable

115

to prevent one of his eyelids drooping in a rakish manner.

Evie said, 'How wonderful you are back in Lymbridge, or as good as. I've just seen that Tricia is here at the races too, and so I would expect her to come in and see you soon – don't you dare look too shocked when you see the size of her stomach! And I'm delighted to report that your mother looks very pleased that you are back here.'

'Evie Yeo – how very fine it is to see you,' Timmy said, and then clasped her in as much of a bear hug as he could manage, causing Evie to lose balance and to laugh with a mixture of ticklishness and embarrassment as she tried to regain her footing in what she hoped was a ladylike manner.

And then the recuperating men who were gathered nearby all laughed jovially when he waved around a list of all the runners and riders and commented, 'If you're quick, Evie, you can nip out and place two bob for me on Sukie to win, and two bob that Dave'll fall off before jump seven.'

Evie said she would.

And then there was a pause, before Evie had to confess that she didn't actually know how to place a bet.

With a roll of his eyes heavenwards, Timmy gave a guffaw before he quickly set to telling her what she had to do.

So, after a second slightly clearer explanation of what exactly she was to say to the bookie, as the betting process hadn't made much sense the first time Timmy explained it, Evie took the four shillings Timmy was holding out to her, and then asked if anyone else wanted a bet placing.

A cheer went up, and it seemed that everybody did. Luckily one of the patients had a notebook handy, and so Evie was able to jot down the various bets and who was making them. She collected the money and turned to head off to the Tote, looking for the one known as Bob Tandy, as Timmy was very insistent that Bob always had the best odds.

As Evie trotted down the grand hallway, she smiled to herself as she heard Timmy explain that Evie was his former fiancée, but she'd seen the error of her ways, and in any case it was probable that his new wife would come by to see him too before very long.

Evie was delighted Timmy seemed much more his impish old self and she was heartened that he was so keen to have a bet. She was certain – although privately she didn't really approve of gambling – that it was a sign that the old happy-go-lucky Timmy of before his injury wasn't completely lost. He still didn't seem to have a whole lot of movement in his body or legs but with a bit of luck this would improve. The other lads in the hospital seemed nice and it was likely Timmy would soon be the life and soul of the party.

Her musings were interrupted when, suddenly, she had the strangest sensation, one so powerful that it seemed as if every hair on her body suddenly had to stand to attention.

For just an instant Evie was convinced she could smell the familiar 'Peter' smell, with his distinctive blend of clean clothes, freshly washed skin and just the vaguest hint of a manly, primal scent.

Evie stopped abruptly and stared around her

117

with eyes flickering from side to side. But she was the only person in the hallway, and aside from the open door from the room in which Timmy and his chums were, through which she had just passed, there was only an empty table at the opposite end of the corridor towards the back of the house, piled high with clean bedding, and several closed doors on either side of the hallway. The glass-paned double front door was propped open on one side so that this afternoon people could wander at will in and out of the grand house that had been requisition as the new re-cuperation hospital.

She breathed in deeply. Yes, what she had sniffed was fainter, but it was still there.

Only Peter smelt that way, she was sure. Peter!

Evie had to put a hand out towards the wall to steady herself. She felt heady and as if she might faint. She was as intoxicated as if she had had a couple of pints of The Haywain's Knock 'em Dead scrumpy.

It was a delicious sensation, but frightening and perplexing too.

She heard a steward's whistle, and knew she must hurry to give herself time to place all the bets. And with that Evie ran out to the air strip and the swelling bunch of local folk who were all excited at the prospect of an afternoon's racing.

## Chapter Six

After she had placed the bets and carefully stowed the precious betting slips in her pocket – she'd wrapped them in a clean hankie to make sure that none fluttered away in the breeze – Evie looked for Sukie to tell her about the overwhelming sensation she had just had.

But her friend was clearly focused on her forthcoming race, gently walking her bay horse on a long rein in a distant corner of the air strip to keep the mare supple and calm, with James looking to be in attendance, presumably waiting to take the blanket from the mare's haunches when Sukie was ready to head to the paddock.

Evie found her sisters, Julia now having turned up, and while the ponies were being mounted by their jockeys the sisters sipped a hasty cup of tea from the WI table, although Evie decided the cakes didn't look up to much now that the evacuees had had their pick, and therefore probably weren't worth bothering with. This was even though the evacuees professed them wonderful (in fact she thought the children were so enthusiastic with their praises because they were angling for seconds, and so to reward them for their ingenuity she bought them each what looked to be a rather literally named rock cake).

Mr Bassett and Mr Rogers wandered across to the Yeo sisters, and then Pattie's beau John arrived,

119

and so it was a rather companionable group that stood together. Evie noted that even Mr Bassett seemed relaxed and to be enjoying himself.

As the pony runners cantered up to have a look at the first fence, Evie surprised herself by agreeing to have a half pint from The Haywain's stall, although she insisted that it should be the weaker scrumpy rather than the Knock 'em Dead.

The race got underway and the ponies went lickety-spit around the course, making it all look very easy with clean jumping and no fallers.

When Evie mentioned she'd been into the hospital and that Timmy's ward seemed lively, Mr Bassett had a word with John, who was technically supposed to be working on The Haywain's table although he'd clearly inveigled a few minutes of free time in order to stand by Pattie briefly. Mr Bassett wanted to say that if the doctors would allow it then he would be privileged to stand the patients at the hospital a round of drinks.

John thought this idea of Mr Bassett's to be very fine, and he promised to arrange this if it were allowed. Without ado Mr Bassett set off smartly in the direction of the hospital to see if he could find someone in authority to speak to, and as she watched Mr Bassett's slim retreating figure, for a minute or two Evie felt a tad contrite that she had so recently written such a damning letter about him to Mrs Smith.

Mr Bassett returned with a satisfied expression on his face as the doctor he had spoken to said he could see no reason why the patients couldn't each have a half pint of beer or scrumpy if they so wished, and he quickly set about organising for eighteen drinks to be transported to the wards.

By now the mares were being led around the paddock, the dipping sun making their winter coats look an array of interesting highlights and lowlights, and the steel of the bits and buckles and stirrups glint and shine.

Evie was gratified to see that Sukie was the bookie's favourite, with short odds of 3/1 against her, with the next closest runner at 6/1. Sukie's enviable figure, film-star face and blonde waves, plus the fact she was working at the hospital, had led to an upsurge of support for her.

Evie decided on the spur of the moment to push the boat out and to put a whole five shillings on her friend to win. She knew Sukie was made of steely stuff and would ride all out; she might look like a cover-plate but she was fiercely competitive and handily, bearing in mind the occasion, a very talented horsewoman to boot.

Evie commiserated with poor James, who was cross with Susan, demonstrated by him kicking a tussock of grass repeatedly. Susan had forbidden him from betting, saying that it was a lousy habit that James had best never start, and in any case fifteen was far too young for such behaviour.

To cheer her brother up, Evie said that once all the races had been run, he could help her hand out the winnings to Timmy and those of his fellow patients who'd made the clever choices; she was sure they'd be very happy to see him.

James brightened at this, although when he saw Robert's happy expression as he was placing his own bet on Sukie, it looked for a moment to Evie as if her little brother might say something pointed to his father, which could potentially be a dampener to a nice afternoon.

Susan was keeping the four evacuees amused but Evie could see that her mother was also watching James like a hawk to make sure he didn't manage to place a crafty bet. Susan was very good at doing several things at once, which the whole Yeo family knew, and so James didn't dare risk stepping out of line. Susan would have had no compunction in calling him out on it, and quite loudly too, no matter who was watching.

True to form, Sukie rode effectively and economically, and won the race by a good four lengths, her mare barely breaking into a sweat.

Evie clapped and cheered at Sukie's victory, as did just about everybody else. There had only been two women riders in this race, and this other woman rider, whose plump physique belied her determination in the saddle, had finished third after a real tussle to pass the horse that had looked as if it would cross the finish in third place. Evie couldn't help but note that several of the men who'd competed against this pair of ladies looked rather crestfallen – this wasn't the victorious ending they'd imagined for themselves. The bookies looked less than delighted too as Sukie had been so heavily betted on.

Julia and Pattie and Evie hugged each other, and clapped with hands held high as Sukie, carrying her saddle, passed by them on her way to the weighing-in enclosure trying hard not to look too smug but failing rather badly.

It was now time for the Hawker Chase, and once Linda, who was the course farrier, had sorted a quick remedial nail on a loose shoe of one of the geldings due to run, the runners were paraded around the paddock and then taken down for their look at the first fence.

Evie wandered over to Susan, who was standing now with Mr and Mrs Smith. The evacuees were milling about with a selection of other pupils from Lymbridge Primary School, watched over by Mr Bassett.

'The grey that Dave Symons is on is the one I fittened – he doesn't like water much,' Evie commented in a conspiratorial tone.

Mr Smith looked as if he knew his way about a horse and then he said, 'His rider had best tuck in behind something honest, then he's less likely to have a stop and a possible dunking at the ditch.'

The white flag was dropped and soon it was clear that Dave Symons had obviously decided on this as his best strategy too, and Evie was gratified to see that her hard work seemed to have paid off as the grey nursed his rider around the jumps in the wake of a bold-jumping chestnut and then accelerated over the last couple of hundred yards, looking as if he had plenty of running left, racing to finish neck and neck with a wiry bay horse ridden by a horsey-faced young woman nobody seemed to know. Evie's grey looked as if he could easily have galloped round all six jumps on another circuit.

The bay horse was said to have won by a nose, but everyone watching could see there were then some heated words from some of the punters, followed by a steward's inquiry, and after what seemed like in inordinately long wait the race was awarded to Dave Symons and the grey. Although the crowd hadn't been able to see clearly as the horses were bunched together at that point, the other rider had impeded the path of the grey at a jump on the far side of the course, apparently – although she hotly disputed this in ringing, upper-class tones – when her mount had allegedly swerved at the last minute just before he jumped. But the steward's inquiry stood, and so it was a furious-faced woman rider who stomped by with her saddle on the way to the weigh-in, while Dave Symons ambled along in her wake with a dazed expression.

Everyone laughed at Dave Symons's shocked face. Nobody had thought he could win, least of all he. The bookies looked much happier than they had when Sukie had won.

Well, there was one person who didn't seem particularly surprised at the outcome of the race, Evie discovered.

Sukie, the dark horse herself, had placed two shillings on Dave to win at long odds of 100/1, it turned out – she had cleaned up by winning back a whole £10 and she'd got her original stake back too. Evie had been feeling quietly smug at her own 15 shillings win, and the return of her stake, but she had to bow to Sukie's clever bet.

Later that evening, Evie and Sukie dissected the three races after all the horses had been returned home and given a good feed, and it seemed that just about all the race-goers had made their way over to The Haywain.

When it came to talking about Dave Symons's unexpected success, Sukie nursed her victory port and lemon that Evie had bought her and said, 'Don't forget that I had inside knowledge of the grey as I'd seen you ride him so much. Although he's not keen on water he's basically straightforward, and I thought that when his blood was up he'd prove honest and so I suggested to Dave that he nip in behind that leggy chestnut as I knew he had won show-jumping classes at county level before the war as he'd beaten me when he was ridden by Ian Messenger – who signed up to fight last year. I thought the grey should go over everything cleanly if he were close enough to the chestnut. And as Dave Symons has heavy hands I told him to grab a handful of mane over each fence to feel secure, rather than hanging on by the reins as then the grey wouldn't be spooked by a surprise dentistry job. I could see the chestnut was carrying too much weight not to fade in the final stages, and so once the last fence was over Dave Symons should just kick for hell. A little bit of inside knowledge can go a long way! I'm not surprised the grey won, but I am surprised that his jockey actually listened to me. Perhaps Dave Symons is not the totally lost cause we've long believed?'

Evie and Sukie caught each other's eye, and burst out laughing. Yes, Dave Symons might have won the race, but it was going take more than that to elevate him in their opinion from being thought of as pretty hopeless generally, and certainly never to the position whereby he could be thought of as possible walking-out material.

Sukie was still wearing her racing colours, although she had let her hair free from the hair net she'd used to keep it tidy under her racing hat,

125

and Evie noticed how many admiring glances were being directed at her friend by the male clientele of The Haywain.

Evie felt plain and dowdy by comparison even though she was actually wearing one of her favourite skirts.

'Sukes,' Evie was just beginning, 'I want to tell you that I had the most peculiar sensation today in the recuperation hospital...'

But Sukie's odd and hard-to-read expression dampened what Evie had been going to say.

Mr Rogers had come up to them clutching the photographs he'd taken at Goosey Fair, and Sukie was concentrating on what he was pointing at in a background corner of the top photograph.

Evie turned to see what her friend was peering at, and almost did a double-take at what she saw.

For Mr Bassett and Julia were deep in conversation, standing much too close and staring deeply into one another's eyes. It looked almost as if they were about to kiss.

As one, Evie and Sukie looked at each other and then turned to peer around The Haywain.

Sure enough, tucked into the very self-same snug where Dave Symons had gleefully informed Evie about Timmy's peccadilloes, were Julia and Mr Bassett, sitting very close to one another.

Mr Rogers chortled openly when he too saw them, saying, 'Looks like cupid's been out and about with his trusty old bow and arrow.'

The harder Evie stared at her sister, who hadn't had much experience with men – actually that was the understatement of the century, as she hadn't had *any* experience at all – the more Julia and the

126

normally withdrawn and silent Mr Bassett now looked for all the world like two old hands in the romance game, as if they could spend all evening delighting each other with what they were saying.

Evie had to acknowledge it was Julia who seemed very much in control of the situation, as she was laughing at whatever Mr Bassett's story was with all the ease of a Sukie (who'd been honing her skills with the opposite sex since kindergarten). And Mr Bassett was seemingly unable to stop smiling back at Julia as he continued to try to win her attention and make her laugh.

Whatever next? thought Evie. And then she and Sukie shared a look of baffled bemusement.

Julia stayed at Bluebells on Saturday and Sunday night, and Evie couldn't help but think her sister was deliberately avoiding her.

But these thoughts were soon to be pushed rudely aside.

For Monday brought with it a terrible shock for Evie.

For Susan – Susan!! – had been arrested and taken to the police station in Oldwell Abbott.

Mrs Smith came to the school at lunchtime to break the news to Evie.

Evie could hardly believe her ears. Her mother arrested! Her mother who couldn't abide the smallest dishonesty or hint of louche behaviour, and who wasn't a fan of either betting or drinking alcohol.

It simply beggared belief.

It was all to do with a map, apparently, and a stranger in the shop reporting to the authorities a failure to follow the correct new procedures concerning maps. It was unbelievable, as Susan was such a stickler for protocol. There must have been some ridiculous and silly mistake, Evie told herself.

Mrs Smith tried to be placatory with Evie as she agreed that what had happened was totally out of character. Indeed she was sure it would all be put right by tea-time. Any other scenario was simply inconceivable.

Mrs Smith then offered to teach Evie's infants that afternoon, provided Mr Bassett would allow Evie to leave school for the rest of the day.

Luckily he agreed, and just as Evie headed out of the school gate as quickly as she could, Mr Smith pulled up in his car to collect her. He had already tracked down Robert, and so the three of them drove to the police station over in Oldwell Abbott, where Susan had been taken.

Both Evie and Robert were at a loss to know quite what to say or to believe. Whatever way they thought about it, it just didn't seem possible.

But it was the impeccable source of Mr Smith himself who had spied the police car at the village shop at about eleven-thirty that morning, and who had witnessed Susan being escorted from the shop before being placed resolutely in the back of the police car.

Mr Smith had hurried into the village shop but he hadn't been able to get much sense out of Mrs Coyne, the elderly woman who owned it. It seemed about the only thing she did know for certain was which police station Susan was being taken to.

At the police station in Oldwell Abbott the three of them were made to wait in the reception area for what seemed an age. Evie looked again and again at the public announcement posters with their mottoes such as 'Careless Talk Costs Lives' and 'Loose Lips Might Sink Ships' that had been attached to the cork board on the opposite wall. There was even a Wanted poster showing the photograph of a despicable blaggard suspected of looting bombed-out houses in Plymouth, and a second grainy image, this time a possible cattle and sheep rustler the police were keen to speak to.

Robert sat quiet and morose, anxiously turning his much-worn hat in his hands as he stared at the floor. Susan would be cross with him, Evie thought, as he'd clearly been so worried about what had happened to his wife that he hadn't thought to change into his smartest clothes before the drive to the police station, or to put some pomade on his unruly hair to tamp it down or even to give his shoes a quick spit and polish.

Evie felt lost for words too, and so nobody really said anything, although she found the solid bulk of Mr Smith to be a calm and comforting presence as he sat quietly nearby, and Evie was very grateful that he had come into the police station with her and her father.

Eventually a plain-clothed detective, who said he was Sgt Mathers, called Robert into an ante-room for a private word.

When Robert returned to the reception area, he whispered in a low voice, as there were now several other people sitting there on other matters, that Susan had been arrested for selling a map without

129

the proper permissions being applied for, while Mr Cleave, the old man who had been looking after Mrs Smith's garden, had been arrested for buying the self-same map.

Apparently Susan hadn't realised that a law was now in place that made it illegal to sell a map to anybody who didn't have the correct paperwork.

She was being charged, as was Mr Cleave, and they would both appear in court in Plymouth the next day. They would be allowed home for the evening, once they had signed their statements.

Goodness.

It was obviously an honest mistake, as anyone who knew Susan would agree.

Sgt Mathers had told Robert that the likely outcome would be a fine, but he warned that it could well be a heavy one.

The story would certainly be reported locally, and possibly even nationally, as the authorities thought their case would be an apposite example to stop anyone else selling a map without seeking the official permissions. Ignorance was no defence in the law, the police were keen to reiterate.

With a sinking heart Evie knew Susan would be terribly upset. It would be bad enough in her eyes that she had done such a thing, but that everyone would know about it too would feel very shameful.

As the three of them went to wait in the car for Susan, having told the desk sergeant where she would be able to find them, Evie realised that it could well be Mr Rogers who would be writing the story the newspapers would publish. Evie had been allowed to make a quick telephone call to Pemberley, where a message had been left for

Julia to take care of the evacuees' tea at Bluebells.

What a state of affairs.

It was a thoroughly chastened Susan who joined them thirty minutes later, close on three o'clock. Evie could see that her mother was visibly shaking with shock and that she was very cold, as she had been arrested and taken to the police car in just the housecoat she wore to serve behind the counter at the shop. Kicking herself that she hadn't thought to bring a coat for Susan to put on, Evie insisted her mother slip into hers and then Evie suggested that her parents travel together in the back seat so that Robert could put his arm around Susan to help her warm up.

Mr Smith asked if anyone had an objection if he also drove Mr Cleave home, as he needed to get back to Lymbridge. Robert nodded, and Mr Smith got out of the car to go and find the elderly gardener.

It was a sombre journey back to the village.

The one good consequence of the day was that it had given Mrs Smith a chance to see Mr Bassett in action as a teacher. As she told Evie later on after Evie had borrowed Mrs Worth's bicycle to go over to thank Mrs Smith for stepping into the breach, it wasn't so much that Mrs Smith felt Mr Bassett to be an incapable teacher as such, but more that she thought he wasn't cut out to be in charge and have the responsibility of running a school. And so she had made a decision.

Mrs Smith would return to be headmistress of Lymbridge Primary School, starting from the following week. She had already cleared it with the local authority.

'After the children had gone, I said to Mr Bassett that I was going to come back to Lymbridge Primary School – which he knew from taking the post was always a possibility – but I suggested to him that I would work two days a week, as I want to have time to spend with Timmy, and Mr Bassett could work the other three days as my deputy, and he seemed happy with that. I didn't say as much to Mr Bassett but it has been intimated to me once again that the education authorities are thinking of merging our school in Lymbridge with at least one of the other primary schools locally, although that is unlikely to happen before next term,' explained Mrs Smith.

Evie agreed that the two of them sharing the teaching of the juniors might be a very good compromise. And she added that if the schools were to merge and Mr Bassett needed at that point to return to teaching full-time, it would give Mrs Smith some time to make sure that he was going about everything in the way that he needed to.

'How did you think Tricia looked on Saturday?' Evie said cautiously as she changed the subject. She realised she felt peculiar talking about Mr Bassett in this manner now that Julia was so clearly smitten with him.

'Well, the baby can't be far away, that's for certain,' said Mrs Smith. She added that Tricia was finishing work at the dairy parlour the next Wednesday and later that same day Mr Smith would drive over to collect Tricia and her belongings. They had decided to wait until then, as the dairy parlour was very close to Tricia's home, and so that meant an easy journey to work for her and back again afterwards.

Phew, thought Evie, I can now let James off the hook as regards moving her possessions. James had been most unhappy with Evie when she had confessed to him that she had volunteered him for the job.

After they had enjoyed a cup of tea, Mrs Smith took Evie upstairs to see the layette ready for the baby, and the new crib which they had brought with them back from London that Mr Smith had placed next to the window. He had also bought an elegant brass double bed for the room, and Mrs Smith had had her woman-who-did make it up already with starched and pressed bed linen, and place a gaily-coloured patch eiderdown on top and a selection of matching towels on the bed frame at the foot of the bed.

It was a bit of a squash to get all the furniture into the bedroom, but it was welcoming and cosy, with lots of space inside the imposing wardrobe and chest of drawers for everything that Tricia and the baby would need – and Timmy too when he came home. Evie could see that it would seem like a palace to Tricia, especially as the cottage's third bedroom was to be converted into an upstairs sitting-room so that the newly-weds could have their own space in which to spend their evenings. Apparently there was a tiny attic room, and this was earmarked for the baby's bedroom at some point in the future. Timmy wouldn't be able to manage the stairs either down to the lower level or up to the baby's room without help from Mr Smith, but this seemed the most sensible use of the rooms for all concerned. If it felt too squashed in the bedroom with the wheelchair, then the wardrobe would be moved onto the landing and the bed turned around, but while Timmy was in hospital Mrs Smith thought Tricia would like to have the wardrobe in the bedroom close to her.

Evie said that they seemed to have thought of everything, and that it all looked wonderful to her. She was sure that Tricia would agree too.

Mrs Smith told Evie that Tricia had been to see Timmy in hospital late in the afternoon of the point-to-point, and apparently he had been joshed by the other patients when they saw how very close he was to becoming a father.

Evie laughed, and agreed that the prospect of fatherhood might certainly be giving Timmy the odd queasy moment.

Just before Evie made to leave Mrs Smith said to her, 'That little Bobby Ayres is as much of a tyke as he ever was. I don't know how he managed it, but by the time I called them in from the play-ground after their lunchtime runabout today, he had managed to find a little bird's nest in the hedge, and he insisted he was going to take it home for his mother to make some bird's nest soup! Would you credit it?'

'Ah, that's my fault, I'm afraid,' confessed Evie. 'I was doing a little geography this morning and was trying to think of an unusual food to go with each continent, and so I told them that in China bird's nest soup is a delicacy. I also said that frou-frou is eaten in Africa, and then the boys tried to tell me that frou-frou was a ballet dress. This is because I'd said to them last week after we saw the hornpipe being danced at Goosey Fair that you could tell a lot about dancers from what they were wearing and that it was possible the white baggy trousers the young sailors wore when they were dancing were based on the old galligaskins, and that women ballet dancers would of course have worn a tutu if they had been dancing a little bit from *Swan Lake* for everyone. I think something got lost in the translation between tutu and frou-frou; and as for the bird's nest soup, well, one can only imagine Mrs Ayres's face if Bobby had presented the nest to her for the supper pot!'

As Evie slowly manoeuvred the ancient cycle across the road to turn in at Pemberley's gate, a large black car pulled up and indicated it wanted to go up the drive also. Evie smiled in its general direction, and went to manhandle the heavy pushbike out of the way.

The car window rolled down, and a voice said, 'Good afternoon, Miss Yeo.'

With alacrity Evie sprang around to look at the car.

It was Peter!

Evie's instant smile of delight faded with equal speed when she saw that beside him was sitting the horsey-faced young woman who had argued so vigorously with the point-to-point stewards about Dave Symons snatching the Hawker Handicap from her clutches, and who was now staring unblinkingly at Evie with what could only be described as a stony expression.

When she thought about it later that evening, Evie was proud of the way she rallied to reply in an overly polite voice, 'Good afternoon, Mr Pipe. How nice to see you back in the area, and looking so well.'

He gazed rather blankly back at Evie, before saying, 'Allow me please to introduce my companion, Miss Fiona Buckley. And Fiona, this is Miss Evie Yeo, who is a school teacher, and a PG at Pemberley. She made me feel very welcome when I was new to the area.'

The two women cast appraising looks at each other. It was clear that neither was particularly enamoured.

Evie was pretty certain that Peter would not have mentioned her to Fiona, and only now had grudgingly introduced them to one another, as not to do so would have made the dreaded Fiona even more suspicious.

But to judge by Fiona's rather sour expression she had already twigged there might be a frisson in the air between Peter and Evie, and her narrowed eyes seemed to be accusing Evie of being almost certainly *too* welcoming of Peter over those late spring and early summer months.

'I see...' The pause felt significant to Evie. 'And will we be seeing you at tea?' Fiona allowed no doubt in Evie's mind that she was emphasising the 'we' so that Evie could be absolutely certain that she wouldn't be welcome to share with them the late afternoon repast. 'Mrs Worth has promised us high tea and then Peter will collect his belongings as he is no longer interested in lodging here,' Fiona added firmly.

Evie felt her belly roil. She hadn't realised but with Peter absent for such a long time, it had

136

been quietly reassuring to her in the meantime that at least some of his possessions had been left in close proximity to her.

'Oh, what a pity!' Evie forced out in a falsely cheerful voice, and then went on with a downright fib. 'I have just been to see my former headmistress, and once I've collected a cardigan from my bedroom I'm afraid I have to be going out again straight away as I promised my mother I would drop in to see her and the family. And so I must say good afternoon to you both as I am running a little late, but of course I hope that you have a very pleasant tea. I'm sure everyone will be pleased to see you, Mr Pipe, and to make your acquaintance, Miss Buckley.'

Peter's face suggested nothing was probably further from the truth.

But Fiona laid a proprietorial gloved hand on Peter's arm as she leant unnecessarily close to him to shoot Evie a phoney smile. And then she said, 'A shame. We'll say good afternoon to you then, Miss Bow.'

Evie noticed the slightest tremor from Peter in the soft skin just below the eye that was nearest to her at the presumably deliberate mispronunciation by Fiona of her surname. And Evie clocked that Fiona had a smear of coral lipstick on the corner of one of her rather prominent front teeth.

Five minutes later, Mrs Worth's rattling bicycle had probably never been ridden so quickly as Evie pedalled hell for leather in search of Sukie. She felt as if she would burst if she didn't speak to her faithful confidante as soon as she possibly could.

Her friend was tracked down as she was making

her way to The Wheatsheaf over in Bramstone, where apparently she had a date waiting (how *did* Sukie manage this with such impressive regularity, Evie couldn't help but wonder). But she was, as Evie had known she would be, wonderfully sympathetic.

Nevertheless Sukie felt that Evie hadn't elicited nearly enough information as to what was going on. Why were Peter and Fiona in the car together? Where were they going? Where was Peter going to be living? And were they engaged? Why on earth hadn't Evie checked the damn woman's ring finger to see if an engagement ring was sparkling on it? And what had Peter been doing that day at the recuperation hospital?

'Honestly, Evie-Rose, you've not been up to scratch at all here. Not by a very long shot indeed. You still know next to nothing about Peter and what's going on!' Sukie sighed dramatically. 'And while we're about it, I want to point out that I don't think you've been quizzing Julia enough about what she's been up to either. When all is said and done, this is remiss and very disappointing of you.'

'I do know one thing,' insisted Evie. 'Just being near Peter still makes my heart flip. And I rather fancy Fiona saw that was the case.'

'I call that two things,' came the pert reply.

# Chapter Seven

Mrs Smith again stepped into the breach to teach the infants the following day, so that Evie could go to court in Plymouth with Robert and Susan. It was quite a squash in Mr Smith's car as of course he also drove Mr Cleave, who didn't have his own motor, and this time Susan was bundled up in her thick coat.

The hearings didn't last long. Susan had a word outside the courtroom with a solicitor whom Mr Smith had arranged, and then when she was called into the courtroom an hour or so later, she pleaded guilty with a mortified look on her face to the offence of selling a map without proper authorisation.

Evie's heart went out to her beloved mother when she saw how carefully Susan had pressed her best clothes and cleaned her shoes; but despite her best hat and gloves, she looked very scared and vulnerable standing in the dock. At least the magistrates didn't rebuke her publically, other than to say that all newsagents and shop-keepers had a duty to make sure they were acting within the law, and that Susan would be fined £20.

Mr Cleave was represented by a second solicitor, also arranged by Mr Smith. As expected, he pled guilty too, and was also fined £20.

In the car on the way home there was an ominous silence for a while, and Evie stared out of the

139

car window wishing this depressing chapter of all their lives was over and laid to rest.

It was raining and under the dreary grey sky Plymouth looked very sorry for itself, with rather a lot of bombed-out buildings and road diversions still obvious on what seemed like almost every soot-coloured street corner, even though the brunt of the bombing had been six months earlier. There were quite a lot of people going about their business but Evie thought they all looked weary and depressed. It was obviously going to take a while for the city to get back on its feet, and the more Evie stared out of the window at the grim state of the punishing Plymouth had taken at Jerry's hands, the more troubled she felt.

Then Mr Smith lightened the mood in the car a fraction by suggesting that he could pay for both fines and the solicitors, and that Susan and Mr Cleave could reimburse him in instalments. At first they both were adamant they would pay their own fines, but then Evie – who knew how strapped for cash her parents felt – pointed out that in effect they still would be paying their fines, just a little more slowly, and surely this had to be a tremendous help as nobody was very flush with money these days?

Five minutes later it had been agreed that Susan could stump up ten shillings a week, and Mr Cleave two bob – although these were small sums, nevertheless they would entail scrimping and saving. Evie thought Mr Smith very probably might have been willing to stand the cost of both fines and not ask for the money back as he was very comfortably off, but he was sensible to have couched his generosity as a loan. Susan and Mr Cleave were proud sorts, and this way enabled them to save a little face.

Evie knew her parents would pay every penny of the loan off as quickly as they possibly could. They would starve themselves rather than renege on a debt. In fact they didn't believe in spending money they didn't have and would diligently save up before buying any new possession.

Mr Rogers had been the only journalist present in court. In a break when a previous case had been paused briefly to give a late witness time to arrive, he promised Evie that although he had to write the story for publication, he would take care that it wasn't scurrilous or unnecessarily sensational.

Evie sighed glumly and nodded to indicate she understood. She thought that was about the best that could be hoped for.

On the way back and just as they neared Lymbridge, Susan declared she would cease working at the shop as the local villagers would never trust her again and she couldn't bear the thought that any customers might think she would diddle them with their change.

Robert and Evie said this would be a huge mistake, and they tried energetically to convince Susan to keep her job, Evie recognising how anxious the prospect of having Susan's income cut from the family's budget – especially with the loan from Mr Smith still to pay – would make her father. Susan seemed too caught up in the embarrassment of her own humiliation to notice the deeply-etched worry lines on Robert's brow or the greyish tinge of anxiety that was now shading

141

his skin.

It was the reasonable tone of Mr Smith that pulled Susan back from the edge of histrionics.

'I completely understand your reasoning, Mrs Yeo, and I might very well feel as you do in your position,' he said. 'But it might be an idea not to be too hasty in this respect. I think the village of Lymbridge may surprise you in its support, and you must give them time to show you this. If they don't, then you can always end your association with the village shop at that point.'

And so it proved to be.

When it appeared, Mr Rogers's story was factual and had no embellishment. In fact it was so pared down that Evie had to hunt through the *Western Morning News* the next day to find it, and it was only on her second pass through the newspaper that she discovered its four short paragraphs virtually hidden towards the bottom of page seven.

And at tea that evening Susan announced herself immensely touched by the number of people who had come into the store especially to commiserate with her. Everybody, it seemed, was keen to show solidarity over what had occurred.

It was a shocking thing to have happened, was the general consensus, and anybody with a brain could see it was a daft ruling. Any invading Germans were unlikely to stop to buy a map in Lymbridge, of all places. Mr Cleave had only wanted the blessed map because he'd managed to secure several gardening and odd jobs in other far-flung parts of Dartmoor and he needed to plot the routes he'd cycle to and from this new work. And Mrs Coyne, the shop owner, clearly hadn't thought to inform Susan of the change in the law, which was bad, as she would never have made such an awful mistake otherwise. And so on.

The silver lining to the cloud was that before they left the shop, virtually all of Susan's supporters made at least one purchase, with the result that when the takings were added up at the end of the day the sum that had passed through the tills was nearly double that of the previous best day's takings.

'It's an ill wind that blows nobody any good,' said Julia in her trademark sensible manner, when the family sat over tea that evening at Bluebells. They all nodded in agreement. All four evacuees were on their very best behaviour, and Evie thought that either Pattie or Julia must have had a word with them.

Susan was very quiet and listless though, and when she had nipped upstairs to get something, the sisters agreed it would take quite some time before their mother was back to her old lively self.

Not too much later that evening the three sisters headed for the Ladies Bar in The Haywain, as they had arranged to meet Sukie and Linda for a quick drink.

They'd tried to get Susan to come with them for just half an hour, to demonstrate to everyone that she wasn't cowed by what had happened and that her family were behind her one hundred per cent.

Susan had declined with a firm shake of her head, although her eyes had darkened with pent-up emotion at the tender care her daughters were very obviously showing her.

It was the lull before the storm, and before the evening would close on this third tiresome day running, the calm world of the Yeos would be shattered.

No sooner had Evie and the four others settled down with their drinks (two shandies, and three lemonades) than the fun and games started.

It all began innocently enough when Linda bumped shoulders with Julia and said, 'And what were *you* doing at the crack of dawn walking down the High Street in Oldwell Abbott on Sunday morning? I was in a lorry being taken to do some sheep's feet as it was the only day I could fit them in – they were in the back making an awful racket – and the window wouldn't wind down for me to call to you, but you were walking along with the biggest smile I've ever seen on your face. You looked so completely in your own world you didn't even notice me waving to you as mad as can be.'

There was a heavy silence that swirled between them all that was suddenly oozing a very perturbing quality.

Julia stared at the floor with two scarlet spots on her cheeks.

Linda faltered as her cheery expression dissolved towards one that was much more pensive as she realised that somehow she had innocently blundered into something unexpected and almost definitely intensely uncomfortable.

Pattie and Evie caught each other's eyes with rather shocked expressions. Clearly they had both thought that Julia had spent Saturday and

144

Sunday nights at the other's home.

What might Linda's observation mean? Was it a cause for concern, seeing that Julia was sitting with them looking more or less just like the ordinary old Julia they knew and loved?

But then they noticed Julia's chin jibbing outwards in an uncharacteristically defiant posture and her eyes had the unusual steely, glittery cast about them that they had started to see occasionally.

Surprised, both sisters shifted their positions to enable them to look more closely at their middle sister, who had now flushed a vibrant shade of beetroot across her neck and décolletage.

Sukie stared glumly down into her drink, almost as if she knew what was about to happen. Linda was fussing around as if she were looking for her hanky; she was making sure she looked anywhere but at Julia.

Evie swallowed apprehensively, and she fancied that the sound of it echoed around the Ladies' bar. 'Julia, Linda made a mistake, didn't she?' Evie's voice was querulous.

'Okay, I hadn't planned for it to come out in this way,' said Julia after what felt like a very long time. She spoke with a distinct touch of aberrant bravado as the colour faded from her cheeks just as quickly as it had slashed across them. 'But I don't suppose it matters. In the long run. And it's not as if it's going to alter anything.'

Evie felt the unpleasant sinking sensation in her tummy that she'd learnt indicated she was almost definitely just about to hear something that was bound to be unpleasant. It was a feeling she'd become all too familiar with.

Julia didn't try and sweeten the pill. 'I spent Saturday and Sunday night in a guest-room at The Griffin in Oldwell Abbott. With Leonard Bassett. In the same bed, and doing everything you could possibly think of. We left here early in the evening after the racing, and went straight over to Oldwell and booked ourselves a room at The Griffin as Mr and Mrs Bassett. You saw me, Linda, when I had left the hotel briefly to make some telephone calls on the Sunday morning to some ladies whose hair I'd promised to do in order for me to tell them that I wasn't coming over to do them until the after-noon. I'd wanted to make those calls from a public telephone box rather than risk the chance of anyone at The Griffin listening in. If I was smiling I had probably made my calls and was thinking that in ten minutes I'd once again be back in bed with Leonard, hopefully to do all the things that we had just done once again,' Julia's gentle but resolutely unapologetic voice belied the shock of her words.

'Julia!' cried Pattie and Linda together in shocked low tones.

Even the normal urbane Sukie looked shaken to her core.

Evie had sat quite still. Suddenly Julia's mysteri-ousness over the past weeks made more sense, as did at least some of Mr Bassett's own peculiar behaviour. She thought with a jolt of the photo-graph of Julia and Mr Bassett at Goosey Fair, and how they had been sat so closely together in The Haywain's snug – how could she have been so blind, so utterly stupid not to see what was staring her slap-bang in the face?

With an icy tremor, Evie realised that she had been so wrapped up in her own thoughts of Peter that she'd not noticed for a moment that her sister had been sneaking around with a man right under her very nose! Evie had always assumed that Julia, over the years apparently so content to follow rather than to lead, would be as keen as she was herself to be a virgin on her wedding night. Now she knew differently, and the thought of her dowdier and plumper and, damn it, younger sister daring to have full sexual intercourse when Evie had never done anything more than kiss was simply too much to bear.

Without quite realising what she was about to do, Evie jumped up and slapped Julia with all her might right across the face.

It was such a hard slap that the sound of it rang out clearly, reverberating around the Ladies' bar and also through to the quite busy main bar across the horseshoe-shaped wooden serving top that divided the rooms.

A significant reduction in normal chatter spread through The Haywain.

Evie had never in her whole life lost her temper before, or at least not in this way.

She didn't know why precisely she suddenly felt this Vesuvius-like sensation of fury rising that was directed at her sister, although she sensed it was something to do with Timmy and Peter, and Tricia's baby, and her own frustration at having mishandled everything and her resulting turmoil of conflicting feelings.

All Evie knew for certain was that at this precise

147

second she could barely contain herself.

'How dare you, you filthy little trollop,' Evie shrieked.

Already quietened by the sound of the slap, at this The Haywain fell totally silent.

Evie wasn't finished. Nowhere near.

As Julia's cheek began to redden in the shape of Evie's hand – the slap having been as fierce as Evie could make it – Evie bellowed loudly, despite Pattie and Linda each grabbing one of her arms and trying to make her sit down, 'As if this family hasn't been through enough already. And now you're acting like the cat who got the cream, when you should be hanging your head in shame, you little … you little, er, TART.'

Evie remained standing, quivering with rage and with her fists clenched by her hips, and she was now breathing heavily. It all felt so out of character, but she didn't seem able to stop. She didn't know where she'd been storing up these words of vitriol, but she definitely felt on the very farthest reaches of being in control.

Julia didn't help the situation. She stayed sitting – even Evie saw with a sneaking respect how calm and resolute she looked – and was able to keep her voice low and steady. Aside from only the very slightest of tremors, Julia's words were brutal, her tones ringingly clear. And equally as cruel, as Julia looked defiantly up at her eldest sister.

'Grow up, Evie, you dangerous, conceited prig. What right have you to judge me? You think you know everything; you always do, and you always have. And you have always thought you were better than everybody else, bossing me and Pattie and James around something dreadful. I can see why you're a schoolteacher, as you've sought out a job where you can be paid to be bossy and a tyrant,' Julia hissed back.

And then Julia let rip much more loudly; now there was no doubt that absolutely everyone in The Haywain could hear every word. 'Yet you were too frigid to let that poor deluded Timmy Bowes do more than kiss you in the chastest of ways, and then you couldn't admit to yourself that your sickeningly prim and smug attitude sent him straight to Tricia Dolby. I'm surprised Timmy didn't do it sooner in fact. He was a lusty young man – we could all see that – and clearly he wasn't going to be content for long with a peck on the cheek, which was about as far as you were willing to allow him to go. And now you're the one on your own in the knowledge that all you're heading for is to be little more than a dried-up spinster. You're just jealous that I'm not afraid to be a real woman, Miss Evie Frigid Yeo.

'Yes, I wanted sexual intercourse, and yes, I wasn't scared to do something about it. And yes, I spent the night with Leonard Bassett. And I enjoyed every moment of it so much that I couldn't wait to do it all over again the following evening, and again each morning, and sometimes more than once! And that is just what you can't bear, goody-two-shoes Evie Yeo, the woman who's locked in a chastity belt of her own design.'

When Julia stopped speaking, a pin dropping could have been heard throughout the public house, and quite possibly throughout the whole of Lymbridge too.

This was entertainment of the highest order, and coming from the most unlikely of sources.

For a second Evie felt violently sick, as if she would vomit on the carpet in front of everybody. She and Julia had never even had a cross word before, as Julia was by nature so placid and over the years she had seemed content to bow to Evie's more forceful opinions and suggestions.

But now Julia's harsh jibes had most assuredly found their target.

Evie knew that in fact she *was* uptight and old-fashioned when it came to sexual mores. And that this had contributed to part of the tussle in her own emotions as regards Peter. There was something about him that had made her want to throw caution to the winds and explore every inch of his body, and he hers, and yet she felt uncomfortable about this to the point that she had given him confusing signals that ultimately had sent him running. And how heavily the burden of her virginity was lying on her now. In short, Evie could see that she didn't know what she herself wanted. And suddenly she understood that this indecision was going to make all of her relationships fail.

With a visible shudder, Evie could see she was a mass of double-standards. Julia didn't know about Evie's feelings for Peter, of course, and so was basing her vicious accusations solely on what had happened with Timmy. But the truth of it was that very probably Evie's determination to keep her legs crossed really had sent poor Timmy into Tricia's arms. What a thought!

Julia's words had contained inaccuracies, sure, but also some painful home truths.

And Evie hated – no, worse, loathed! – the fact that Julia hadn't been happy merely to rein in her own feelings and desires too and remain a virgin, in the frustrated, cramped-up manner that Evie had forced and subjected herself to.

Evie realised that she was nothing short of furiously jealous of her sister. How amazing it would be to find oneself the sort of woman who would go all the way out of wedlock, and then not feel an iota of shame. Evie couldn't imagine what that might feel like, and nor could she credit that it was dull and dowdy Julia who had proved to be by far the braver of the two of them in this respect.

Evie searched for the most spiteful thing she could think of to hurt Julia. 'And for you to do this and act as if you have been brought up in the farmyard when Father and Mother have been so upset about the court case, you selfish little witch, you!' She knew how much Julia loved her parents; Julia would be devastated if she thought her actions might hurt them.

Evie added for good measure, 'And all for such a dreary and dull man, can you believe? Someone whose most interesting conversation is about the "poetry" of leather on willow. Give me strength! You must be blind as well as stupid, Julia.'

Sukie was on her feet now. She put an arm around Evie's shoulders, saying firmly, 'That's enough now, Evie-Rose. The Haywain doesn't need to hear any more of your private affairs, and Julia is obviously aware now of you being very angry with her.'

But Evie shook Sukie away with an angry push. Sukie stumbled back into a chair that fell over,

151

and she had to be swiftly grabbed by Linda in order not to crash to the ground herself.

With a quick lunge forward Evie pulled Julia, who had remained staring boldly up at her, to her feet and started to shake her vigorously.

All the tension and anger of the past year were concentrated at this moment into Evie's out-of-character actions. Julia was like a rabbit being worried in the mouth of a dog, her hair whipping wildly this way and that, and Evie could hear her sister's mouth and lips slapping against her teeth.

And then Julia planted her feet more firmly beneath her on the ground, and she started to push Evie back. In a trice they were grappling like two fishwives as they fell together onto the table top around which just a minute or two before they had been happily sitting, knocking beer mats and glasses down to shatter noisily as they hit the stone-flagged floor.

Up until then, Barkeep Joss and John had been watching events unfurl with amused expressions on their faces as they paused in their serving of drinks, but now with unnecessarily dramatic sighs they slithered over the bar-top and gently elbowed Sukie, Linda and Pattie aside as they went to separate the sparring sisters.

Once they had been parted, Evie shook herself and shouted, 'I'm going to tell Mother and Father, and then I'm going to tell Mr and Mrs Worth of your foul, wanton behaviour. Morals of an alley cat, that's what you have. They'll all be ashamed of you. And then you see how much you like your nights with Mr Bassett after that, when everyone you know sees you for the hussy you are!'

'You do just that, Evie, you *virgo intacta,* and with my permission,' screamed Julia back. 'I don't care a damn what anyone thinks of me – and I mean anyone. At least I can sleep tonight knowing the truth of what a man can do to a real woman, which is something that's *never* likely to happen to you!'

With Julia's words ricocheting around her head, Evie gave a heartfelt cry that combined horror, fury and frustration, and then she turned and ran from The Haywain, with Pattie in pursuit, furious sobs erupting from deep within the eldest Yeo girl.

Sukie and Linda set to righting the chairs in the ringing silence that was reverberating around the public house, as they helped Barkeep Josh and John tidy up the decimated Ladies' bar and pick up all the broken glassware.

All the while Julia could be heard crying loudly in anguish in the lavatory where she had now locked herself.

The pregnant hush was interrupted by a male voice ringing out from the main bar, 'Whatever those ladies are having, when you're ready, Barkeep; they've earnt it.'

'Very funny, I don't think,' Sukie called back. 'But seeing as you're asking, I think I'll push the boat out and make mine a very large port and lemon.'

Over at Bluebells, the minute Evie ran in, closely followed by Pattie, their eyes bottomless with suppressed feelings and their hair messy from running, and with Evie's skirt damp and stained from scuffling in the spilt drinks, Robert realised instantly that something extremely grave had happened. He sent the evacuees straight away upstairs to bed even though they hadn't yet finished the game of cards he had been teaching them. Catherine and Marie trotted off willingly enough, but Frank and Joseph started to protest, although when they saw Robert's unusually stern expression, which was brooking no argument, they contented themselves by just giving dramatic groans as they left the room.

Susan looked horrified, and scared too at the sight of her daughters; she had never seen them so upset or so dishevelled.

Punctuated by gulps and sobs, Evie blurted out Julia's grave indiscretion.

At first she tried to gloss over how harshly she had shouted at her sister, but then she remembered that Pattie had been there and was now standing behind her, and as Evie burst into hot tears of remorse she admitted, 'I told Julia she was a trollop, and I slapped her. The whole pub went quiet as she called me a prig and frigid, and then we fought – we pushed and shoved each other – and I called her a tart and an alley cat and a hussy.'

Evie looked down at her shaking hands, and was struck silent when she saw she had pulled out a slim shank of Julia's hair. It was still caught between her trembling fingers.

Pattie filled the silence by saying, 'It was awful. None of us knew what to do. And Julia wasn't the least bit embarrassed or ashamed about what she had got up to with Mr Bassett, and I think she'll do it again the moment she can.'

James came in, and was immediately told by

Robert to go out again. His look was comical, but he suggested that if he had to make himself scarce then he could perhaps go to the offie half-door of The Haywain and get himself something there, if his father were to advance him a little money.

Robert realised he couldn't send James to The Haywain as this would be the very worst place for him to be just at the moment, and so he said he'd changed his mind and that James had better sit by the fire but that he wasn't to say a word no matter what he heard.

Evie had fully expected Susan and Robert to be vocal and equally as indignantly furious at Julia's blatant poor behaviour as she herself was.

Instead they treated the news of Julia's two nights with Mr Bassett at The Griffin with a clipped resignation, and a refusal to be drawn further on it.

Putting on a united front to their children, Robert and Susan obviously weren't happy about this turn of events, their furrowed brows suggested, but their muted verbal response was most disappointing to Evie. She had expected a reaction much more explosive.

Instead, to Evie's chagrin, they seemed much more concerned with Evie's own behaviour at The Haywain than whatever Julia had been up to, shaking their heads and gravely asking Evie whatever on earth had come over her? Had she quite taken leave of her senses? Hadn't they brought her up to know better than that?

Then – and Evie hadn't considered this for a second, her temper had been running so high – they pointed out that she had a position of responsibility and authority at the school, and what had just happened might lead to irrevocable and unpleasant consequences for her, and possibly even her removal from her post. And if that were to happen it might very well lead to Evie never being able to get another job as an infants' teacher as her references wouldn't be worth the paper they'd be written on.

Robert and Susan disappeared into the garden, with their overcoats thrust over their shoulders, where they could be seen in the evening murk standing close to Robert's largest vegetable patch on the edge of the orchard, deep in conversation for twenty minutes. Neither James, Pattie or Evie said anything at first, while the kitchen clock seemed to tick with an ever-louder tock.

Soon Evie had a splitting headache, and felt quite unwell. Her lips were dry and sore, and she was dizzy.

Until six months previous Evie had always believed herself to be an even-tempered, generally cheerful person, and in her whole life she had never been angry like she had been earlier.

She'd always had, she thought, good relationships with all of her family, and she had never been prone to flashes of ill-humour or bad temper. Her behaviour that evening in The Haywain was scary and quite inexplicable to her. She felt ashamed. More ashamed in fact than she could ever have dreamt possible. And, looking back to her behaviour over the summer and how she had treated Peter, it all added up to prove her to be nothing better than a common hypocrite. What a disgrace she was to the Yeo family name.

When Robert and Susan came into the kitchen once more, Evie realised she hadn't said a word in all the time her parents were in the garden, that she'd been oblivious to both Pattie and James and so she had no idea if they had been talking about her or to her, or if they had stayed as tight-lipped as her.

'We will have a word with Julia, but it will be in our own time, do you all hear? Nobody is to say anything in any way to Julia on the matter, and that means nobody. I want that understood as crystal clear by all of you, and you especially, Evie. Not a comment, not a jibe, nothing,' said Susan emphatically as she and Robert stood united inside the back door. Pattie slipped by them on her way to put the kettle on.

Robert explained he would go over immediately to tell Mrs Smith what had happened. And then he would go to see the Worths at Pemberley.

Evie's heart sunk at his words. 'Daddy, must you? Daddy, I don't want you to go. Can't we just let what happened earlier die a death? The least said soonest mended and all that, as you've always said to us,' pleaded Evie. She hadn't called Robert 'daddy' for more than ten years.

'Evie, your words were careless and crass, and you created a simply unforgivable scene,' Robert said firmly.

'Mrs Smith needs to know what happened – you work at the school, as does Mr Bassett. And although he wasn't there, he is obviously implicated in what has occurred. And the same goes for Mr and Mrs Worth – both you and Julia live under their roof, as does Mr Bassett, you seem to be forgetting. Mrs Smith and Mr and Mrs Worth won't like what I have to say, I don't doubt, but it's best they hear it from me and not as rancorous village tittle-tattle, gossip that will be spreading around Lymbridge like wildfire as we speak. And they will then have to make up their minds what they should do with you.

'And, young lady, don't you dare leave Bluebells or speak to anyone outside this room – you have done quite enough damage for one night. You will wait in this kitchen until I return, and I expect you to be here, Evie.'

And with that Robert gave the contrite Evie a harsh look and stomped out. He had never had occasion to admonish her in this way before, and Evie really didn't like it. Not at all.

Susan refused to look Evie in the eye, and she went upstairs to see what the evacuees were about. Evie heard an undignified scrabble and so she guessed the evacuees had been sitting on the stairs trying to eavesdrop.

James and Pattie looked at each other with mirrored quizzical looks, and Evie couldn't fail to notice their excited expressions. It was most unlike Robert to speak as he just had done, and so the whole family felt knocked out of kilter.

Evie put her head into her hands. She felt too low and humiliated even to cry.

Then there was a feline 'purp', and Keith jumped up onto her lap. Somehow Keith had realised her soothing presence was needed and had made her way the half mile or so through the village to Bluebells.

Evie held her close and this time she allowed

healing tears to purge her, body and soul.

Robert didn't return until after eleven. Susan, Pattie and James had all gone to bed, and Evie was sitting on her own in the darkened kitchen, in just the light of the orange embers of the range.

It was one of the first frosts of the season, and Robert's nose was red as he explained that Mrs Smith had naturally been very shocked at hearing Evie was at the centre of such a furore, and she had told him that Evie was to stay away from the school until the following Monday. Evie would receive a formal written reprimand, and would be docked a fortnight's salary, Mrs Smith said. Robert added that the Board of Education would decide if further action should be taken against her, but Mrs Smith thought that most probably that wouldn't happen and that as far as she was concerned Mrs Smith's punishment would be the end of the matter as regards Evie, although of course she couldn't guarantee that the BoE would take the same view. As for Mr Bassett, that was quite another kettle of fish, but Mrs Smith hadn't given any further intimation of what would happen as regards him.

Without further ado Robert had then gone to Pemberley. He had spoken to the Worths in private, and then to Mr Bassett.

Julia had meanwhile locked herself in her and Evie's bedroom, and it had taken Robert over half an hour to get her to open the door to him.

After a minute or two of trying to brazen it out, Robert said, Mr Bassett buckled and became very remorseful. He apologised immediately for allow-

159

ing Julia to suggest, and for his own acquiescence to, their spending the two nights at The Griffin. He said he had nothing to say in mitigating circumstances, and then he confessed to a long-term psychological problem that led to risk-taking behaviour and mood swings between the extremely excitable and the very low. It had caused him problems in the past, he explained, and he found it very difficult to settle to any one thing for long. He had come to Lymbridge as he and his family had hoped that a quiet life in a moorland village might be the thing he needed to restore a more balanced equilibrium. He was a capable teacher, he felt, but he had found his concentration increasingly hard to muster over the past month or two.

Luckily, Mr Bassett said, he was fortunate to have a private income that could support him and Julia too, if she so wanted, and so he would resign from the school with immediate effect. His behaviour had been inappropriate and he didn't know what he had been thinking of, and so he apologised without reservation to Robert. He added that his physician had discussed medication with him that he'd been reluctant to try, but now it was maybe time he reconsider.

However, he had been insistent to Robert that he and Julia loved each other deeply. They had taken to sneaking time together at Pemberley from the morning after he had moved in. They hadn't wanted their growing attraction for each other to become public knowledge, as Mr and Mrs Worth would have insisted he move out. Although it was very regrettable that his and Julia's relationship had been exposed in this way, they had been planning to bring it into the open, although not quite the extent to which it now was.

Then Mr Bassett, after apologising once more for putting Julia in a compromising position, asked for Robert's permission to request Julia's hand in marriage, which Robert grudgingly agreed to, feeling that if Julia wanted to and they were to marry quickly then perhaps not too much harm had been done.

After Julia had squealed with delight and accepted, Mr Bassett had set off with a hastily written resignation letter for Mrs Smith, after assuring the Worths and Robert that he would stay at The Griffin.

Mrs Worth requested that both Mr Bassett and Julia move out at once. Robert agreed that until they were married it was best if Julia moved back to Bluebells, although he begged Mrs Worth to find it in her heart to let Julia stay one last night at Pemberley, and Robert would keep Evie at Bluebells.

Mrs Worth agreed reluctantly, but said that she would like a word with Evie the next day before she decided if Evie would have to move out too.

As Robert finished describing his evening to Evie, she felt simply terrible. It hadn't occurred to her that she might need to find a new home too. And if that were Mrs Worth's decision, where would she go if Julia were back at Bluebells? It was inconceivable that she and Julia could reside under the same roof.

When her father asked his eldest child once again what had driven her to behave as she did, all Evie could do was to shake her head at him with brimming eyes, unable either to understand fully or to articulate her actions.

Evie was further shamed when she noticed how exhausted Robert was, and how extremely disappointed he was in her. Evie was used to her father being quietly supportive and admiring of her, and so to see him look in her direction with such a disillusioned expression was almost more than Evie could bear.

Unsure of what they should do now, both she and Robert agreed it was time for bed. It was now well past midnight, and he had to be up early for work the following morning.

Keith snuggled in to Evie when she pulled a blanket over them both as she lay in the clothes she had worn all day on the uncomfortable sofa in the parlour. What a perfectly foul few hours, but although Keith's drone of a purr and her constant paddy-pad of her paws with their sharp claws kept Evie awake, the trusting cat and her open affection made Evie feel just a smidgen better as she gently stroked Keith's furry round belly.

It was a short-lived respite though, as Susan's frosty attitude the next morning told Evie that everything wasn't suddenly going to be all right between mother and daughter, with events of the previous night brushed under the carpet as Evie had so hoped they would be.

Her mother's sour look left Evie in no doubt at all that she had thoroughly disgraced herself, and by association, the whole of the Yeo family. Evie would have to do a lot of bridge-building to make amends was the message sent through Susan's

162

tense shoulders and lack of chitchat.

Message received and understood, thought a very chastened Evie.

It felt most peculiar not to be going to the school, and Evie wasn't sure what to do. She knew that Mrs Worth wanted to see her at three o'clock, but she didn't have anything to occupy herself with until then.

She wandered round Bluebells. It was familiar, but somehow not. And without all the people she cared about coming and going, as everyone had either gone to school or work, she was slightly taken aback at how shabby the place looked. There was something about her family that made the rooms seem warm and welcoming when everyone was there, but without them present the rooms lost any sense of invigoration, leaving everything threadbare and unappealing.

Evie decided to pay Tricia a visit. She would have moved into Mrs Smith's cottage the previous day.

To her horror, Evie mis-timed her walk over to Tricia's. She had only gone a little way when Julia cycled by, her Post Office bag bulging with post to be delivered, studiously avoiding acknowledging Evie.

Evie didn't know what to do, and so she looked at Julia, and then quickly averted her eyes. Evie felt a hot blush sweep across her and her hands perspire.

Julia didn't seem at all bothered either way, to judge by the determined set of her shoulders and her slow, steady cycling.

Evie felt that this resolute silence was most awkward, almost worse than if they had said a few more sharp words to one another.

By the time Evie was knocking on Mrs Smith's door her lower lip was trembling, and when Tricia finally opened it, all Evie could do was stand there with blobby tears starting to run down her face.

Tricia had obviously heard what had happened the night before to judge by her rather hard stare. Then her expression softened and she patted Evie on the arm surprisingly gently and kindly, before manoeuvring her into the kitchen for a cup of tea.

'Let it oot, Miss Evie. I 'eard abut t' set-to last night – it mus' 'ave bin full-on an' frankly I didn't know you 'ad it in yer. It sounds a right ol' ding-dong, but anyhow it's gud that Lymbridge folks 'ave somethin' else to do their worse wi' rather than me an' ma belly,' commiserated Tricia.

And for some reason Evie found Tricia's words to be the most rib-ticklingly funny thing she'd ever heard, and instead of crying she began to laugh.

And Tricia, who although at first was a bit con-fused and shocked at this reaction, soon saw the funny side too (even if she wasn't a hundred per cent sure precisely what it was that she was actually laughing at).

And so the pair of them sat on either side of Mrs Smith's well-scrubbed kitchen table laugh-ing their hearts out. For just a minute or two, it felt wonderful.

## Chapter Eight

Evie decided she should try to seize a tiny piece of initiative before her rather dreaded meeting with Mrs Worth later that day. She went to the village shop and bought her landlady a couple of magazines as a peace offering, Susan still giving her the cold shoulder when she went to the counter to pay for them. When Evie headed for Pemberley, she took extreme care to arrive there at three o'clock precisely.

She entered through the familiar front door and found Mrs Worth counting her best linen napkins in the dining room. Evie said simply, as she put the magazines on the table and gently nudged them an inch or two in the older woman's direction, 'I am ashamed of myself, Mrs Worth. I cannot begin to explain what came over me, or fathom what you might think of me. And whatever you are thinking of me, I am sure I deserve it. I really do not have anything to say in my defence. It goes without saying, of course, that I will quite understand if you want me to move out of my lovely room in Pemberley, although I very much hope that you will allow me to stay as I have had such a happy home here with you all.'

Evie had her fingers crossed that Mrs Worth wouldn't want her to leave; the uncomfortable night on the hard sofa in the chilly parlour had shown her that life at Bluebells, now that there were four evacuees there as well as her parents and Pattie and James, would be less appealing than life in the rather grand Pemberley with its gracious, high-ceilinged rooms and impressive gardens. She had, she realised, rather got used to a more moneyed way of life than Bluebells offered. Evie wasn't proud about this, of course, but she felt very differently these days to the inexperienced Evie who had first moved to Pemberley earlier in the year.

Evie also hoped that with the sudden loss of Julia and Mr Bassett as PGs, Mrs Worth might be keener to keep her as a lodger than she would otherwise; there'd be the issue of the loss of income through the empty rooms, and also the threat of the authorities wanting to use Pemberley in some other manner in the war effort if the bedrooms weren't filled.

Mrs Worth looked at her coolly for a long moment, and then said in an admonishing voice, 'Evie, I don't quite know what to say to you, really I don't. This is a respectable household, and I don't like to think of the behaviour of yourself, or Julia, or Leonard Bassett for that matter. None of you have covered yourselves in glory. On the other hand up until now you have been an exemplary member of the household, and I have become very fond of you over the past months. Indeed I have come to think of you almost as the daughter I was never able to have...'

Mrs Worth's soliloquy was interrupted by Evie being unable to hold back her frazzled emotions. Her lower lip was wobbling uncontrollably. She realised that she had grown fond of the Worths too, and that she would miss them if she had to go.

She looked up to apologise again, and was surprised to see that the usually very controlled Mrs Worth also appeared to be on the brink of breaking down. Her landlady's eyes were very shiny and she was fiddling with a scrap of lace-edged hanky.

They stepped towards each other, and gave each other a heartfelt hug. They didn't really need words to communicate the conflicting feelings they both obviously felt. It was a rotten situation but not necessarily an irrevocable one, was what Evie sensed in the embrace. Evie felt both comforted and relieved; she didn't think Mrs Worth wanted her to move out after all.

It was a much less pleasant meeting that was to take place two hours later at Mrs Smith's house. Tricia had the good sense to make herself scarce while Mrs Smith berated Evie every which way for a good twenty minutes, Evie having the grace to take the scathing words on the chin and to keep quiet, determined to say nothing on behalf of herself. For there really wasn't anything she could say in her own defence, was there?

Evie mused over her behaviour while Mrs Smith told her at great length how disgracefully disappointing Evie had been. Evie agreed she had now seen the shocking depths to which she could sink, and with the words of her parents, Mrs Worth and now Mrs Smith hitting home, she understood that nobody could say anything to Evie that she hadn't thought about herself or her actions already.

'And the worst of it is, Evie, that with Mr

Bassett having resigned I had to teach the whole school as one class today, which wasn't a good thing on any level – it means that whether I like it or not I now have to come back to school full-time, when until Christmas I had been planning on spending quite a lot of time at Timmy's side,' said Mrs Smith. 'You must start back again on Monday as there is such a woeful shortage of qualified teachers these days, and although you and myself will say no more on this troubling and painful matter after this evening – unless I am instructed to say something to you by the Board of Education – I want you to understand that your card is well and truly marked, young lady. One more mistake and you'll be out on your ear and out of your teaching career more quickly than you can say Christopher Columbus wears colourful pyjamas and knitted knickerbockers.'

Evie didn't dare smile.

After what felt about the right amount of time, Evie suggested that Tricia come down to join them in the warm kitchen. Evie stayed long enough at Mrs Smith's to make sure that both Julia and Leonard Bassett would have had time to move their things out of Pemberley, and then she walked back to the guest house at a rattling pace as she really didn't want to run into any of her family or anyone else she knew on the way back to Pemberley.

Mrs Worth told Evie that Sukie and Pattie had called in to see her but had decided not to wait for Evie to return. And Julia wasn't at all pleased that she was to move back in with Robert and Susan. Mrs Worth also mentioned that Mr Bassett had taken a room somewhere over in Bramham.

Julia had apparently boasted to a scandalised Mrs Worth just before she left, James helping her with her bags, that although the previous night she had been very excited to accept Mr Bassett's timely proposal of marriage, following a night to sleep on it, Julia had come now to a different decision.

After reassuring Mrs Worth there hadn't been 'any hanky panky or funny business' under the respectable roof of Pemberley (Mrs Worth admitting to fanning herself with one of the women's magazines that Evie had bought her in relief at hearing this assurance), Julia had gone on to say in an extraordinarily calm but firm manner that the reality was she felt that she and Mr Bassett didn't know each other very well yet.

Although she was sure that if they both continued to feel as they had the previous weekend then they would go on to marry at some point. However, right now, she didn't want to rush into a legal obligation about which they both might cool.

Julia claimed too that she wasn't too bothered about a ring on her finger, and so she was contemplating the two of them possibly moving in together soon, regardless of their lack of a marriage certificate. If this were to happen, then she would call herself Julia Bassett even though they wouldn't legally be man and wife.

When a still shocked Mrs Worth repeated this conversation, Evie didn't know what to think. She had never heard of a man and woman choosing to live together without being married. The feisty Julia of this week seemed a very far cry from the

169

placid Julia of last week. And the fact it was such a taciturn, unlikely man who had proved the catalyst for such an outpouring of turbulent emotion didn't make much sense to Evie either. How could somebody as difficult as Leonard Bassett make someone like Julia so bold and forthright? It was an extraordinary state of affairs.

Throwing caution to the wind as regards politeness and the holding back of discussing such a scandalous turn of events, Evie and Mrs Worth pulled up chairs to the kitchen table, and over several cups of tea each, they debated whether Mr Bassett and Julia would find they were actually able to rent a home together, if it went that far. Gossip spread like wildfire and country areas were by nature conservative in their beliefs. It wouldn't be every landlord who would rent to an unmarried couple, they decided.

Evie thought to herself that if Julia were serious (and of course she might not be in a day or two, once she had had a chance to better think through all the ramifications of such rash and irrevocable actions), then one thing would be certain, which was that neither Robert or Susan would know what to do about it if Julia really was determined to live in sin with Leonard Bassett.

In the face of a village scandal, her parents might turn out to be a whole lot less resigned to what had happened and what was potentially about to happen than they had appeared the previous evening.

Evie didn't think they would cut their ties with their daughter or give her some sort of ultimatum, as some families undoubtedly would, but they wouldn't be at all happy and they would feel that Julia was being very foolish. Still, if that was what Julia insisted on, there probably wouldn't be anything that they could do to prevent it.

Goodness, it was an extremely challenging situation that Julia was deliberately creating – and by association, she had dragged Mr Bassett, and also Evie herself, into whatever was going on (even if Mr Bassett was a willing party, and even if Evie had fanned those flames by her own immensely stupid behaviour at The Haywain).

However one looked at it, it was impossible not to think that the Lymbridge rumour mill was all set for a continuing treat at the expense of the Yeos.

Evie thought that after Susan and the court case, this was the last thing her family needed.

The next morning Evie decided to go and see Timmy. She still felt nauseated every time she recalled her and Julia screaming at each other face to face as they had done, and she thought he would prove to be a distraction.

The unbroken sky was a deep turquoise and the sun felt almost as warm as it had during the summer, although the air felt cold in any shadows, and as she walked over to the recuperation hospital Evie discovered that it was hard to be too downhearted in the orangey low sunlight. At one point she stopped and closed her eyes as she turned slightly to face the sun as best she could, enjoying the warmth on her face. Evie dawdled a while and smiled to herself at the sight of a herd of moorland ponies who lifted their heads from grazing to look inquisitively in her direction as she passed by. The foals had lost their baby looks, and their mothers were fat after a summer gorging on the springy moorland grass. They were now all quite hairy as their winter coats had grown in ready for the icy weather that would inevitably arrive very soon. The stallion was keeping a watchful eye over his family, just in case there was another marauding stallion nearby who fancied adding the mares to his own herd.

Evie thought that Robert was rather like the stallion she was looking at, being a proud and morally robust man. He did everything he could to protect and look after his family, but sometimes events would spiral beyond his control. Robert would be thinking very seriously about his middle daughter and what might happen to her, Evie was sure, and he'd be very possibly thinking equally disturbing thoughts about his oldest daughter too.

Timmy had a bored expression on his face as Evie entered his ward but he perked up considerably the moment he saw her.

'Well, Evie, I'm hoping you've come to tell me in full and gory detail all about what went on at The Haywain the other night. It's all around the area, and it sounds as if I've missed a right show,' he chuckled. 'You'll have made Barkeep Joss's year.'

Evie sighed, and nodded miserably in acknowledgement.

'Yes, it was a show, all right. I made a right fool of myself, is the truth of it, and so did Julia. Before the point-to-point the rest of us had no idea what Julia had been up to, or even that she and Mr Bassett had noticed each other let alone were thinking of the other one in *that* way. And quite how far they had taken it came out very suddenly, when Linda blundered into stormy weather with a silly question, and I don't know, er, but, er, I suppose that without meaning to, I just lost my temper with Julia when I was told what she'd been up to, which was the last thing I was expecting to hear. I think if she had been the slightest bit contrite or embarrassed, I wouldn't have felt so geed up. But she was just so ... er, so ... er, brazen and so pleased with herself for what she'd dared to do, and it really got my goat. She and I had never even argued before. Not once in all our years! I'd had tiffs with Pattie, but Julia and me had always appeared to get on, and she seemed to like to agree with anything I said,' remarked Evie.

Timmy raised an eyebrow pointedly at the last comment, pausing Evie's description, before he added, 'Evie Yeo! I always suspected there was a passionate woman under your cool exterior–'

Timmy's jokey tone was silenced by Evie interrupting with a sharp, 'Now, don't *you* start – I'm absolutely beyond caring what anybody else thinks.'

Timmy was wise to raise both hands in supplication and keep whatever he'd been planning to say next under wraps.

They chatted for a pleasant half hour, Evie thinking it funny how much better they got on now that Timmy was married to someone else.

Timmy thought it prudent to change the subject and so he started to tell her about life in the hospital, and that he had met a nice fellow who occasionally would wander about there, bringing

173

Timmy and the other patients cigarettes, news-papers and books.

'But that's all very well – I've asked him for some ladies and some alcohol, but no luck on that so far.'

Evie laughed and thought that Timmy would never change. Tricia was probably going to find him a hard dog to keep in the front garden. Timmy wasn't the sort of chap to let a major head injury and what looked, at the best-case scenario, to be paralysed legs to get in the way of him living as full a life as possible.

One thing Evie mentioned was raising money towards a Spitfire. Timmy had a good suggestion which was that perhaps the hospital should be involved in some way as it might well be that with a bit of official clout behind a campaign, it would be more successful. He'd have a ponder and maybe a chat to one or two of the doctors.

And when Evie mentioned that Linda would be getting married in a week's time, but still had no wedding shoes, Timmy had a second good idea (Evie could hardly believe this – she hadn't thought he had it in him to be so imaginative for one usable idea, let alone two). 'Why don't you ring the *Western Morning News* and ask them to write about it? I bet that would dredge up a pair of shoes from somewhere that Linda could borrow,' said Timmy.

Evie said just before she made her goodbyes, 'Timmy, I hope you don't think I'm interfering–' cue Timmy's second pointed look of the visit aimed at Evie, at which she smiled '–but you must remember to help Tricia settle in with your mother and Mr Smith. I don't think it's going too badly so far, and from what I gather everyone is trying to be very polite around one another, but maybe you should tell Tricia about one or two of Mrs Smith's little foibles or, to put it another way, what you think your ma will expect of Tricia. I've been able to beg, borrow or steal a couple of dresses for Tricia from various ladies in Lymbridge that will see out the end of her pregnancy in a reasonably respectable manner – well, actually, Julia did this after I asked her, back when we were speaking to each other before our Words. She had a quiet chat with some of her ladies in the village when she was dressing their hair and they came up trumps with what was needed until the baby arrives. But Tricia is also going to need new clothes once she starts getting her figure back as nearly everything she owns just isn't smart enough for her to be seen out and about now that she's Mrs Smith's daughter-in-law and your wife.'

Timmy agreed, and said he would have a word to reassure Tricia, and that he would say something to his mother too. 'Damn, Evie, I feel bad that I've not thought about this. She's been coming over to see me almost every day and yet I'd not really thought about what it's really like for her. She's quite a card, and a lot sharper than I gave her credit for. I can't tell you how much I wish I were well enough to be at home with them all.'

The Lymbridge sewing circle was still meeting regularly at Pemberley, and it had had a welcome injection of enthusiasm with the arrival of Annabel as a PG. They found her professional experience

175

most useful to call on, and she appeared happy to be more or less always on hand to advise and suggest things.

Now that Linda's wedding garments had been all but finished, the focus had shifted slightly away from needlework and more towards knitting. It was the time of year when one's thoughts turned towards scarves and gloves, warm cardies and cable-knit woollies.

Evie was a very skilled knitter and she was happy to tutor Annabel in this as Annabel's ability with knitting or crochet needles didn't match her skills as a seamstress, and Tina and Sarah were rather good knitters too. Soon, everyone – even Mr Worth and Mr Rogers! – could at least do the basics.

Julia was no longer part of the group, and her name was never mentioned to Evie, even by Pattie.

Julia's absence meant no more Mrs Sew-and-Sew, Julia and Pattie's party piece of a bossy imaginary lady who told the others the whys and wherefores of sewing, which Evie thought a pity. Nobody at Pemberley ever dared to bring up the subject of the argument in The Haywain, although if somebody strayed too far in this direction as they chatted while they sewed there would be an uncomfortable silence as the members of the sewing circle bent their heads to their work.

Robert and Susan remained firmly tight-lipped about what had been said by them to Julia, or what they really thought about Julia saying that she and Leonard Bassett didn't need to marry after all but would just act as if they were man and wife. Pattie told Evie that Julia, who was having to sleep in the draughty parlour, was walking around with a determined look on her face, but that Julia had told Pattie that Pattie needn't think she was going to discuss anything with her either. Pattie said she'd felt quite rebuffed at this.

Evie avoided Bluebells, and she felt time weighing heavily on her hands now she was spending less of it with her family. Pattie passed on the occasional snippet of family gossip, such as Julia having slept at Bluebells every night, or that James had been seen holding hands with a pretty young lady in Oldwell Abbott, ironically, by Linda again as she was being driven through the town on the way to a farm.

'Linda says she's going to put a blindfold on the next time she goes through Oldwell Abbott, just in case another Yeo is up to something or other,' laughed Pattie. 'James is naturally denying everything.'

Still, Julia's presence was sorely missed at the sewing evenings, as even though most people would have thought of her as quite a quiet person who didn't necessarily say a whole lot, except when she was larking about with Pattie as Mrs Sew-and-Sew, somehow Julia *not* being there with the rest of them at Pemberley made every session a bit less cheerful and pleasant.

They were busy knitting scarves, jerseys, balaclavas and thick woollen socks as the government had asked for sets of these, both for the Naval servicemen and also for the brave sailors in the merchant navy who were facing such heavy losses as the German U-boats were targeting them heavily in an effort to stop supplies reaching home shores. Plymouth was a major port for ships in the merchant navy, and so any loss felt very close to home for those who lived on nearby Dartmoor.

The government had also asked for volunteers to help make netting for camouflage webbing, but according to Tina and Sarah (who were still dithering as to whether to stay at Pemberley or to go) this was a hellish business that simply ripped one's hands to shreds. They had spent a Saturday and Sunday doing it somewhere in Plymouth after which they had both declared, Never Again. Pattie was also struggling with her knitting as her rough farming hands tended to catch on the wool.

Knowing how much the seaman's woollies were needed, Evie hesitated to mention Tricia and her need for clothes.

Eventually Evie took the plunge and said to the members of the sewing circle that she and Timmy were going to help Tricia with her clothing problem. And while the government-requested woollies were the priority, might it be possible for them to find a little time to do something for Tricia too?

There was a palpable sense of tension being released. It had obviously been preying on people's minds that they must be extremely careful not to mention Timmy or Tricia to Evie.

It wasn't long before Evie was able to tell them how Timmy was getting on in hospital (surprisingly well, all things considered, with his headaches decreasing in intensity and number) and how Tricia was settling in at Mrs Smith's (Evie wasn't sure, but Mrs Smith and Tricia were each cautiously polite when talking to Evie about the other one).

The upshot of all of this was that the sewing circle agreed with one another that although the main focus of the knitting would remain the woollies for the servicemen and merchant sailors, if Evie could scavenge the wool, they would combine efforts to make sure that Tricia had three or four nice cardigans to wear once the baby had been born.

Evie was very pleased at the response of her friends, and she thought with a warm heart about how generous of spirit people could be. Evie felt that she should probably make a greater effort with Tricia's garments than the other members of the sewing circle should – perhaps this would in a small way atone slightly for those terrible minutes in The Haywain – and so Evie decided that she would go all out to find some material to make Tricia two blouses for when she was getting her figure back after the birth of the baby, as well as some clothes for the baby.

There was one moment though as they sat around Pemberley's huge dining-room table, that made Evie shift about on her hard chair, although she wasn't sure if it was a wiggle of pleasure or of pain.

This occurred when Mrs Worth began speaking about Peter and Fiona. Clearly she had no idea about Evie's feelings for Peter.

'Peter was as charming as ever, and it was very pleasant to see him. Apparently he is working on something he can't talk about, and he didn't give any indication as to where he was moving and of course I didn't like to ask, even though I gave him the opportunity to be a little more forthcoming.

But enjoyable as it was to see Peter, I would be telling an untruth if I didn't admit that I wasn't at all sure about his lady friend, as she just wasn't what I expected, not that I had really given much thought to what I should be expecting.'

Mrs Worth went on, 'Miss Buckley talks down to one, if you know what I mean, and she rather took over the tea, acting somewhat as if this were *her* house rather than mine, which was an attitude I didn't particularly take to. Peter quickly made himself scarce as he disappeared off on the excuse that he needed to load up the car, but in his absence I was interrogated rather forcibly as to how life as a PG at Pemberley went on, and who Peter would speak to. I told her that as far as I had seen Peter spent most of his free time with his nose immersed in a book, and she looked most disbelieving when I said that. I added that you, Evie, would be sorry to miss having tea with them, and I explained what a difficult month or two you had had with your intended being so badly hurt and the end of your engagement.

'When I went out to wave them off, Peter did make me and Mr Worth a lovely gift of an extremely useful set of gardening tools, which will come in very handy as my shears have just about given up the ghost, and meanwhile Miss Buckley did make some nice comments about how lovely the wisteria must have been and so maybe she's someone who improves the better one knows her.'

Evie made sure to look up at Mrs Worth at the mention of her name, but otherwise she kept her eyes firmly fixed on the sock she was knitting, dipping her head downwards to stare intently at

180

her handiwork as if she were finding the heel of the sock she was working on a bit fiddly to sort out.

For days Evie had been aching to grill Mrs Worth about that teatime with Peter and Fiona, but she hadn't dared to do so in case Mrs Worth came to suspect Evie of any ulterior motive as regards to Peter, and with that the suspicion there might have been improper behaviour under her roof.

Now it looked as if Evie's wish was about to be answered. She absolutely wanted to hear as much as possible about Fiona; Evie told herself she would have been inhuman to feel any other way. After all, this not particularly attractive, long-faced young woman was the preferred alternative to herself, and Evie wanted to puzzle out why. And she was pretty keen that in any comparison between the two of them, Evie would be able to convince herself that she came out on top.

Good old Pattie. Evie's desire for further information was inadvertently granted when her sister came to the rescue by starting to probe Mrs Worth a bit more closely about Fiona, with questions along the lines of what was her figure like, and her clothes, and what had she said exactly that had evidently got under Evie's landlady's skin?

Although Evie and Pattie had seen Fiona ride in the point-to-point they hadn't really paid her much attention as they hadn't realised at the time who she was. Evie had only seen her the once up close, which was when Fiona had been sitting next to Peter in the car, and she hadn't been able to do more than cast the occasional scrutinising glance in her direction at that fraught time, when of course what she'd really wanted to do was give Fiona a very close inspection and once-over.

Evie hadn't much liked the little of Fiona she had seen – of course she damn hadn't! – and she desperately wanted more grist to feed her anti-Fiona mill.

Mrs Worth replied that Fiona was thinnish, and quite well-spoken, which were two things about her that Evie had already gleaned.

Fiona had nice hair apparently (seriously? thought Evie), and she sported expensive clothes and shoes, and she wore a lot of make-up (you can't make a silk purse of a sow's ear, was Evie's next rejoinder to herself).

Mrs Worth had found out that Fiona's family had properties in north London and an extensive farm close to Torquay, and they had made their money banking. Fiona had done a lot of hunting before the war in Hertfordshire, having been blooded at some ridiculously young age, and of course she claimed to be absolutely fearless on a horse. Then Mrs Worth added that Fiona seemed to treat Peter as if he should be happy to cater to her every whim. There was something snooty about her attitude that wasn't appealing, was their landlady's final comment.

Good. None of these attributes were particularly endearing, decided Evie, as she still made sure she was paying extra attention to the turning of the heel on the cream woollen seamen's sock she was working on. What on earth did Peter see in her? Possibly the fact that Fiona was obviously well bred and from an affluent family might be a boon in some people's eyes, but Peter had never given Evie any sign that he was this sort of man, and so it was all something of a mystery to Evie.

Fiona must have some good points, Evie supposed, but Peter had many more. How aggravating it all was.

Then Evie gasped as by mistake she had plunged the tip of her knitting needle painfully into the forefinger of the hand holding the sock.

It was all Evie could do not to hurl the knitting across the dining room in a fit of pique.

## Chapter Nine

Timmy's idea about the plea for help to be published in their local daily newspaper proved to be very sound. In fact Evie was rather impressed that something Timmy had said had gone on to prove truly useful, which wasn't a feeling she usually associated with her former fiancé.

On the Saturday before the marriage ceremony Evie had had a word with Mr Rogers about the urgent need for some rather large-sized white or cream shoes to go with Linda's wedding dress.

Then Evie showed him the *Western Morning News* clipping about Linda from earlier in the year, before he had arrived in Dartmoor. It was a story about how she had to spend a couple of weeks in hospital following a strafing by a lone German aircraft on an exposed hilltop farm a long way south of Lymbridge. Linda and the farmer had been leading the farm's two massive workhorses into the yard for a routine foot trim and replacement of their not-yet-too-badly worn metal shoes. As the plane swooped, seemingly from nowhere, they were caught on a very open piece of land where there was unfortunately no cover. The mare, Mabel, had been killed instantly with a bullet to her head, her body falling to the ground with a tremendous crash. At that unexpected sound the gelding, Hector, had quite understandably panicked. But by mistake he had knocked Linda to the ground as he whirled around in distress, catching a hoof against her chest and thereby puncturing her lung. True to form though, Linda wouldn't hear a word against faithful Hector afterwards.

Mr Rogers agreed that the potential disaster if Linda couldn't be sorted out with some appropriate footwear for Saturday was something local people would want to know about, and then he added he was sure the readers of the *Western Morning News* would help out if they possibly could.

He told Evie it was very hard for newspapers to find 'lighter' stories these days. Nobody wanted to read anything too flippant, but then neither did they want to read about constant doom and gloom either, and therefore a story like this, which had the added bonus that it could be accompanied by a picture of a most attractive young woman, was perfect.

Evie went to fetch Linda, and fortuitously the day had turned fantastically sunny by the time they returned to Pemberley. They then walked into the village where Mr Rogers took a nice photograph of Linda perched rather precariously on top of a wobbly five-bar gate at Switherns farm that opened on to some spectacularly beautiful countryside, with the moorland tors standing impressively in the background. Linda was wearing her jodhpurs (as Mr Rogers had instructed), but she was waving her bare feet in the air as she pointed to them, and happiness radiated from her smiling face as the bright autumn sunlight glanced most becomingly off her shiny hair.

When the story ran the following Monday, accompanied by the headline 'Heroine Blacksmith Needs Wedding Shoes Saviour', Linda found that before the day was out she had several pairs of suitable shoes to choose from, all of which Mr Rogers dutifully delivered back to Pemberley when he came home from work on the Wednesday so that they could be tried on along with the rest of the wedding get-up.

And on the Thursday evening when she dropped into Pemberley to collect her wedding outfit, Linda was very touched to see a stack of a dozen or so good luck cards that complete strangers had kindly sent to the *Western Morning News* to be passed on so that she and Sam could read them together at the wedding breakfast.

However, Mr Rogers had a condition of him giving Linda his newspaper's help in finding the shoes: he would run a second photograph of her, this time wearing the shoes, taken on the actual wedding day.

For mid autumn the weather was keeping very clement. On the morning of the wedding this was good news, as the borrowed shoes Linda liked best were satin and summery, and really wouldn't have been suitable if it had been raining. Linda had kept another of the loaned pairs that Mr Rogers's story in the *Western Morning News* had gleaned standing by just in case. But she preferred the satin shoes as they were so delicate and dainty, and such a complete contrast to her sturdy and usually muddy boots she wore almost all of the time.

Nevertheless there are two flies in the ointment, thought Evie as she put on her beloved dogtooth-check suit that she had made in the spring and then pinched her pasty cheeks to bring a little more colour to them.

The first was that she wasn't at all sure how she and Julia would react when they saw each other later on, and this made her feel tense and apprehensive.

She and Julia were each very good friends of Linda's, and of course this meant they would both be at the church, and at the reception at Lymbridge's church hall afterwards (incidentally the hall was looking very pretty, as well as smelling divine, as Sukie and Evie had spent the previous teatime sprucing the perennially dusty hall up and decorating it with lots of evergreen branches to smother its more familiar, slightly musty aroma with something much fresher and pleasant smelling).

Evie was certain that neither she nor Julia would do anything to spoil Linda's wedding day, as this would be a simply unforgivable crime and absolutely couldn't be countenanced. But things would remain awkward between them in all likeli-

186

hood. It wasn't a very enticing thought.

The other thing that was causing a niggle of even queasier-inducing apprehension in Evie's tummy was that Keith seemed to be missing.

Nobody was quite certain when the little cat had been seen last, but it was certainly several days ago. To be honest, Evie hadn't noticed for a day or two as she was so wrapped up in her own woes these days, but just after lunch the day before, Bobby Ayres had demanded at full voice, as only a six-year-old can, 'Miss, MISS, where's KEITH? 'e's not bin 'ere for ages, Miss. 'As 'e? D'you think 'e's died?' And after that Evie had given Keith a loud call, which ordinarily would have been enough to send the tabby charging to find her to see what Evie wanted and if there might possibly be food involved in Evie's plans.

But call and call as Evie did there was only an aching absence, and Evie started to feel a flicker of concern. She told herself not to worry as such, as perhaps Keith was mousing in the field behind the school, but there was still no Keith after school when she banged a side plate with a fork, and Evie couldn't help but feel her hopes begin to plummet; it was so out of character for Keith to miss a meal.

After she and Sukie had prepared the church hall and there'd been another unsuccessful name-call and tapping of the plate with the fork, Evie had spent a considerable amount of time wandering around Lymbridge, checking every place she could think the little puss might have gone.

Even though it was a cloudy night and intermittently pitch black, she searched carefully in the

187

blackout all over the school and the school grounds, wishing she could cast the light of a torch's beam this way and that, including inside the Nissen hut, even though nobody had been inside there for at least a week. Her worry was such that she didn't allow herself the luxury of remembering the gossamer kisses that she and Peter had shared in the Nissen hut on the day of the summer Revels. This was the first time she had not done so when looking at the Nissen Hut since that unexpectedly wonderful afternoon back in July.

Next, Evie checked all through the hedgerow that marked the school field's boundary in case a fox had caught and killed Keith, hoping to God that she wouldn't find the remains of a mangled feline corpse. Then she searched over at Switherns too (well, the little bit of the farm and its wall and hedge that was close to the road, as it was very dark and Evie felt too scared to stray onto the unlit farmland). Finally Evie walked slowly from the school right over to Bluebells on the far side of Lymbridge, checking both sides of the road, which hadn't been lit since the start of the war, in case Keith had come to grief under the wheels of a car and had crawled into the roadside hedge to die.

But wherever Evie searched, and no matter how often she called, there was no happy 'purp' in answer and no sign of the tabby and white cat, dead or alive. It was as if Keith had been quite magicked away.

After her own breakfast on Linda's wedding day and another thwarted visit to the school just in case Keith had turned up overnight, Evie wrote a notice describing Keith and saying that she was missing, and at the bottom she put Pemberley's telephone number.

She felt most concerned. Increasingly it seemed as if something distressing must have happened to the cat, and Evie realised she had grown very fond of her. Keith loved her food, and had never been late for a meal before, and so for her to miss several days of feeds was distinctly out of character, and very probably didn't bode at all well.

Evie knew that her infants would be devastated if Keith were never to return, and she started to think of tactful but honest ways that she might break the news to her class on Monday.

Daring to make her first visit in over a week to Bluebells, Evie trudged across the village and knocked at the front door and waited, rather than going straight in as she would have done just a fortnight earlier. When Susan came to answer the knock, Evie remained standing on the doorstep and said she couldn't stay and so it wasn't worth her coming inside.

Susan didn't try to insist, although Evie was gratified to see that she seemed slightly more pleased to see her eldest daughter than she had right after the dreadful night in The Haywain. After confirming with a regretful shake of her head that Keith hadn't visited Bluebells since the night described by her mother euphemistically as 'the when one you slept in the parlour with her', Susan promised to place the notice in the shop's window on her way to the church for the wedding.

Of Julia there was no sign, and Evie decided it prudent not to mention her, and presumably Susan thought the same too as she didn't say anything directly about Julia either. Then Susan said she hoped Evie was feeling better now and had taken time to do some serious thinking about what had happened.

Evie didn't risk saying anything as tears never felt far away these days, but she nodded at Susan's words and then quickly turned to go.

An hour or two later at the lichen-roofed village church, Rev. Painter officiated a very happy wedding ceremony.

When Evie thought back afterwards, she decided that Linda had looked strikingly beautiful, indeed the best she ever had, and so stylish that nobody would ever guess that the wedding outfit was made from bits of this and that, and hadn't been at all expensive. As Evie remembered the beaming bride, she was proud of what the sewing circle had been able to concoct from little more than scraps of fabric, and a couple of lucky hand-me-downs.

Sam scrubbed up as surprisingly dashing too – who'd have thought that?! Pattie whispered in passing to Evie as everyone took their seats at the wedding breakfast – in large part as Sukie had managed to seek out a doctor at the hospital who was about Sam's size, whereupon she had made short work of persuading him to loan the groom his smartest suit.

In short, Linda and Sam looked very much in love with each other, and Evie found herself dabbing her eyes with her hankie in the church, but at least for once these were tears of happiness. She felt only the tiniest twinge of envy.

During the service, school caretaker Mr Cawes

was sitting in the pew behind Sukie and Evie – he was a churchwarden and so had bagged himself a place towards the front of the church so that he could hear what was going on as he was quite deaf these days, and getting more so by the week – and he made Evie turn around to look at him in surprise when he grabbed her shoulder in a sharp clench at the point in the service when Linda and Sam were repeating their vows to one another.

In a loud whisper that caused several other members of the congregation to look over at him too, he said, 'You mark my words, missie, those two'll be makin' a babbie tonight. You jus' see if I ain't be right, Miss Evie Yeo.'

And with that Mr Cawes gave a knowing wink, and then evidently was so impressed with what he'd just said and done, that he ducked his head in a significant manner as he cocked an even more elaborate wink in Evie's direction, accompanied this time by giving his sizeable hooter of a nose a knowing pat or two with his forefinger.

Evie could only imagine Linda's horrified face if she had heard the school caretaker's stagey whisper, and she turned back to face the altar while trying to suppress an outright laugh at the thought, although a giggle bubbled up and threatened to escape and had to be brutally stifled by a cough when Sukie pressed her elbow into her friend's ribs with a quiet 'you mark my words, missie!' hissed at Evie between only slightly parted lips.

There had been no sign of Julia outside in the churchyard prior to the ceremony as Evie and Sukie stood chatting to various old pals before they had gone inside to sit down. And in fact Julia didn't put in an appearance until literally a matter of seconds before Linda made her grand entrance.

As there were the muffled sounds of the bride arriving and sorting herself out just on the other side of the church door, from the corner of her eye Evie noticed Julia and Leonard Bassett slip unobtrusively into church and slide into a pew right at the back of the nave, where they sat down next to each other as bold as brass and as if this were the most everyday thing in the world for them to do.

Evie glanced towards the pew to her left where Robert and Susan, and James and the evacuees, were sitting, all squeezed together in a motley line of varying sizes of people who were each looking to be staring straight ahead. She couldn't tell if her parents had noticed Julia arrive, but in spite of a twinge of anxiety at seeing her errant sister, Evie found herself grinning at the sight of the evacuees, who all looked so cleanly scrubbed and well behaved that it was as if butter wouldn't melt in their mouths.

Linda entered the church and paused, and everybody stood up and looked in her direction to watch her being walked down the aisle by her father, with Pattie just behind as her bridesmaid (or was it maid of honour? Evie and Sukie had been debating this question) and looking very smart in Sukie's fawn-coloured suit that the Lymbridge sewing circle had made for her when Sukie landed her job at the recuperation hospital.

As everybody smiled at the bride, Evie realised that they couldn't avoid seeing Julia and Leonard

Bassett standing together, although further back in the church than Linda and her father.

There could be no doubt that now every single Yeo in the church was acutely aware of Julia and Mr Bassett using the wedding as their first public outing together. And probably nearly everybody else in the church was trying to snatch a quick gawp at all the Yeos too to see what their reaction was to Julia standing so calmly and brazenly beside Leonard Bassett, Evie sighed to herself in a resigned manner.

She knew that a high proportion of the Lymbridge villagers would know what had happened at The Haywain and believe Julia's attitude towards Leonard Bassett to be very scandalous, and probably the more so as she had never really done anything to step out of line previously. And it could be that later the odd pointed comment would be made to Robert and Susan, very probably along the lines of they should have taught their middle daughter to know the difference between right and wrong.

On the plus side, all would be well for the next hour or two as politeness would be forced on everybody because of the sense of occasion, Evie was pretty certain.

Nonetheless she and Sukie exchanged pensive glances, and Evie decided that immediately after the wedding breakfast she would head back to Pemberley to ensure she kept herself out of trouble and couldn't feel tempted to leap to her parents' defence or to speak critically of her sister if provoked.

Although she in no way approved of what Julia

193

was up to, Evie acknowledged she was very disturbed that they had argued so ferociously and that by now she was missing Julia dreadfully.

Evie had arranged a surprise for Linda for after the service, and she was very much looking forward to watching her friend's face when she saw it. It was a surprise that had turned out to take an inordinate amount of planning and manoeuvring, and Evie had reflected as she made her bed first thing in the morning that if she had known at the beginning how difficult all of that would prove to be, then she might not have been so keen.

Knowing how horse-mad Linda was, Evie had arranged that Hector, the giant gelding that had caused Linda's lung to collapse when the German plane had strafed them, would be brought to the churchyard to stand at the end of the guard of honour through which the bride and groom would pass as they left the church. And so, if all had gone to plan and Evie's various instructions had been followed to the letter, Hector should by now be waiting patiently outside having a nibble of the grass close to the lichen-covered gravestones.

Linda was always saying that she thought Hector an absolute poppet. 'He's a complete sweetheart, and the closest thing to a gentleman that it's possible to be on four legs, and in fact he's more gentlemanly than most gentlemen on two legs,' she had declared only the previous week. 'He's got the sweetest moustache on his top lip, and I think he knows that something life-changing happened when we were together that day with darling

Mabel, as he always neighs out as loud as he can when he sees me.'

His owner had been under strict instruction from Evie to hide Hector behind the church until Linda had gone inside and then to walk him to the church door across the grass so that his hoofbeats couldn't be heard on the flags of the church path. The poor farmer had had to go a very long and meandering way around even to get Hector into Lymbridge as Evie hadn't wanted to risk Linda seeing him come down the road through the village. On Evie's stern instructions the farmer had given Hector a bath, oiled his hooves, and brushed his mane and tail out until they shone, and the gentle giant looked very smart, although also very big when he was up close. There were two extravagantly large white satin ribbon bows (the ribbon coming from Bobby Ayres's mother, who had been at school with Evie and Linda), one placed jauntily in his forelock and one at the top of his tail.

The moment Hector glimpsed Linda as she left the church clutching on to Sam's arm, he gave a vibrating whicker of greeting and tossed his mammoth head in pleasure.

Linda's own head shot up and she looked quickly around. And when she saw the perpetrator of the whicker, even though her wedding guests were milling around the church doors wanting to congratulate the happy couple and clap as she and Sam walked through the guard of honour of school pals of the couple, she ignored them all and ran straight to Hector to fling her arms around his neck and bury her nose in his winter coat in order

195

to take a deep sniff of her favourite horsey smell.

Having wound on the film in his camera, Mr Rogers had a quick confab with the horse's owner, and then with Linda and Sam. The result was that Hector was led to a pretty area of the church yard, and once she and Sam had gone through the guard of honour, Linda was given a boost-up so that she could sit on Hector's broad back side-saddle-style, while Evie made sure the satin ribbon bows were pulled and puffed about so that they looked as showy as possible.

A bashfully grinning Sam clutched the reins to the horse's bridle, and Linda's borrowed wedding shoes were clearly on display as her legs hung down, as was the white fur wrap and the blue clasp James had made from the costume jewellery against the dark bark of the trees behind.

Hector adopted a majestic position as he looked quizzically at everyone with his gentle brown eyes; his head was held high, his ears forward. It was as if he was an equine model who was giving his very best pose for the camera.

Linda looked the epitome of happiness as Mr Rogers snapped several photographs to accompany his latest story on Linda and the outing for the borrowed oyster satin shoes for the *Western Morning News.* Evie thought that whoever had lent the shoes would be very gratified that they had.

The wedding breakfast at the church hall was an array of sandwiches and tiny cakes in paper cases, with beer for those who felt like it, and tea or lemonade for those who didn't.

The wedding speeches were funny and erred just pleasantly on the decorous side of raucous, and to judge by the whistles and clapping, it was clear that everyone thought that Linda and Sam had each just made a very good match. Certainly they couldn't stop smiling, and even Evie found that after a while her own cheeks were aching with beaming, although that might have been a little from tension too. She was so intent not to look around the church hall to see where Julia and Mr Bassett might be. She absolutely didn't want to catch the eye of either of them as she wouldn't know what she should do in response.

Fortunately it wasn't a long reception. Mr Smith had promised to drive the new Mr and Mrs Torrence to the train station so that they could catch a train for a two-night honeymoon in the unspoilt Georgian town of Truro in the adjacent county of Cornwall, and the blissful couple had said to him that they wanted to arrive there by early afternoon.

As the guests began to gather in readiness to wave the newlyweds off, Sukie and Evie saw Julia, who'd been making sure to keep in the background, suddenly chivvy Mr Bassett to walk right up to Susan alongside her, whereupon Julia introduced him formally to her mother. Susan's face was impossible to read, and Mr Bassett didn't look at all comfortable, but Susan did shake Mr Bassett's hand without any show of reluctance, Evie noted. Robert must have been standing somewhere behind Evie, as she heard him snort quietly as he watched what was happening, although he made no effort to go over to intervene or to say hello, or to stand by his wife.

Before Evie could say anything to her father,

197

Sam clambered into the back of Mr Smith's car, and waited for his wife.

'Single ladies, may the best of you win,' called Linda. And with that she threw her small bouquet of winter blooms over her head backwards. Whoever caught it would be the next to marry, as was the tradition.

There was an undignified scuffle as various eager young women jostled for position. Evie stayed where she was and tried to spy in a casual manner what Julia and Mr Bassett were doing now.

But after arching gracefully above the heads of the young women leaping to catch it, the bouquet fell straight down and right into Evie's hands, almost as if by higher design.

Evie stared at the bouquet in shock as she was congratulated by several of those who had fought hard to capture it for themselves.

Evie headed back to Pemberley almost before Mr Smith's car had disappeared from view, and when she went straight to her room at the top of the house to change out of her good clothes, there was a wonderful surprise.

Keith had made a nest just beneath Evie's pillow on top of her eiderdown, and there she was lying curled around three beautiful kittens who were nestling at their mother's tummy. There were two tiny black and white kittens, and a tabby and white whose markings bore an astounding resemblance to her mother's. Keith narrowed her eyes in happiness when she saw Evie, and then gave her familiar purp.

The new mother pressed her nose towards each

of her litter of mewling and trembling babies; it was an adorable sight. Keith had never been to Pemberley before, but somehow she had been able to find her way there and seek out the safe haven of Evie's bed.

'You minx of a naughty madam, you!' Evie said to Keith in a low and soft voice, as her heart filled with wonder and pleasure at the sight of the care the devoted mother was giving her little family as she gently washed the head of the nearest kitten while they all suckled greedily. 'Clearly you're another one who's been up to no good in the bedroom department. At this rate I'm going to be the only creature left in Lymbridge who wonders what it's all about.'

The following afternoon Evie headed for the recuperation hospital. She went quite early in the afternoon as the nights were really drawing in now, and even if she didn't stay for too long it would probably be getting quite dark by the time she arrived back at Pemberley.

Obscuring her view of Timmy's bed was a metal-framed room divider on wheels, with gathered cotton covering the frame that was hemmed at its top and the bottom. And as Evie walked around the screen she could hardly believe her eyes.

Timmy was laughing – that wasn't unusual, of course, as he was by nature a sunny-natured fellow – but what was beyond Evie's wildest imaginings was that he was sharing the humorous moment with Peter.

And although Peter had his back turned towards Evie, he appeared to be apparently equally amused with whatever it was that either one of them had just said. They were each smoking and there were cards laid out on a table beside the bed, and an ashtray with a collection of cigarette stubs heaped within it and two cups that had presumably had tea in them, and so it looked as if Timmy and Peter had been enjoying a very convivial time for quite a while.

Evie wished the ground would open up and swallow her. She tried to scuttle backwards and reverse around the screen so that it would seem as if she had never been there.

But Timmy was too quick for her, and with a beneficent and garrulous wave of his hand, he beckoned her over, with a loud, 'Evie Yeo, old gal! There you are! Pull up a chair and meet my new chum, Peter. You'll like him, you just see if you don't.'

Peter was still turning to face her, and when Evie saw the laughing expression on his face change instantaneously into one she could only describe to herself as shock that quickly degenerated into abject terror, she realised with a thunk that Peter had previously no idea that the talkative character he'd been whiling away a cigarette with was really the man who had caused them both so much upset over the summer.

Peter was a smart chap and so he obviously had, of course, jumped immediately to the correct conclusion that Timmy had to be Evie's former fiancé, as he would quickly tot up the clues of a local serviceman with a terrible back injury with the significance of Evie's presence and Timmy's relaxed and familiar words to her.

Evie had kept Timmy a secret from Peter for months, and now Peter had been kept unintentionally in the dark by Timmy himself as to who he really was.

No wonder Peter wore such a pained expression.

The one good thing was that Timmy wasn't paying any attention to Peter, and of course in any case he was oblivious that Evie was in love with Peter.

And so Timmy prattled away, making both her and Peter cringe inwardly. 'Peter, my dear chum, you must say hello to Evie. Stop hanging back there, Evie – there's a surfeit of seating so pull yourself up a pew. Anyway, Peter, Evie and myself were engaged and actually we still would be if I hadn't managed to blot my copy-book with a not–'

Oh no!

An already fraught situation was now made infinitely worse by Tricia's rounded belly coming into view around the screen, closely followed by Tricia herself. She was so big she was now waddling rather than walking, and it was very obvious that the baby she was carrying was all but ready to be born.

Tricia's unhappy and tense-looking face showed she had heard Timmy's most recent words and, understandably, she was surprised and hurt.

Timmy stared at his wife with an open mouth, his words dying on his lips as he was unable to disguise the look of guilt creeping across his face. Goodness, whatever had he been just about to say, Evie wondered? Tricia looked towards Timmy with a thunderous expression, and then turned almost as hard a look and flinty eyes in Evie's direction. Peter glanced between the three of them.

Suddenly Evie wanted to laugh. Nobody was saying anything now, and there was a simply terrible pause.

All Evie could think as Timmy and Tricia stared accusingly at each other once more, and she and Peter did their best *not* to look at each other, was that they were all at that moment caught up in a moment of ridiculousness that was very akin to a hammy French farce.

Timmy then peered questioningly in the direction of Evie. Something was up, and he wasn't sure what, his look now said, but it was very probable that something to do with Evie was at the bottom of it. Tricia looked as if she could cheerfully have aimed a punch in Timmy's direction, and quite probably one at Evie too.

Evie thought she'd better say something. 'Tricia, do have my chair, dear. You must feel as if you could do with a sit-down.' Evie manoeuvred Tricia into the seat she had just got for herself. Peter half rose in politeness until Tricia was sitting down.

Evie decided that if she remained standing it would be easier for her to make an escape as soon as was feasible.

She went on in an effort to sidetrack Tricia's wounded air, 'Peter and I were PGs together at Pemberley for a while, Timmy, and so we know each other already, although it's now been simply months and months since Peter moved out. And Peter, this is Tricia, who is Timmy's wife, the new Mrs Bowes; they got married during the summer. Tricia has recently moved into Mr and Mrs

Smith's house. And as for myself, I came over to see Timmy today, Tricia, as I wanted to talk to him about two things, one of which was about raising money for a Spitfire, and the second was to do with Timmy's clothing coupons, which I thought might come in handy for you, Tricia.

'But Timmy, I know you mustn't allow yourself to get too tired, and so I'll make myself scarce and come back another time when it's a bit less busy here. Tricia, would you like me to drop in on Mr Smith on my way past to see if he can come to collect you?'

The tension seemed to have evaporated a little from Tricia's posture, replaced by a slump that suggested that she was verging on being too weary to speak. It was a while before Tricia nodded vaguely in Evie's direction in a forlorn and disconsolate manner.

With a breezy, 'Have a lovely afternoon, won't you?' Evie concentrated on doing the buttons up on her coat instead of looking directly at anyone, and then she turned tail and virtually ran from the ward, her heels beating a brisk clickety-clack on the wooden floor, and without a backward glance at any of them, even Peter (much as she wanted to).

In the corridor outside Evie realised she'd not really been breathing for the past few minutes, with the result that she now felt faint. She stood for a moment and closed her eyes, the fingers of her left hand resting on the hall wall.

Her dizzy sensation heightened when she felt a hand slipped under her elbow, and Peter in one fluid movement deftly unlocked and then opened

203

a door that was all but camouflaged in the corridor wall as it had been covered with the wallpaper adorning the plaster walls of the hall, its unobtrusive door handle right next to Evie, she now saw, and then he swiftly urged her down a flight of stairs to a basement level. Peter whisked her past a room with an open door through which Evie could see strange upright contraptions and what looked like maps that had several young men staring at them in deep concentration, and into a mess room next door where he released her with what felt like a gentle push.

Evie half stumbled towards a rather battered sofa, where she collapsed somewhat inelegantly, staring at Peter's face all the while.

His expression was fractious, there was no doubt about it. His temper had, if anything, brought the gold flecks in his eyes into even sharper relief than when she and he had kissed in the sunlight several months ago, although back then Evie had found the flecks to be the brightest and most alluring things she had ever seen.

Peter gave her a hard look without any hint of romance in it, and then he turned and poured small shots of whiskey into two squat and chunky cut-glass tumblers.

A thought flashed through Evie's mind that whatever was going on down here in the basement of The Grange, trouble had been taken to ensure that the resting conditions of those who were thus occupied beneath the hospital were as comfortable and well-supplied as possible.

Peter pushed a surprisingly heavy glass into Evie's hand and flung himself down so that he was sitting beside her with a frown wrinkling and distorting his brow. He then noticed there was only about nine inches between their thighs, beneath which Evie could see the rather prickly covering of the distinctly worn brown 1920s sofa on which they were sitting and also a little bit of a multicoloured crochet blanket that presumably she was sitting on too.

With what could best be described as a squeak of emotion, Peter quite literally sprang a further foot away from her along the sofa cushions. He slugged his drink back in one gulp, and then leapt up to pour himself another.

All thoughts of going to find Mr Smith to send him back to get Tricia had gone from Evie's head.

She and Peter still hadn't said anything to each other and Evie was increasingly feeling as if they were trapped in a surreal and distinctly disturbing dream.

'Evie, it seems we are destined to make fools of ourselves with each other.'

There was a moment when Peter looked at the carpet with a serious expression on his face and Evie nodded in agreement, before he continued, 'Obviously I had no idea before you walked around the screen that the Timmy here was the person you had been engaged to. And probably if I had done, I would have assumed that you wouldn't be visiting him now that he is married to somebody else.'

Evie felt a hot sensation course through her body. That last comment felt snide and unfair. The afternoon had just dropped another notch as she realised that Peter thought she was harbouring vestiges of amorous feelings for Timmy and so she had come to visit Timmy behind his wife's back to spend a little playful time on her own with him.

'Peter, stop it, for goodness' sake, and grow up,' Evie cut in in a tone that managed to convey both grumpiness and exhaustion. She had never talked to Peter so forthrightly before, and his injured look in return suggested that he didn't like it much. Evie went on, 'This is getting us nowhere. And I think you should be putting away your wounded face. Yes, that was awkward, up there in Timmy's ward. And yes, you were uncomfortable, as was I. But you seem to be forgetting that I had likewise a very difficult minute or two when you and Fiona were in the car at the bottom of Pemberley's drive.' Peter looked a little contrite at Evie's passionate outburst.

Unfortunately she couldn't quite contain her next comment of, 'And that snidey "Miss Bow" still rankles with me, if you want the truth, as I'm sure your Miss Buckley slipped that out on purpose.'

Peter's expression had been relaxing slightly, but at the reminder of Fiona's deliberate rudeness he looked tense and unhappy again.

Evie couldn't resist one last dig. 'When I arrived on the ward this afternoon it looked like you and Timmy were having a high old time. And I very much doubt that the same shall ever be said in the case of your intended and myself. As it turns out, I did want to talk to him about the Spitfire and Tricia's wardrobe, but frankly it is irrelevant to me whether you believe that or not.'

To cover her surprise at how prickly and prim

her voice had become, even to her own biased ears, she downed her whiskey in one as Peter had done, and then spent quite some moments spluttering at the unexpected sensation of swallowing a neat spirit, which she had never done before. It was very undignified, not helped by Peter's rather indignant sniffs and impatient sighs.

When Evie had got her breathing more or less back to normal, although not her red face and watery eyes, she stood up and nodded a curt farewell roughly in Peter's direction. She didn't dare say anything more. Peter was now sitting on the far end of the sofa, his head in his hands.

Unfortunately she was halfway up the staircase to the hospital corridor before she remembered her handbag, which was still on the floor of the mess room, tucked in beside the brown sofa.

'Drat and double drat,' Evie berated herself, as she steeled herself to go and get her handbag. 'And drat again!'

## Chapter Ten

After retrieving her handbag – she and Peter taking care not to acknowledge each other – Evie hid in what was now earmarked as the ladies' lavatory until she felt more composed. This took some time as wave after wave of painful emotion threatened to get the better of her.

In fact she had to sit in the white-tiled cubicle for long enough to become chilled right through before she felt she was calm enough to contemplate being seen by anyone who might be about.

Cautiously Evie ventured out and as she made her way from the hospital she didn't know whether she was pleased or upset that there was no sign of Peter. But as she headed for home, her gait became charged with pent-up tension, her feet angrily hitting the ground and her curls jiggling as if they were just as furious and out of sorts as she was, and so Evie thought she should have waited for a further five minutes in the seclusion of the lavatory.

The weather had turned decidedly nippy in the last hour and she felt shivery as she marched furiously along, keeping her head firmly down and turned away from the occasional gust of brittle wind. What she really wished would have happened, Evie now realised, was that she had taken a leaf out of Julia's book and had kissed Peter with a heady abandon while they were sitting on the hideous sofa, Fiona or no Fiona.

Evie quickened her pace in an attempt to dispel these hypocritical feelings. If Julia had felt half as aroused by thoughts of Mr Bassett as Evie did by just being near Peter, then suddenly Julia's bold move to allow herself to be seduced became much more understandable.

With a small groan of frustration, Evie hurried out of the drive and onto the road, where she came across Tricia, who was making her way towards Lymbridge much more slowly than she, and at the sight of Tricia's rounded belly Evie felt a rush of guilt as she remembered that in spite of her promise to try and arrange it (which she had meant sincerely at the time), there'd be no Mr Smith about to drive around the corner to collect an extremely pregnant and probably still tetchy Tricia, who was almost certain to be wondering just why it was that Evie seemed to spend quite so much time with Timmy.

And sure enough, Tricia gave Evie a suspicious and thwarted look as if she expected the worse.

'Tricia, I'm so incredibly sorry but I got ... er ... waylaid just now, and the bad news is that I completely forgot to telephone Mr Smith. And as you can see, I haven't yet walked past his and Mrs Smith's cottage – which is of course also your own cottage – so I've not been able to pop in to ask him. And so our dear and usually so reliable Mr Smith won't be coming to pick you up after all, I'm afraid.'

There was an unashamedly defeated sigh from the other woman. Evie studied the ground in front of her feet, and when she dared look up it was to see that Tricia's expression was frosty and sceptical still, although it was now tinged with a note of grave disappointment too.

Evie decided to clarify things. 'I only went to see Timmy to talk about raising money for a Spitfire, and also about his clothing coupons...' Tricia managed now to combine a world-weary sigh with a sniff of disbelief. 'I know that was really pre-sumptuous of me when you are perfectly capable of asking Timmy about his stupid coupons your-self, but for a hare-brained moment it felt like the right thing to do, Tricia, and I was only trying to be kind and welcoming to you. Anyway, I apolo-gise. I am very sorry if I have stepped out of line in any way or offended you. It was absolutely the last thing I wanted to happen.'

Tricia's continued silence on the matter confirmed to Evie that she had been rambling and not particularly coherent, and that Tricia was blaming her for something, even if it wasn't quite clear to either of them as to just what it was. Looking at the grey tarmac of the lane, Evie gave a defeated sigh in sympathy with Tricia's, and then attempted to rally one final time.

She slipped an arm under Tricia's elbow. 'Come on, Tricia, let's head back to our village together, and you can tell me what it is you'd most like to get to wear once the baby is here and you've got your figure back; and then when Timmy lets you have his coupons we can see about the sewing circle sorting that out for you. I know everyone is looking forward to making something new that's just for you after the baby is here. What are your favourite colours?' Evie said cajolingly, although even to her own ears her voice sounded false and slightly too jolly.

Tricia didn't say anything in reply although she did cast Evie a sideways look as she sluggishly began to plod forward in the direction of Lymbridge. She didn't shake off Evie's hand under her arm though.

Evie tried again, although this time in what she hoped was a genuinely warmer and less gung-ho manner, even making so bold as to touch Tricia briefly on top of her arm with her other hand, which brought Tricia to a halt, at which point she turned to peer silently and disconcertingly right into Evie's eyes. Evie's hand slipped out from under Tricia's arm.

'Tricia, please don't you worry in the slightest about me seeing Timmy, not at all. It's true I like him more now than when we were engaged, but not in *that* way, I promise you with all my heart. In fact I'm not at all sure that I ever liked him much in *that* way–' Tricia's sceptical eyebrows were now raised to an almost pantomime height '–and I'm convinced that we only get on now a bit better because there's absolutely NO romantic feelings between us any longer. And I really did want to speak to him about the Spitfire, and to remind him to donate his clothing coupons for you, as I explained when you came upon us all at Timmy's bedside earlier, I promise you, on my mother's life.'

At this Tricia looked very slightly mollified and as they turned for Lymbridge she allowed Evie to slip a tentative hand once more under her arm (although this was more for warmth than to comfort Tricia, if Evie was being totally honest with herself, as her fingers were by now quite frozen).

At little more than a snail's pace they began to walk more companionably along the road, with Tricia huffing and puffing beside Evie, and demanding frequent rests during which time she would knead her lower back in what an increasingly impatient Evie soon considered to be an unnecessarily dramatic fashion.

Dusk was falling and it was cold, and there was still a fair way to go as the lane stretched ahead before them. Evie was just thinking that at the rate they were going it would take them a considerable time to wend up the steep incline into

Lymbridge when a black car with a low purr of an engine came up behind them, headed in the same direction. It drew to a halt beside them and the window wound down.

Peter's voice said dejectedly, 'Evie and Mrs Bowes, you'd better get in. It's getting cold and dark, and it looks like rain.'

Without a word Evie climbed into the rear seat, making sure she didn't pay any attention to Peter, although she couldn't resist rubbing her hands together rather pointedly and blowing on her fingers to warm them, almost as if to chide him for taking such a long time to do the right thing and come to pick them up.

Evie was so intent on Peter (while making sure that she looked anything but, naturally) that for a few moments she didn't notice that she was the only one who had done what was expected.

Peter was gazing mournfully across the moorland as he slowly drummed silent fingers on the wide-diameter of the thin-rimmed steering wheel.

Evie adjusted her skirt to make sure it was pulled demurely as far over her knees as it could go as she waited for Tricia to follow her lead and climb into the car.

But there wasn't any corresponding sound of Tricia doing just that, and so Evie looked towards her with a questioning expression flickering around her eyes. As Tricia had been making such an uphill struggle of their walk back to Lymbridge Evie would have expected her to get into the car quickly so that there was no danger of her being left behind.

Instead Tricia seemed to be frozen in mid-step,

with what Evie could only think was a horrified look on her face.

Then Tricia shifted her weight so that she stood with her feet planted about eighteen inches apart, her eyes staring ahead now but unnaturally wide open, her mouth hanging somewhat slackly and her bottom protruding rather further behind her than was usual.

Suddenly she clutched at her belly and let out a noise that sounded more animal than human.

Evie had never heard anything remotely like it, and with her heart now beating rapidly, she and Peter looked at each other with apprehension, and they both leant forward in a strangely mirrored gesture of incomprehension.

There was the sound of liquid hitting the ground and Evie's eyes also widened and her own shoulders lifted in tension. It was hard to avoid the thought that Tricia was wetting herself right in front of them both. Oh, the shame!

But Tricia's anguished cry cut abruptly across any such thoughts.

'Evie ... ugh... Miss Evie! Help me. Aargh... The babbie, I can't 'old 'im in any longer. 'E's comin' right enough, and there don't seem a thing I can do to make it otherwise, right 'ere in middle of t' road! Eeeowh...'

And with that Tricia grabbed on to the still-open car door and made as if she was about to squat right in the road in front of them. She looked as if she were in a primal world of her own, a place of life and death that Evie and Peter could only imagine.

For just a split-second Evie found there was

something undeniably magnificent about Tricia, despite her grimacing face, uncomfortable-looking posture and the strange lowing sounds emanating from her. Although obviously in pain, she looked brave and indefatigable, very much a strong and somehow noble vision of womanhood.

'Peter, do something!' yelled Evie at the top of her voice as she wriggled across the car seat so that she could get out of the vehicle on the opposite side and then run around its rear end to get to Tricia, who had planted herself in the way of both of the car doors on the side she was standing. 'Peter, we must help her.'

'Yes, yes. No! No. Yes, you're right. Er? Um. Evie, I don't know what to do,' came the strangled reply.

'Yes, you do! You always know what to do, Peter. Think!'

Evie was now standing in front of Tricia, who was looking back at her as she painfully clutched at both Evie's arms just above her elbows, and then used Evie's slender frame to support her weight and to help her balance as she started to strain and squat lower.

'Okay. Okay. We can do this,' said Peter more to himself than to either Evie or Tricia. The anxious timbre of his words belied what they were saying.

Tricia let out another roar, and Evie winced as Tricia's grip slowly tightened on her arm. (Yes, this was possible, even though it wouldn't have seemed to be so a moment before.)

This latest sound of Tricia's distress and her clearly advancing condition seemed to do the trick though, as suddenly Peter became more like the

Peter who had helped organise the summer Revels. He told Evie in a businesslike manner that he thought the cottage hospital in Oldwell Abbott was the best bet for them to head to, as it was between doctor's shifts at the recuperation hospital and there was only a skeleton nursing staff on duty there until the evening medication rounds, and actually 'skeleton' might be to oversell it because it was Sunday afternoon and none of the patients were critical and so the most likely scenario was that there wouldn't be anybody suitable around there who would be able to help them...

'If that's the best you can offer us, Peter, then shut up. I don't want to hear it, and neither does Tricia,' interrupted Evie peevishly.

Peter looked put out for a second. Then he got out of the car in a more hangdog manner than was normal and went to help Evie manhandle Tricia rather ungraciously into the car with quite a forceful push to her rump on his part, and then more gently Peter leant in to ease the distressed young woman backwards until she could lie down across the whole of the back seat.

Evie indicated to Peter that she wanted his jacket, which he took off with only the slightest shiver and handed it over. She folded the garment into a pillow with the satin lining facing outward, and she placed it under Tricia's head.

Evie looked at Peter and shook her head at him – he felt she still found him wanting in some manner, although he was unclear what else it was that he should have done – before she squeezed herself into the back of the car, perching a buttock on the edge of the seat alongside where Tricia was

215

lying as she gesticulated for Peter to get a shifty on. Evie also wasn't sure where she felt Peter was falling short, just that he seemed somehow lacking in his actions at that particular moment.

Peter hurried to get in behind the wheel and then he did an agonisingly slow fifteen-point turn to manoeuvre the hulkingly large car around in the narrow road so that it was facing back the way he had just driven. He put it in gear, and then stalled, the car bucketing to an abrupt standstill. Evie gave what could only be considered a growl, while Tricia moaned in what sounded like agony. Evie then remembered the two glugs of Scotch she had seen Peter down not so very long before. He wasn't too drunk to drive safely, was he? Heaven's above, this was a testing Sunday afternoon!

Peter didn't dare look anywhere other than at the car's bonnet, and he tried briefly to hum to distract himself from Tricia's predicament. He dropped his head, took a couple of slow breaths to collect himself, and then he was able to turn the ignition key, put the car in first gear and drive forward much more smoothly. After the first corner he put his foot down and then they were whizzing like the clappers towards the cottage hospital on the outskirts of Oldwell Abbott.

When she dared, Evie looked at Peter's eyes in the car mirror and she saw him glancing back at her every second or two. They both had very anxious expressions, she could see, although as far as Evie was concerned this didn't detract from how very attractive she found Peter, even when he was looking so perturbed. Although it was a very strange situation the three of them found them-

216

selves in, right at that second Evie didn't want to be anywhere else in the whole wide world.

Bringing her thoughts back to Tricia, Evie mouthed silently in Peter's direction in the car rearview mirror, 'I hope there's a doctor on duty at the cottage hospital,' to which Peter replied by holding up two crossed fingers in agreement and sending the car off its course with a lurch, causing Evie to frown and to raise her shoulders vigorously in an unspoken attempt at getting Peter to hold the steering wheel with both hands.

Tricia didn't need to hear that Peter had nearly driven them into a roadside ditch. And neither did she need reminding that a country area late on a Sunday afternoon was never going to be the ideal place to find medical help, and certainly not on a bleak winter afternoon in wartime with darkness rapidly settling around them.

Evie said a short prayer to herself, asking that Tricia and the baby be kept safe. And as an afterthought she added a rider to the prayer in which she hoped God was ensuring that Tricia wasn't thinking about the likely lack of medical knowhow in the immediate vicinity. And a third quick prayer was to say that she hoped Peter hadn't gulped too much whiskey to be able to drive safely.

Never had the journey to Oldwell Abbott seemed as long or as tortuous.

And as they got nearer to the market town than to Lymbridge Evie berated herself at the sudden realisation that really the most sensible thing for them to have done would have been to take Tricia the short distance to Mr and Mrs Smith's house rather than risking this madcap chase on the steep

217

and windy road across the moors. It was almost certain that arrangements would have been made already by Mrs Smith for a local midwife to be on stand-by at all times, ready at the drop of a hat to attend the birth of Timmy's baby.

What a hellish pickle it all was, and Evie hoped this latest chapter of her up-and-down life would end well. She would never forgive herself if anything bad were to happen to either Tricia, or to Tricia and Timmy's baby.

As the car bombed along the not too well tarmacked rural road Tricia kept her eyes closed tightly as she lay across the whole seat, with her knees up and tightly closed together, as she gave intermittent whimpers of pain. Evie was now more or less wedged into a crouching position in the footwell in front of the leather-covered seat so that she could give Tricia as much room as possible, while remaining on hand in case she could help in any way.

After a while Evie realised that Tricia hadn't made a sound on the latest part of the journey, other than to give a now mercifully quieter moan each time they went over a bump, which was quite often, unfortunately. Evie could see, however, that Tricia's breathing was irregular, and that quite often she seemed to be holding her breath. She was pale, although her cheeks were red, and there was perspiration on her brow that was glinting in the gathering gloom.

Evie looked down and was surprised to see that she and Tricia were holding hands. When had that happened? Evie really didn't know but then she thought that the peculiar thing was that she was almost definitely more reassured by holding Tricia's hand than Tricia looked to be having Evie hold hers.

After what seemed almost a lifetime, the car swung around the last hairpin bend on the final drag into Oldwell Abbott.

Evie felt a burst of relief. But just at that moment Tricia hollered and suddenly sat forward and wrenched her hand from Evie's so that she could pull down her knickers.

Evie's corresponding frantic cry spurred Peter on, and the wheels and tyres to the car screeched as he drove through the gates to the cottage hospital as rapidly as he could.

As he brought the car to a stop with a judder as close to the main doors of the hospital as could be, Evie was horrified yet simultaneously fascinated to see for an instant a glimpse of the top of the coming baby's head, before it seemed to be sucked back up inside Tricia again.

'Peter!' Evie screamed. 'The baby's nearly here and she's going to have it in the car!'

'Evie, why does anything you are involved in come accompanied by supreme drama?' said Peter in an unbelievably tense and tight-lipped voice as he slammed his hand on the car horn to sound it again and again. He absolutely didn't dare look around to see what was going on in the back of the car. It sounded very gruesome though, and there was a strange metallic smell.

Tricia was panting furiously, her breaths interspersed with loud cries.

Evie ignored Peter and told Tricia that she had just seen the baby's head, and although she couldn't tell whether it was a girl or a boy, there certainly looked to be a baby coming with a very good shock of dark hair. This didn't seem to cheer Tricia up much.

Peter dipped and then rested his head on the steering wheel in horror as he sounded the car horn even more furiously.

'Tricia, don't be frightened. We're at the cottage hospital now, and you're doing wonderfully well. I think you're the bravest person I know,' Evie tried to reassure Tricia, even though her voice was squeaky rather than soothing, and in reply Tricia quickly snatched Evie's hand to her bosom. Evie had no idea what is was that she should be doing.

After what seemed an unimaginably long time but which was probably only a matter of seconds an orderly came to see what all the fuss was about.

At the sight of Tricia he ran much more speedily back inside the hospital, and soon a woman nurse was gently nudging Evie into the other footwell at the back of the car as she started to tell Tricia what to do.

And when a doctor came too and leant into the car to see what was going on and started to orchestrate proceedings, Evie said to Tricia that she was going to get out now to give everyone some room, but that Tricia should remember that she was now in good hands and that it wouldn't be long before she would be a proud mother.

Tricia looked at Evie with dark and oily-looking eyes and then reluctantly released her. Evie then wriggled backwards out of the car, although not before she planted a quick kiss on Tricia's slick forehead just as another nurse hurried towards

Peter's car with an armful of towels and blankets, her other arm hefting a black bag that presumably contained various medical implements.

Evie found Peter leaning with his back against a wall about fifty yards away, trying and failing to light a cigarette with shaky hands. Her own knees were wobbly so that she was more tottering than walking as she headed his way.

'May I have one of those, please?' said Evie in an emotional voice, nodding towards Peter's packet of cigarettes.

'You don't smoke.'

'I know,' she agreed gravely, as she took one anyway and waited with trembling fingers for Peter to strike another match so that she could light it.

That evening, once the dust had settled on the dramatic happenings of the afternoon and she was feeling a bit calmer, Evie felt compelled to go to see her parents at Bluebells. The past couple of hours had felt momentous, to the point that although Peter had driven her back to Lymbridge, she had remained completely silent in the car, lost in her own thoughts and quite oblivious to the fact that she and Peter were alone and sitting next to each other. Peter hadn't said anything to her either.

When Evie arrived at Bluebells, Julia was in the kitchen with Robert and Susan, writing what looked to be a letter, but she refused to cast even the merest glance towards Evie.

Evie barely noticed. Whatever Julia was doing, or not doing, seemed of little importance now.

221

Instead she felt hot and heady at the memory of what she had seen that afternoon in the hospital car park.

Susan took one look at Evie and immediately understood that yet again something out of the ordinary has happened, although quite obviously not of the same ilk as the terrible night of the fight in The Haywain. Taking off her pinny, Susan waved Robert and Julia away so that she could be on her own in the warm and softly lit kitchen with her eldest daughter.

'Oh Mother, I was so scared,' Evie confided softly. 'Tricia seemed in such pain, and it was un-dignified and noisy and messy. The nurse told me later that the fluid pouring to the ground must have been Tricia's waters breaking, and I doubt I'll ever forget that sound. But there was something amazing about it too, and there was something extraordinary about Tricia – she seemed so strong and almost heroic. And when there was that little first cry from the baby, I couldn't help but cry too, and Peter looked as if he wanted to as well, although of course he didn't. And later I held the baby for a minute, after Tricia had been put into a bed on the ward and the baby had been weighed and cleaned up. I didn't know a new-born baby girl would be so perfect, or so small, or so beautiful.' Evie words were wobbly as she spoke.

'Yes, giving birth is one of life's mysteries. A new life coming is to be thanked in any circum-stances – and I don't think there's anything to equal it,' agreed Susan. 'It must have been very strange for you though, especially seeing as this was Timmy's baby. But it sounds as if you have

222

been very brave, and as if you did all that you could. How lucky that Tricia wasn't alone, and how fortunate that Peter had just stopped to pick you both up, as if he hadn't, it doesn't really bear thinking about.'

Evie went on to say once again that the baby was a little girl, and both mother and baby seemed well, although Tricia was complaining of being sore (Susan nodded at this with a knowingly sympathetic expression). The hospital staff said the birth had been very quick and straightforward, indeed very much so for a first baby, and that Tricia had done very well. Mother and daughter would both be kept in hospital for about a fortnight as was normal, but unless anything untoward happened in the interim there didn't seem to be any reason why the pair should be hospitalised for longer than that.

Evie told her mother that after she and Peter had had a cup of tea to steady their nerves, she had been allowed to phone Mrs Smith from the hospital office, and Timmy's mother had sounded shell-shocked at the news, as Evie had expected she would. Tricia had been gone for such a long time they had just been starting to get a little anxious about what possibly could be keeping her, and Mr Smith had driven along the road to the hospital and of course there had been no sign of the new Mrs Bowes even though Timmy had said she had left a long time before. Mr Smith had returned home, and he and Mrs Smith had just come to the conclusion that perhaps Tricia had paid her parents a visit after she had seen Timmy, considering they lived quite close to the recuperation hospital, when Evie had telephoned.

Evie rang off so that they could get ready to go and see Tricia (Matron at the cottage hospital had seemed very strict about visiting hours and so Evie wasn't at all certain they'd be allowed to see her so late on a Sunday, but she hadn't had the heart to mention this to Mrs Smith). Then Evie telephoned the recuperation hospital so that a message could be passed on to Timmy that he was now a father of a bonny baby girl. Evie thought Mrs Smith would probably leave a similar message too.

After that Evie was allowed back into the hospital ward to see Tricia briefly before she left, and she was pleased to find Tricia sitting up in bed, quite happily munching on a slice of toast and with a cup of steaming tea on the bedside table next to her. There was no sign of the baby, but Tricia explained to Evie that she had now been taken to the nursery, where a nurse had described to Tricia placing her in a crib, the fifth in a line of four other newborns. Tricia added that she had been told that at nine o'clock she would be allowed to try feeding her. Apparently the first feed was very important.

Mr and Mrs Smith arrived at the hospital just as Evie and Peter were leaving, Peter having waited patiently on a chair in the hospital hallway while Evie made her telephone calls and visited mother and baby. As Evie buttoned her too-thin coat up against the cold, she told Mrs Smith what a beautiful granddaughter she had, and then she and the older woman shared a heartfelt

224

and emotional hug.

Now the drama was over, Evie dropped her head as she said to Susan in the kitchen at Bluebells, 'I feel exhausted, Mother. I don't know why when I didn't have to do anything much, but I do feel quite jiggered.'

Evie's voice was now much fainter than her usual ringing tones.

When Susan put her arms around her, it felt like the only place in the whole wide world that Evie wanted to be.

And although she was absolutely tuckered up, there was a flame of happiness flickering deep within Evie's breast that had sprung to life at the sight of Timmy's baby daughter.

She was perfect and lovely, even though she did have the slight look of Winston Churchill about her face, which Susan said knowledgably was common to all newborns. After all the ups and downs and the doubts of the past months, now that she had seen the baby girl, Evie was certain that everybody would love her.

Sometimes it seemed that there were miracles in everyday life, Evie told herself, and she was convinced that this was one of them.

The baby had initially been an unwelcome surprise, but now it looked as if she was very welcome. One might almost say that everything looked to be working out for the best.

Everything, that is, except for her own life, thought Evie as she closed her eyes and rested her head against the familiar smell of her mother's everyday hand-knitted cardigan, allowing Susan's heartfelt words about her and Robert's desire that

Julia and Evie be reconciled to wash over her. Evie nodded so that Susan knew that she had heard what her mother was saying, and in response Susan hugged her tighter. If only Julia felt the same way about reconciliation, sighed Evie.

The following morning it was Evie's first day back at school since the dreadful argument in The Haywain (thank goodness she and Peter hadn't got around to talking about that as Evie didn't care to remind him that she had a touch of the fishwife about her that evening), and naturally she made sure to be punctual and as professional as she could be. The wind was blowing briskly as Evie made her way from Pemberley, and as she looked at the shrivelling green on the moors, which was giving way to the much darker shades of the yuletide season, she fancied she could veritably smell winter coming.

The children seemed lively and very pleased to see her, which was gratifying, and Evie asked them what they had been doing in class during the days she'd not been with them.

It took a bit of wrangling but over the course of the morning Evie was able to award everyone at least one star for good behaviour or for putting their hand up to answer more than three questions or for drawing a lovely picture of a donkey – the list went on – and as she pasted up the final few stars, Evie realised how much she had missed being allowed to come into the classroom during her purgatorial time of being requested to remain at home.

Despite theoretically still being a bit cross with

Evie over The Haywain incident, Mrs Smith looked immensely pleased when Evie saw her, although the older woman admitted to being tired too.

Apparently she and Mr Smith had stayed at the hospital the evening before until quite late, Matron sensibly recognising that they weren't going to go until they had seen both Tricia and the baby. After that they had driven to the recuperation hospital where they had been allowed to have a word with Timmy to relay Tricia's rather unnecessarily graphic and bloodthirsty description of the birth (Mr Smith having to make his excuses at this point and leave the ward, as hearing the details once already had been one more time than he would have liked).

Evie laughed, and then gave her version, omitting how very close she had been to seeing the baby actually slither out of Tricia.

'Have Timmy and Tricia decided on a name yet?' Evie asked.

'I think they are thinking of Henrietta, after Tricia's mother, and then Rosalie after me, and finally Evelyn after you, as Tricia wanted to recognise the help you gave to her in the car,' said Mrs Smith. 'I think the plan is to call the baby Hettie as her everyday name. Of course if they had chosen my name as the first name, then she could have been Rosie, as I was as a child. But Tricia explained, and I would have to say rather sweetly, that they hope by doing this that Tricia's mother will think more kindly towards the baby.'

Although Evie had been at the joint wedding of Timmy and Tricia, and also Mr and Mrs Smith, she realised with a start that she must have been thinking of something else – almost definitely Peter – when the older couple were taking their vows as she didn't know that Mrs Smith was called Rosalie, or Rosie. She was a little taken aback at the gentleness of the name for such a stout and determined owner. Mrs Smith didn't look like a Rosalie (although precisely what a Rosalie might look like eluded Evie, only that it wasn't someone at all like the sturdy Mrs Smith), and Evie could only think of her headmistress as either Mrs Bowes or Mrs Smith.

Evie smiled to herself as she realised that Mr Smith obviously wouldn't call his wife Mrs Smith when they were sitting on their own in the parlour at home, when presumably he called her Rosalie, or maybe Rosie, not that Evie had ever really noticed him call Mrs Smith by anything at all, other than Mrs Bowes before they were married.

Anyway, Evie was very touched that her own name was going to be honoured by Timmy and Tricia. She hadn't really done anything to help little Hettie's way into the world, but as she explained to Sukie over a cup of tea just before the sewing circle started a furious hour or two of knitting later that evening, it had definitely felt as though she had been privy to something very special. And Evelyn did have a very nice ring about it, was that not so?

## Chapter Eleven

The end of term was starting to loom and there were only several weeks to go until the Christmas holidays would begin. Evie felt very busy; there was a lot she needed to do before the year ended.

She had decided to employ all of her Make Do and Mend skills to create for her friends and family, and Mrs Worth and Mrs Smith, and Hettie too of course, small Christmas presents. This meant that every spare moment of these long and dark winter evenings as November drew towards its close was spent with the wireless broadcasting softly in the background and the fire hissing in the grate as Evie busily embroidered a hankie or ran up a tea towel or crocheted a nice hair snood or, in the case of Hettie, knocked up a bundle of nappies from old towels to go with a set of safety pins Susan discovered hiding on the bottom shelf at the village shop.

Lunchtimes at school were jam-packed too as Evie was rehearsing with all the children at the school so that they could sing a broader repertoire of carols. She had asked Mrs Smith's permission to take the children to Lymbridge village hall early one evening in the final week of the Michaelmas term for a carol concert, with the funds raised beginning a collection she could put towards the Spitfire fund.

And with Evie keeping all the children occupied

thus with their carol singing for forty minutes or so after she had raced them through their lunch, it meant that Mrs Smith, who had bought a second-hand bicycle, could pedal like the clappers over to the recuperation hospital. She would only have time to spend five or ten minutes with Timmy, but if she could go, she would (and it had to be raining *very* hard to keep her at the school instead). Day after day, Evie was rather awe-struck at her head-mistress's dedication to Timmy, not least as the steep hill back up into Lymbridge was quite a challenge, even for the fittest of cyclists.

Mrs Smith chose to cloak her substantial frame in a rather mannish woollen cape for these excursions with a not quite matching tweed cap and some ancient driving goggles, as cycling into the cold wind made her eyes water. On bitterly cold days there was a lengthy woollen scarf from yesteryear wrapped bulkily around her neck too. The sight of this idiosyncratic get-up brought a smile to Evie's face each time she saw Mrs Smith freewheeling her bicycle across the playground, but she would never have mentioned how very much like a tweedy owl her headmistress was looking in her cold-weather bicycling outfit – especially when once, in the road through the village, she stood up as she pedalled hard to get a bit of oomph powering her bicycle and the wind billowed into the tawny-hued cape which puffed up her silhouette alarmingly.

Evie hoped that Timmy appreciated the effort his mother was going to on his behalf. She thought he probably did, but that he would stop short of actually telling his mother so, which was a pity, and so Evie would always try to smile warmly at Mrs Smith as she left, and to ask Mrs Smith to please pass on her warm regards.

The children hadn't looked particularly enthusiastic at the idea of the carol concert after school, especially the older ones who more obviously felt that such a commitment would be eating into their free time – to lose valuable running-around, kiss chase opportunities at lunchtime was bad enough, but to plan something additional for an evening was ridiculous their faces seemed to say. Evie explained it had to be in the evening so that their parents who were working would be able to come and see how wonderfully they sang, to which one of the older lads called back, to the odd hoot of laughter from his fellow pupils, that 'they must all be deaf then'.

Seeing her explanation hadn't quite done the trick, Evie then had to resort to bribing the children, with the promise of going to see Keith and her kittens a day or two *after* the carol concert (to stall dropouts), as long as everyone promised to be quiet as mice in order not to spook the new mother or her little ones. This was a much more successful ploy, as there was much less muttering or downright grumbling the next time Evie mentioned the carol concert.

Regarding the formal arrangements for setting up the Spitfire fund-raising, Evie talked to Mr Worth and Mr Rogers at Pemberley, and then to Mr Smith about it, and finally to Timmy.

And the upshot of all of this chitchat was that they decided to have a meeting for interested parties at the recuperation hospital in one of the still-empty wards, the location being chosen so that Timmy could attend, in order to discuss various ideas, such as who would be fund secretary and so forth.

Mr Rogers said that as £6,000 to buy a Spitfire was such a substantial sum, they needed to work out a way that they could band together with other like-minded people and organisations, so that the fundraising campaign could run across the whole of Devon and Cornwall, and possibly Somerset and Dorset too. Mr Smith said they would need to open a special bank account for the money. And then Timmy hadn't helped matters at all by blundering forward with a suggestion that Peter seemed the right sort of person to be involved too.

Early one morning as she was on the way to school, Evie bumped into the Rev. Painter, who had got wind of the Spitfire campaign. He suggested that bearing in mind how wonderfully efficient Evie had been in organising the summer Revels, maybe she should think about planning a New Year's Eve dance in the village hall, and thereafter a monthly dance, perhaps on the last Saturday of every month, with the money from these dances going into the fundraising box rather than into the church's own fund.

One thing Rev. Painter was clearly blissfully unaware of was the contretemps between Evie and Julia, as he mentioned that he thought Julia would be a wonderful lieutenant to Evie's captaincy in arranging these 'musical shindigs'.

Evie tried to look casual as she sidestepped responding to this comment with the sense of horror that she felt. Her first inclination was to say no to the reverend's idea about the dance on New Year's Eve, as she didn't feel in the right sort of mood to organise dances, and particularly on a regular basis. But then the more she thought about it, the more it seemed to have sound possibilities for swelling the fund, and so Evie came to the conclusion that perhaps she shouldn't be too hasty in saying an outright no to the proposal.

In any case, Evie had a more pressing matter to get out of the way first: she wanted to make a Christmas cake to share between those living at Pemberley and Bluebells.

The only recipe book in Lymbridge, it seemed, was *Mrs Beeton's Everyday Cookery*, which had been a wedding present to Susan and Robert, and this faithful tome was well thumbed and possibly even had a couple of pages missing as several of its quires were a bit loose.

Unfortunately Mrs Beeton's recipe for a Christmas cake demanded a whole half pound of both butter and caster sugar, and equally generous amounts of currants and sultanas, as well as a pound of flour and four eggs.

Pattie tried to look on the bright side by pointing out that it only needed six ounces of candied peel, although she had to confess straightaway that she had no idea what candied peel was, or glacé cherries either, come to that. Evie admitted she was a bit hazy about these ingredients too. The sisters laughed together as they acknowledged they were poor cooks – Susan had taught them the merest basics, but they hadn't shown much interest beyond that.

Then Evie said quietly, 'I wish Julia were here – she's so much better at this sort of thing than either you or me. And the sewing circle just isn't the same either. There's no Mrs Sew-and-Sew hectoring and lecturing and posturing, and telling the rest of us what to do in her own inimitable manner. I really miss Mrs Sew-and-Sew, and I miss Julia too.'

'Yes, she has left rather a gaping hole, hasn't she? It's just not funny if I try and be Mrs Sew-and-Sew on my own,' agreed Pattie quietly, as one of Keith's kittens attempted to climb gingerly over her foot while the sisters sat around the kitchen table at Pemberley. Pattie's instep must have seemed almost a mountain to the tiny black and white kitten, thought Evie as she watched the determined little mite make quite a good stab at it. 'Maybe if I have a word with Julia once again it will encourage her to soften a little,' Pattie added after a pause.

There was a silence as the sisters watched the kittens explore, and listened to the sound of the ticking kitchen clock. The week before, Mr Worth had found a strong wooden box that had once contained beer bottles, and a bed had been made up for mother and kittens close to the kitchen range, with an old cardie that Evie didn't wear much any longer being donated as a comfy lining for the box. Keith had chosen to give birth on this woollie by dragging it close to Evie's pillow after it had been thrown askew onto Evie's bed one morning when she'd had problems deciding what to wear, and Evie didn't much fancy the thought of putting it on after that, even though it had washed quite clean. Mrs Worth told Evie that Keith had done that because the cardigan had smelt of Evie, which Evie found rather sweet.

Now, basking in the always warm kitchen, Keith would occasionally lift her kittens out of the box for a few minutes so that they could sit on the kitchen mat. Evie noticed that Keith would let them sniff and sit down for a little longer each evening, and then the mother cat would gently bite the scruff of each of their necks so that she could lift them up one by one back into the box when she thought they had had enough. They were still too tiny to explore the whole room properly, and their eyes had only just opened and right now looked to be a cornflower blue. Despite being a first-time mother Keith seemed to know what she was doing in educating her brood as to the ways of the world.

Evie loved the kittens and secretly hoped that at least one of them would become a permanent fixture at Pemberley, although Mrs Worth seemed curiously unmoved by the idea, huffing extravagantly as she would very obviously step cautiously around the kitchen mat, and saying it wouldn't be long before those blues eyes were as green as Keith's and then there would be all sorts of mischief from those kittens, which she wasn't very enamoured at the thought of. That is, if she hadn't trodden on them first, mind.

Evie had tried pointing out that at least any mice would be having second thoughts about setting up home at Pemberley, to which Mrs Worth had told her scathingly, 'Pemberley has *never* had a problem with rodents, large or small. Evie, I cannot believe my ears at hearing you even think to mention such a thing.'

Evie was certain she had seen something grey and mouse-like scuttle into one of the outhouses across the yard during the warmer autumn weather back in October, but she thought it wise not to draw attention to that in case Mrs Worth took further umbrage towards the kittens.

Now, Evie looked on as Pattie smiled and used a feather-light finger to stroke the head of the kitten who was now perched on her foot, Keith keeping a careful eye on her piebald youngster all the while.

And then Pattie confided to Evie that Julia was still very quiet as she went about her days at Bluebells, and she seemed to avoid initiating conversation if she could help it.

Pattie presumed that Robert and Susan had had a serious discussion with her about what was going on between Julia and Mr Bassett (too much! thought Evie with almost as much fervour as she had *that* night in The Haywain), but they didn't seem to want to talk about the state of affairs between Julia and Mr Bassett any further, or at least not with Pattie.

The truth of it was that although nothing more had been said about them setting up home together, Julia and Mr Bassett seemed very involved still, from what Pattie could gather, and just this last weekend Julia had spent a night away from Bluebells. She hadn't asked permission or told her parents where she was going; instead she just hadn't come home one evening, and the next day offered no explanation for where she had been.

Apparently Pattie had suggested to Julia only the evening before in as gentle a manner as she could think of that perhaps the stand-off between her and Evie had gone on for long enough, and with Christmas drawing close and with it the time for families to be united together around warm fires with the smell of holly drifting across the hearths, wasn't it high time that the pair of them made up? Whereupon the only reply Pattie had been able to elicit from Julia was a darkly muttered 'over my dead body', followed swiftly by 'and don't you take it on yourself to interfere, Miss Nosey-Parker, you'.

Evie wrinkled her brow at hearing this and rubbed her temples. She would give almost anything to have Julia nearby, her sister's full lips widening into her gentle smile as she told them a funny story about something that had gone on earlier in the day while she was on her postal round or had been doing a shampoo and set on one of her 'ladies' in the village. Evie felt her eyes prickle with the threat of tears – things were no longer as they always had been between them.

Evie tried to rally with little success when Tina and Sarah joined the Yeo sisters at the kitchen table, the scrape of the chairs against the flagged floor making Keith put all the kittens back in the box with undue speed before she lay on her side in the box beside them so that they could nurse, Keith's loud purrs soon clearly audible. The kettle was on for another cup of tea, and Annabel was folding laundry at the far end of the room, ready for ironing.

The fact that the two WRVS girls weren't strictly family didn't deter Evie from confiding to her sister that she wished desperately that the argument in The Haywain had never happened.

'I don't think I'll ever be able to live it down, not really. And I'll never be able to show my face in The Haywain either.' Evie's voice cracked slightly as she went on to describe how very much she was now missing their old nights out, and that she felt a fool for showing herself up so by her own impulsive and harsh behaviour that terrible evening.

There was a silence as everyone gazed at the kitchen table.

There was an obvious attempt to lighten the atmosphere when Tina and Sarah assured Evie that she wasn't to worry so much as this would all blow over, things like this always did. Then they said why didn't they all band together to make the Christmas cake? And if they could beg, borrow or steal enough sugar for some icing too, even if only for the cake top, then perhaps Julia could be persuaded to ice it, which might set the wheels turning for a reconciliation.

Evie felt exhausted at the very idea, but she didn't want to sound too down on it when her fellow PGs were going out of their way to be kind to her. In fact, she thought, she probably couldn't be bothered with the Christmas cake either, after all. Somebody else could make it or they could go without.

Suddenly all thoughts of the Christmas cake problem were abruptly pushed to one side as hurried footsteps down the hall heralded the unexpected arrival of Linda, bright and jolly after her honeymoon (Mr Cawes probably had been right about the 'babbie-making' to judge by the sparkle in her friend's happy brown eyes, Evie decided) and Sukie, who looked to be full to bursting point with some news.

'But, Evie-Rose, I'm not going to say a thing until you have braved The Haywain this evening,' said Sukie, studiously ignoring Evie's answering grimace. 'I know you're going to say no, but I'm simply not going to listen. Honestly, you're the only one who cares a jot about what happened between you and Julia the other night. And anyway by the time I was leaving The Haywain when all the drama had ended, Barkeep Joss was boasting to me that your and Julia's tiff had livened things up no end, to the point he'd ended up having the best weekday's takings that evening since war had been declared,' said Sukie cheerfully, being able to read Evie's reluctant expression with the ease of reciting her A.B.C. 'Come on, Evie-Rose dear, get your coat and scarf on, lovey, we've got time for a quick one and then we can be out of the Ladies' bar and heading homewards by eight o'clock as we all have to be up early for work.'

Evie didn't want to go, but then she saw the others were making moves to stand up. She realised that she didn't want to stay at Pemberley either if everyone else was going out. And it looked as if they all were, to judge by the mass donning of coats and gloves.

Without more ado, Sukie was holding Evie's coat open for her, and Evie smiled in defeat with a tilt of her head towards her friend and a raising of eyebrows in an effort to show she was only giving

239

in reluctantly. She slipped her arms inside the open coat and buttoned it up as quickly as she could as though she were giving herself Dutch courage.

Sukie gave Evie a lightning-quick hug and a kiss on the cheek as she said, 'Chin up and shoulders back, Evie-Rose – remember you've nothing to be ashamed about as far as The Haywain is concerned. Most of the old soaks there aren't fit to lick your boots. And Julia's been in there at least twice since your quarrel, so I hear, along with Mr Bassett, and with absolutely no problem. And so Julia's two visits mean that you have quite a lot of catching up to do on the I-didn't-really-create-a-scene-and-even-if-I-did-then-I-can't-say-as-if-I-much-care front.'

And so it proved. When Barkeep Joss spotted Evie trying to fade into the background by standing unobtrusively at the rear of the group of friends as they gathered around the bar in the Ladies' room, he said in a loud voice so that everybody in the public house could also hear, 'Miss Evie Yeo, and about time too; it's far too dull here without you, and we've been hoping you were going to be joining us once more before too long. Now, what are all you young ladies having? It's on the house, just this once.'

Evie began apologising for her behaviour, but Barkeep Joss cut her short with, 'There's plenty round about who've got up to worse in here and so don't you give it another thought.'

She smiled gratefully at him, and went to sit demurely by Sukie. While the others were distracted by sorting out the drinks, Evie realised that

Sukie had something urgent to say to her, and so she smiled at her to let her know she was listening.

Apparently, Sukie began in a whisper that only Evie could hear, there were Top Secret goings on in the basement of the hospital, and to all intents and purposes whatever was going on down there looked like something to do with Peter.

Evie thought back to the rooms she had spied when Peter had taken her down to the hidden sitting room on the lower level of the recuperation hospital, the room where he had given her the whiskey after that embarrassing minute or two they had had to endure on the hospital ward along with Timmy and Tricia.

'It's all very hush-hush and on the Q.T., we're told,' said Sukie, 'and of course I'm going to try to get to the bottom of what is going on. But what I do know is that Peter and the rest of them have a special entrance at the back of the house so they don't have to go down there via the main hallway through the hospital. But from my keeping an eagle-eye on comings and goings, I can say that Peter definitely seems to be at work in the basement every day, although the word has gone out that we're not to ask anyone what is going on or to mention anything at all to people outside the hospital about it. The powers that be would be absolutely furious if they knew I was speaking to you, of course, but I'm not going to think about that. Anyway, I've seen a couple of RAF chaps hanging around their entrance, waiting to be let in, as fortuitously it's just below the window beside the filing cabinet where I file the patients' records.

'And when I ran into Peter today, who'd been

241

sitting with Timmy, can you believe,' (yes, Evie could, unfortunately) 'the first thing he said to me was that he couldn't say what he was doing at the hospital and so I wasn't to ask. And the next thing he said was had I seen you since Tricia had given birth?'

'And what did you say?'

'I told him I knew that you were very touched that one of the baby's names was going to be Evelyn, after you. And then he looked like he wanted to say something else. But he didn't, and then I had to go back to work.'

As gossip went, really this didn't amount to much, concluded Evie. Aside from the separate entrance and it looking to be something to do with the RAF, the only thing she'd discovered in addition to what she knew already was that Timmy and Peter were still spending time together.

Sukie said next that she was trying to come up with a plan that would throw Peter and Evie together, and kick Fiona into touch. Then she admitted that so far it was an empty plan, as she hadn't been able to think of anything. The two friends looked at each other for a moment, and then shared a laugh. Evie felt comforted to know that Sukie had her back; even though it wasn't going to make any difference in the long run, at least the feeling of being united in a common aim was cheering.

Evie and the others stayed at The Haywain for longer than had been planned that evening, as not long after Sukie had finished spilling the beans, Mr Rogers arrived with several of his *Western Morning News* colleagues and also a few other newspaper friends, who had come down to the West Country to cover the first aeroplanes landing and taking off at the air field, which was slated for the next day or two.

The whisper was that Mr Rogers had promised his chums that Lymbridge was the best village in Britain to find pretty women. As Evie stared around The Haywain, it looked like his chums rather agreed with that ludicrously far-fetched claim, although it was also true that both Sukie and Linda looked to be rather on top of their game in the looks department just at the moment.

Anyway, there was a rumour that some aircraft would be flown in perhaps as early as the following week by women pilots, who would be delivering them from the manufacturers.

Women flying aeroplanes!

What a thought, Pattie and Evie agreed, and they then decided that after Christmas they should ask Robert if he would teach them to drive, if they could work out a way of getting a little petrol for Robert's car, which was currently parked up in the garage. The more independent women were, the better, the sisters assured each other.

The air field and the navigation tower weren't quite finished yet, and nor were the buildings that would eventually house all the pilots who would be based there. In the interim it looked as if there were going to be several months of special sorties needing just a few pilots, with the result that these men were being put up in a dorm in the attic roof space of the recuperation hospital.

The delay was partly due to negotiations still

taking place with a local church that didn't want to remove its spire, even though there were concerns that the height of its current spire might cause an accident for aeroplanes taking off or landing, explained Mr Rogers.

An hour or so later, Evie walked home to Pemberley in a much more cheerful mood than when she had set off for The Haywain.

Nobody had batted an eye at her presence there. And, even better, two of Mr Rogers's colleagues were going to take Sukie and herself dancing in Plymouth on Friday night.

The following evening saw the inaugural Lymbridge Spitfire Fund meeting taking place in an empty room at the hospital.

Timmy was now able to sit up, and so he was taken to the meeting in his wheelchair, with a blanket tucked around his knees to keep him cosy, and another over his shoulders. Evie was surprised at how touched she was to note that under his plaid dressing gown with its twisted cord tie-belt, he was yet again wearing the pyjamas she had made him back in the summer when he had first been admitted to Stoke Mandeville hospital.

Also present at the meeting were a couple of the doctors from the recuperation hospital, and several of the more able-bodied recovering patients; and there was Robert and James and Mr Smith, Mr Worth and Mr Rogers, the Rev. Painter, and Evie, Pattie and Sukie, and of course Mrs Smith and Mrs Worth.

They were just deciding that Mr Smith would chair the meeting and Mr Worth would take the minutes when Peter bustled in too, followed almost immediately afterwards by Mr Bassett.

Evie and her sister and her friend exchanged meaningful glances as Mr Bassett pulled up a chair at the large table, which meant there was a fair bit of shuffling along this way and that in order to make space for him.

While everyone got themselves sorted Evie risked a glance in the direction of Mr Smith. She had felt very awkward around him since she and Julia had argued as she felt he would have expected better from her. His benevolent expression as he looked back with slightly raised eyebrows at her seemed to combine reassurance with the gentlest of remonstrations against any bad behaviour, she decided. And the more she looked across the table at the calm demeanour of Mr Smith the more Evie felt fortified, and it wasn't long before she was doing her best to concentrate on what was being discussed.

And what was being decided was all good stuff. Mr Smith led the meeting skilfully – he was obviously used to this sort of thing – and Mr Worth took notes with what looked like great efficiency as various ideas were discussed.

In only a matter of minutes plans were hatched whereby the doctors would try to link in various West Country hospitals to the fundraising, Mr Worth would see what he could do with local businesses to generate interest, while Mr Rogers would try to bring local newspapers on board with the fundraising, such as the *Cornishman,* the *Cornish Guardian* and the *North Devon Journal Herald,* as well as his own *Western Morning News.*

If the editors of those newspapers 'nibbled,' he would extend the fundraising into the press of Somerset and Dorset, Mr Rogers said.

Timmy and Peter said they had other useful contacts, and Mr Bassett offered to be fund treasurer, working alongside Mr Smith, while Peter volunteered the use of the safe in the hospital basement for any funds waiting to be banked.

There was a moment when Evie and Peter caught each other's eye, and the immediate hammering of Evie's heart and the flush she could feel spreading across her collarbones was, she was sure, a ready admission for anyone who might be looking her way of how very close to the surface her passions were whenever Peter was near. Evie took care not to look directly at Peter again and instead contented herself with risking small sideways glances at bits of him, such as his knees or how he turned his fountain pen this way and that as he listened to what was going on, or once, when he bent forward to push a piece of paper in Mr Bassett's direction, at the soft skin at the back of his neck. After that Evie felt Timmy might have shot her a curious look, and she had to stare intently at the table in order to calm herself down and act as if nothing untoward had happened.

Luckily Pattie and Sukie came to the rescue when they added they would speak to the Women's Institute and would help plan local events that would involve the women in the community, at which Evie nodded her agreement too, causing Peter to look at Evie once more, his own neck slightly pinker than normal, she thought.

Then Mrs Worth said she'd think of schemes to rally the local women who didn't belong to the W.I. to see what ideas they could come up with, and Mrs Smith said she would speak to local head teachers, and the Rev. Painter said he would speak to all the clergymen locally then those rectors could talk to their local publicans and town or village bigwigs and also to any groups affiliated to their churches who hadn't been covered by any of the above.

In fact they were so organised that the meeting took barely thirty minutes to decide all of this, and to schedule a second meeting for a week's time. Short as the meeting had been though, it was enough to make Timmy look tired out, and, noticing this, Peter said he would wheel him back to the ward.

Evie realised later that she had hardly acknowledged Peter and Timmy leaving because suddenly she was very undecided as to whether she should speak to Mr Bassett or not. Still, she did note the gentle care with which Peter rearranged Timmy's blanket and the trouble he took to manipulate the wheelchair through the door without knocking into the frame or jarring Timmy in any way, and Timmy's answering grin of gratitude in Peter's direction.

As the Worths had agreed to drive the Rev. Painter back to Lymbridge, Mr Smith had promised the young ladies a lift home, but for the moment one of the doctors looked to be deep in conversation with him.

Suddenly, on the spur of the moment, Evie found herself heading towards the man who had

247

been dominating her thoughts over the last few minutes.

'Good evening, Mr Bassett,' she said cautiously, aware that Pattie and Sukie were watching her every move, ready to step in if need be, although to do what would be anybody's guess.

'Miss Yeo, or Evie, if I may, good evening,' he replied stiffly but not quite in an unfriendly way.

There was a pause.

'I want you to know that although I think you have encouraged Julia to behave in a manner that I have found, er, unexpected – I'm sorry, but I can't say otherwise, Mr Bassett – I do not want any bad feeling between us to continue,' Evie said. 'I behaved extremely poorly when Julia told me about your relationship, and I wish very much I hadn't allowed my feelings to get the better of me. It was a disgraceful scene that I caused, and I am aware that the public brawl between me and Julia was something no respectable family member should get into. I didn't mean it as a slight to you or to her personally, but it was more the result that I felt Julia had been behaving in an imprudent fashion. Since then there isn't an hour that passes when I don't regret that things have irrevocably altered between me and her, and I don't have words to express how much I miss her.'

Mr Bassett didn't say anything to Evie. Instead he nodded gravely in her direction, before he turned sharply away, as if he would head briskly to the door. But instead he stopped and then turned to face Evie once more. She couldn't help but notice that his eyes looked clear and his forehead relaxed; he didn't seem to be deeply morose in the way he so often had been when he was teaching at Lymbridge Primary School. Maybe Julia was the reason for this lightening of spirits.

'Miss Yeo. I mean, er, Evie, I too wish more than anything for there to be no ill will between our families. Julia knows this, but I am afraid she is still very angry and upset. I must shoulder the whole of the blame for these events, I am aware, and naturally I too wish it all had unfolded differently. I do, however, care for your sister very much and I would like you and all of your family to know that I see my life going forward with Julia at my side,' he said. Then, without further ado, Mr Bassett turned on his heel and headed out of the door, his footsteps soon sounding noisily on the stairs.

In the chilly car on the way home, his comments were pulled this way and that by Evie, even though Mr and Mrs Smith were there, as well as Pattie and Sukie. Just before Evie got out, she said it was clear that Mr Bassett cared deeply for Julia, and so it was a good thing that at least Julia had cast away her reputation on a man who looked as if he was willing to stay the course with her. Not that she approved of what Julia had done, added Evie.

As Mr Smith allowed the car engine to idle, the exhaust fumes clouding in the brisk autumn air, Mrs Smith agreed that Julia had been impetuous and hot-headed. And then she alluded to what everybody was thinking at that moment. 'But who am I to comment? Look at my Timmy and Tricia, and how they behaved. I was very angry when I discovered what they were up to, as I'm sure you must have been too, Evie. But now when I look at that angel, our little Hettie, I can barely remember any of that. Whatever the situation is with Julia and Leonard Bassett, time will heal, Evie, I am sure of it, and so do remember that, dear.'

## Chapter Twelve

The next day after school, Mr Smith was in his car waiting in the lane outside the gates. He was taking Evie to see Tricia and Hettie in Oldwell Abbott. Mr Smith was about to return to work full-time following his period of reduced hours in order that he could be with Mrs Smith when Timmy's life had hung in the balance. He would now be in London quite a lot, and so he had said to Evie when they were at the recuperation hospital the evening before that she had better take advantage of his offer of a lift to Oldwell Abbott as he wouldn't be so readily available in a week or two.

Evie had been up late when she had got back from the Spitfire Fund meeting, hastily finishing off a knitted bonnet for Hettie that had a more complicated shell design than she had bargained for when she first skimmed the pattern, with the result that she had spent part of her lunchtime earlier that day neatly threading through a narrow ribbon at the front to make a tie for the bonnet.

As Evie entered the maternity ward the first thing that struck her was how well Tricia looked. She was sitting up in bed and had draped around her shoulders a very flattering dark-green knit that was complemented by beautiful tortoiseshell buttons down its front.

Evie had never thought that Tricia was a particularly good-looking woman, but now that she looked rested and less care-worn than she had when working in the dairy parlour, Evie noticed how fine her skin, teeth and eyes all were, and how thick and healthy her hair, and Evie realised with a small wrench that with well-cut clothes and a trace of make-up it wouldn't take very much at all to make Tricia look like an appropriate wife for Timmy, as far as Mrs Smith would be concerned. Evie recognised that she had assumed for a long time that Tricia was more homely and less attractive than she in fact was, and this made Evie feel a bit peculiar. The thought struck her for the first time that she had very possibly liked a bit too much the fact that Tricia was lower down the pecking order in the looks and deportment department than she. If Tricia was found to scrub up well, would she herself feel so warm towards her, Evie wondered with a little ripple of shame.

The rather posh green knit was already testament to the fact that Mrs Smith was working behind the scenes to this effect.

'Miss Evie!' called Tricia cheerfully when she noticed Evie staring at her, and Evie gave herself a shake and tried to plaster as warm a smile as possible onto her face.

Tricia went on, 'That was a rum do, wasn't it? In Peter Pipe's car–' as if Evie could have forgotten this already '–an' I baint never seen a chap wi' such a white face afore as that Peter. To tell 'e the truth, Evie, I 'adn't felt right all day, an' when I got there I knew that I shouldn't 'ave gone to t'ospital to see Timmy, as 'Ettie were pressin' sommat dreadful on me waterworks. An' when I started back to Lymbridge wit you, it all got too much, and I couldn't 'old my 'Ettie in no longer. I were a right state, I were. An' you were too, I daresay! Everyone 'ere tells me that was the quickest first birth they've 'ad in this 'ospital. But I was glad you and 'e were there rit enough.'

'I'm sure it was the quickest birth for Dartmoor! I know nothing about birthing but it seemed very fast to me. My though, it's good to see you, Tricia, looking so fine. And I love the cardie on you – that green is very much your colour,' said Evie, trying to ignore the fact that Tricia's country dialect was so ingrained that Hettie was unlikely ever to be anything other than 'Ettie as far as Tricia was concerned. Evie couldn't help wondering if this would in time rankle Mrs Smith, as she was the type of class-conscious person who always slightly over-emphasised the fact that she could pronounce her own Hs in what she deemed to be a more middle-class manner than was often the case with those who spoke with the more rural local accent.

Tricia seemed genuinely delighted with the gift of the tiny bonnet Evie had made. The two of them definitely had a sense that despite their rocky beginnings they had been brought closer by sharing a momentous event, and so Tricia and Evie chatted quite happily for fifteen minutes or so, with Evie saying to her that she had heard from Mrs Smith how delighted Timmy had been at the news of Hettie's arrival and that his wife and baby were doing well. Tricia said that the minute she and Hettie were allowed home, a visit to Timmy would be the first thing on the agenda.

And although Evie was very aware of Mr Smith right now waiting for her on a chair in the somewhat grim and draughty corridor, when the nurse interrupted their chat in order to deliver Hettie to Tricia's bed for a feed, and after Tricia indicated she didn't mind at all if Evie wanted to stay and watch the baby suckle, Evie found she couldn't quite pull herself away.

Little Hettie looked very content with life (although still alarmingly like Winston Churchill) and she guzzled away greedily while making a variety of sweet wheezes and sucking sounds. Evie was fascinated as she watched, not least as Tricia's pendulous breasts were mottled by dramatic blue- and green-coloured veins, and her dark brown nipples looked enormous. Evie was surprised that Tricia didn't seem to be in the least embarrassed, but then she thought that maybe Tricia remembered how very close Evie had been to seeing Hettie make her way into the world, and so that perhaps this feed seemed small fry in comparison.

Evie risked a glance downwards towards her own quite small chest, and looked up guiltily when Tricia laughed at her. She'd been rumbled.

Tricia seemed very matter-of-fact and not the least put out; perhaps this was because she had been a dairy parlour maid. 'Me titties are 'uge, baint they? Like t'udders on t'old cows I milked, I think to meself twenny times a day. I daresay they'll shrink in time, an' t' nurses keep sayin'

253

that me feedin' 'Ettie'll tuck ma belly aways too in no time, but I 'ope I goes back natural an' not all floppy and wrinkly. Sittin' yere, I feel if you 'ung a bell round my neck I cud take a place in t' parlour with the other milkers, but they say that's normal. I see you lookin' at yorn bosom, but they'd come up like these if you were with yorn own babbie, as I was never big afore.' And so on.

As Tricia described the various other symptoms of being a new mother, Evie found she was both impressed that Tricia was so circumspect, but also rather put off the idea of having her own children one day. The picture of motherhood that Tricia was painting was unabashedly graphic, and sounded painful, messy and not a little inconvenient. It was true all the same, thought Evie, that somehow she and Tricia were finding a common meeting ground between them, and they might be on the verge of realising that in fact they rather liked each other.

Still, Evie wasn't quite prepared for when Tricia leant across and in a rather workmanlike manner plonked a now napping Hettie onto Evie's lap, following a very emphatic burping. Evie stiffened for a moment but when she felt the baby's heat radiating through the crochet blanket and saw how Hettie was very happy to nestle down in her arms for a comfy doze, Evie relaxed a little. As she looked down at the utter trust Hettie was bestowing on her, suddenly Evie's apprehension was cast aside as she understood that perhaps one's own baby might make all the disadvantages and physical discomfort seem worth it.

Not that she wanted to put this to the test any

254

time soon, of course.

As Mr Rogers's friends were taking Evie and Sukie dancing on the Friday evening, Evie made sure that on the day that wrapped up what had felt like a very long school week, she trotted across the playground towards the school gates as soon as she decently could, even though Mrs Smith had seemed intent on describing to her (again) the various wonderful things there were about Hettie.

Up in her bedroom beneath Pemberley's eaves it all seemed rather depressing, Evie thought as she looked around her. The light's glow seemed dimmer and gloomier than was usual. Keith never ventured upstairs as far as this any longer, not now that she and her kittens were so close to the warmth of the kitchen range in their comfortable box, while Julia's bed looked to Evie's eyes to be accusingly empty.

Evie realised she was still downcast by her sister's absence, and she longed for their night-time gossips just before they would drift off to sleep.

The room was cold enough to show Evie's breath in little puffs of cloud as there was no heating in the attic rooms, and Evie hurried to slip on her best outfit for dancing, which was a gun-metal crepe tea-dress Sukie had given her after she had decided it didn't suit herself and made her midriff look plump (it didn't, but Sukie wouldn't hear otherwise).

Evie had had to do some nifty reshaping to make it sit well on her own waist and hips (annoyingly she was both much shorter and slightly bonnier than her tiresomely sylph-like friend).

Earlier in the week Evie had added a maroon velvet collar and cuffs to the dress – the velvet had once been an ancient cushion from the 1920s at Bluebells, but Shady had ripped a hole on one side of it with his sharp claws when trying to bury a dog biscuit in Robert's favourite chair – and she was gratified to see that her deep-red lipstick, the posh one in the gold-coloured case that Mrs Smith had given her, was almost the same colour as the velvet, and that it really lifted her outfit into one that was verging on the swish for an evening of dancing and making merry.

Evie's date for the night was a dark-haired printer called Ted, while Sukie's was Bob, one of the sub-editors at the *Western Morning News,* and they came to Lymbridge in a delivery van emblazoned with the name of the paper on its side to collect the girls.

On the way to Plymouth, Evie, who had never been to a large dance like this one promised to be, told them all to keep their eyes open for tips she could use in turn for putting on her own New Year's Eve dance in the village hall. She had finally agreed to Rev. Painter's request that she should do this, but she hadn't yet actually started to set the organisational wheels in motion as making the Christmas presents, seeing Tricia, and the Spitfire meeting had eaten up so much time. The Christmas cake definitely wasn't going to happen this year.

But the more Ted and Bob told Evie how very late she was in organising such a dance, especially on such a special night of the year, as all the good local bands were very probably booked elsewhere by now, and as there'd been no publicity for the event, it was likely that many people would already have made alternative arrangements to welcome in the new year, and so on, the more Evie felt a growing sense of dread at the thought of the dance. It was bound to be a failure, she could only conclude, and so perhaps she'd best not bother.

Sukie sensed Evie's falling spirits and squeezed her hand to buck her up, and then Sukie did what good friends do, and distracted Ted and Bob with the question of whether it was true about the controversial American socialite and politician Nancy Astor dancing with ordinary sailors on the Hoe. (It was, they said, and there were photographs at the offices of the *Western Morning News* to prove it.)

Although it was windy and extremely cold the four of them walked along the Hoe to take a look at the inky-black sea dotted with small whitetops, and then they turned to head for the dancehall with shining eyes and rather pink noses from the biting wind.

Rather to her surprise Evie very much enjoyed her evening. Ted and Bob proved to be very able dancers, and they each danced quite happily with both Sukie and Evie, swapping partners as and when. Ted was surprisingly good company as he was naturally a very amusing chap who was also an extremely good mimic, and he kept the four of them laughing.

Evie and Ted were getting up from their table for probably their seventh or their eighth dance

257

when Evie, who was still giggling from his latest impression of Mr Rogers, found herself barged into and then nudged out of the path towards the dance floor.

She looked away from Ted's rather sweet grinning face right into the distinctly less pleasant visage belonging to Fiona, who was holding on proprietorially – yet somehow also ostentatiously – to Peter's arm.

As her heart began to bump painfully within her ribs at the unexpected sight of Peter, Evie was pretty certain that he and Fiona had only just arrived as she felt her own acute Peter-radar would have alerted her to the fact of his presence if they had been there for any length of time.

'Why, it's Miss Snow, isn't it?' boomed Fiona across to Evie in a snootily cut-glass voice as Peter visibly shuddered and pretended to scan the dance floor. There was a sea of people dancing, many of the men and also the women wearing their military uniforms, while the energetic band looked quite hot and sweaty on their raised dais.

Yes, thought Evie, you *are* deliberately mispronouncing my name. You almost had the benefit of my doubt the first time we met, but now it's just plain rude.

Fiona went on, 'I was just saying to Peter how quaint a provincial gathering such as this is, and how heartening it is to see local people being so ready to wear fashions of a season or two ago. Wouldn't you agree?'

Evie didn't dare look at Peter, although she was privately awarding him a black mark for not doing anything to stem Fiona's poisonous comments.

She felt Ted's grip tighten slightly on her own arm. He couldn't know what was going on, but nevertheless he had obviously detected something of an atmosphere between the two women.

'Yes, I would quite agree with you, Miss Buckley,' Evie said through gritted teeth. 'And I see that it must be so very dull for you to have to spend time with the Devon hoi-polloi.'

Evie felt her irony was probably being wasted on Fiona, who was peering at her with a look on her face that seemed to say that she was someone for whom irony didn't apply.

Evie tried to stare coolly back at her, but it seemed an age before Fiona retaliated in the sweetest voice imaginable as she attempted to strike a confiding tone. 'I do hear, and perhaps you can tell me all about it, that there's very lively entertainment to be had midweek these days in the Ladies' bar at The Haywain.'

That dart most assuredly hit home, and Evie was left speechless and with an open mouth, as a liquid feeling of shame slithered through her to the very tips of her fingers and toes.

With a brusque 'good evening' shot in Evie and Ted's direction, to which Ted replied quite tersely (and in a deliberately dumbed down and downright common voice, Evie was sure), 'Evening', Peter fairly pushed Fiona in front of him and then prodded her to walk before him away from Evie and Ted. There looked almost to be the slightest of tussles as Peter quite obviously had to take a prompt side-step in order to prevent Fiona being able to look back over her shoulder in Evie's direction or to make one final quip before she was out of earshot.

The speed of Peter removing Fiona from the scene was evidence, Evie felt, that her own shame was public knowledge. She had been secretly hoping that Peter was unaware that she had been involved in a brawl with her sister. Clearly this had been a vain hope.

But as smooth as golden honey dripping from a waxen comb, Ted swept Evie onto the dance floor, taking care to pull Evie close to him as he whispered in her ear, 'Whatever you're thinking, let it pass, as it's making you look cross. I've no idea what was going on there between the three of you, but I can tell you that you are twice the gal that, er, creature is. And now I'm going to make that chap who was too scared to tell her to be quiet regret standing back from what she said. When he sees me dancing with you he'll feel jealous as a pig wanting to get to the mud and the potato peelings, but finding himself locked in his sty. And we'll make that hoity-toity excuse for a woman hopping mad as well, as she'll see the look he gives you. Your job is to smile and go along with what I do.'

And with that Ted led Evie to a spot not so very far from where Peter and the dreadful Fiona were now sitting as they watched the many people who were dancing.

Skilfully keeping in time to the music Ted pro-ceeded to move Evie flashily this way and that, once even daring to tip her a long way back-wards, her head feeling as if it wasn't far above the ground at the lowest point of the move, as Ted bore down above her.

Although ordinarily Evie would have felt such

ostentatious dancing to be brazen and that it simply wouldn't be for her, now she threw herself wholeheartedly into the experience, even sliding her hands quite obviously across Ted's muscular arms and torso as he twirled and whirled her about. She took care to paste a merry smile on her face and to let out at every opportunity what Sukie would have called an annoyingly tinkly laugh.

For Evie had realised that from the angle she was certain that Peter and Fiona were watching from, it could look very much as if she and Ted could be sharing a glancing kiss each time he flipped her backwards.

In fact as they were dancing she cast a scrutinising look over Ted's cheerful face, and decided he was very easy on the eye, as well as wonderfully fun to be with.

And so the next time he swung her backwards, she did kiss him, tentatively the first time, but enjoying it more the next time, almost to the point where she was hardly caring if Peter and Fiona were looking her way or not.

What fun it was to be so wanton, Evie told herself, unaware for the moment at least that it hadn't been that long since she had been screaming as loud as she could at Julia about how very important it was to demonstrate decorum and good behaviour at all times.

When Sukie and Evie enjoyed a cup of tea together the next morning at Pemberley to buoy themselves up for a Christmas shopping trip to Oldwell Abbott, they talked about the evening's dancing as they stifled the occasional yawn – it had been past midnight by the time they had been delivered back to Lymbridge.

Sweet and very gentlemanly as Ted and Bob both were, the friends decided, the night out as a foursome was to be a once-only experience.

Evie especially felt that if she were to agree to see Ted for another evening, it would only give him the wrong idea. She had had fun, and it had been good to flirt and then kiss him when Peter and Fiona had, with a bit of luck, been watching, but she didn't have any real desire to repeat the experience. Fortunately Ted had realised from the off that the kisses they'd shared weren't proper kisses but were for show only, although this might be a harder feat to carry off if she were to see him another time.

The pals then talked about Fiona. Sukie hadn't been able to hear what she and Evie had said to each other, but she had seen Evie's face as the women stood before each other, and so she knew it hadn't been good. And when Sukie had noticed the flamboyance with which Evie was dancing, which was so out of character, she'd then upgraded the 'not good' to 'pretty dreadful'.

Their musings didn't last though – Evie actually felt there was a lot more that she wanted to say on the subject of Fiona, but she had to keep these thoughts to herself as Tina and Sarah bustled into the kitchen with the news that a fox had got into two of the chicken coops on the village green, and had killed all of the chickens within them.

By the time the four of them had got down to the village green, there was quite a crowd standing around and the dead chickens were being divided out between the village's families. The meat wouldn't keep for too long, and so it was important that not a scrap of it was allowed to go to waste.

The fox may have taken a chicken for himself, but what everybody was exclaiming at was that he had run amok until he had made sure that every single chicken he could get at had been slaughtered. This went way beyond hunger, and seemed verging on the demonic.

Luckily none of the geese that had been purchased at Goosey Fair, or the ducks, or the chickens in the other coops had been got at. Christmas dinners of the geese or the ducks would still be able to go ahead as planned. Nevertheless, steps were being taken, overseen by Robert and James, to reinforce the wooden houses of the remaining poultry as it was thought that the fox would come back now he knew where such a tasty meal was residing.

'Isn't it horrid?' said Tina, who wasn't used to country ways, having grown up in the city of Exeter. 'That fox didn't want to kill because he was hungry. Once he'd had his fill, those chickens were killed just because he could.'

Mr Cawes was standing over James, checking that he was making a good job of nailing in some planks of wood.

When James saw Evie and Sukie, he removed the three nails he'd had in his mouth as he'd been hammering to describe seeing the first woman to land an aircraft on Dartmoor.

Evie and Sukie had to smile when he was somewhat incredulous as to how smooth the aeroplane had been brought down, and the efficiency with which the pilot had then taxied to the edge of the runway.

'Next you'll be telling us that you then saw a woman doctor in an ambulance driven by a woman,' Sukie joshed Evie's brother, who went slightly pink at the attention she was giving him.

'Women,' muttered Mr Cawes, 'bane of a 'onest workin' man's life...'

Evie wasn't sure if he was joking or not. Robert, she noticed though, was listening with a wry look on his face, although Evie was pretty certain he'd have been careful not to seem quite so amused if Susan had been nearby.

Meanwhile, as the breaching of the livestock pens were put to rights, there was talk of the terrible battering Britain's merchant navy ships were taking at the hands of the German U-boats. Imports were being radically restricted, and because many of the merchant sailors lived locally, as Plymouth was a strategic port for the merchant navy, there was a very sober mood amongst the villagers of Lymbridge as Evie and Sukie eventually set off for their delayed shopping excursion. They talked about how it seemed that while Britain's forces were fighting in foreign lands the real offensive was going on at home. It was imperative that everyone worked as one, as allies united against the Jerrys.

When they alighted from the bus in Oldwell Abbott, they saw something that made their hearts rise.

There was a poster at the bus stop about the Spitfire fundraising campaign, and then later they saw several others in local shops. It looked as if Mr Rogers and Mr Worth had been able to start things rolling, and Sukie said to Evie, 'This is largely down to you, you do realise?'

They wandered around, not really buying very much as their hearts didn't really feel in it, and then decided on the spur of the moment that they should go to see Tricia at the cottage hospital.

To their surprise, they discovered that Tricia was up and dressed, and was just getting Hettie ready. Mr and Mrs Smith were coming to take them both home. Evie couldn't believe how much bigger Hettie looked; she had obviously been tucking into lots of nutritious milk.

'I can't wait, I tell 'e both,' said Tricia. 'Every time I goes to sleep, I gets awoken to feed 'Ettie, it feels like. And then it's 'er nappy. She gets fractious when the other babbies cry, and that's no good. But she does like her grub, that's sure enough.'

'Come on, Tricia,' Mrs Smith interrupted. She had crept up on them unawares. 'Let's get this little princess over to see her daddy.' Mrs Smith tore her eyes away from the baby to look at Evie and Sukie, and then she added, 'This is the first time Timmy will get to see Hettie, and he may even be strong enough to hold her for a little while.'

'Timmy will be thrilled,' said Evie. 'What a lovely day for him.'

She and Sukie caught the bus back to Lymbridge. It had been a bitty day, where they didn't really feel they'd achieved anything, and Evie was feeling increasingly tired following her antics of the evening before. She was looking forward to an early night and for once wasn't to be thwarted in this aim.

## Chapter Thirteen

That night Evie had a dream in which the men of the village had the chance to win a cake in the shape of a Spitfire as part of the fundraising project. Peter was there, wearing a frilly pinny over a floral housecoat, making ready to hand the cake, resplendent in its grey icing, over to the lucky winner. Evie was unmercifully chivvying everyone around (even though she was somehow aware that she was dreaming, she cringed even in her dream at how exceptionally dictatorial she was). And then Evie had had to show Peter none too gently how to wrap the housecoat over across his front and then to tie the strings of the pinny placed on top of the housecoat in a large bow, while saying bossily to him that the thing about a young woman like Fiona was that she would have no idea how to go about something useful like putting a housecoat on, a statement that Peter had nodded wisely at, although even in the dream Evie felt it was very odd that he kept on nodding long after Evie had stopped talking.

Evie woke up with a start and then smiled to herself at the thought she hadn't allowed the Lymbridge ladies to have a chance of scooping the cake jackpot – why on earth not, she wondered? –

and then at what a psychologist might have to say over the housecoat and the pinny and the Peter part of the dream, which was nothing she'd want particularly to hear, she was pretty certain.

Then Evie lay for a while in bed wondering if a raffle a little like this might be possible, although open to all local residents, of course. She decided it wouldn't, at least not how she had dreamt it – there were a whole host of practicalities as to why not, not least the logistics of keeping such a cake fresh while the raffle tickets were sold, or the poor chump who would have to make and ice it, let alone the dreaded search for said ingredients (she gave a small grimace as she thought about how readily she'd given up totally on making the Christmas cake after she'd read the extensive list of ingredients). A minor issue was that Evie herself was a very poor baker, but all the same she thought she might have the germ of an idea on how to raise some money on broadly the same theme regardless. It was early still, and she lay in bed eager for sounds of the other residents getting themselves up.

At breakfast Evie buttonholed Mr Rogers, and he suggested that Evie should meet with the home economics editor at the *Western Morning News*, who might be able to help. He also said that he would pitch a feature to his editor on Evie and her efforts in galvanising local interest in the fundraising.

After morning church, Evie decided to head for the recuperation hospital as she wanted to leave a note for Peter, and it meant too that she could drop in to say hello to Timmy.

She arrived just as the hospital padre was finishing prayers with the patients, doctors and nurses. She hung about in the hallway until she could see that he had finished and that most of the patients and the hospital staff were going about their daily routines once again.

Timmy was perhaps not quite as pleased to see Evie as she had expected. But that could well have been because she arrived at his bedside just as he was trying to persuade a rather pretty young nurse that it was his day for a bed bath. 'It most certainly isn't, Mr Bowes, as you well know,' Evie heard the nurse saying back to him in a prim voice, before showing she knew how to handle a patient like Timmy, 'and in any case, and I'm sure you know this already, it's Nurse Hatch who is on bed-bath duties today and for the whole week to come.'

Evie knew that Nurse Hatch was nearing sixty if she was a day, and she was brusque and seemingly unashamed by having quite a whiskery, untended chin.

'Oh well, Evie, I shall have to make do with you then,' said Timmy with a dramatic upward roll of the eyes.

'That's the ticket, Mr Bowes,' said the nurse as she gave Evie a fleeting wink on her way to attend to another patient.

'And, Timmy, don't even think of suggesting that *I* give you your bed bath...' Evie said in what she hoped was a suitably firm manner.

Although it was a cold day, it was sunny with little or no breeze, and Timmy persuaded Evie that she should take him out on to the terrace in his wheelchair. Evie agreed, as long as he was warmly wrapped in blankets, and she set to bundling him up in a manner that would have withstood an Arctic blast.

Outside, Timmy was keen to show her how he was learning to control the wheelchair and push himself along and turn himself about. He was surprisingly cheerful, given that he then confided to Evie that the doctors had told him that unfortunately it was virtually certain he wouldn't be able to get any further movement back below his waist and that he would certainly never be able to walk again.

'Still, it could be worse,' he added. 'I can build up my upper-body strength, and the docs say that there isn't any reason that I shouldn't be able to live a long and rewarding life, or be a good father to Hettie. They've said it won't make any difference as far as she is concerned – she'll only ever know me in a wheelchair, and apparently children are much more accepting of this sort of thing than adult family members tend to be. The docs have also said that when I am allowed home I'm to insist that Ma and Tricia treat me as normal, and that they don't make unnecessary allowances for me or do too much for me. I'm going to break the news to Ma later, and tell her that I wonder if we should think about building a specially designed cottage for me and Tricia and Hettie at the far end of the garden. As it's not going to be a case of me getting back on my pins, I don't now think that us being squeezed into those upstairs rooms at home will work in the long term, although it will be good for when I first come out and Tricia has to learn to look after me. I want to be independent, and I want to be able to wheel myself out of my own front door and along to The Haywain if I fancy a swiftie.'

Evie didn't really know what to say, although she thought privately that Mrs Smith would have a difficult time trying not to do everything she could to help Timmy, and to pander to his every whim and wish.

Evie leant over from the stone bench she was sitting on and patted his knee in what she hoped was a comforting manner. She then realised with a jab of horror that very probably he couldn't feel her touch if the nerves in his legs were damaged, and so she squeezed his arm instead.

Timmy's eyes were bright as he looked at her. He knew what had just happened – of course he did – and he touched her briefly on the back of her hand to let her know that it was all right. Evie dropped her head on to his shoulder just for an instant; it seemed so unfair that such a vigorous young man should be cut down in his prime. And then Evie said softly, 'I'm sure Barkeep Joss wants you to be able to wheel yourself over to The Haywain too.'

They laughed as Evie sat back up and then they stayed quiet, side by side, staring out across the airfield to the moorland beyond. Two pony stallions were warning each other off with anxious neighs and a lot of pawing at the ground and baring of teeth and posturing half-rears, while a group of mares and foals were gazing on in what looked like at best only mild curiosity as to what might happen.

The smaller of the stallions backed reluctantly away, and the mares took to nibbling the grass again, although the stallion spent several minutes rounding them up and herding them into a tight knot as if he was reminding them they belonged to him.

The breathtakingly beautiful view in the low winter sun across the moorland to the dark-grey tors was soothing, and as they stared at the many hues of colour in the bracken, heather and granite before them, slowly the various troubles they each faced felt a little more manageable.

After a while they began to chat companionably about this and that, and Evie was gratified to see that Timmy seemed very proud of Hettie and that he was speaking of Tricia if not yet quite in an affectionate way, at least respectfully and with a certain warmth. They agreed that Evie should take Tricia Christmas shopping in either Plymouth or Oldwell Abbott, provided Mrs Smith would mind Hettie, and Timmy promised that he would make sure that Tricia had a generous amount of money to spend.

They watched as Mr Smith's car drove into the hospital car park and reversed into a parking space, and Mr and Mrs Smith got out, as did Tricia and Hettie. They waved as they saw Timmy and Evie on the terrace and made their way directly over to them.

A minute or two after they had all said hello to one another, Evie said she should go as she needed to drop off a note for Peter. She was very mindful that she should make it clear to the Smiths and Tricia that this was the real reason she was at the recuperation hospital. She sneaked a glance at Tricia, who smiled gently back with a much more accepting look at Evie than she might have done previously.

Before she left, Timmy explained to them all that he was keen Evie and Tricia should have the opportunity to go Christmas shopping together, and as expected Mrs Smith immediately volunteered herself as being very excited at the prospect of looking after Hettie for a little while. Tricia appeared a bit reluctant at the thought of leaving her baby, but once Timmy promised her a whole £5 to spend on whatever she wanted, as well as his clothing coupons, she said she was looking forward to the outing, as long as it wouldn't be for too long as she was of course still feeding Hettie herself.

Evie was just making her way down the steps from the terrace to look for the back entrance Sukie had told her about – in fact Sukie had drawn a map, even though Evie didn't need one, because 'Evie-Rose, you need all the help you can get!' – to the lower part of the building where Peter was working when Peter himself came around the corner.

'Evie, I thought I heard your dulcet tones. Might you have time for a cup of tea downstairs?'

Evie thought Peter must be joking as her family had often asserted that she had rather a strident, loud voice. But she couldn't be sure, and so she said, 'Great minds think alike – I was just hoping to drop off a note for you.'

Her heart was beating uncomfortably quickly, but she told herself to relax and that there was nothing for her to be het up about. It was the first time she and Peter had seen each other since the dance in Plymouth, but what of it? Peter was with Fiona now, he'd made quite clear to her, and she was fine about that. More or less. Actually a bit less than more. But fine. Definitely.

In the mess room she sat on the old brown sofa with its crochet blanket in exactly the same place she had on her previous visit, but this time Peter didn't look at all angry with her. Instead he asked a young woman in uniform if she might bring them some tea. He then turned to Evie and said he was pleased that she had come there today as he wanted to apologise to her for letting Fiona be so rude.

But before Peter had got very far Evie interrupted and said actually she wanted to apologise to *him*. She was, she went on quickly, very embarrassed that she'd not thanked Peter at all for helping her on the day that Tricia had given birth to Hettie, or for driving her home afterwards from the cottage hospital in Oldwell Abbott. She couldn't believe she had just climbed out of the car back in Lymbridge with little more than an incomprehensible murmur in his direction, and had wandered away from him in nothing short of a daze, but there it was – that was what she had done, even though Peter had been very kind. And she did appreciate how he was making an effort with Timmy, and she wanted Peter to know that although she and Timmy were no longer together, she did still want the best for her former fiancé, and so the fact that someone like Peter seemed to like the Timmy who was now stuck in the dratted wheelchair was important to both of them, not that Timmy had any idea that she and Peter had ever been anything more than the merest of friends, of course. Finally Evie said, in a tone that she could hear sounded contrite, that she knew she had been ill-behaved and ill-mannered in not at least paying lip-service to making Fiona feel a little more welcome in the area. And with that Evie's long apology ran out of steam.

There was a silence dominated by the ticking from an old brass-faced wooden clock on the mantelpiece, and then Peter, who was still standing on the far side of the room looking at her with a hard to read but intent look on his face, said weakly, 'Oh Evie.' He lit a cigarette and then repeated what he had just said, followed after another pause by, 'You, of all people, don't have anything to apologise for. And Fiona – who is much nicer when you get to know her than you might at present believe, I assure you – really hasn't been very pleasant to you at all. And Timmy seems a very nice person – in fact, a top-hole chap – and it would be inhumane of me not to try to cheer up our wounded servicemen who have paid a much higher price in the name of King and country than I could ever imagine paying myself. And as for that afternoon with Tricia, well, it ended happily enough, although I'm not sure the same can be said for the back seat of my car, and I don't mind confessing that it was an experience that I am in no hurry to repeat.'

Evie didn't really know what to say.

Peter came and sat on the sofa next to her, and he added that he felt bad too as he could see that it must have all been very hard on Evie, and

274

indeed Sukie had intimated as much to him only the other day, at which point Evie cut in to say that she thought it was time for them to change the subject.

They smiled tentatively at each other, and as the uniformed young lady came in just then bearing a battered tin tray on which rattled a teapot and two mismatched cups and saucers and a small jug of milk, suddenly the atmosphere in the room lightened into something more pleasant, being almost quite convivial.

Evie allowed Peter to fuss around with the teapot and the teacups, and then she added that she knew he couldn't say what they were working on in this hotchpotch of lower-ground-floor rooms, but she assumed it was important work and that the contraptions she had spied in adjoining workspaces on this visit and the last looked to be very impressive, although not like anything she had ever seen before. Peter nodded, acknowledging that the work was vital to the war effort, and that without going into any detail it was something to do with helping pilots fly better, but Evie absolutely mustn't breathe a word to anyone and he was only telling her because she was, well, Evie.

They then began to talk over less contentious matters, namely about how the fundraising for the Spitfire looked to be shaping up, with Evie even risking confessing to Peter about the pinny dream to do with him that she had woken up to that morning, at which he gave a hoot of laughter. And when Evie admitted she was very behind in organising the New Year's Dance, Peter said he'd be happy to help, if she wanted him to. Evie said she'd think about it but she didn't want to cause any awkwardness between him and Fiona, to which he said it wasn't a problem, it really wasn't. A short silence then suggested that actually neither of them quite believed that statement.

At last Evie stood up to go, and Peter offered to drive her back to Pemberley. Evie felt that she had been in a play for the last half an hour that had demanded a high level of acting. She had tried to convince Peter, and herself too, that they could behave with one another as platonic friends. But the frisson that thrilled her as they stood up and Peter briefly touched her back as they headed towards the door of the mess room told Evie a very different story. She was most definitely still deeply in love with him, even though she knew it could never be.

Later, when Evie thought of the morning, she realised it was precariously balanced between being a hugely pleasurable memory (being so close to Peter was always wonderful) and terribly painful (because it all felt so unresolved and hopeless between them).

There was no school the next day, as myriad local Home Guard units from all over the West Country were converging on Lymbridge Primary School. It was to be the centre of operations for a dummy run of some sort of mass defence exercise. Mrs Smith had been livid when she had found out about this late the previous week as she felt the authorities weren't taking the pupils' education seriously enough by being so cavalier as to allow the school to be so commandeered. She calmed a

276

little once Evie told her what Robert had said, which was that the Home Guard felt a weekday was needed as different things went on during the week and a range of working people would be out and about, and previously all the practice operations had been at weekends, and now they needed a real-life run-though of what it might be like should there be a German invasion on a weekday. In the New Year, apparently, there would be a further operation, which would take place during the hours of darkness.

In fact Evie was rather pleased to have an extra day to herself, although she could see it would present difficulties for some of the working parents, who would have had to hastily arrange for someone to look after their kiddies.

Evie popped over to Plymouth first thing in the morning with Mr Rogers, where she then spent a very profitable hour at the *Western Morning News* with the women's page editor, Miss James, and the home economics editor, Miss Farr.

They talked through various ways to run the competition for a Spitfire cake, and Evie realised quite soon into their discussion that the newspaper saw the competition as a means of promoting itself too, whilst also trying to help a good cause. Evie supposed she'd been naïve to think there wouldn't be mixed motives from the point of view of the newspaper, but she was still slightly surprised. But then she told herself firmly that business was business after all, even in wartime, and her job was to try and mould business interests into a means of doing good and raising money for the Spitfire fund.

And so the three of them decided the entrants would have to donate two shillings to buy a raffle ticket. The plan involved the newspaper obtaining donated ingredients from shopkeepers, and the provision of a specially written recipe for the cake, which Miss Farr offered to put together along with a drawing on graph paper showing how to construct the cake in the right shape. The owner of the winning raffle ticket would then receive the ingredients and the recipe and the cake construction instructions, and the whole competition would be drawn to a close by the winner having a photograph taken and a story written about them in the *Western Morning News* once they had made and iced the cake. Then hopefully the cake would be donated to some good cause, such as a children's home or something similar, and another story could run the following day with a photograph showing the cake being eaten.

Evie thought it sounded workable as an idea, and the three of them decided that in terms of timing, it would be good to do this in January, or even early February, as the paper found it hard to get good-news stories at that time of year, and so they would be able to devote lots of space to the competition's promotion.

Miss James also suggested that after Christmas, Evie might like to think of organising a series of fundraising talks that they could also promote. She suggested maybe a lecture somewhere in Plymouth given by, say, the BBC radio drama department's sound-effect team on how they made sounds like a storm or a bicycle cycling along or grass being cut, which might go down well, or a

278

cookery demonstration by one of the official war-time dieticians and recipe makers. Evie found herself getting ideas too – Frank and Joseph loved the BBC broadcasts that had been so popular with children in the 1930s and that were occasionally re-run, of Grey Owl, who spoke of conservation and the First Nations' way of life from his cabin, Beaverlodge, on the Ajawaan Lake in Canada, and she wondered if maybe she could organise a day of these old broadcasts aimed at children. There were bound to be other ideas too, Evie was sure.

Anyway, the early start meant that Evie was back in Lymbridge by lunchtime, and as arranged she went straight to the Smiths's cottage, where she shared a simple but nonetheless hearty soup with Mr and Mrs Smith and Tricia, after which every-one got in the car ready for the shopping trip to Oldwell Abbott as Mr Smith manhandled a shiny new perambulator into the generous boot of the car. It had to lie on its side and Mr Smith had quite a wrestle to get it in, despite the largeness of the boot, and so Evie thought the perambulator wouldn't be taken out in the car too often. Tricia deposited a bag into the boot that contained blan-kets and nappies. The plan was that Mr and Mrs Smith were going to take Hettie for a stroll along by the river while Evie and Tricia visited the shops.

'Let's be organised, Tricia,' said Evie, as they were dropped off on the High Street of the market town. 'We've clothing coupons for you, and Timmy has given you some money too.'

'An' I'd best get Timmy and 'Ettie a Christmas gift, an' Mr and Mrs Smith too,' said Tricia. 'I've never 'ad money for Chrissy presents afore.'

279

Evie was touched by Tricia's unembarrassed and unapologetic confession. She realised she was rather getting to enjoy spending time with her. Evie could never guess quite what Tricia was going to say, which was fun, and Evie was suddenly determined that Tricia would have a good first Christmas as a married woman.

'Do you have any idea as to presents?' said Evie. Tricia shook her head. 'Well, Mr Smith would probably like some tobacco, don't you think? And I'm sure Mrs Smith would appreciate some writing paper,' suggested Evie.

Tricia agreed, and then said she'd like to get Timmy a book, but that she'd need Evie's help in choosing the right one, and that she wasn't sure at all what to get Hettie.

Evie suggested they look around the shops as they might get inspiration as far as Hettie was concerned.

It all turned out to be much easier than they had expected. In a newsagent's they were able to get the tobacco for Mr Smith, writing paper for his wife, *and* an illustrated book on the ins and outs of car engines for Timmy. And then just as they were leaving the newsagent's Tricia spied a smallish wooden picture frame that she liked, and Evie said that if Tricia bought it then she would get Mr Rogers to take some photographs of Timmy, Tricia and Hettie as a family group – she'd pay for the development of the photos as her Christmas present to the new Bowes family, Evie said – and then Tricia would have a very special present to mark her daughter's first Christmas, even if it wasn't strictly a Christmas present for Hettie.

With the gifts safely stowed in Mrs Smith's best shopping bag that Tricia had been loaned, they then went to a shop that sold wool and material, where they chose some patterns and then used Tricia and Timmy's clothing coupons for a selection of materials and wool, with Evie promising to show Tricia what to do. Tricia gave Evie a sceptical look, and they both laughed. In fact, Evie was so prudent with her advice that there were enough coupons leftover to get Tricia a new pair of shoes, and at the shoe shop several doors along the High Street she chose some smart wooden-soled lace-ups that had a rubber hinge in the sole to make walking easier; the shoes had been dyed a lovely rich navy blue and Evie was left feeling more than a little envious.

'Evie, I used ter 'ate the very idea of you, and yet look at us now,' said Tricia with a smile. 'I don't know wot I'd a dun withou' you these pas' months.' And with that she gave a surprised Evie a quick and rather awkward but obviously well-intentioned hug.

They arrived back at the car at exactly the same time as Hettie and her grandparents, and then Tricia got into the car to give the baby a quick feed while the others remained tactfully standing outside, with their backs to the car. Evie described just what sensible and in fact jolly good shoppers they had been, while trying not to have memories of Julia and Mr Bassett, stirred up by the sight of The Griffin's hand-painted sign swaying gently in the wind directly opposite where the car was parked.

Although they hadn't been in Oldwell Abbott

very long at all, not really that much more than an hour, it was dark by the time they got back to Lymbridge and Evie was dropped off at Pemberley. The December weather was feeling distinctly wintery with the temperature plummeting.

Evie was looking forward to a cup of tea and a half hour in front of the fire with the latest copy of *Woman & Home*, which had been her treat to herself from the newsagent's. Her *only* treat that day as she had been determined to keep the focus on Tricia.

Mrs Worth was in a state of high anxiety though, because earlier that day Sarah and Tina had given their notice as PGs, saying they were bound for London. And with the Wallaces not having been replaced yet, and with the sudden loss of Mr Bassett and Julia, Mrs Worth was very worried about the low occupancy of Pemberley if the authorities were to come poking around as there was only Mr Rogers and Annabel Frome, and Evie too, of course, as PGs.

The two WRVS girls had been quick to reassure their landlady that they weren't moving out until the first week of January, in large part as they wanted to attend the New Year's Dance that Evie was organising.

Evie felt she ought to confess that there might not be a dance in the church hall on New Year's Eve. She had done absolutely nothing about it, and she knew that until the coming Friday she was going to have to concentrate all her efforts on the carol concert with the school pupils, unfortunately. She'd not really put enough work into that either, and she could see an embarrassment looming that evening if she didn't make a last-ditch attempt to up her game. Evie didn't mention that Peter had offered to help with the dance, as she didn't want to risk muddy waters over Fiona or why it was that Fiona might not like Peter getting involved.

'Right,' said Tina and Sarah, after Evie had described the sorry state of the New Year's Dance plans. 'All hands to the pump then,' was the rallying cry.

And by the time the crumpets were toasting for tea, it had been decided that everyone in the sewing circle would be mustered to help organise the dance and find a band and so forth, leaving Evie free to concentrate on the carol concert.

Also, the services of Mr Rogers would be called on to try and fill the empty rooms at Pemberley. It really was very useful having a journalist on hand and it was amazing how often a judiciously placed story in the local press could reap dividends.

### Chapter Fourteen

What Evie had kept very quiet about at Pemberley was that the day of the carol concert was also her own twenty-first birthday. Twenty-one! But try as she might, she didn't feel like making much of a song and dance about her birthday, to be honest, even though it would be her key-of-the-door year. The previous twelve months had felt like a bit of a rollercoaster, with plenty of challenges along the way. Evie certainly didn't feel she was yet grown-up enough to be joining the adult world, as she knew she had taken several wrong turns over the past months. And in any case, it seemed wrong to be celebrating something essentially so frivolous when Britain was still very much at war with Hitler.

Over the next few days the weather got colder and colder, with the moorland air feeling crisper than Evie thought she could ever remember. When a prisoner, an allegedly vicious 'lifer', broke out of Dartmoor Prison, locals were told to check fields and outbuildings for him as he might not survive in the harsh weather unless he had been able to get off Dartmoor to head for lower countryside, or else had taken shelter somewhere to ride out the icy snap.

The errant prisoner was captured on the Thursday morning, as luck would have it, by Robert's Home Guard unit, who were checking telephone wires as dawn broke before they all went off to work.

As Robert said to Evie later, it was the highlight of any of the manoeuvres carried out by the Lymbridge Home Guard, although to be fair it had to be said too that the prisoner, who'd only had his indoor prison garb on and worn plimsolls with no socks, had been so frozen he'd actually come out of his hiding place with his hands in the air when he'd heard their Jeep driving gingerly along the moorland lane and he had begged them to take him back to prison. They'd had to stop at Bluebells on the way to Dartmoor Prison to give the escapee a cup of tea and a blanket from Julia's bed to warm him up a little, his teeth were chattering so and his hands were quite literally blue with cold.

Meanwhile Sukie came to see Evie with the suggestion that she would love to get a group of friends together to go out at the weekend to celebrate Evie's important birthday.

Despite Sukie's protestations to the effect that Evie needed to let Sukie step in and nudge matters along both with the birthday celebrations, and also with Peter, Evie shook her head firmly, putting the dampeners on Sukie's well-intentioned offers. Evie insisted that although most people were excited about reaching the age of majority themselves, personally she felt completely unexcited at the prospect; and certainly there was to be no attempt to alert Peter to her birthday, or for Sukie to try and engineer more convivial relations between Peter and Evie.

Evie added that she expected Susan would give her a low-key tea-party the day after the carols as there wouldn't be time on the day of the performance. And that would be her birthday marker, and low-key was fine with her as Robert had remained worried about foxes breaking into the poultry houses on the village green in the cold weather, and after lunch on Saturday he had already co-opted Evie and Pattie, and Tina and Sarah, to help Frank and Joseph lug some old bricks over to the green so that he and James could set about reinforcing the henhouses with some brickwork. Susan's tea party would take place after that.

'Be still my beating heart – the glamour of a

winter's Saturday in Lymbridge!' said Sukie, adding, 'Evie-Rose, I never had a maid like you down to be such a killjoy when it comes to a Saturday night and a birthday celebration. I'm in danger of falling into a swoon at the shock of it.'

'Shame on you for even assuming that I'd be asking you to celebrate my birthday with me, even if I had fancied sampling the staggering array of delights in Oldwell Abbott of a weekend evening,' said Evie with a defiant toss of her hair. 'Which I don't.'

Sukie pushed her lower lip forward in a brief moue of petulance, and then she brightened as she thought of something else and asked Evie if it was set in stone that the school carol service had to be at the church hall?

'Why not let me see if the carols can take place at the recuperation hospital?' said Sukie. 'I think the wounded men would love to sing the carols they'll remember from their own childhoods along with the local children from your school, and I suspect too that the pupils' parents would like the patients to feel they were being supported by the village. What do you think?'

What Evie thought was that her tummy had done an uncomfortably energetic somersault at the unexpected mention of the recuperation hospital, namely because that was where Peter was. Sukie was a minx, and was obviously determined that Evie and Peter would be thrown into each other's orbit, or else Sukie would have Evie's guts for garters.

But what Evie actually managed to say to Sukie in a demure and only slightly strangled voice was,

286

'Hmmmn, you might have a point, Sukes, as I can see that to shift the – to quote Rev. Painter – "shindig" there would make the service a little more special as a fundraising evening. Tell me, is there a suitable room that's large enough inside the hospital, which will ideally have some vestiges of heating? And do they have a piano?'

Sukie said to Evie that she wasn't fooled for a minute by her friend seeming to be so casual about Sukie's suggestion. And the answers to Evie's questions were yes and yes. There was actually a bona fide ballroom at the house, which Sukie claimed wasn't being used for anything much and actually few people knew it was there as it was tucked away in a side wing. And in it there was a grand piano that one of the patients had had a go at tuning the other day.

In fact, Sukie confessed, she had already had a word with the powers that be and there was no problem at all about changing the venue, even though there were only a couple of days' notice.

Evie could only roll her eyes as she let Sukie know that she thought Sukie's desire to engineer as many meetings as she could between Evie and Peter to be Very Tiresome Indeed.

Sukie's pointed look back left Evie in no doubt that Sukie knew the truth of it, which was that Evie felt distinctly excited at the prospect.

Rather to Evie's surprise it proved very easy to move the carol service to the recuperation hospital, even though time was short to be making such a shift. In fact Mrs Smith thought it a wonderful idea, saying that she couldn't believe that neither herself nor Evie had thought of it. With barely a pause to collect her thoughts further Mrs Smith steamrollered the hospital administrator into agreeing to the plan, and then she cleared it with the Rev. Painter too, as she didn't want him to feel affronted by the rejection of the church hall, and then Mrs Smith told all the parents on Evie's behalf of the eleventh-hour alteration to the agenda. That would sort out any last-minute quibbles, Evie acknowledged.

Susan thought the change of venue to be a good idea too, and she made sure all the visitors to the village shop knew where they had to go instead of the draughty church hall.

Evie had a slightly dicey moment in the shop at one point when she was there at the same time as her father. Taking advantage of Susan not being distracted by any other customers, as he and Evie were the only ones in the shop, Robert said in his quiet but serious manner that he very much hoped that Evie and Julia would soon mend the broken bridges between them. They were setting a poor example to James and the evacuees, he went on, and although Julia was still being hot-headed, he didn't think she was as affronted as Evie had said she had once been. Grabbing hold of her mother's hand across the counter, and then Robert's, Evie said to her parents that she agreed; it was time the two sisters buried the hatchet, although as yet she wasn't quite sure how this would be achieved.

'It is my problem though, Mother and Father, and so please do let me and Julia sort this between ourselves,' said Evie. 'I behaved childishly, and so did she, and now we must resolve our argument as adults, and without the help of anyone else.'

For the first time in weeks Evie was able to bask in genuine smiles from her dear parents. It was a good feeling.

Meanwhile Pattie insisted that her beau, John, told all and sundry during his stints serving at The Haywain where the carol concert would be. Mr Worth hired a charabanc at his own expense to transport the children, and Evie and Mrs Smith too, over to the recuperation hospital, and Timmy said he would make sure all the pilots and crew at the airfield knew about it.

As Evie confided to Sukie about thirty minutes before the audience started arriving on the day of the concert, and after a surprisingly slick dress rehearsal, Sukie had given Evie a wonderful birthday present by having an idea where, for once, Evie ended up not having to do any running around to make it happen, but was nevertheless able to take all the credit for a scintillating plan.

Sukie had replied with what she probably thought was a modest expression on her face, had it not been for the twinkle in her eye. 'I'm a clever thing that way, as you should well know by now, Evie-Rose!'

Mr Cawes had been despatched, grumbling as usual, over to the recuperation hospital first thing that morning, and in spite of his mutterings he had done sterling work in constructing a tiered platform with the help of some of the crew from the airfield, so that all the members of the audience would be able to see each and every pupil of the school, no matter how big or small, and

289

regardless of the size of whoever might be standing in front. The piano was placed in a prominent position to the side of the stage, and there were even some elementary lights rigged up that would shine on the performers.

Rows of chairs had been put in place for the audience. Evie had told Mr Cawes to put out fifty chairs, if he could rustle up such a large number, but when the parents and villagers started to arrive, having braved intermittent sleety flurries, it was obvious quite quickly that this was an underestimate of the number of attendees, and so there was a flurry of activity while as much extra seating as possible was found. The ground crew from the airfield leapt into action and proved to be very inventive with sturdy planks supported on wooden beer crates.

Timmy and several other servicemen in wheelchairs were placed to one side of the ballroom, with them joking between each other that at last they had discovered an advantage to being in a wheelchair: they had somewhere to sit. And where they were had a damn good view to boot.

In fact there were so many people who wanted to watch the service that Evie was very gratified at the frequent sound of coppers, threepenny bits and silver coins hitting the bottom of the fund-raising bucket.

Soon, it was standing-room only, and Evie had to suggest that even though there was the occasional flurry of snow outside, perhaps a window could be opened a smidgen or two, as she was a little worried about members of the audience fainting if they had to stand for too long and the room got too warm with all the people there.

Before the carols got underway, the hospital administrator welcomed everyone, and gave a short speech about the important work that was being done at hospitals like this for the returning wounded servicemen. A representative of the airfield then said a few words about Spitfires and what great little fighting machines they were, followed by an old buffer from the Home Guard, who droned on rather too long. Mr Rogers spoke in a welcome snappier manner as a representative of the *Western Morning News,* outlining Evie's idea for raising what they all hoped would one day swell to become the £6,000 needed to buy a Spitfire, and the way they were all working together to get as many local groups as possible all pulling together.

'If we manage to raise more than £1,000 for the fund by Easter, it will be a feather in all of our caps. For there will be other parts of the country doing likewise, and we can pool our money, and before we know it we'll be showing our brave boys how very much we think of them,' Mr Rogers said, finishing on a stirring note. After that, Rev. Painter spoke for a minute or two of the value of the Christmas message, and the feeling of renewal and hope that would come with the New Year.

Evie then took to the stage.

'I'll be brief,' she said, 'as we have a lot of wonderful carols to get through tonight, and I know that each and every pupil from Lymbridge Primary School can hardly wait to sing their hearts out to all of you tonight. There are some copies of the words to the carols, courtesy of lunchtime copying by our wonderful juniors over the past couple of weeks – please forgive any small spelling slips as they had to do them very quickly – and so do sing along too, although please note that we would like to perform for you the final carol with no accompaniment from the audience. Meanwhile I would like to thank you all for coming, and for digging so deeply into your pockets, purses and wallets for such generous donations. We wish you and all your loved ones, near and far, a very merry Christmas, as well as a happy and safe New Year. We must embrace the love of our families at this special time of year, and make amends for any wrongs we have done to them. God bless you all, and God Save the King!'

There was a round of applause as Evie stepped back to allow the pupils to line up in their allotted places. Hettie had been having a snooze and Evie saw her open her eyes in alarm at the unfamiliar sound of the applause, but she quickly settled down again when Tricia moved her to the other arm and cuddled her gently. Evie couldn't see Julia or Leonard Bassett, but she hoped they were there and had heard what she had said about the value of reconciliation and family love.

But before Evie could start to feel maudlin, Mrs Smith began to bash out 'While Shepherds Watched their Flocks by Night' (with James making sure he caught Evie's eye as he sang 'While shepherds washed their socks at night', as was his wont), followed by all the traditional festive favourites one would expect. Generally the school pupils sang pretty much in tune, which wasn't a claim that could be made of the audience who were singing along with perhaps a little too much out-of-tune shouting at times. But what the audience lacked in finesse, they made up for in gusto. However, by the time of 'The Holly and the Ivy' it was all going a bit awry on the stage as Evie's infants in particular were by now getting a little over-wrought at having to stand still for such a long time and concentrate so hard, and Evie had to fight manfully not to catch the grinning faces of Sukie, Linda and Pattie, who were doing their level best to make her smile at the duff notes.

Then the lights dimmed and Joseph stepped forward with a serious face. He stood in a patch of light to sing the final carol. It was 'Silent Night' and his eerily bell-like choirboy's voice soared out high and true across the room. Evie had only recently discovered that Joseph had such a wonderful voice and that he could carry a tune with confidence, and she had been audacious enough to suggest that he sing without the piano, which he now did with extraordinary panache and stage presence. It was a tremendously affecting performance, and it absolutely stole the show. Unexpectedly, Joseph's elder brother, Frank, had a much less appealing voice – everyone at Bluebells claimed poor Frank sounded like nothing so much as a foghorn, an accolade that Evie had thought previously to be hers alone. The audience were so caught up in the beauty of Joseph's voice that by the time that he had finished singing Evie saw many a hanky being pressed to moist eyes by many abashed and burly grown men as well as a high proportion of the village's womenfolk. Evie discovered she had a real lump in her throat too, and that her own eyes were misted over.

Mrs Smith was an experienced trooper in this sort of situation luckily, and without further ado she stepped forward to lift the mood of the evening as she announced in her familiar imperious voice that she was going to let everyone in on a closely guarded secret, at which point she put her finger to her lips and looked around with eyebrows raised as if she were auditioning for a pantomime.

Evie thought immediately, darn it! How silly she was not to have thought about putting on a panto, or, more to the point, suggesting that someone else put on a panto. It could have been a lot of fun to stage and to watch, and could have been a popular money-spinner. If, heaven forbid, the war was still going next Christmas, this would be top of her agenda as a fundraising project, most certainly.

Then Mrs Smith said to a loud chorus of oohs and aahs that the secret she was going to let them in on was that this very day was Evie Yeo's twenty-first birthday, and so could everyone please join in with the traditional rendering of 'Happy Birthday'. Evie's modesty would be preserved by not being given the bumps, said Mrs Smith, but of course all the schoolchildren were welcome to make as much noise as they wanted.

Evie was overcome – this was a complete surprise, as were the Hip Hip Hurrahs then said in her honour. And there were quite a few catcalls, and lots of stamping of feet and clapping. She was hot and blushing furiously when she took a quick bow, and then made everyone laugh by fanning herself extravagantly with her hand, but not before she had seen Hettie's horrified face at the noise and Tricia's prudent dash for the nearest door with her held high so that her wail of disapproval didn't dampen the moment. Clearly the pupils of Lymbridge Primary School didn't need asking twice when commanded to make a hullaballoo by their headmistress.

To Evie's surprise it turned out that a makeshift male choir had been cobbled together from people involved with either the recuperation hospital or the airfield, and as Evie slid into a seat at the end of the front row where people had budged up to make enough room for her, Peter took his place at the piano and accompanied the choir as they belted out a medley of contemporary popular songs.

It finished with everyone singing 'We'll Meet Again', before standing up to close the evening with a rousing rendition of 'God Save the King'.

As everybody clapped for a final time, it was clear that a thoroughly good time had been had by all.

Tea and buns were provided, and The Haywain had donated the services of John (which pleased Pattie, of course) as well as some scrumpy and ale, and also what the hostelry claimed was 'mulled wine', although when Evie had a cautious sip she decided it was a very odd festive beverage and not one that was particularly pleasant or that she'd care to sample again.

Now that the pressure of a public performance was over, the children milled about excitedly, and Evie suggested that Joseph and Frank carry the collecting bucket around, giving the coins the odd clanking shake-up to encourage the adult members of the audience to make one final donation.

Not too long after the bucket had been delivered back to Evie, along with the money taken for the various drinks and the buns, Timmy and his fellow patients were told it was time for them to retire in order that they didn't find the evening too taxing. Quite quickly after that the room began to thin out as members of the audience were aware that this was a working hospital and so the patients should be allowed to get a good night's sleep. Evie was pleased to note that Tricia, carrying Hettie, looked to be accompanying Timmy back to his ward, and that they must have been sharing some sort of joke as they were each smiling broadly.

Susan and Robert were busy organising getting the four evacuees into their coats ready to head back home in the squally winter weather, Linda and Sam had left as soon as the singing was over as Sam's mother had a chesty cold and they were a little concerned about her, and Sukie didn't seem to be around any longer so Evie guessed she was probably diverting herself with one of the crewmen from the airfield. Julia and Leonard Bassett were notable by their absence for the whole evening, which was disappointing. Annabel Frome, Tina and Sarah, had already left for The Haywain with a gaggle of the aircrew.

Evie chatted for a while with the Worths and the Smiths, who had got birthday cards for her, but before too long she made her excuses and went to help stack up the chairs and put the room to rights.

As Evie worked she felt restless and slightly out of sorts, with a nagging headache and shooting pains in her back, the way one often does after there's been a surge of adrenalin, and so she wanted to expend a little more energy, which spurred her on to work at a faster rate than the other people who were helping tidy up.

It wasn't long before Peter sidled over in an un-necessarily nonchalant manner, and after a moment or two of indecision, Evie allowed herself to bask in his attention as after he had wished her a quick happy birthday, Peter told her it had been a very enjoyable carol service, and that he thought the funds of the Spitfire coffers would have been nicely swelled.

'Yes, considering it was all completely from scratch as to venue and of course there were all those speeches that I hadn't quite expected before we could get going, I thought we all acquitted ourselves rather well,' agreed Evie with a small smile as she peeped up rather coyly at him.

Peter then went slightly pink when Evie added how good it had been to hear *him* playing the piano once again as he really was the very best pianist that Lymbridge had ever seen. And at the sight of his reddening cheeks, for a moment Evie was reminded of the gauche, bashful and peren-nially awkward Peter she had first encountered over the breakfast table the morning after he had moved into Pemberley, which was only a mere seven or eight months ago. Then, he had been a young man with poor skin and a pronounced stammer. It was a world away from the still sometimes shy but generally much more assured and confident Peter of today. His skin had cleared over the spring months, and Evie realised that he rarely stammered these days, or at least not in her presence.

Peter touched her arm briefly, and enquired whether Evie would like to use the mess room downstairs as a quiet and private place to count up the funds raised, which he could then enter into the official Spitfire fundraising ledger, and finally both the ledger and the money could be locked away from harm in the metal safety box.

Evie realised that this was an opportunity to be alone with Peter on her birthday, even if just for a few minutes, and it was what she had really wanted to happen all along, although it was a prospect that she hadn't dare allow herself to hope for.

She tried to nod in agreement to his suggestion casually and without too much enthusiasm, and she thought she had succeeded.

But then there was an awkward moment when they each caught each other's eye.

It felt like they were teetering on the precipice of something. It was a glance that felt illicit. It felt daring. It felt exciting.

This wasn't a feeling that lasted. Just a minute or two later, once they were actually alone together in the mess room, she was teetering on having second thoughts.

Her headache seemed that bit more persistent and she told herself that wouldn't she be little better than a trollop if she allowed herself to take advantage in any way of the situation? Especially bearing in mind that she had been so vitriolic over the questionability of Julia's morals.

With a small quiver that travelled the length of her tense back, Evie felt heady as she found herself thinking less well of both herself and Peter, and the way they had managed to inveigle a little time alone together, and suddenly she wasn't at all sure what she would do if he did make a move towards her. The way he had asked her to join him in the mess room might have appeared innocent enough, as would her acceptance, but she felt distinctly uncomfortable and less than innocent now that she was actually *in* the mess room with Peter nearby.

Fortunately Peter helped her relax by being the same old Peter. He didn't do anything untoward or sit too close to her, and he helped her count out the money.

Perhaps she had been reading too much into them being alone, Evie thought, as it didn't seem as if anything else was on the agenda. Now, to her shame, she felt a tinge of disappointment.

Counting the large amount of coins took quite a long time to get to a total they both agreed on as there were a lot of threepenny bits and pennies and halfpennies to tot up, and it meant there had to be a couple of recounts. But eventually they were able to agree that the event that evening had netted a whole £25 17s. 6d for the Spitfire fund, which was excellent news as Lymbridge was by no means an affluent area.

Peter wrote the sum in the ledger, with 'Lymbridge Primary School carol service' proudly beside it, and the date, and then as Evie stared at the ledger's page with this as the first sum for the Spitfire Fund, she couldn't help but think as she gazed at the large white expanse below Peter's rather elegant writing what a long way they had to go before anything close to £6,000 could be raised, or even the £1,000 target by Easter. Peter popped out of the mess room. He had gone to find a very large and strong envelope into which the coins were then painstakingly placed (it looked like some sort of internal memo envelope as Evie could see various names crossed off on the front of it), the envelope was sealed and then the seal covered with a melted red wax blob into which Peter pressed the signet ring he always wore on the little finger of his left hand, and the same heading and total sum was written on the front of the envelope. Finally, the ledger and the envelope were carefully placed in the safety box which Peter then locked.

'Evie, I'll drive you home, of course, but would you like to have a small whiskey with me first?' he asked.

Evie said she would, although she took care to take only small sips this time as she remembered how she had coughed and spluttered the last time Peter had given her some whiskey.

Taking care to sit at opposite ends of the sofa they talked a little about their plans for the Christmas week – Evie was having Christmas lunch at Bluebells, while Peter would be in London for the festivities (Evie didn't have the nerve to ask if Fiona would be in London too for the festivities) – and then they got down to some serious discussion of the New Year's Dance, and Evie jotted down some ideas. There was a second whiskey and when Evie stood up to go, she tottered a little, being unused to imbibing strong spirits.

Peter took her arm and gently guided her up the stairs. They seemed to be the only people still up and about in the building.

'What time is it?' whispered Evie to Peter, her mouth close to his ear.

'Late, I think,' he whispered back. Evie shivered when she felt his warm breath on her neck.

She had to wait for him to unlock the door so they could leave the building, and for him to lock it again. He offered her his arm as they headed to the car. The snow had stopped and the sky had cleared, leaving a full moon hanging luminously above them, although the windscreen remained icy.

'Peter,' said Evie as she slid into her seat, emboldened by the two whiskies, 'why aren't you with Fiona tonight?'

There was a silence. 'I don't know,' he replied at last in a tense-sounding voice.

They drove slowly towards Lymbridge, and Peter brought the car to a gentle halt just down the lane from the bottom of the drive to Pemberley. He turned the engine off, and they sat there each staring out of the windscreen in front of them.

'I'm not sure what to do or to say,' said Evie after a while.

Peter sighed, and dropped his head downwards. He reached out with his left hand towards Evie, but stopped short of touching her.

'I'd better go,' said Evie.

She got out of the car but she couldn't quite

bring herself to walk away. Peter thought how beautiful she seemed in the moonlight as she turned to look at him once more.

Peter opened his side door and came to stand in front of her. They were only inches apart. The moon went behind a cloud and small swirls of snow started to cascade gently down as they stared into each other's eyes, feeling that they were seeing deep into the other's soul.

Every fibre of Evie felt as if it was quivering and desperately alive as she watched the occasional snowflake land on Peter's hair.

Then there was the sound of a car engine towards the other end of the village, and the electric connection between them was shattered.

Evie turned abruptly and stepped swiftly into the safety of Pemberley's drive, and within moments she heard Peter gently close the car door and turn on the ignition of his car.

Dawn was sneaking its first tendrils across the leaden sky and it was almost breakfast time before Evie was able to close her eyes without reliving the heady experience of standing so close to Peter. She felt hot and confused, and her brow felt clammy.

They had behaved perfectly respectably – the questions about why Peter wasn't with Fiona that evening and precisely why Evie had been so pleased to share what felt like stolen seconds in secret with Peter standing at the roadside – and yet it felt like something extremely improper had occurred between them.

## Chapter Fifteen

The autumn term ended with something of a whimper as the children generally seemed over-tired and tetchy as, to be honest, did their teachers, although Evie was very touched to be given homemade Christmas cards by all of her infants and, to her surprise, by quite a lot of the juniors too.

Evie thought the short days in the run-up to Christmas had taken a toll on everyone, as it was only just getting light by the time school began and after lessons were over for the day the children were then wending their way home in thick dusk, if it wasn't black as pitch already. The sleety snow had given way to a cold but dampish snap that meant constantly drifting mist and fog that would shroud the bracken and heather in tiny white droplets, alternating with persistent drizzle.

Every time Evie went to put on her coat and hat they were damp and unwelcoming, and she felt constantly cold and shivery. At night-time there might be a few clear hours where the stars and moon could be seen clearly, and the moors and craggy tors would look mysteriously imposing and shadowy. But these beautiful night skies merely meant even further plummeting temperatures and frost forming almost before one's eyes.

It certainly wasn't Evie's favourite time of year, although she did agree with Sukie that there was something to be said for the Ladies' bar at The Haywain as Barkeep Joss always made sure there was a welcoming log fire burning in the blackened old iron grate and he'd throw a few pine cones on too so that there was a pleasant evergreen aroma in the bar.

The final afternoon at school had been a riotous one of games and a rowdy singalong, with Mrs Smith belting out the tunes on the school's piano, and everybody was allowed to run around and make a huge amount of racket until they were quite worn out. There were crackers to pull, and the children were encouraged to wear the paper party hats and to read out the jokes. And then each child was sent home clutching a wooden jigsaw, with larger pieces for the younger ones and much tinier pieces for the older children, as well as a Christmas card for every child that both Evie and Mrs Smith had signed.

The jigsaws and crackers were by way of Mr Rogers, who had written a story on a storeroom that had had water damage in Plymouth earlier in the year, when a bomb dropping next door had caused a fire and the firemen's water hoses had unintentionally doused the storeroom. He had been able to do a very good deal on the salvaged jigsaws and crackers, most of which only had negligible water damage, and for well over a month they had been sitting in boxes in an unused outhouse at Pemberley. As Mrs Smith said, ordinarily the school funds wouldn't be used for something frivolous like this, but it had been a difficult year and so she thought that, just this once, the children would benefit more from a treat rather than spending the money on something more practical for the school.

Evie felt exhausted. In fact she didn't really think that she'd felt quite herself since that terrible night in The Haywain when she and Julia had argued so vehemently. Her equilibrium seemed out of kilter, and since the carol service she had started to wake up in the mornings with feelings of worry and anxiety uppermost in her mind. She'd become prone to headaches and was at a complete loss as to what she could do to restore herself to the happier, more even-tempered Evie of old.

She'd even said as much to Mrs Smith first thing on this final day of term, when the headmistress commented that Evie looked ready for her Christmas break. Mrs Smith acknowledged tactfully that with Timmy's injury and his marriage and Hettie arriving all crammed into the space of just a few months, and with the argument concerning Mr Bassett, it had been a testing time for them all.

'Evie, I am hoping you will feel this is good news, and I had been waiting to tell you at the end of the day, although perhaps right now is a more appropriate time instead. The long and short of it is that I am hoping that you will stay on with us to teach again for the spring term, although I am not in a position unfortunately to be able to promise you the summer term too. Next year is likely to bring the school a whole new set of challenges as it seems almost definite that early in the New Year some of the moorland primary schools are to be merged. But frankly, if we are going to face turbulent times, I don't think there is anybody else that I'd rather have by my side than you as we prepare to do battle, in the educational sense, on our beloved Dartmoor,' said Mrs Smith rather grandiosely.

Evie surprised both of them by being unable to prevent hot tears welling up. She had a pain in her chest too, and the more she tried to hold her sobs in, the less she seemed able to, and she could feel her shoulders quaking as she attempted to gulp back her emotions, and the squeezing pain behind her eyes seemed almost unbearable.

'Evie, my dear, whatever is the matter?' fussed Mrs Smith, as she passed across to Evie a neatly pressed man's cotton handkerchief.

Evie mopped her face and blew her nose loudly.

'I'm hoping those aren't tears of sadness at the thought of teaching alongside me once again next term,' Mrs Smith went on in the slightly strange tone she was apt to employ when making a joke as it was apparent that Evie was still unable to speak, although Evie did manage to shake her head to convey that she wasn't crying because she didn't want to come back to Lymbridge Primary School in the new year.

Mrs Smith took Evie's shoulders and turned her towards the toilet block, and gently propelled her forward as she suggested that a few quiet moments and an opportunity to wash her face might be the ticket that would set Evie up for the final push of teaching.

It did the trick, but only to a certain degree, as Evie remained pale and quiet until home time, and she kept taking her cardigan on and off as she couldn't seem to get comfortable, even though she tried putting a brave face on during the end-of-term Christmas hi-jinks. But as out of sorts as she felt, she remembered to smile warmly when Bobby Ayres and April Smith were awarded oranges – what a treat as they were so scarce these days – for having been given the most stars for good work in Evie's class during the autumn term.

The next day it was obvious that Evie had come down with influenza. She vomited first thing and then was unable to stand up without feeling dizzy, and so Mrs Worth insisted she was to stay in bed and not have contact with any of the PGs or the Worths as she didn't want influenza racing through Pemberley. Evie's temperature was alarmingly high, her throat sore, and she was achy all over, with a pounding head, and disconcertingly she was now managing to feel both hot and cold at the same time.

In fact, Evie was so poorly that Mrs Worth told Susan she was very worried about her, with the result that Pattie, who was renowned in the family for never being ill or picking up coughs and colds, no matter how closely one of her relatives would splutter nearby, was despatched to Pemberley to share Evie's room for a few days to keep an eye on her. Mrs Worth made it clear to Susan that while she was anxious that Evie be looked after properly, she couldn't herself keep running up and down the stairs to Evie's bedroom to tend to her needs.

It was a very boring sojourn for Pattie. Quite heavy snow had fallen overnight and was lying across the moors, and so she wasn't able to work. It was the first major snowfall of the winter and Dartmoor appeared bleak and very eerie in its virginal-looking blanket, and sounds carried for miles across the white-cloaked countryside. Several small herds of ponies looked disconsolate as they pawed at the snowy ground in order to reach the vegetation beneath. The sky felt low and heavy, with its promise of nothing other than more snow to fall. In fact the snow that had come already was deep enough that even the most stalwart members of the village's sewing circle were crying off leaving their homes for one last session around the large dining table at Pemberley, citing having to get ready for Christmas and make up beds for visiting relatives.

And poor Evie was no fun at all, decided Pattie. When she wasn't coughing or sniffing, or saying she was feeling nauseous, she was sleeping fitfully, often tossing and turning and occasionally muttering something about a mess room, although her youngest sister could never quite make sense of what she was saying. Pattie encouraged her to drink as much water as possible, but she couldn't get Evie to eat.

Pattie had to wear layer upon layer of clothing herself, as their attic bedroom didn't have a fireplace, and the central heating in the cast-iron radiators that Mr and Mrs Worth were very proud of had only been installed on the ground floor, in the two grandest bedrooms and on the first-floor landing. Pattie found that in spite of her many garments she was often so cold that she had to creep under the woollen blankets and feather eiderdown of Julia's old bed. It was definitely too cold for sewing or knitting as within minutes Pattie found that her fingers felt stiff and frozen, and so she spent several days listening to the wireless and reading a selection of rather gripping Agatha Christie whodunits.

On the afternoon of her second day Pattie escaped for an hour to go to Bluebells to fetch some clean clothes and to call in to see Susan at the village shop, but Susan made it clear that Pattie should return to be with Evie pronto as proper influenza could become a very nasty business, and the hospitals were so stretched these days that it was important Evie's condition didn't worsen to the point that she had to be admitted to the cottage hospital in Oldwell Abbott, and she sent Pattie off with some aspirin for Evie and the instruction that Evie was to drink a large glass of water every hour.

Linda and Sukie both called at Pemberley, but Mrs Worth wouldn't let them go up to see Evie. Pattie had yelled down to them as she hung out of the bedroom window as they were getting ready to wheel their bicycles down the drive that it wasn't worth it anyway, Evie was out for the count, but she could meet them for a very quick drink in The Haywain at six.

Grouped around the open fire in the Ladies' bar the friends had a pow-wow about the New Year's Dance. The upshot was that they decided to plough on without Evie. If they waited for her to get better, it would then get all mixed up with Christmas, with the result there'd be a real danger that it wouldn't happen at all. In fact the arrangements were all running so badly behind schedule anyway that secretly nobody believed an actual dance would be able to take place.

Sukie thought Evie had better hurry up and feel well, as there was no better time to fan the flames of an old romance than Christmas, the season of mistletoe and kisses. But she took care to keep her friend's secret, although when Pattie mentioned Fiona briefly, Sukie enjoyed pointing out that she wasn't a great beauty.

To Sukie and Pattie's relief, Tina and Sarah had already been hard at work making the posters, and so, wrapped up warmly, they plodded around the local villages putting them up, with Annabel Frome also stepping in to help. Linda and Pattie said they'd get to grips with giving the village hall a thorough clean and tidy, with Sukie offering to persuade Mr Cawes to do his bit in helping them too. Sukie popped over to The Haywain to sort out the prerequisite liquid refreshment and the loan of some glasses, and then she arranged for James to be the doorman for the evening, taking money for the tickets as they didn't have time to pre-sell any. When James heard that Sukie would be the cloak-room attendant, and that she would be sitting alongside him, he fairly leapt at her suggestion. Sukie mused that in a slack moment she must remember to quiz James about the young lady Linda had seen him with in Oldwell Abbott during the autumn; it had been very quiet on that front.

After only a little prevaricating Julia agreed to help set the dance up, saying she was only getting involved as the fundraising cause was such an important one for the war effort and this meant that family rifts must be cast aside in order that everyone could pull together, and so she offered to organise sandwiches and fancies that could be sold as refreshments. Julia added that she thought a lot of the ladies whose hair she was doing at weekends would help her in this. (Julia also declared to anyone who would listen that she doubted she and Leonard would be there for the actual dance. On hearing this, Sukie, Linda and Pattie all said at different times that it was time the hatchet was buried and Julia and Evie made their peace, to which Julia would shake her head in disagreement, although a little less vehemently each time.)

Meanwhile Robert, perhaps the least likely person to demonstrate an artistic awareness, said he would make sure that the Home Guard pulled their weight by hanging the church hall in a swathe of paper chains and streamers and other suitable decorations. He also suggested that they have a radiogram there so that they could hear Big Ben ring in the new year from London, and he offered the loan of the slightly battered old faithful one at Bluebells.

This was all very well and good, and for a day or two it seemed there would be a dance after all. But pretty soon it was apparent that the real issue in danger of scuppering their plans was the band, or, more exactly, the utter absence of anything approximating a band.

Proper dance bands were expensive, and when Sukie did a phone-around she discovered that the popular local ones all seemed to be booked in any case. She asked the bands she talked to, and indeed just about everybody else she could think of, if anyone knew or could think of an alternative. The saying 'and some fell on stony ground'

311

was something Sukie would say to herself when she heard negative response after negative response to her question. The reality they were left with was that while they had a gramophone and a rather good selection of records, they wanted some live music to generate a better party atmosphere. But live music looked a forlorn wish in Lymbridge for the New Year's Eve of 1941.

It was Mr Rogers and his trusty job at the *Western Morning News* that got them out of a hole. This was getting to be a habit, Linda joked with him, but it was quite a good habit that shouldn't be thrown over too easily. He wrote a funny story, accompanied by a photograph of Sukie and Pattie, both looking very glamorous, as they pretended to search around the yawningly empty church hall for a band. There was a second picture of Sukie, a close-up of her face this time, as she appealed for a band to come forward and offer their services for free, seeing that the bash was to be a fundraising effort for the Spitfire Fund.

The day the story was run, Mr Rogers was telephoned by the leader of a very good brass dance band from Bristol. The man had been contacted by his mother, who lived in Bovey Tracey and who had read the story and had thought of him and his pals. The venue they had been going to play at had just cancelled their New Year's Eve booking because the son of the publican who was putting the dance on had been killed in action, and understandably the publican couldn't face opening over Christmas or new year. This meant that the band was unexpectedly available; and they would be happy to supply the music for the event for free if they could be put up for the night afterwards, and if they had their transportation to and from the village provided.

Mr Rogers said he was sure they could arrange the transport, and fortuitously there was lodging at Pemberley that the band was welcome to use (he crossed his fingers as he said this, as he knew Mrs Worth could be touchy on occasion if she felt guests were foisted on her).

So it seemed the various problems were solved by Evie's friends while she lay feverish and with a hacking cough in the damp and twisted sheets of her sickbed.

On Christmas Eve Evie began to feel just a little better, and so she persuaded Pattie it was time that Pattie went home to Bluebells. While Evie herself didn't feel well enough to get up yet, she didn't feel at death's door any longer either, and she knew that Susan and Robert would make sure that Bluebells would be a fun place to be over the festive season and that it would be a real shame if Pattie had to miss this, as it was traditionally a time when everyone was good-tempered and nice to be around. Pattie was reluctant to leave her sister, but then Evie reminded her that there would be Midnight Mass at the church, preceded by a candlelit carol service. The family would go to church again on Christmas morning, stopping off at The Haywain for a drink on the way back to Bluebells where a large roast lunch would be consumed late in the afternoon. They would listen to the King's Christmas Day message, of course, and round off the day playing parlour games and charades.

Pattie thought Evie still looked ghostly pale and she couldn't seem to stay awake for long. But after helping Evie have a bath, and then changing the sheets on the bed and making sure Evie was tucked up again warmly, wearing a clean nightie, bed jacket and bed socks, and after Evie had managed a slice of dry toast (her first food for five days) and a large cup of tea, Pattie felt a bit more sanguine about leaving. So, with the wireless playing softly in the background and the pile of Agatha Christies handily close to the bed, Pattie kissed her sister goodbye and fairly trotted off back to Bluebells. She felt rather as if she had been let out of school after a detention once she was able to inhale the fresh air – it smelt *snowy*, if air could smell of such a thing, Pattie thought – as she headed swiftly down Pemberley's generous drive.

The next morning all the Yeo family, including all the evacuees, traipsed up the several flights of stairs to Evie's room to wish her a happy Christmas. Julia put her head around the door but withdrew abruptly, leaving Evie to wonder if she had in fact imagined seeing her sister's familiar but very missed face. The contingent from Bluebells were on their way to church, and in a scratchy voice Evie insisted they stay on the far side of the room as she didn't want to pass on whatever it was that she had. Susan could see the good sense in that, especially when she heard how painful Evie's chesty cough still was and noticed how very thin Evie had become. Susan said she would pop back after their Christmas lunch with some treats.

Evie thanked her mother for the kind thought, but insisted that Susan should put her feet up and stay by the fire at Bluebells. It was a Yeo family tradition that once the lunch had been cooked, Susan did absolutely nothing for the rest of Christmas Day and all of Boxing Day – Susan was to pretend she was a queen who was waited on hand and foot, and to take the opportunity of a well-deserved and long-overdue rest. Evie added that Mrs Worth had promised Evie a Christmas lunch on a tray in her room, and so she would be well provided for. Susan looked at her eldest daughter for a long second, and then said they *all* wished Evie a speedy recovery and as good a Christmas as Evie could have under the circumstances.

Evie felt her mother had included Julia in the 'all' and she was heartened, although she couldn't prevent a pang when she heard her beloved family troop down the stairs. Evie had always spent Christmas with her nearest and dearest, and it felt very strange not to be doing so this year. But she wasn't at all well, she knew, and it wasn't long before she had drifted off to sleep, after a momentary thought of how Peter and Fiona might be celebrating their own Christmas Day right at that moment. Then she told herself that actually it was probably best not to know.

## Chapter Sixteen

Evie's influenza was reluctant to leave her be, and so it wasn't until 29 December that she was able to get dressed and gingerly join the Pemberley PGs for tea. Although she was only up for a couple of hours, she felt shattered, and was back in bed by seven o'clock.

The next morning was a washout too, with Evie staying in bed all day, much to her chagrin. Every time she tried to get up, she felt weak as a kitten, and eventually she gave in and reached for her part-read Agatha Christie.

After lunch things took an upturn. Sukie had a day off, and so she came to see Evie, bearing several women's magazines, and so they had an enjoyable couple of hours reading out snippets and beauty tips to each other, with Evie lying in bed and Sukie sitting in a chair she pulled over to the bedside, cocooned in the pink eiderdown from Julia's old bed. Sukie made herself very useful by running up and down the stairs, to get tea or a hot water bottle or some toast, and soon Evie was feeling decidedly more cheerful.

'Evie-Rose, I am only doing this in order that you can be well enough to come to the dance to-morrow night,' Sukie admonished as they got to the end of the magazines. 'It's going to be a pretty poor show if the star guest isn't there, the star guest being you, of course. And especially as it felt like I had to move heaven and earth to try and find a band, which of course wasn't down to me in the end. And actually everybody *has* moved heaven and earth to turn the church hall into a dance hall worthy of the name. I have hurt feelings, therefore, and you are the only person who will be able to cheer me up tomorrow night.'

By now Evie was feeling distinctly worn out by the full force of Sukie's attention, and Sukie's obvious scheming as to the dance and how it all might go, and so Evie said in a rather weak voice, 'Sukes, you are a complete dear and you've been absolutely wonderful today. Do you think though that maybe I need to try and get a good night's sleep tonight, as that might well help me feel stronger tomorrow?'

So with one last trip downstairs to make Evie a hot honey drink – the antiseptic qualities of honey being very good for bad throats, apparently, if the nurses at the recuperation hospital were to be believed – Sukie was at last persuaded to leave Evie in peace.

Maybe it was the honey drink, or maybe it was due to almost a fortnight of lying inert and feeble in bed, but the next morning Evie felt if not exactly chipper, then a whole lot better than she had since the final day of term.

Pattie came by after breakfast to see how Evie was, and she suggested that Evie, who was still wan of face, should go back to bed for the rest of the day until teatime. Then Pattie would come over late afternoon to help her get ready, in order that she could at least put in a token appearance at the Spitfire dance, as it would be a tremendous

317

shame if she wasn't there at all.

'Everything is in hand for tonight, we think,' Pattie said soothingly, 'and on my way over to Pemberley I saw The Haywain delivering the drink and glasses to the church hall. And Rev. Painter stopped me to say he has had lots of telephone calls about the tickets and so I am assuming that lots of people plan to come, and then I bumped into Mrs Smith who told me that Timmy was able to sort out something with a Bristol airfield, the result of which is that the band are being flown here, can you believe, in a plane that was going to come from Bristol to Lymbridge in the New Year anyway; they brought the delivery forward by a couple of days to make the drop-off. And it's been arranged that the band are going to go back by train on New Year's Day. There's more snow forecast, but it doesn't look as if it will be heavy enough to cut Lymbridge off. And I think Mr and Mrs Worth are quite excited about having the band staying here later – he's whistling, anyhow, so I hear, and she's happily bossing Tina and Sarah about as they are helping her make up the spare beds. You really don't need to worry about a thing, other than which dress you want to wear.'

Evie relaxed; it really did seem as if she was superfluous to requirements.

After making sure that Evie's clothes for the evening were all ready (her dress with the crimson velvet collar she had worn to go dancing in Plymouth), and that she had new stockings (Pattie's Christmas present to her) and a new lipstick (a flattering coral colour that was Mrs Worth's Christmas present to Evie) all neatly laid out, Pat-

318

tie said she was off but that she would be back later.

Rather to her surprise, Evie went to sleep almost immediately, and was only gently shaken awake six hours later by Pattie saying she had run Evie a bath and Mrs Worth had slopped a little slosh of bath essence into it, so it smelt divine.

As Evie and Pattie prettified themselves, Pattie made Evie laugh. The band had turned up, and Mrs Worth had been totally lost for words when she bustled to the front door to greet them, only to find that all five members were black! Although black people were very occasionally to be seen in Plymouth or Exeter, neither Evie or Pattie could think of a time that a black person had ever set foot in Lymbridge.

Mrs Worth had collected herself pretty quickly, and had been very gracious as she showed the men to where they would be sleeping, although Tina had heard her saying to Mr Worth later in the day that of course Bristol had a long history of negroes living there but, although she and Mr Worth were broad-minded to the extreme, it could be that the band would cause many a raised eyebrow over the forthcoming evening by more easily shocked local people.

'Oh my goodness!' said Evie. 'I do hope the band weren't offended if they heard her. They are giving their time for free after all, and I would hate to think they hadn't been made welcome.'

'Well, the two I saw lounging about in the sitting-room just now were extraordinarily fine-looking chaps, and they looked as if they had made themselves at home. Annabel and her fiancé,

319

Derek – he's an odd cove, by the way – were telling them about the funny Lymbridge ways. I think the local young women will be making sure they feel *very* welcome,' said Pattie. 'And if their prowess with their musical instruments in any way matches their looks, we're all going to be in for a treat.'

Evie was eager to say hello to the band before they left for the church hall, and so she hurried Pattie up. Within fifteen minutes they were dousing themselves in cologne and heading off to the sitting room, where now all five members of the band were sitting with Mr Rogers and Mr Worth, enjoying a snifter in the best chunky cut-glasses. There was no sign of Annabel or Derek, but Mr Worth seemed perfectly happy, and he made a great fuss of introducing Evie and Pattie to his guests.

'This band has made Mr Worth's year,' Mr Rogers hissed to Evie, as he stood up to brush cigarette ash off the sharply pressed crease running down the legs of the trousers to his smart suit. 'He'll be dining out on it for months, mark my words.'

And then in his ordinary voice Mr Rogers offered to go and fetch his camera so that a nice photograph could be taken of Mr and Mrs Worth standing in front of the grand fireplace, surrounded by the band, in order that the occasion could be marked.

Tina and Sarah came in, looking very spruced up, and there was a very pleasant twenty minutes or so as various members of the band chatted with the young ladies.

Mr Rogers then said he'd drive everyone over

to the church hall in relays, but it was probably sensible if he dropped Evie and the other young women off first so that they could check everything was as it should be before people started to arrive, and then he would come back for the band, before making a third journey for their instruments and the Worths.

Evie still felt more than a little wobbly on her pins, and when she saw how fantastic the church hall looked she felt her lower lip wobble with emotion, which she put down to not yet quite being back to her old self.

The church hall looked simply wonderful, Evie thought as she gazed about her. And to think it had all happened with her lying supine and oblivious in bed. She now had a hard lump in her throat, and she hoped nobody would say anything to her for a minute or two as she felt tears hovering dangerously close.

She concentrated on looking intently around, and waited for the welling-up of emotion to subside, which fortunately it soon did.

Someone had been able to get hold of copious amounts of muslin (goodness knows how, although if Evie had to guess, it was likely to have come from one of the local dairies and would have to be returned there for cheese-making), and the muslin had been pinned across the width of the hall just at the point the walls gave way to the pitch of the roof, and also interleaved from front to back. The effect was very pretty and it gave the impression of a lower ceiling and a more intimate and welcoming space for the occasion, and Evie thought she could detect the imagination of Annabel Frome behind this. The muslin canopy also had the huge advantage of masking the odd damp patch in the roof as well the occasional bit of peeling ceiling paint.

Robert and the rest of Lymbridge Home Guard had really gone to town with the promised decorations. Evie gazed above her in wonder at the row upon row of jauntily coloured paper chains, looped about across the whole spread of the muslin, with strategically placed steamers hanging copiously from the chains. Every now and again there was a sprig of mistletoe hung by a cheery length of red wool, presumably to tempt a final burst of festive kissing.

Some oil-fired heaters had been left on in the hall for the day, and so despite the snow lying still inches deep outside, which had frozen with a hard crust of ice on it since the afternoon, the hall felt pleasantly warm, with the rising hot air making the streamers gently flutter and the bunches of mistletoe slowly circle around.

On the wall directly opposite the door, so that everyone arriving at the hall would see it as they came in, there was a giant poster that had a drawing of a Spitfire with 'Lymbridge welcomes you – and wishes a very merry New Year to all' written in large letters beside it. Evie recognised the artwork as that of Tina and Sarah, and so she caught their attention and smiled warmly in heartfelt appreciation as she nodded towards the poster.

The tall, stately windows were covered by blackout blinds, of course, and every generous-width windowsill was adorned by fragrant decorations of holly, evergreens and fir cones, sprinkled with silver glitter and with tinsel intertwined, and in one corner of the room a Christmas tree decked with tiny glass red and green baubles stood proudly in an earth-filled bucket that had been shrouded in paper patterned with tiny Santas and reindeers. The rather harsh electric lights on the walls were surrounded by protective cones of coloured paper, which made for a dimmer and much more appealing sense of atmosphere. Evie was pleased to see that the large electric lights hanging from the ceiling had been left switched off, even though some of the elder guests might feel the room was rather dimly lit.

The stage was set up for the band, and one of James's friends, a somewhat dopey lad called Sid, was standing on it to one side and already playing dance tunes on the gramophone with the sound turned up as loud as it would go. On the opposite side of the stage was a small table and on it the square wooden wireless ready for listening to Big Ben. Next to the wireless was a giant clock positioned so that everyone could see the final hours of the old year slipping away.

One side of the room was devoted to the provision of beverages and snacks, and some tables and chairs had been set out nearby so that people didn't have to stand around while trying to balance precariously a drink and a small plate of food. It was obvious that Julia had been busy with 'her ladies' as there were many tempting-looking cakes and sandwiches sitting piled on large dinner plates, mostly covered by lightly moistened tea towels in order to keep them fresh. At each end of the table were two quite high piles of freshly ironed napkins, and Evie could see too a selection of bread loaves waiting to be sliced and some pats of precious local butter.

Clusters of chairs around small tables – Evie had no idea where these had come from as she hadn't seen them before – were dotted about the rest of the room here and there, each with an ashtray in the middle, while the old wooden benches from the church hall were lining any free space along the wall, so that there should be lots of space for anyone who wasn't dancing to sit down. The open dancing space was sizeable though and occupied the middle part of the hall.

James and Sukie had positioned themselves just inside the inner entrance door, although hopefully out of the way of the chilly gust of icy air that blasted in each time the outer door to the porch was opened, ten feet or so away from them. James was sitting at a table with a metal petty-cash box, a notebook, and several books of pale pink and light green numbered raffle tickets in front of him. Evie wondered what was going to be raffled.

Sukie was now sitting down next to James, holding a book of raffle tickets of a different colour (Evie couldn't tell if they were white or lemon yellow from where she was standing) and a large pin cushion. She had her own petty-cash box too, and so she looked all set to take money for hanging coats on a couple of makeshift rails that Evie now spied had been set up behind her, empty coat hangers hanging waiting.

When Sukie saw Evie, even though she had only just that second sat down, she bounced up and ran over to Evie to envelope her in a bear-hug, saying softly in her ear, 'I'm so, SO glad you are here, Evie-Rose. I was more than a bit concerned you wouldn't be up to scratch and able to make it. Pattie told me to keep away, but I was thinking about you all afternoon.' And then Sukie added in a stage whisper, 'James and I are each wearing *two* vests, can you believe?! It's simply perishing near the door. And I saw Peter at the hospital this morning, and said our fundraising needed him, most definitely, to be here tonight.'

'I'm ignoring what you just said about Peter, as you seem to be forgetting the dreaded Fiona, and I don't want to know what he said back to you. Well, I do, but you know what I mean, and I'm still too woozy to make much sense, so you'll have to do what I say in sympathy with me being poorly. Anyway, to change the subject, poor you and the double vests. You'll have to make sure you do lots of dancing to warm up afterwards,' Evie said with a smile, and then gave Sukie a less bearish hug and a squeeze.

'And have you met the band yet?' asked Sukie. 'I hear tell they are *quite* the event. I can't wait to see them.'

'Mr Worth is certainly preening – it's the first time he's talked to black people, I believe, and so he's very proud of himself as he's discovered they talk back in English that's *just like his,* although with a different accent. Goodness knows what he'd been expecting, but now he's quite effusive with them, which he doesn't realise isn't necessarily the point in his favour that it'd be if he'd just treat them as he would you or me. And I

325

believe Mrs Worth is feeling rather excited too, to judge by the number of times she's pointed out to them where the downstairs lavatory is beside the dining room, and where the bathroom is on the landing, or how warm the radiators are – I think she's very keen they appreciate Pemberley's plumbing,' said Evie with an affectionate smile.

'And as it turns out, Pattie and I did say hello to the band just before coming here, and I can confirm that they all seem very nice, certainly, and that they all appear to have quite strong Bristol accents, which surprised me as I rather expected them to sound American, although I'm not quite sure why. Maybe it's because they look showy enough to be from America, or I've seen too many films from Hollywood. Anyway, I think they are used to being gawped at by people who aren't used to seeing such dark skin, as they all laughed in what seemed like a genuinely amused manner when I said to them on the quiet while Mr Worth was refreshing their glasses that we'd not seen the like previously, and that we were very parochial and so they'd have to forgive us for our rude village ways and they should make allowances for our blinkered view of the world. Although to be fair, I then added, the same could have been said of *any* dance band coming to Lymbridge, we're such country mice! Anyway, they'll be here in a minute and you can judge for yourself,' Evie concluded.

And with that the band arrived at the exact moment Evie stopped speaking, almost as if she had conjured them up by magic.

They removed their overcoats and scarves, and

James leapt up to hang them on the rails. The band members looked dazzlingly smart in their black suits, white shirts and white bow ties, and Evie was amused to see Sukie's obvious nod of approval as she pursed her lips in a knowing manner and fluttered her blackened eyelashes.

After a look around the church hall, the band had a quick chat with Evie and Sukie, after which their instruments arrived and they carried them to the stage. They took out their trumpets and trombones, and a much pared down set of drums, and carefully stowed the black travel cases behind the curtain at the back of the stage.

Then they indicated to Sid that they'd like a brief rehearsal so that they could see how the sound would travel, and once he had turned off the gramophone, they lifted their instruments and without further ado played a tune that was so catchy it was impossible not to tap one's toes.

Evie and Sukie nodded at each other – it was immediately obvious that this was a tight and exceptionally skilled band that augured very well for the night's dancing ahead.

The band moved its members around the stage a little, until they were happy with where everyone would stand in order to get the best sound, and the drummer fussed about a bit with the seat he had brought with him. Then they put their instruments away and told Sid to start playing the records on the gramophone once again so that the first people to turn up for the dance wouldn't arrive to a yawning silence.

The leader of the band, Wesley, who had mentioned that he also sang on some of their numbers,

327

came up to Evie, Sukie and Pattie, who were now standing with Tina and Sarah, holding a tray bearing an array of small glasses filled with a clear spirit.

'Join us, please, ladies, in a pre-show drink – we always have just the one before we go on stage, and we would be honoured if you all would share a toast with us,' Wesley explained.

But before the drinks could be quaffed Mr Rogers said this would make a good photograph for the paper, and he bustled about as he arranged the band and the young women in front of the large poster with its painted picture of the Spitfire, and then asked Wesley to hold the tray of drinks up, and could everybody give a big smile, please?

No sooner had a couple of photographs been taken, with the bulb having to be replaced after each exposure, than the first people were through the doors. Evie realised that the volunteers who had put on the night hadn't bought tickets to be there, and so she quickly made a circuit of the room with a bucket, asking all the volunteers and the band members if everybody could make a financial contribution. She asked so sweetly that people dug well down into their pockets or their purses. And with that the night began.

An hour later Evie was amazed at the number of people who had turned out in their best bib and tuckers to support the Spitfire Fund. There was no lower age limit and so many people had come with their whole families. Most of the pupils and the parents from Lymbridge Primary School were there, it seemed, as was just about everybody else

328

Evie knew locally. There was a good showing from the older members of the village, with Mr Cawes and Mr Cleave demonstrating how well they scrubbed up. Mr Cawes even daring to suggest playfully to Evie that she save the last dance for him.

Robert and Susan had paid for tickets for all the evacuees at Bluebells, and also for Pattie and Julia and Leonard Bassett, although there was still no sign yet of Julia or Leonard.

Pattie said to Sukie, when she had made sure that Evie was safely on the other side of the room, that while her parents didn't condone what had happened, it was clear that they were trying to welcome Leonard into the Yeo family fold. But he was undeniably a tricky chap to deal with, claimed Pattie, and he didn't seem to make much effort with Robert and Susan. He was one of those very up or very down people, and so the Yeos were never quite sure which was the Leonard they were going to get when he did visit. He seemed fond of Julia though, and she still appeared very taken with him, although there hadn't been any further talk of them moving in with each other, despite their occasional night together. And, apparently, he had been doing some teaching at a small private school close to Oldwell Abbott.

Mr and Mrs Smith arrived with a very smart-looking Tricia and baby Hettie in tow. Mrs Smith's dressmaker had run up a dress for Tricia from some of the material they had bought on the day they went Christmas shopping in Oldwell Abbott, and it was very flattering; in fact it would have been hard to guess that Tricia had had a baby so recently, the dress was so well cut. Evie went over to say hello, although she made sure to keep a good distance from Tricia and Hettie just in case she still had the odd influenza bug that she could pass on.

As expected the band were causing lots of excitement. They hadn't yet started to play, but they were going out of their way to be very affable and to chat with anyone who looked friendly. Lymbridge villagers were intrigued. Evie and Pattie had been right – it seemed as if these might indeed be the very first black people to set foot in the village.

There was a prolonged gust of cold air and Evie looked over to the door. The crew from the airfield had arrived, and the RAF pilots had brought with them the more able-bodied of the servicemen recovering in the recuperation hospital. Several were walking unaided by their compatriots, although they were leaning heavily on walking sticks and moving very slowly.

And then Timmy and several others who were confined to wheelchairs came in, all of them smartly dressed in their service uniforms. Evie was gratified to see the fuss that was made of Timmy by his former drinking buddies from the various hostelries that he used to frequent; led by Dave Symons they all encircled Timmy with an obvious bonhomie. She felt it was important that his old pals thought of him as more or less the same old Timmy (well, perhaps a Timmy who was a little more able to keep his flies buttoned when he saw a willing local lass); he might be in a wheelchair but he was otherwise just the same.

Tricia was hovering nearby, holding Hettie, and Evie was pleased to see that Tricia was gazing at Timmy with what looked to be a genuine expression of happiness.

The band climbed to the stage for their first set, and Evie joined them, staring out into the crowd as she stood in front of the band. Just before she started to speak she saw Julia and Leonard Bassett slip through the doors and go to stand close to the coat rails where Sukie made sure to give them both a welcoming smile.

'Welcome everybody and what a wonderful turnout we have tonight. Thank you all so much for coming,' said Evie, once Mr Smith had hushed everybody. 'We have a treat for you. We are very fortunate to have with us a dance band called The Swingtimes, and in a month or so I am told they are going to London to record their very first record, and so we are lucky enough to hear them *before* they become a household name. They all live in Bristol, although band leader Wesley's mother is currently residing in Bovey Tracey. I was lucky enough to hear them run through a warm-up tune earlier, and I very much hope that you have your comfy dancing shoes on as you are going to be very, very sorry if you haven't. You are going to be on your feet for a lot of the evening. Without more ado, I give you The Swingtimes.' And with that Evie led the applause and then quickly removed herself from the stage.

For the first twenty seconds or so the audience looked transfixed at the band and remained standing stock still in spite of the jaunty dance tune emanating from their instruments. Evie's tummy

331

sank as nobody looked as if they were going to dance – and if they didn't, the evening would be a disaster.

And then Linda led Sam onto the dance floor, and Mr and Mrs Worth stepped forward, and also Mr and Mrs Smith. With that there was a swift exodus from the sidelines and soon there was a mass of couples moving rhythmically with one another. Many of the women had to dance with women as there weren't enough men to go around, but everybody was used to that these days.

Evie's head spun and she felt faint, and so she quickly found a bench to sit on. She was too hot and she leant back against the cool wall and closed her eyes as there seemed too many colours swirling about for her to look at.

Now that she had done her bit it was probably time she went home – she was still recovering, after all, and so she had probably exerted herself to the point of giddiness, although she did want to stay for just a little longer. She opened her eyes to see that Susan was leaning over her.

'Evie, I want you to know that your father and I are very proud of you. This was your idea, and just look at how much people are enjoying themselves,' Susan said. 'I'm sorry you are obviously still feeling a bit peaky and so it probably won't be the night you personally had hoped for. And I'm sorry too that you have had such a bumpy few months generally; life is like that sometimes. But remember, Evie dear, that what doesn't break you makes you stronger. Robert and I think the Spitfire Fund will be nicely swelled by the money taken tonight.

You are looking pale though; do you want me to find Robert so that he can take you home?'

Evie said that would be nice, but she thought she might have a lemonade first and sit there quietly for just a little longer. 'I can't quite bear the thought of leaving when there are still people arriving. It seems so feeble somehow,' she added.

Susan beckoned Frank and Joseph over, and asked them to get Evie a drink and a sandwich, and she gave them some money.

Evie realised she was hungry. She hadn't eaten anything since breakfast, which she had only picked at, but now she felt ravenous.

'Mother, you are an angel. You've always seemed to know how we are all feeling, whether we can tell you so or no.' Evie smiled at Susan, although her lips felt tremulous.

Susan was on her feet already, keeping an eye on Catherine and Marie as they were still so little, but she leant over, kissed Evie quickly on the top of her head, and said to her once again, 'We're very proud of you, Evie dear. Very proud, remember.'

Susan wasn't a particularly demonstrative woman, and so Evie felt most special.

'Mother, I want you and father to know that I still feel bad and very ashamed about the show I made of myself and Jul–' Evie's words were interrupted by Susan telling her to sssh, and to think forward now, rather than backwards.

Evie rolled her eyes as if to say 'easier said than done', and then mother and daughter shared a complicit smile before Susan turned to go.

Frank came back with Evie's drink and her plate of food, and he sat down and chatted happily as she ate.

Soon Joseph and some other boys from the village came by to spirit Frank away, and Evie decided it was time that she should find Robert, so that he could make sure she got home safely.

She stood up, and was taken aback to see Julia actually standing quite close. They were each clearly shocked when they realised that by mistake they were looking directly at one another. Julia turned abruptly, and put her hand very obviously on Leonard's arm to nudge him towards the dance floor.

Evie felt downcast. She and Julia had been so close in the past, but now it seemed as if they would never be allied as sisters against the world again.

She sighed with unhappiness, and looked around for her father who, annoyingly, was now nowhere to be seen.

As Evie peered about her, it was another dreadfully mistimed moment, as this time she spied Peter and an overdressed Fiona speaking to James at the door. They had clearly just arrived and Evie watched as they handed their coats to Sukie, who greeted them with a warm-looking but (Evie fancied) rather false smile as she jabbed the pins through the raffle tickets to denote the coats as theirs before hanging them up together on the same coat hanger. Once Peter and Fiona had moved away, Sukie then looked over to Evie and gave a small shrug.

Evie waited until Peter and his horsey-faced companion were at the refreshments table, and then she made to walk forward. But now her path was blocked by a smiling Tricia holding a snoozy Hettie, with Timmy beside her in his wheelchair. Evie was perturbed to see that while Tricia was cheerfully talking to Evie about this and that, Timmy was casting over Evie a scrutinising look, and then he pointedly looked over to Peter and then back to Evie, this time giving her a questioning expression with raised eyebrows.

Evie sighed. It was obvious that Timmy had picked up intuitively that there was something awkward and unexpected going on between her and Peter and Fiona. A friend of Tricia's came over to say something to her, and Timmy turned his wheelchair slightly so that he was obviously blocking Evie's exit. Evie sat back down on the bench, on the principle that she should get the next minute or two over as otherwise she'd spend too much time wondering what Timmy had to say on the matter. She was going to have to hear it at some point, and so it might as well be now, she supposed.

Deftly Timmy suggested that Tricia go and show Hettie off to the gaggle of Tricia's friends who were standing in a group on the other side of the room, very clearly discussing the handsomeness of the band members. Evie saw that these were the young women who'd been with Tricia months earlier, on the evening when Evie and her own friends had run into them in the pub, and it had become woefully apparent to all that Tricia was in the family way.

'So Evie...' Timmy began.

'What?' was her bolshie reply.

'I detect something of a frisson,' he said, 'al-

335

though it's not yet clear to me whether it's that nice Peter Pipe who has brought the colour to your cheeks, or the sight of that angular woman with the large teeth and expensive dress he's brought with him. Whatever it is, I don't think I've ever seen you with quite this look on your lovely face before. There's a saying about someone looking on with a face like a baby's slapped behind, and now I look at you I know what it means!'

'Shut up, Timmy. I've been ill, and I have a headache, that's all.'

'Ah. I see everything now. You and Peter have had a moment, or possibly more, and now he's with *her*, and you're not happy,' said Timmy. 'He looks uncomfortable, and she is watching him like a hawk at the same time as she is looking around the room for someone. You, I guess. But you're, very cleverly, hiding by sitting down and talking to me.'

'Not in the mood, Timmy.'

There was a silence. Evie had always thought Timmy to be on the dim side, and emotionally illiterate. But actually he'd been spot-on in his assumptions.

'I'll take that as a yes then,' he added in a deliberately helpful voice.

'Give over, Timmy. As I said, mood, and not,' sulked Evie.

'Well, Evie Yeo, I had you down as someone with a bit more backbone,' said Timmy. 'If he is the chap who's caught your eye, what are you doing sitting down out of the way? You need to make a fight of it. *I'd* choose you over that woman.'

'That is a silly thing to say. On so many levels.'

'What have you got to lose? Repent at leisure and all that,' said Timmy as Tricia returned and he reached up to bring Hettie down onto his lap.

Evie stood up and said 'excuse me' to Tricia. Timmy had been as annoying as usual, but she thought there probably was a germ of truth in what he had said to her. By meekly avoiding Peter and Fiona as she was wont to do, she only seemed to make Fiona gloat and to give her that bit more power to rankle Evie. Perhaps it was time the worm turned, just a little.

Emboldened, she headed towards Peter and Fiona, who looked to be deep in conversation over what drinks to have.

'Good evening to both of you, and I hope you are having a pleasant time,' Evie managed to utter bravely as she looked at their faces directly (but, she hoped, without too much of a challenge).

Fiona looked coolly at Evie but didn't say anything, and Peter tried to smooth over the awkward moment by commenting that the church hall was practically unrecognisable, and what a daring band The Swingtimes were to have been booked, and that Evie and her friends must all have been working very hard.

Evie smiled at him to show she appreciated the effort he was making. She turned to Fiona and said with as much warmth as she could conjure up, 'I must apologise to you; I was saying to Peter the other day that I feel bad that I haven't made you feel more welcome to the area. It has been very remiss of me.'

Fiona looked towards Peter, who now had a slightly stricken expression. 'That was a conversation that you thought not to mention?'

Evie realised she had made things worse, rather than better. She backtracked, saying the first thing she could think of in her nervousness. 'Oh, it was only a casual comment in the mess room after, I think, I'd been to see my former fiancé, Timmy.'

'A conversation in the mess room?'

'Well, it might have been that time, or possibly the other time when we were counting the money there after the carol service, or maybe when we had to take Timmy's wife Tricia over to the cottage hospital. She very nearly had the baby in the back of the car! I've been ill, Miss Buckley, and so I'm hazy as to details, I'm afraid.'

'Peter hasn't been ill at all, and yet, strangely, he's apparently had complete amnesia as to these mess room tête à têtes, certainly as far as I am concerned. And there's been no mention of the near miss with the baby in the back of the car. Do tell me more, Miss Yeo.' There was a steeliness behind Fiona's words that sounded dangerous.

Peter's shoulders were drooping. He refused to look either woman in the eye as he bent over to light a cigarette.

'Or perhaps you'd like to fill me in, Peter?' Fiona said through gritted teeth as she turned an angry face his way.

'Anyway, I'm still feeling poorly, and so I'm going now. I just want to say good evening before I left,' Evie said hurriedly.

Peter and Fiona were now staring at each other, and it didn't seem like they'd heard Evie. She tried to surreptitiously make herself scarce. That discussion had gone about as badly as it possibly could have.

Evie took a couple of steps backwards, and then she turned and headed with alacrity towards Sukie and the coats, while making sure she threw Timmy a thunderous look. He waved back cheerfully, which was almost beyond irritating.

The sound of the band playing merrily as they blasted out their upbeat dance numbers jarred gratingly with Evie's dark mood, and instead of being pleased at the sight of the veritable sea of people who were enjoying themselves as they shimmied this way and that, Evie felt raw and in pain.

'Don't ask!' Evie said in response to Sukie's questioning look, as she hurriedly pulled on her coat and hat. 'Can you do both the door and the coats while James makes sure I get home safely? I can't bear being here a moment longer and don't want to have to spend time looking for Father.'

James looked up dozily and not particularly happily towards his sister. He was clearly enjoying spending so much time with Sukie, and thought Evie's assumption that he would take her home an imposition.

As Evie did up the last button to her coat she turned around as she felt a sharp tap on her shoulder. It was Fiona, who looked fuming.

'I don't know what has been going on between yourself and Peter,' she said in a slightly too-loud and unnecessarily carrying voice. 'But I have one thing to say to you. Hands off! Keep away from my intended, Miss Nosey-Parker Yeo. Do you hear me?'

Evie didn't know what to say.

Fiona leant forward so that her face was now close to Evie's. 'This is the *one* warning I will give you. Steer clear of Peter Pipe from now on, do you understand? After this, I will not be held responsible for my actions if you persist in pursuing the man I intend to marry. I will not be cast aside for the mere likes of you, Evie Yeo.'

Those closest to the door were now starting to look around with interest. It wasn't so much that Fiona had shouted, because she hadn't. But her stance was forceful and strange, and she looked aggressive. It felt very out of keeping for what one would have expected at a village dance on a wintry New Year's Eve, and so it was interesting because of that.

Evie was at a loss, and to make matters worse she felt suddenly as if she were about to keel over. She didn't feel able to breathe, and she couldn't think of a single thing to say in her defence.

Fiona obviously wasn't used to such a seemingly placid reaction.

And so she jabbed Evie quite forcefully with pointed fingers right on the breastbone where it hurts, saying more forcibly, 'Do you hear me, Evie Yeo? Or are you deaf as well as stupid?'

Suddenly Fiona was swung around by a hand gripping her shoulder. It was a hand with which Evie was very familiar.

'Leave my sister alone! How dare you speak to her this way! Evie has done nothing – I repeat *nothing*, do you understand? – she need reproach herself for.'

Evie felt as if she was dreaming. It was Julia – Julia! Yes, Julia!! – who had sprung to Evie's de-

340

fence, although she had done so in a louder tone than ideally Evie would have hoped for. Whatever, the two sisters caught each other's eye with an expression of familial loyalty, and then Julia gave the smallest flick of her head to one side to indicate that Evie should go.

Mindful of how rapidly the scene in The Haywain had escalated, Evie turned quickly and fled while Fiona was otherwise occupied by staring open-mouthed at Julia's unafraid face with a look that suggested Fiona was most unused to not having her way or anyone daring to stand up to her, Evie slipping silently out of the large outer door to the church hall just as she spied Peter heading swiftly in Fiona's direction, presumably to calm things down.

James hurried after Evie, pulling on his scarf and coat as he gambolled along, and as quickly as they could on the icy road they hurried towards Pemberley, with James doing his level best to reassure Evie that very few people would have noticed what was going on.

Evie didn't believe him, and once she was home she walked heavy-footedly up the stairs and went straight to bed. What an awful evening.

Several minutes later she heard the welcome purp of Keith, who jumped up to deposit one of the kittens on Evie's bed. Within five minutes all three kittens had been collected and were having a night-time suckle while Keith's booming purr was urging Evie towards a fitful sleep.

Evie woke up in the middle of the night to find Keith nestling close. She felt comforted although still desperately unhappy. The air in the bedroom was polar though, and so Evie felt around until her fingers touched her loose-knit pink bed-jacket that had been slung on the counterpane when Evie had got up at teatime. Trying not to disturb the feline family, Evie then draped the knit over the mother and kittens to keep them warm, and then tried to go back to sleep once more.

It was now probably the New Year, was Evie's last thought before she drifted off. What was the next year going to bring for them all? And what had been raffled? Then she realised she didn't much care about any of it, she felt so miserable.

## Chapter Seventeen

The next morning Evie thought she might as well brave everyone at the breakfast table. If her reputation were mud – and if it were, then it was pretty certain that Mrs Worth would expect her to move out, bearing in mind the Julia/Leonard Bassett debacle – then she might as well hear the worst sooner rather than later.

However, very much to her surprise, everybody sitting around the breakfast table seemed to be in alarmingly good spirits, with the dance declared a tremendous success and without any hint of suggestion that Evie had overstepped an invisible social convention. Apparently Fiona's outburst hadn't been as obvious as Evie had feared as they all assumed that Evie had merely gone home early because she was still recovering from the influenza, and so Evie decided not to disabuse them of the notion.

Slightly fortified, Evie decided that she must grasp the nettle and go to see Julia in the next day or two. It was time to clear the air, she decided. The one good thing to have come out of the previous evening as far as Evie was concerned was that she was certain that Julia had forgiven her and was ready to be friends, if Evie made an overture to her.

Evie turned her attention once more to her fellow PGs. The carousing had gone on into the wee small hours, she was told, and a very good time had been had by all. As midnight drew near, the music had halted and the radio had been turned on so that the chimes of Big Ben could ring out across the dance floor, and then everyone had joined together to sing 'Auld Lang Syne'. New year kisses had been freely exchanged by all and sundry, and then The Swingtimes kept being asked back onstage to perform yet another set. It was past four a.m. by the time the instruments were being packed away and the final merrymaker was pulling on their coat and making to leave.

Mr Rogers had done his ferrying back to Pemberley in reverse, and had also brought all the evening's takings back too. Over breakfast, and after Evie had wished everyone a Happy New Year, he told Evie that he'd got the short straw by having to work on New Year's Day and so very soon he would be leaving for his late-morning to early-evening shift at the *Western Morning News*. But, Mr Rogers went on, if it were helpful he could drive Evie and the money over to the recuperation hospital on his way to work, where it could be counted, logged and then locked in the safe.

Evie didn't really feel like it, but she agreed this was a good idea. At best she'd be able to find out from Timmy what had really happened after she left. He loved a bit of gossip, and he would have been keeping a weather eye out. And at worst, she and Peter would argue, although Evie doubted he would be there or that they had much more to say to each other on any matter at all.

As Evie was waiting in the hall at Pemberley, warmly wrapped in her coat and hat, and was just putting her knitted gloves on, the band came down the stairs and headed towards the dining room. She had completely forgotten they were guests at Pemberley, so wrapped up was she in her own affairs.

'Thank you all so much,' Evie said warmly to Wesley and his friends. 'You were amazing and fantastic and fabulous. I'm sorry I wasn't up to staying for the whole evening, but we were very, very lucky to have you celebrating the new year with us in sleepy Lymbridge. We'll never be able to match such a fantastic evening in that draughty church hall.'

They smiled and said it was they who should be thanking her – it was one of the best audiences they had ever played to.

Evie and Mr Rogers climbed into his car, and then Evie realised he might be a little hungover as they had nearly reached the bottom of the drive before Mr Rogers remembered that he had forgotten the evening's takings. She had seen Mr

Rogers enjoying the Knock 'em Dead with Ted and Bob, who had come to Lymbridge from Plymouth for the evening and had later allegedly made free with two of Tricia's friends.

Mr Rogers reversed back up the drive, the car swerving this way and that on the ice, and he ran inside to retrieve the bucket that was clanking with coins. On top rested the petty cash boxes from the door takings and Sukie's cloakroom.

As they drove through Lymbridge, Julia and Leonard Bassett were just leaving Bluebells. Evie asked Mr Rogers to stop the car, promising she wouldn't be a moment.

The sisters hurried towards each other, and held each other tightly as they said in a mixture of crying and laughing how sorry they each were and how very much they had missed each other.

Evie was just starting to thank Julia for stepping in to deal with Fiona when there was a toot of the car horn, and Evie turned to see Mr Rogers tapping his watch as a signal he was running late.

'Julia, dear, I must dash as I want to get the money from last night to a safe and it's too heavy for me to carry to the recuperation hospital. But can we have tea later, and catch up properly?' Evie called as she headed to the passenger door, with a wave. As Julia clasped Leonard Bassett's arm, she smiled happily at her sister, which Evie took for agreement. How good did that feel? Very good indeed, decided Evie.

When Evie climbed out of the car at the hospital, she was surprised all over again at how heavy the bucket was, especially further burdened as it was with the petty cash boxes.

She peered into Timmy's ward, and he looked up. He was a bit bleary, and so Evie surmised he'd not drunk lemonade all night.

'What time did you stay out until?' she asked.

'We saw the new year in,' Timmy replied, a small wince convincing Evie that, sure enough, he had a headache and might be regretting imbibing quite so much the evening before. But he was able to continue. 'I also watched while you went to talk to Peter and his companion, and I saw her come over to be a pest to you as you made to go. I wasn't close enough to hear but she looked hopping mad. But once Julia was involved, then it was very clear that she didn't approve of Fiona – that is her name, isn't it? – looking down her nose and thinking ill of you. As you left, that drip Leonard Bassett tried to calm Julia down, but she wasn't having any of it, and it was only when your pa gave her a stern look that she quietened. Fiona looked thunderstruck at someone having the effrontery to take her on – I don't think that's happened often – and then I saw Peter more or less manhandle her out of the door. So it was all good fun, with the bonus that your reputation survives intact for a little longer.'

'I was going to wish you a Happy New Year. But you're having too much fun at my expense. I am very pleased though that you felt well enough to put on your glad rags and brave the snow to come out last night,' Evie replied.

'Best japes I've had in ages,' repeated Timmy to Evie's exasperated sigh.

After Evie had said goodbye to Timmy, she left by the front entrance and immediately lugged the heavy bucket around to the rear of the hospital, banging the bucket against her knees in the process, where she rang the bell to the entrance of the part of the building where Peter worked.

There was a lengthy wait, during which time Evie thought that perhaps nobody was working, and if that was the case what on earth was she going to do with all the money they'd raised? How annoying, especially as it was too heavy for her to be able to walk back to Lymbridge with it.

Eventually, though, Evie heard someone come to the door, and when it was unlocked she saw it was a wan-looking Peter. She didn't know whether to be pleased or angry.

He took the bucket from her without a word and fairly stomped off back down the stairs. Evie shut the door and pulled the bolt across and dolefully plodded after him.

It seemed they were the only ones in the warren of rooms, as they were all dark other than the mess room where it looked as if Peter had been reading a book on the uncomfortable sofa. Evie tipped the mound of coins onto the table in its corner, when eventually Peter broke the silence by asking Evie if she would like a cup of tea.

After what seemed an age Peter returned with the tea and sat down on the other side of the table to Evie. He looked haggard and had dark shadows under his eyes. There wasn't any milk to go in the tea.

'Evie, I have really made a mess of things, with the result that by now I have made you, Fiona and myself all very unhappy,' he said.

Evie kept quiet, but sipped at her tea as she wondered where this was leading. Peter stared morosely deep into his cup.

'I shouldn't have resumed my old relationship with Fiona in the first place. We've never been particularly well suited, but you can see how persistent she is, and I think that when we began to spend time together once more she could see her future mapped out, rather than it being a situation where she had any particular feelings for me or me her. And then when I discovered you were free and that I still loved you, I should have had the courage to end things with Fiona,' he said dejectedly.

'Fiona is very forceful, too much so, and my family and hers think we are a good match, and I've never been very good at saying no to any of them as it's only since I lived at Pemberley that I realised I *could* say no to them if I wanted, although I've not yet actually done so. Anyway, they all seemed convinced Fiona and I should have a future together. Meanwhile you weren't there and I thought you'd be thinking poorly of me following our discussion at The Ritz, and so I took the easy option and let things drift. I hate myself for that. It was weak and unforgiveable, but it seemed too much to think about when I was so busy with this new project, which really is important to the war effort.

'But I can't forget you, Evie. And so I told Fiona last night that it is you I love, and that my relationship with her is over. She replied that I had another think coming if for a moment I thought it was going to be quite so easy to get rid of her. She said she thought we were obligated to be with each other and I would be breaking a contract if our relationship ended.'

For a moment Evie felt blasted through with delight. Peter loved her.

But Peter went on, 'And so this morning I made a decision. I know what Fiona is like; she always wants to be in control and she doesn't like to be thwarted. I can certainly make sure that she and I are no longer in a relationship. But what I really want is for you and I to be together. However, given the fact that I don't think I am worthy of a special person like you, as I am weak and selfish, I don't believe you would have me. But even if you would, I know that Fiona would be so vitriolic that she would make it her life's work to ensure that you and I could never be happy together.

'I want to protect you, and so the only solution I can think of is that I ask the War Office for a posting abroad so that I can continue in peace, although not in happiness, to work further on the amazing advances we are making here. If I am not around, I think Fiona might decide to return to London, and then you might be able to carry on your life in peace too.'

Evie sat still as a statue as she listened to Peter's long speech. A cold feeling was seeping into her spine.

Then she wriggled in her seat and opened her mouth to tell Peter that she thought that she and he should have an honest discussion with each other about their feelings, and that they should plan on being together.

But Peter cut her short, and then went on quickly with, 'Please. Please don't say anything, Evie. My mind is quite made up and in fact I have already written to the War Office and posted the letter.'

Evie didn't know whether to be happy or sad.

Peter had said quite clearly that he loved her, words she had craved for months to hear.

But he seemed intent on going away, leaving her bereft, and there didn't seem much she could do to prevent it.

His expression was one of resolution and determination, and there looked to be a sense of peace about him now that he had come to a decision. But it was a look that no longer seemed to include her, and that felt appalling.

Evie leant forward and laid her hand on Peter's arm. He looked at her, and then deliberately lifted her hand and slowly placed it on the red chenille cloth covering the table at which they were sitting.

In silence he began to count the coppers into shillings. Peter refused to look at Evie, and after a while, she stopped staring at him.

It was with an unbearably heavy heart that she also began to count the pennies and halfpennies.

This was a bad – no! – a very, very bad start to the new year indeed.

The publishers hope that this book has given you enjoyable reading. Large Print Books are especially designed to be as easy to see and hold as possible. If you wish a complete list of our books please ask at your local library or write directly to:

**Magna Large Print Books**
Magna House, Long Preston,
Skipton, North Yorkshire.
BD23 4ND

This Large Print Book for the partially sighted, who cannot read normal print, is published under the auspices of

## THE ULVERSCROFT FOUNDATION